For the original Lana Ashwin, a glamorous dark-haired actress and one of my mother's close friends who rented a flat in the same building in Kensington. She and her husband, actor Michael Ashwin, endured the London Blitz along with Mum and Dad.

To all Dr Barnardo's children during the Second World War who were the inspiration for this series.

Lastly, to all the animals who were used in the war – they had no choice. If you haven't been, do go and see the monument, Animals in War, on the edge of Hyde Park, London. It's a powerful and moving tribute to the thousands of animals who suffered and died in service.

An Orphan's Wish

Molly Green

W F HOWES LTD

This large print edition published in 2019 by
W F Howes Ltd
Unit 5, St George's House, Rearsby Business Park,
Gaddesby Lane, Rearsby, Leicester LE7 4YH

1 3 5 7 9 10 8 6 4 2

First published in the United Kingdom in 2018
by AVON

A CIP catalogue record for this book is available
from the British Library

ISBN 978 1 52885 435 1

Typeset by Palimpsest Book Production Limited,
Falkirk, Stirlingshire

Printed and bound by
T J International in the UK

BEFORE . . .

Mellanby, North Yorkshire

Lana read Dickie's letter for the umpteenth time. It was dated 23rd August 1941.

My darling dearest girl,

I hated leaving you for yet another tour but I'll be home before you know it. I can't wait to see your lovely face again, to bury myself in that wonderful hair of yours, but all I have at the moment is your photograph. I'm gazing at it now as I write this.

I miss you so much, Lana. When I get my next shore leave we'll go on long walks, hand in hand.

Keep safe for me, darling. I long to hold you in my arms again. I love knowing my grandmother's ring is nestling between your breasts, but it's hidden, and I want to put it on your finger to let the whole world know we're engaged to be married – the sooner the better. I know you prefer to wait so we can tell your parents together, but it's so frustrating with this damned war.

Give my love to them, and if you get time, I know mine would love you to call in at number 10. You're always welcome – you know that. If you let them know ahead, Mum will make your favourite liver & bacon dish.

Will close now and try to get a couple of hours' kip before the next shift. Will write again soon.

I love you so much.

Dickie xxx

Lana blinked back the tears. Her dearest love. He'd worked in their special code – created by them because of the severe censoring of all letters between members of the armed forces and their parents, wives and girlfriends. She loathed liver, but it meant he'd be docking at Liverpool, and his parents' address at number 10 meant he'd be home in the tenth month – October. She couldn't help smiling as his parents' number had changed more than once to suit his homecoming date.

Her hand automatically touched the ring – Dickie's ring that she'd put on a fine gold chain and worn around her neck ever since he proposed to her on her birthday, 6th August. Today was 4th October, the month he said he'd be home. As usual, the letter had taken several weeks to arrive.

This was October, yes, but the year was now 1942. Fourteen months since his proposal, she calculated, and the diamond and ruby ring was still around her neck.

CHAPTER 1

February 1943

'Is there something wrong, dear?' her mother said, her voice anxious.

'The ATS won't accept me for driving,' Lana said dully, as she slid the sheet of paper back into the envelope.

Her mother's eyes widened. 'Why not? An intelligent young woman – healthy—'

'Seems I'm not.'

'What—?'

'They say I've got flat feet. I'd never be able to march. They might be able to find me a job in an office as a *civilian* – well, they can forget that.' She rounded on her mother, the gold in her hazel eyes flashing. 'The woman who interviewed me more or less said they'd welcome me with open arms as an experienced driver. Some welcome.'

'Well, at least you haven't got anything serious,' her mother said calmly. 'You had me worried for a moment.'

'You don't understand, Mum. Joining up was going to change my life. Pay back those bloody Germans for killing Dickie.' She absentmindedly fiddled with her engagement ring, now on the third finger of her left hand.

'Don't swear, dear,' her mother said mildly. 'I know how you must feel but if I may say so . . . and don't get cross with me, but that isn't quite the right spirit. You want revenge for Dickie's death but that's going to keep you bitter. Not all Germans are Nazis. I'm sure many of them don't want to fight any more than our boys. I *do* understand your feelings but—'

'I'm sorry, Mum, but you don't understand at all,' Lana said, her voice rising as she sprang to her feet. 'I'll never forgive them – never!'

Knowing she was behaving badly but not being able to stop herself, she rushed from the room.

'You shouldn't take it personally, Lana,' her father said when she'd calmed down a little and stepped into her parents' grocery shop a quarter of an hour later. 'They haven't rejected *you* – it's just one of those things.'

It was pointless to argue with her father. She knew he was right anyway. But it didn't make it any less hurtful.

'Your mother and I have been talking. The last thing we want is to keep you at home now Mum's getting better. Working in the shop is not for you – it would be a waste of all your training. Now Marjorie has left to join up, I've put an advertisement in the paper for a replacement assistant.' He glanced at her, and she saw the love and concern

6

reflected in his eyes. 'You have to decide now what you want to do. Personally, I think you should go back to teaching. Your mum says the same.'

'You sound like Dickie,' Lana said, more than a little annoyed.

'I'm not surprised. Dickie was right. We all know how the children loved you. I reckon they thought you were a little eccentric – different from any of their other teachers – but that was why they adored you.' His eyes twinkled with humour and she couldn't help giving him a small smile in return. 'I think that's where you're needed. Not fighting Jerry.'

She couldn't think of a reply so she busied herself undoing a box of tinned sardines that had just been delivered.

'Any eggs this week?' she asked, more for something to say, as there wasn't much hope of any.

'We're expecting our allowance tomorrow,' her father said.

'Well, at least that will stop Mrs Mason from her perpetual moaning.'

Her parents' words tumbled over in her mind the rest of the morning. Maybe they were right. Maybe her strength lay in teaching. And if she was honest she'd missed it terribly these last few months when she'd come home to look after her mother. A severe case of influenza had turned into pneumonia. Lana closed her eyes for a moment. It had been touch and go. At one stage she'd thought she was going to lose her mother as well as her fiancé. Now her mother was finally regaining her strength, Lana had some thinking to do. She was uncertain as to whether the headmaster would give her back her old job, even though they knew her slightly unconventional ways and couldn't deny how much the children responded to her.

She remembered standing in the headmaster's office when she'd asked him if he could hold her position by having a temporary teacher for the time it took her mother to recover. He couldn't guarantee it, he'd said. It depended upon who came in her place. What their situation might be. He wouldn't look her in the eye. At that moment in his office she'd made up her mind never to go back to that school, whatever the circumstances.

'Even if he offered it to me it would be going backwards,' she said aloud as she checked the list of items they were waiting to be delivered. She'd always taken pride in trying something new if things didn't turn out as expected or if she was unhappy. Begging for her old job would be admitting failure.

When Marjorie Drake had suddenly announced to Lana's father that she was joining the Women's Auxiliary Air Force and would be leaving in a week's time, Lana had felt a spurt of envy. She'd decided then and there to join the Auxiliary Territorial Service. To fight Jerry. For Dickie's sake. But now that had been cut from under her.

★　　★　　★

8

'The library was shut today,' Lana grumbled to her father after supper a few days later when her mother had retired early. 'Staff shortage, I suppose. It's so annoying. I've finished my book and I've got nothing else to read.'

'Try these.' Her father put down his newspaper and tossed a couple of magazines over to her. 'Mrs Randall-Smith dropped them in this afternoon when she came to see your mother. You might find something of interest.'

They were sitting in opposite easy chairs in the parlour, which they used more these days since her mother had been ill. Lana had lit a fire but the room was still chilly even though the ugly blackout curtains were disguised by a second thick pair of richly flowered ones. Lana shivered. All the curtains did was give the impression the room was cosier than it felt.

Lana flipped through one of *The Lady* magazines her mother's friend had left, then looked up. 'No response yet for an assistant?'

'Not yet. Everyone seems to have joined up.' He looked suddenly contrite. 'Sorry, love. That was a bit tactless of me.'

Lana gave a rueful smile. 'Don't worry, Dad. I'm all growed up now.'

Her father's face broke into a grin. 'You certainly are, Topsy. I'm hoping it won't be long before we have some replies – then you'll be free to continue your own life.'

It was her father's old nickname for her when

9

she was still a child. Impulsively, she sprang to her feet and kissed her father's cheek. 'You're the best father in the world,' she said, 'but you're encouraging me to be the most selfish daughter.'

'Not at all,' he said, giving her an affectionate kiss back. 'You haven't had an easy time with this war and—'

'No different from thousands of others,' Lana interrupted, her expression grim. 'I so badly want to get back at the Germans for what they took away from me, Dad, but Mum thinks I'll end up a bitter and twisted old maid.'

'Did she actually say that?' Her father looked at her in surprise. 'Doesn't sound like your mother.'

'Not exactly those words but that's what she meant,' Lana grimaced. She went back to her chair and picked up the magazine again, but she couldn't concentrate. She sat thinking while her father quietly read his paper, until he folded it and yawned.

'I think I'll turn in,' he announced.

He'd been a handsome man, she thought, as she watched him struggle to his feet, but the strain of another war – the first one where he'd lost a brother, and now two sons away at sea – had begun to tell on his features. His mouth had lost some of its fullness and his cheeks were a little sunken, but his eyes still held their teasing sparkle. A lump came to her throat.

'G'night, love.'

'Night, Dad. Sleep tight.'

'And don't let the bed bugs bite,' he finished, smiling.

It was how they'd always finished saying good-night when she was a little girl.

She grinned back.

In bed, she opened the magazine and read a couple of articles, wrinkling her nose at the 'Let's Make Do & Mend' article. If this war went on much longer she'd need to improve what little sewing skills she had. Idly, she turned to the 'Situations Vacant' pages and her eye roved down the columns. Her attention was caught by one, enclosed in a box.

Urgently seeking temporary headmistress for village school in Bingham, nr Liverpool. Must be an experienced teacher and willing to supervise small team while headmaster is abroad fighting. Pls reply to Mr G. Shepherd, Box 3032 at The Lady.

Lana's heart turned over. Dickie's home port had been Liverpool. She'd been there once to see him off and had been horrified at the devastation in the city. It had looked every bit as bad as London, having only just suffered its own blitz. Beautiful buildings turned into heaps of rubble and debris, people picking their way through it, children playing games amongst it, and what had been people's pets looking dazed by the way their world had changed in an instant, ribs sticking through their unkempt coats, foraging for scraps.

Lana shuddered, remembering how every bombed building, every church destroyed, every ship struck, had all brought home to her the danger Dickie faced every day. She'd caught the train home on the same day, not only sad at parting from Dickie but also frightened on his behalf, and thoroughly depressed about the ruined areas of the city that he and his friends seemed almost to accept as part of war.

Safe in what had been her old bed at home, she pulled the blanket up further so she could tuck the ends around her shoulders. The room was so cold it was difficult to think straight, but she knew that was true for most of the nation. She wondered how far Bingham was from Liverpool and for the children's sake she hoped this place was miles out in the sticks.

She shook herself. Why did it matter how far the village was from the city? She wouldn't dream of applying. A headmistress was different alto-gether from a teacher. It would be far too big a leap and she wasn't going to put herself through more humiliation by being rejected – this time for not being experienced enough. A pity, really. If they'd been advertising for a teacher she might well have been tempted to apply.

A few days later *The Yorkshire Post* forwarded two letters to her parents for the part-time assistant vacancy.

'Trouble is, we can't pay much,' Lana's father

said as he came through the shop to the kitchen for lunch. 'But I'd still have thought there'd be at least a half a dozen replies from married women who only want part-time.' He held out the two opened letters for her.

'I'll have a look at these after supper tonight,' she said, then hesitated. Should she say anything? She knew her father wouldn't let it go further if she asked him not to. 'Dad, in one of those magazines Mrs Randall-Smith left for Mum there was quite an interesting advert.'

'Oh, what was that?'

She felt her father's eyes studying her closely.

'They want a headmistress for a school. Apparently, the headmaster has joined up and gone abroad. It's obviously only for the duration of the war.'

'Have you applied?' her father asked casually as he picked up the tray with a bowl of lentil soup and bread and margarine, ready to take to his wife.

Lana shook her head.

'What are you waiting for? It sounds right up your street.'

'Because I don't have any experience of being a headmistress.'

'You could do it standing on your head.'

She grinned at him. 'You've always had such faith in me, Dad. But it would be too terrifying.'

'Nonsense. Can I see the advert?'

'Let me take Mum's tray.' She took it from her father's hands. 'She's probably got it.'

She was back in moments and handed her father the magazine.

'Hmm.' Her father looked up. 'It only says an experienced *teacher*. It doesn't mention anything about being an experienced headmistress.'

'I know, but *I* wouldn't feel confident organising the other teachers – telling them what they have to do.'

'Darling, you've been in teaching long enough to know how it all works – the duties of the head-master. And you'd be releasing a man to fight for his country.'

'He's already gone,' Lana said.

'There you are, then. Why don't you apply and see what happens?'

'It's too far away. Near Liverpool.'

'Straight through on the train,' her father said. 'Mind you, you'd certainly see some action there, if that's what you're looking for.' He spooned up the last of his soup. 'If you *do* decide, for heaven's sake don't let Mum know how bad it is. Jerry regularly bombs the docks, from what I read in the paper.'

'It's not in Liverpool itself – it's in a village called Bingham. I'm not sure how far away it is from the city . . . but I shan't apply.'

'Her father gave her a sharp look. 'Because the docks are so near?'

'No, not that at all,' Lana said quickly. 'It's because I'm needed in the shop.'

'Not true.' Her father set the tray down on the

14

kitchen table again. 'Both women who applied for the job sounded nice, so we're bound to pick one of them.' He looked at her, his eyes smiling. 'Your country needs you more than we do, Lana.'

'But the ATS won't accept me—'

Her father ignored her. Instead, he said gently, 'That goes for the school kids as well.'

'Did you reply to that advert in *The Lady*?' her mother said unexpectedly one afternoon when she was reading her book in the front room. Lana had just brought her a cup of tea and a digestive biscuit.

'Dad shouldn't have mentioned it.'

'Well, he did. He thinks you ought to at least apply. I agree.'

'Even though it's in Liverpool?'

'Yes. Being a headmistress would give you a sense of purpose, which is exactly what you need.' She looked up at Lana and smiled gently. 'I know Dickie would approve.' From the bowl she scooped a tip end of sugar and stirred it into her tea. 'Except for the rationing we've had very little to put up with, except the time when that little row of cottages was struck and that whole family was killed.' She shook her head. 'That was terrible.' She took a sip of tea. 'Sometimes I think we should be doing more for the war effort.'

'Don't tell the villagers that, Mum. They wouldn't know what to do without you and Dad for their food supplies.' She looked at her mother's pale face. 'You need to eat more. You've lost quite a lot of weight since you've been ill.'

'You're changing the subject, dear. We were talking about the headmistress job. It would be a marvellous opportunity for you.'

'I'll think about it.'

'If you don't answer soon you'll be too late. Mrs R-S gives me *The Lady* after her daughter's read it.'

'I'm sure it won't have gone,' Lana said. 'Most people seem to be doing proper war work.'

Her mother gave her a sharp look. 'Lana, get it out of your head that you wouldn't be doing proper war work, as you call it, if you went back to teaching. All right, you wouldn't be in the military, but your job with children would be just as important. Imagine how they must feel – terrified most of the time, I should think. You'd be bringing some fun into their lives, and some stability as they won't have their fathers coming home every night. And some of them, poor little kids, will lose their fathers forever.'

'Oh, I don't know, Mum.' Lana looked across the room at her mother, a sob catching in the back of her throat. 'I don't know anything any more.'

'Believe me, love, life's too precious to waste. This war is taking far too many of our young people.' Her mother blinked rapidly. 'I think about your Dickie every day.'

Even at this distance Lana could see her mother's eyes fill with tears and she knew she was also worrying desperately about her sons, Geoff and Nick, Lana's beloved brothers, so far out at sea, not knowing from one day to the next if they were safe. She went and knelt by her mother's chair.

'Write the letter this evening,' her mother said, stroking Lana's head. 'Will you promise?'

Lana nodded. 'All right, Mum, if it makes you happy.'

The reply came through swiftly. The position had already gone, Mr Shepherd informed her. *Thank you for your interest and I wish you good luck in seeking a suitable alternative position,* he finished.

Her hands made fists. Another rejection. She knew it wasn't personal – for heaven's sake. The man didn't know her – had never heard of her. But it felt like another slap in the face. She tore up the letter and threw the pieces onto the fire, enjoying the flames rising as the strips flared, then burned into ashes. It was meant to be that she didn't go to Liverpool. Mr Shepherd and the successful applicant had made the decision for her. What a relief!

CHAPTER 2

She'd left it too late by dithering. As each day passed Lana became more annoyed with herself for not taking action. It would have been a marvellous opportunity to gain experience as a headmistress, albeit temporarily. Nothing was permanent in wartime anyway, but it would have looked good on her work record. At least she now knew what she wanted to do. She'd thought she'd wanted to join the ATS, that was true, but teaching was in her blood, and as soon as her parents employed an assistant for the shop she'd start applying to other schools.

Another week passed and Lana was kept busy with deliveries and serving in the shop while her mother built up her strength and carried on doing the bookkeeping. There were times in the evening, though, when Lana just longed to go out with a friend to the pictures – anything to relieve the relentless tedium. But most of her friends had joined up if they hadn't already been conscripted. She would have been pleased to take her mother so she could escape to a world that didn't consist of the constant round of cooking, cleaning, washing and all the other domestic chores on top of the accounts for the shop. But her mother always shook her head, her chin quivering with fright at the thought of venturing into the outside world. Lana gave a sigh of frustration.

The only bright spot was that the nights were drawing out and it was already March. The month when spring began. When the primroses showed their yellow faces along the verges. She'd already spotted snowdrops three weeks ago when she'd gone for a walk up the lane. Her heart lifted for a few moments and then the memory of Dickie's face blocked out everything else, and an overwhelming sadness filled every part of her body. Her love had been extinguished by some nasty little Austrian's megalomania, and his hatred of anyone who didn't fit his bill of a perfect blond-haired, blue-eyed German. If Hitler had those physical traits it would be slightly more understandable, but he was the very opposite of what he ranted on about; yet no high-ranking German, from the little they were told, seemed to mock it, or even question it.

Dickie had only been the second serious boyfriend in her life. She'd never told her parents or they would have been shocked but she'd lived with the first one, Keith Travers, for two and a half years. She'd been twenty-five and old enough to know better but had been totally infatuated. He was every girl's dream – handsome, intelligent, fun, successful at his job as a property developer . . . she could go on listing the things that had appealed. But he'd invested in the wrong company who'd done the dirty on him and he'd lost almost all his money. He'd changed overnight, becoming morose, angry, argumentative, even lazy about his appearance . . . No matter how she'd tried to help him and encourage him, he'd turned her away, shouting at her that she didn't understand what a failure he felt.

Something flickered at the corner of her mind. Wasn't that how she was feeling right this minute? She'd accused Keith of having no backbone, but wasn't she acting exactly the same? Giving up, instead of gritting her teeth and getting on with it. It was over a year now since that terrible day when she'd had the telegram confirming Dickie's death and most of her friends thought it was high time she pulled herself together and got on with her life. She wasn't the only woman who'd lost her fiancé in the war, they reminded her. She'd immediately felt guilty, as two of them had lost their husbands, leaving little children without their fathers.

She swallowed hard as her thoughts rolled back to Keith again. To when she'd finally made a decision to be responsible for her own life.

An only child, his parents doted on him and she'd simply carried on doing everything for him. But one evening when he'd flounced out and, she presumed, gone to the pub, which he did most nights, she packed her clothes and her few small valuables, and left him a brief note on his pillow. Her friend, Belinda, had mentioned a spare room in a house she shared with two others if Lana should ever need it. But Keith hadn't accepted it was the end of their relationship. He asked her to go back and after a solid month of begging, she'd given in. It had been a disaster and six weeks later she'd left for good.

Biting her lip she flinched at the memory and her own foolishness, but one good thing had come from the failed relationship: Keith owned a car. It was the one thing he'd managed to hold on to. Although her brothers had taught her to drive in their old Austin 7, it was Keith who showed her how to change a tyre and check the oil and water, and do basic maintenance work.

When she looked back she realised she couldn't have truly cared because she'd got over him quickly. Dickie was different. She'd known he was special straightaway – and they'd hit it off as true friends. It had been a slow lead-up to love, but when the spark had burst into flames she knew she was happier than she'd ever been in her life. Now he'd been taken from her. By the bloody Germans. She swallowed but she couldn't stop the tears flowing.

This morning the customers were even more demanding than usual. She was tired of reminding them that there was a war on.

'Make us a cup of tea, love,' her father said at ten past ten. 'I'm that thirsty I can't wait until eleven.'

She gave him a fond look. His eyes were drooping, not masking the lines of strain around them.

'All right, Dad. I could do with one myself.' She nodded over to the two boxes of biscuits that had just been delivered. 'I'll sort them out when I come back. There might be a few broken ones that we couldn't possibly sell to our customers.' She grinned. 'Not to the adults, anyway.'

Her father chuckled and carried on stacking the shelf with the dozen tins of soup. No doubt they'd all have disappeared by the end of the morning, Lana thought, and who knew when there'd be another delivery.

She picked up an envelope her mother had left for her on the kitchen table and studied the handwriting. She could hear Mum upstairs and smiled. It was changing-the-beds day and nothing would alter her routine even though Lana had told her not to do it by herself. That she'd be there in a few minutes to help. Sliding the blade of a knife underneath the flap she pulled out a typed sheet of paper and glanced at the signature at the bottom. *G. Shepherd.* Curious. Her eyes lifted to the beginning.

18th March 1943
Dear Miss Ashwin,
   I'm writing to you to inform you the situation has changed regarding the position for a temporary headmistress. Therefore, if you are still interested I would be very pleased

to arrange for you to come for an interview as soon as possible.

I look forward to hearing from you shortly.
Respectfully yours,
G. Shepherd

Lana read the letter through twice to be sure she'd understood it correctly. Reading between the lines Mr Shepherd sounded worried. It was obvious the other person hadn't turned out as he'd hoped. She laid the sheet of paper on the table while she filled the kettle and prepared the tea tray, her head spinning. What should she do? She wasn't ever going to pass her medical for one of the services, so that was out. There was no doubt about it – she'd loved every moment of teaching before she'd come home to give her parents a hand. It was just that joining one of the forces had seemed the only way to fight Dickie's murderers and keep faithful to his memory.

She took her mother's cup into the front room and read Mr Shepherd's letter out.

'There you are, love,' her mother smiled. 'I told you something would turn up. You just need patience.' She looked at her daughter. 'I hope you'll write back straightaway and fix a time to see him.'

'I think I will,' Lana said slowly as she folded the letter and tucked it back into the envelope. 'Yes, I will.'

CHAPTER 3

Five days later Lana was on the train to Liverpool.

It had been a long journey with a delay of over an hour when they were close to Liverpool. A siren had shrilled and the train had immediately stopped. Most people in the carriage carried on reading or chatting as though this was a normal daily routine, but Lana's heart thundered hard in her chest. She flinched at the half-dozen explosions, even though they were muffled, but the train shook with the vibrations, causing her glasses to slip down her nose as she doggedly attempted to read her book.

She'd had no lunch and her stomach rumbled. Now, the pouring rain added to her misery as she waited for the number 42 bus outside Kirkdale station. At least in the train she'd been inside. Drops of water ran under her collar and seeped into her shoes. *How much worse could it get?*

'Expect bus'll be late as usual,' the woman in front said to her companion. Their umbrellas bobbed as they talked, their accent so strong it was difficult for Lana to catch everything.

''S'not their fault, Mags,' the second lady said as she moved a little to the side to escape her friend's umbrella spokes. 'They've gorra lot on their plates what with all them holes in the road. I don't know how they do as well as they do.'

'It's your sort who never get things made any better,' the first woman retorted. 'You see the good in everyone. It's ones like me who complain and get changes made. Then you cop the benefit but I end up the stirrer.'

Lana gave a start. It sounded as though the two were about to go into a full-scale row. To her relief the other one chuckled. 'That's true. They just think what an old dragon you are and what a lovely woman *I* am.'

'If only it were true.' Mags gave her friend a little push.

So they were only poking fun. She'd have to try to understand their humour if she did end up living here. But she wouldn't think that far ahead. No point in getting her hopes up.

'Bingham,' called out the conductor as the bus slowed to a halt.

Lana glanced at her watch. Already three o'clock. Nearly an hour late. Not a good impression to give.

'Is the village school very far?' she asked him as she alighted.

'No, pet. Not five minutes. It's just up the road ahead of you. Low red-brick building on the other side. You can't miss it.'

25

With the trains often delayed interminably, and sometimes not running at all, Lana had decided to stay the night in a bed-and-breakfast one of her customers had recommended. Her heart gave a little skip of freedom at the thought of being in a place where she wasn't known. She wouldn't have to force herself to smile when someone she hadn't seen for a while enquired, 'How's that gorgeous fiancé of yours?'

When she explained, the person would be embarrassed and clearly wish they'd never asked. She'd have to mumble some excuse to rush away before they saw her tears.

She braced herself now and stepped down from the bus, thanking the conductor, relieved to see the rain had eased. The school building came in sight after only a few hundred yards. A sign pointed to 'Office' and she hurried through an arched entrance that opened onto a haphazard garden of concrete path, flower borders and patches of vegetables, with one dejected-looking tree stuck in the middle. The path led to a door with a notice: 'Please ring the bell and enter'.

She found herself in a hall about the size of her parents' front room. To one side was a recess with a protruding sign: Office. A woman of indecisive age, her hair scraped back into a severe bun, sat peering through a glazed screen, looking Lana up and down before she spoke.

'Miss Ashwin?'

Lana nodded.

'You're very late.'

Not the warmest welcome, Lana thought, as she shrugged off her damp raincoat, giving herself time to respond.

'I'm really sorry,' she said, folding her raincoat and laying it across her arm. 'The poor driver had to make so many detours with all the damaged streets. I don't envy them their jobs at the moment.'

'That's as maybe,' the woman said with a sniff. 'Mr Shepherd has been waiting I don't know *how* long. I'd better let him know you've *finally* arrived.'

Lana looked around, longing to sit for a few moments after her long journey but there was no seat provided. They obviously didn't want to let visitors linger too long, she thought, biting back a grimace. What a sombre place. She almost decided she wouldn't bother seeing Mr Shepherd, but could hear her mother telling her not to be so rude. Well, she'd meet him and be quick about it, saying she realised Liverpool was just too far away, then make some excuse that her parents needed her as they hadn't been able to find a suitable person to help in the shop. Anything to escape.

These thoughts were churning around her head when she heard someone call her name.

'Miss Ashwin?'

She swung round to see a figure limping towards her.

'George Shepherd.' She held out her hand and he shook hers briefly. 'Come this way.'

She followed him along a corridor and another

short passage where he opened a door on the left and ushered her in.

'Sit down, Miss Ashwin. Expect you've had a frightful journey.'

He spoke in a crisp tone like a military man and didn't seem to expect a response to his comment. She nodded and took in a breath.

'Damned nuisance, this bloody war,' he said, then smiled at her reaction. 'I do apologise, Miss Ashwin. Too used to being with chaps all day long. Not used to females in the least.'

She smiled, the tension dissipating a little. 'Don't mind me,' she said, thinking he must have been a soldier injured in the war.

'I don't work here, God forbid,' he said, grimacing. 'I'm from the council – Education Department. The school is understaffed with everyone rushing to do their bit but we *must* keep the schools going. These nippers need a bit of continuity in their lives, poor little buggers.' He looked across the desk and made a tutting noise. 'Oh, sorry. Am in bad habits.'

'There's no need at all to apologise, Mr Shepherd, but coming here I realised Liverpool was much further from home than I'd thought. I wanted to tell you in person that I'm afraid I've wasted your time. I know you haven't offered me the job as I've only just arrived, but I'll be catching the train home tomorrow. I see now that I should stay a bit closer to home.'

Mr Shepherd's skin tone changed colour. 'You

mean we're both on a wild goose chase. Shouldn't you have thought of that before I arranged the interview?'

'It's my turn to apologise,' Lana said quietly. 'It's hard to know how one would feel upping sticks and leaving family behind. I can't see myself being happy here. And if I'm not happy then the children won't be. I'd be doing them a disservice.'

'I believe I'd be the best judge of that.' George Shepherd tapped his pen on the desk. His eyes, a strange mixture of brown and green, caught hers.

Lana squirmed in her chair, feeling seven years old and being told off by her teacher. She was just about to say it was best to know sooner rather than later how she felt when he came out from behind his desk and opened the door. For an instant she thought he was sending her off with no further ado, but instead he called a passing lad.

'Young man, please go to the kitchen and ask them for a tray of tea . . . cake, too, if they've got any.'

He went back to his chair and a smile twitched on his lips. 'Can't send you away with nothing inside you,' he said. 'Have you eaten?'

'Not since breakfast.'

'Hmm. You'll waste away if you carry on like that.' He looked at her gravely. 'While we're waiting, tell me about yourself. Humour me. Even though you've turned down a job I haven't yet offered you.'

Lana couldn't help a small smile. He had a dry

sense of humour, which she liked. She explained a little of her circumstances without mentioning Dickie but again, as though he knew she was holding something back, he barked: 'Husband? Boyfriend?'

'I had a fiancé,' she said with only a faint tremor. 'Had?'

'His ship was torpedoed by a U-boat only a few days after leaving Liverpool. Most of them survived but not Dickie.'

'Bad luck. How long ago?'

'Forty-one. He left on 23rd August and went down on the 28th.' She swallowed hard, desperate not to allow her voice to waver. His mother and father had told her as much as they knew, both of them with tears pouring down their cheeks. She'd never spoken about it to anyone else, not even her own parents, except to say he'd drowned.

Mr Shepherd's eyes widened. 'On the *Otaio*?'

Lana gave a start. 'Yes. How on earth did you know?'

'I was also Merchant Navy. That's how I got this gammy leg.' He appraised her for a minute. 'Why didn't you join up? Help get the buggers.' He grinned. 'And this time I won't apologise for swearing in front of a lady. It's the only name that suits them.'

She gave a weak smile back. 'I agree. I wanted to but failed the medical in the ATS.'

'Oh? On what grounds?'

'Flat feet,' she mumbled. It was as though she

had something to be ashamed of, she thought, crossly.

'Sorry to hear it but of course it wouldn't affect your teaching abilities.'

There was a knock at the door and a maid entered holding a tea tray.

'Please thank Cook and ask her for a round of sandwiches for the lady,' Mr Shepherd said.

'Yes, sir.' The girl bobbed her head and vanished.

'You're very kind,' Lana murmured.

'Not at all. I just want to know what I can do to persuade you to stay here and do the vital job of educating children.'

'Teaching is what I love,' Lana said cautiously. 'It's just that Liverpool is so far away.'

'From your parents?'

Lara nodded.

'Are they ill?'

'My mother's been very ill but she's much better now. No, it's not that. They own a grocer's shop and it's too much for them now the assistant's joined up and my mother is having to run the house as well as do the bookkeeping.'

'They could always sell up and come to Liverpool. Be near their daughter.'

'They couldn't do that. You see, my mother doesn't even go out, so she'd never move.'

'What do you mean?'

'She has a condition. Agoraphobia.' She rarely told anyone this as they had either never heard of the condition or found it impossible to understand,

31

and she was tired of hearing people say her mother should buck herself up. But she felt she owed Mr Shepherd an explanation for all his trouble.

'She was always on the nervous side,' she continued, feeling his gaze on her, 'but going through the Blitz has made her far worse. She began to get nervous attacks and now she's too frightened to catch a bus into town on her own – or even go into our village by herself.'

'I'm sorry to hear that,' George Shepherd said, steepling his hands. 'Not a nice thing to have to deal with. But she wouldn't want that to hold you back, would she?'

'Oh, no,' Lana said truthfully. 'She wants me to live my life to the full. In fact, both my parents encouraged me to apply for this job, even knowing it was near Liverpool.'

'Well, then . . .'

They were interrupted again with the welcome sound of the maid bringing in a plate of sandwiches. George pushed the plate over to her.

'Yours,' he said. 'And Cook's custard tarts. You'll feel completely different with one of those inside you.' He chuckled. 'Don't talk. Just enjoy it.'

He poured her a cup of tea and she drank it down gratefully. The two triangles of egg and cucumber sandwiches slipped down easily, and Mr Shepherd was right about the cook's custard tarts. He insisted she eat the second one as well. They were delicious.

'Better?' Mr Shepherd said.

'Much. Thank you.'

'Well, then, why don't I show you round. It's an interesting building and you've come all this way.'

She loved seeing different schools, getting a measure of how they ran, seeing if there was anything they did that would improve her own school – not that the headmaster at her last school had ever taken any notice of her suggestions.

'I'd like that,' she said as she rose from her chair.

'I'll show you a couple of the classrooms,' he said, limping by her side. 'This one's Miss Booth's mathematics class.'

Lana peered a few moments through the glazed door to see a blur of children sharing desks. An older girl suddenly caught her eye. She sat at the side of the class halfway between the children's desks and the teacher at the front. The girl raised her head and looked through the glass. To Lana's surprise she threw Lana a look of utter despair, then bent her head down again, scribbling rapidly in her notebook.

She was obviously extremely nervous about something. How odd. She was a pretty child, but those eyes had registered such misery for someone so young.

Just as Lana stepped back, the door opened and a young woman stood there, brown eyes warm with welcome.

'Do come in,' she said. 'Are you the new headmistress? Oh, I do hope so.' She didn't stop for Lana to say otherwise. 'The children are so excited to have a new headmistress. They weren't all that fond of Mr Benton. He was terribly strict. Like some Victorian master.' Her hand flew to her mouth. 'Oh, dear, I shouldn't talk like this in front of you, Mr Shepherd. You'll get me sacked.'

'I doubt that.' George Shepherd smiled as he lightly touched Lana's arm to guide her in. 'Teachers aren't two a penny any more, so we may be stuck with you.' The teacher chuckled. 'Anyway, I've brought Miss Ashwin to have a look round the school. And yes, I'm trying to persuade her to take the position of headmistress.'

With a loud scraping of chairs thirty-odd children scrambled to their feet. Lana noticed the older girl was the last one to stand up.

'Children, this is Miss Ashwin, come to say hello.'

'Good afternoon, Miss Ashwin,' they chorused.

The older girl didn't move her mouth.

'Sit down, children,' the teacher said in a raised voice. She smiled and put out her hand, saying quietly, 'Wendy Booth. Seriously, please think about the position. We're a friendly bunch when you get to know us, and we need someone like you desperately.'

'I haven't made up my mind yet,' Lana said, lamely.

'What have you been saying to put Miss Ashwin off?' Wendy Booth grinned mischievously at George Shepherd.

'On the contrary, I'm doing my best to encourage her.'

'In that case, don't take her next door. Mrs Parkes has had to cope with a very unruly child who's disturbing the others. Not a good scene for Miss Ashwin to see.'

'I've probably seen worse,' Lana said fervently. 'That sort of thing doesn't put me off. But we're keeping you from your class,' she finished as she noticed the sea of faces watching them curiously.

'Yes, I'd better get back,' Wendy Booth agreed. 'It's been lovely meeting you, and I do hope you'll join us.'

Lana smiled and turned before the teacher could discern her tears. She felt Wendy could be a friend. It had been too long since she'd had someone to confide in. To lay the past to rest. To think of the future.

George Shepherd took her round the rest of the school and even introduced her to Meg, the cook, who bustled about, but had a smile for her when Lana thanked her for the sandwich and custard tarts.

'I didn't mention the salary,' George Shepherd said when they returned to the office. 'Four pounds a week plus accommodation in a two-bedroomed cottage in the grounds with Janice Parkes, the history teacher Miss Booth mentioned.'

It was more than she'd expected. It seemed that a headmistress was generously rewarded for the added responsibility. She hesitated, not knowing how to answer.

'And you'd be running the show,' George Shepherd cut into her thoughts slyly, 'making sure you were one happy family, kids included. I think you'd make a marvellous success of it.'

'As I explained, I've never held the position of headmistress.'

'That's not a problem,' Mr Shepherd said immediately. 'But we did want someone with more than a couple of years' teaching experience, and you've had three times that.'

Lana was silent. Mr Shepherd was waiting for her to answer. She began to feel uncomfortable.

'Where do the children come from?' she asked, more for something to say.

'Mostly Bingham, but some from the neighbouring village, which is even smaller. One twelve-year-old, Priscilla Morgan, lives at Bingham Hall – that's the Dr Barnardo's orphanage, half a mile away – but she attends school here. I'd like to talk to you about her in particular. She desperately needs help. Mr Benton was not the kind of person she could talk to. She's an orphan but won't believe it. It's had a devastating effect on her studies as she's been removed from the girls' grammar school in Liverpool where she'd been doing very well up until then.' He took his glasses off and polished them with a soft cloth before pushing them back on his nose. 'Didn't you say you taught eleven- to thirteen-year-olds?'

Lana nodded.

Mr Shepherd was watching her closely. She was

sure he was talking about the girl who had given her such a look of hopelessness.

'She's got wonderful potential,' Mr Shepherd continued. 'She's a difficult child – not naughty, really – it's just that she doesn't trust anyone any more. I think you'd be able to help her. She deserves it.' He leaned back in his chair, his eyes unwavering. 'So what do you say, Miss Ashwin?'

CHAPTER 4

The return journey on the train was even more fraught than the one going to Liverpool. It stopped at every possible unnamed town, and sometimes in between for no apparent reason. No sirens had gone off and the guard hadn't explained the reason for the hold-ups. He probably didn't know himself. Lana's frustration was fuelled by her thoughts, which were spinning out of control. The children needed a headmistress in place of this Mr Benton. Deep down, she knew she was capable of doing the job, though it would be a challenge – a big step up. She wished she could have met Janice Parkes who she'd be sharing the cottage with. That was important. She wouldn't be able to stand anyone who was morose, or worse, didn't stop talking. She couldn't help a wry smile. Mrs Parkes was more than likely a perfectly nice person and *she* would be worrying herself sick as to who was about to step into what she'd probably considered to be *her* cottage.

She wondered what Dickie would say if he could see her now. How she missed him. Her eyes stung with unshed tears as she tried to block out the recurring nightmare of the torpedoes that struck his ship, leaving him to drown or be blown up – she'd never know for sure. Even so, it felt too much to bear. Such a wasted life. And all the others, of course. Later she'd learned there were many survivors, and that had made her even more upset. Why couldn't Dickie have survived?

For the hundredth time she wondered what his last terrified thoughts had been. She gulped. She mustn't break down in front of the other people in the carriage.

'Promise me you won't join up.' She could hear his voice at their last parting. 'I couldn't bear to think of you in any kind of danger. No matter what happens to me, I want to think of you teaching children. That's where your heart is. And I love you for it.' He'd looked at her and grinned. 'Besides, with that red hair of yours and a quick temper to match, I can't see you toeing the line or taking orders.' When she'd opened her mouth to protest he'd kissed her lips to hush her. 'I probably know you better than you know yourself. The kids need someone original like you to give them hope in this crazy world. They are the future now.'

But my heart's no longer in it, she wanted to scream at him as she sat on the carriage seat squashed between two women in the ATS. Three airmen were standing close by and smoking. Her eyes began to water. *That rotten stinking Hitler and his friends caused you to die and I'm going to do everything in my power to help pay them back, so help me God.*

The people in the carriage were starting to throw her curious looks. She turned her face away and wiped her eyes with a handkerchief.

When she finally arrived home her mother bustled into the kitchen to heat up her supper. Lana followed her, watching as her mother put the plate over a saucepan of boiling water and a lid over the top.

'There . . . that won't take more than a few minutes to heat through,' she said, looking round and smiling. 'Go and keep Dad company. We've had ours . . . and we're dying to hear about it.'

'Your mother's been on tenterhooks all day, wondering how you were getting on,' her father said.

'Well, he's offered me the position,' Lana said, as her mother put a plate of macaroni cheese in front of her. 'More money – four pounds a week and all found. Sharing a cottage with another teacher. I didn't meet her but I met one – the mathematics teacher. She was awfully nice.'

'What about the man who interviewed you?' her father said.

'Mr Shepherd? He was nice too. He doesn't work there – he's from the council – but he interviews prospective staff.'

'Have you decided?' her mother said, smiling encouragingly.

'Not really.'

'What did you tell him?'

'I said I'd think about it and let him know either way by telephone by the end of the week.'

Her father nodded. 'Very wise, dear. It's a big decision. But if you say you'll take it, your mother and I are right behind you. The change of scenery would do you the world of good and you'd do a marvellous job. Those children would flourish. But only *you* know what would suit you best.'

'Thank you both.' Lana gave them a relieved smile. They were the dearest parents in the world and she wanted them to be proud of her. She shrugged. She didn't know what she wanted, but she couldn't bear to be in limbo for much longer.

It was the afternoon. She'd been watching her father attend to several customers who were plainly upset with their meagre rations. The egg delivery that was promised definitely for today hadn't come in, and one lady had grabbed an orange from the half-dozen in the basket clearly marked 'For Children Only', saying she wanted to give it to her daughter who had just had a baby. Dad had explained the oranges weren't for babies but for children who could peel their own fruit. The lady lost her temper and said it wasn't fair and she was sick of queuing for what little was left when she finally got to the top of the queue . . .

And then someone opened the shop door making the bell jangle. A man walked in. He was the same height and build . . . same chestnut hair . . . same narrow face. For a fleeting moment, in the dim electric light, she thought Dickie had come back to her. Her heart jumped and she had to put her hands on the edge of the counter to steady herself. But this man didn't have Dickie's heart-melting smile. As her pulse slowed, the man gave her a brief nod and put his list on the counter.

But it was too late. That initial reaction jogged her memory of when she'd first met Dickie. She'd come home from teaching for the summer holidays and had just brought her father and Marjorie a cup of tea. She saw the appreciative smile as the man looked at her, then lowered his eyes to her hands, giving a slight nod. It was the summer before war was declared.

'He came in every day for a week,' her father told her, smiling. 'Poor chap. You should see the look of disappointment on his face when he sees you're not there. He's been in just now and asked me to give you this note.'

Lana laughed. 'It's like something out of a Jane Austen novel,' she said as she picked up the letter opener her father always had handy in a jam jar on one of the shelves behind her.

Dear Lana, (it's what your father calls you so I hope you don't mind)
I keep hoping to see you when I go in the shop, but I've now run out of things to buy!

42

So I prepared this note in case the same thing happened today – and it did. You weren't anywhere in sight.

I was wondering if you fancy going out somewhere where we can talk. I would like to get to know you better and hope you feel the same. If so, we can go to a little restaurant in York where I know the owner. The food is very good.

What about this Saturday? Say, 7 p.m.?

Do please say you'll come.

Dickie Knight – maybe your knight in shining armour!

She'd laughed at that and taken a chance, though she'd been wary. She knew nothing about him but her father vouched for him saying he'd been a regular customer for the last three months and was always polite and well spoken. As if that made him a good person. Lana gave a wry smile. But her father prided himself on being a good judge of character.

Six weeks later Dickie told her he had fallen in love with her. Then the following week Hitler invaded Poland, and three days later Britain declared war on Germany. Dickie joined the Merchant Navy the following day.

He loved the sea – she knew that. It was her only major concern. She'd have to be prepared for long absences. But in a way it suited her independent spirit. It was always romantic when he came home on shore leave – as though they were meeting for the first time.

It had taken a year before he'd mentioned marriage.

'I've decided when this blasted war ends I want to settle on shore. I've already seen enough sea to last me the rest of my life. And enough terrible things.'

He'd always refused to give her any details.

'You don't want to know,' he'd said, tenderly smoothing the hair away from her forehead and kissing it. 'But I've realised I want to be with you always. Will you marry me, darling Lana? I promise I'll be a good husband.'

'You'd damned well better be,' she laughed. 'And the answer is yes, I'll marry you. But only when the war is over.'

'Why wait? We're not a couple of kids. I'm thirty-two and you're twenty-nine.'

'Don't remind me,' she'd said, chuckling. 'All right, then, we'll marry the next time you have at least three days' leave. I'm determined to have a honeymoon, even if it's only two nights.'

Feeling the tears well at the memory she rushed from the shop, leaving her father to serve the man who'd reminded her so much of Dickie. She had to get away. Dickie was right. She'd be far more use teaching children.

Lana could almost see in her mind's eye Dickie's triumphant grin when she telephoned Mr Shepherd to say she'd decided to take the position as temporary headmistress.

'When can you start?' he asked immediately.

She thought quickly. It was 29th March. 'What about the beginning of May? Easter is late this year so I could come after that.'

'What about the first of April?' Mr Shepherd didn't pause.

Lana grinned to herself. 'And risk being an April Fool?'

This time Mr Shepherd clearly hesitated. Then his voice came over the line. 'The second, then. Would that be possible? I can't tell you how desperate we are, and we think you'll be the perfect choice.'

'You're not giving me much notice,' Lana said, reluctantly. But what notice did she really need? Mrs Brooke, a young widow, had started that morning in the shop and appeared quick to learn and was delightful with the customers. 'All right,' she said. 'The second of April it is.'

His sigh of relief blew down the telephone wire, making her smile. 'Good. I'll get the paperwork ready for you to sign when you're here.' She could picture him now, relieved the headmistress vacancy was resolved. 'It will be a three-month probation period to make sure we're happy on both sides. I'm sure we will be. The salary will be five guineas a week, all found, with most Saturdays and every Sunday off. One week's holiday pay a year.'

Lana hesitated. She'd have to say something.

'Five guineas a week sounds wonderful, but you told me at the interview it was four pounds.'

'My fault. I was looking at the teachers' salary. You'll be the headmistress but I appreciate you telling me.' He paused. 'Does that sound fair?'

'Very.' Strangely she felt a huge relief as though an inner part of her was settled.

'Any further questions?'

'Do any of the children board?'

'No. It's strictly a day school. But with this war we know that could change at any minute. We have a couple of large upper rooms that could easily be turned into dormitories, should the need arise.'

She could sense that Mr Shepherd wasn't about to make any idle chat. He'd got the replacement and simply wanted to get on with matters. That suited her very well.

'Thank you very much, Mr Shepherd,' Lana finished. 'You've been most kind.'

'We will look forward to seeing you in four days' time, then.'

'Yes, four days' time,' she repeated.

Maybe things were finally falling into place.

CHAPTER 5

April 1943

Her body bent in an ungainly position, Lana struggled with her suitcase up the short drive to the school. The case was so heavy she'd had to keep changing hands. Most of the weight was in books. A few for herself, a couple of teaching books and a good dictionary, just in case the school didn't have a decent one.

She rang the bell and stepped in the hall as she had the first time, but George Shepherd was nowhere in sight. Neither was the woman with the tight bun behind the glazed screen. Instead, a tallish woman with no-nonsense dark brown hair tied back strode towards her and stuck out her hand.

'You must be Lana Ashwin. Janice Parkes. How do you do?' The woman's voice was as clipped as her manner.

Lana put her hand into the woman's larger one, inwardly satisfied to note she was that bit taller than the teacher.

'Very pleased to meet you.'

'I believe you'll be sharing my cottage,' Janice Parkes said.

Did she detect a cool note in the teacher's voice? Maybe the woman was just tired. Lana would have to give her the benefit of the doubt. She put on her brightest smile.

'Yes, so Mr Shepherd said. I do hope you won't mind too much.'

'Too bad if I do, apparently,' Janice Parkes said tartly.

So she hadn't imagined things. The history teacher was definitely resentful. Why hadn't she insisted on meeting the woman she'd be sharing the cottage with before she'd agreed to make the move? It was too late now, and she'd have to make the best of it. She decided to ignore Janice Parkes's last remark.

'Would it be possible for me to go over to the cottage and unpack my case?' she asked.

Janice Parkes glared at the case as though it were a child who was misbehaving, then looked at her watch.

'You'd better come with me this minute, as I have a class in ten minutes.'

She turned on her heel and marched out of the entrance door. Lana followed closely and cursed under her breath to think she had been so naïve as to assume the teacher she'd be sharing with would be pleasant. Janice Parkes hurried along a path at the side of the building and round the back where a pair of plain brick semi-detached cottages stood. The teacher went up the path of the nearest one and turned a key in the door. She pushed it open, pocketed the key, and turned to Lana.

'Just pull the door to when you leave.' And with that she stalked off.

Lana was glad she had. She needed time to compose herself. To think what she'd done. If Janice had given her the same warm welcome that the nice mathematics teacher Wendy Booth had, she knew she would have felt completely different. Why did it have to be Janice with whom she had to live in such proximity?

Lana put her case down and stepped back a few feet to take in the outside before entering. It was a plain exterior, which she felt would be vastly improved by cleaning the murky sash windows and repainting the orange front door that clashed horribly with the red brickwork. It could be a sweet cottage but had the air of one that had been neglected. Her gaze fell on the adjoining one. It was in complete contrast with its crystal-clear windows and green door, the colour of ferns. Lana's eyes stung with tears. The cottage was exactly like the one she and Dickie had dreamed of. She'd suggested renting a flat when they'd first started to talk about where they'd like to live because it was cheaper, but Dickie had insisted on a little house with a garden.

'All that time seeing nothing but sea,' he'd said.

'So when I'm home I must be able to step out onto grass and see trees and flowers.'

She'd happily agreed even though she knew little about gardening. Her father loved pottering about in his vegetable plot as a way of relaxing after standing so many hours in the shop. Lana's mother preferred roses and shrubs. But since the war started the flowers had had to make way for more vegetables.

The cottage next door's garden, with its recently painted white picket fence, was neat as ninepence, with an area dug over presumably ready for planting, whereas Janice Parkes's garden was nothing but a mass of choking weeds and unruly ivy climbing the wall and doing its best to work into the roof.

After stepping into the dark cramped hallway Lana pushed open a door . . . and gasped. Presumably it was the living room though it was hard to tell. There wasn't one inch of floor space or any other space. Every possible surface that could hold something was piled high. A sofa indicated someone had slept on it recently, by the way there were two pillows on the floor beside it, and a pile of blankets. A dirty cup was turned over on its side. The one other chair in the room was overflowing with clothes and shoes, which surely should have been in a bedroom. Is this how the woman lived? She'd given the appearance of a neat, clean, conservative teacher but her home said something quite different.

Lana put her case down and came back to the small hall. She strode through to the dining room and gazed round. This was the same. What should have been a dining room table was loaded with books and newspapers and a dirty wine glass. The three dining chairs were piled with more papers. A modest pine dresser, which should have been a striking piece of furniture, was practically obliterated by the crockery and dishes and even a couple of saucepans, and the smell from several overflowing ashtrays dotted around the room caused her to wrinkle her nose in disgust.

How could people live like this?

Not only would Janice resent being told to tidy up her things, but she would also take issue with the fact that the request was coming not from a teacher, but from the new headmistress.

Pulling a face, Lana stepped through an arch to the kitchen. At first appearance, it wasn't quite so bad. There was a stack of dirty dishes in the sink and another pile that looked clean on the wooden draining board. Any work surface was home to items that didn't belong in a kitchen, such as a pair of binoculars and a book: *Birds in your Garden*, but the small kitchen table covered with a pale blue cloth actually had space for two people to sit, and the kitchen chairs were empty of belongings.

Even if she decided not to take up the position, she'd have to spend at least the night here so she had a chance to talk to Mr Shepherd and explain her reasons. Grimacing, she hauled her case up the gently curved stairway to the landing.

One door at either side. She opened the left-hand one. Janice's. The same untidy heap. Clothes all over the bed and chair, dressing table choked with so much rubbish you couldn't possibly see your reflection in the mirror, Lana thought, with a curl of her lip. She shut the door quickly and opened the door on the right. It was tidy although the bed wasn't made up, but there was a stack of sheets and pillowcases and towels on the chair. She looked in the wardrobe where there were half a dozen wooden coat hangers mournfully swinging on the rail when she pulled open the doors. No dressing table at all, though there was a sink with a decent mirror over. The room was smaller than Janice's but she didn't care. At that moment, she doubted she'd be staying more than a night.

There was another door at the far end of the landing and she opened it to find a bathroom with Janice's things tossed all over the place, though upon inspection the toilet and sink and bath were all reasonably clean. But it was the general feel of the place. An atmosphere that Lana wasn't used to at home.

She set to and made up the bed, worrying about the waste of clean linen if she didn't take up the position. Hurrying over to the schoolhouse, her stomach rumbling at every step, she glanced at her watch. Goodness – ten past three. She'd had nothing to eat since her porridge that morning.

Maybe the cook would give her something to tide her over until supper.

'Here you are, lass.' Meg put the tea and toasted currant bun in front of Lana. 'You'll feel better for something inside you. Why didn't you say you'd had nowt?'

'I've only just realised, Cook,' Lana said.

'Oh, just call me Meg. It's nicer.'

Meg was a short dumpy lady, somewhere in her fifties, Lana guessed, although her cheeks were smooth, the blue eyes clear and bright, as she stood over her like a hen guarding her chicks. 'Do eat up. As it's your first evening I'll leave the two of you some supper.' She paused. 'Janice is not one to cook so I doubt she's got anything prepared for you.'

'No, I don't.' Janice's frame filled the doorway, a mocking smile on her lips. 'I was relying on you, Cook.'

'Your luck's in then,' Meg said briskly, going to the oven and removing a large dish. 'Shepherd's pie.' She placed it on the kitchen table, assessing it with a critical eye. 'You can easily heat it through. And there's plenty for second helpings for both of you.'

'Thank you, Meg.' Lana was aware of Janice watching her closely.

'We call her "Cook".' Janice Parkes's tone was knife sharp.

'I told Lana to call me Meg,' Cook said, folding her arms and not taking her gaze from Janice.

'Fine, if that's what you want,' Janice Parkes said. 'I'll see you later.' She nodded to Lana and vanished.

'She'll come a cropper one day,' Meg said after her disappearing back. 'Shame. She used to be quite a nice woman.' The cook sighed. 'Oh, well, better get back to work. You stay right there, Miss Ashwin, and finish your tea.'

'Lana, please, if I'm still allowed to call you Meg after Janice Parkes's glare.' Lana grinned.

'She's her own worst enemy,' Meg said, her back to Lana as she reached up to pull a large enamel bowl off the shelf.

'Why do you say that?'

'Well, when she first came she was as nice as pie. But since—' Meg stopped, and pressed her lips together. 'No, I shouldn't say anything. Let her tell you herself if she wants to. But it's changed her and she's often snippy and her manner doesn't have a good effect on the children, even though her heart's in the right place.'

Lana was silent, digesting the information. Something awful must have happened to Janice Parkes for her to change so radically. But why should she put up with someone who was permanently angry? It was making her feel uncomfortable.

Suddenly, Lana heard her grandmother's voice in her ear when she was fourteen or fifteen.

'Lana, my dear, you can do anything you set your mind to, but you're apt to run away when things don't suit you,' her grandmother would frequently tell her. She'd fix her tired grey eyes on Lana and nod as though to emphasise her words. 'You'll find through life that many things won't be to your liking – some things you can change and some you can't. But it's up to you to give, more than take. That's what will teach you to have empathy for others and the backbone to stand you in good stead.'

Lana closed her eyes, picturing her grandmother standing at the old stove, making a delicious stew to tickle her taste buds. How she missed the old lady's wisdom.

Meg gestured for her to pour herself another cup of tea.

CHAPTER 6

'The children will be going home soon,' Meg said, as she glanced up at the kitchen clock.

'May I ask you something?' Lana said.

'Of course, lass. It won't be the first question you'll want answering.' Meg sat on a seat opposite. She gave Lana an encouraging smile.

'I was wondering about the older child in Miss Booth's class,' Lana said. 'I noticed her when I came for the interview. She was sitting away from the other children. Mr Shepherd said she needed help.'

She waited tentatively for Meg to answer.

'That's Priscilla, poor love,' Meg said, crossing herself. 'One minute she was a happy girl with two loving parents, and next breath her mother and father were walking back from the cinema in the blackout and a car with no headlights, of course, ploughed into them. They were killed outright.'

'Oh, how dreadful. Poor Priscilla. Where was she when it happened?'

'The children were rehearsing a play at her

school,' Meg said. 'Priscilla was in it. Leading light, I believe. Her dad was going to fetch her after the rehearsal. He never turned up, so she refuses to think they died. They were both mangled, apparently . . .' Meg drew in a shaky breath. 'There's never been a proper service. It's all so sad.'

Lana shuddered. 'How long ago was it?'

'Must be two or three months. She's now living at Bingham Hall – the orphanage. From what I hear, she's most unhappy. But then who wouldn't be, becoming an orphan overnight? But you mustn't use that word to her or she goes barmy. I feel so sorry for her.' Meg gathered the dirty cups and plates. 'The trouble is, the shock seems to have affected her brain. She's a bright child, really.' Meg took the dishes to the sink. She turned round to Lana and wiped her hands on her apron. 'The police had to break the news to her about her parents but she doesn't believe them. She thinks if she is very, very good they'll be restored to her.'

'Oh, what a heart-breaking story,' Lana said, tears springing to her eyes as she pictured the child trying to take in such terrible news from strangers.

'It was a shame Mr Benton hadn't joined up before it happened,' Meg went on. 'He was a strict headmaster and was not the best person to help Priscilla in those first dreadful weeks. She needed love and kindness and understanding – which is where you'll be able to help, I'm sure.'

There was simply no possibility for Lana to tell this nice cook that nothing was definite. Not after seeing the despair on Priscilla's face and Meg telling her the child's background.

'Changing the subject, what did you think of the cottage?' Meg asked.

'A mess,' Lana answered without hesitation. 'And that's being kind.'

Meg chuckled. 'Yes, Janice is not the most house-proud woman.'

'It was so bad I almost decided there and then I couldn't stay,' Lana said, smiling. 'But I'm looking for a challenge, so I might reconsider.'

'Now you're talking,' Meg said, putting the shepherd's pie into a basket. She set it on the table in front of Lana. 'Well, this evening will give you the chance to get to know Janice. Her bark's often worse than her bite.'

Lana walked back to the cottage, keeping the basket steady, all the time thinking about Priscilla and Janice. She realised she hadn't thought about her own anger over Dickie's death all afternoon. Maybe this was just what she needed. To stop thinking about herself and be aware that other people were going through misery of their own. And poor Priscilla was still only a child – so much for a young girl to bear. Was it meant to be that Lana had come to the school to help her?

She didn't believe in fate so that was nonsense. And anyway, she had to face Janice first of all.

She'd soon know if Janice was going to thaw out or not if she didn't respond positively to Meg's delicious-smelling pie.

Feeling a little silly, Lana knocked on the door, then tried the handle. It swung open. She could hear scuffling in the kitchen.

'It's me,' she called, but there was no response. A smell of cabbage wafted through. She gave a wry smile and went into the kitchen. Janice had set the table for supper.

'Oh, you're back,' Janice said, glancing up, then lifting the lid of a saucepan. 'Just dump the dish on the table. I've made some cabbage to go with it,' she added unnecessarily.

'I'm hungry just smelling everything.' Lana set the dish on a tablemat. 'I meant to bring a sandwich for the train but forgot, and breakfast seems a long time ago – apart from Meg's toasted bun, that is.' She smiled but there was no response from Janice who was frowning as she tried a shred of cabbage.

'I think it's done,' she said, turning off the gas, 'so we may as well eat early.'

Janice was very quiet during the meal, not inviting conversation. Lana could hear herself swallow. It unnerved her. How on earth could she even contemplate sharing a cottage with such a woman? And yet . . . Meg had said she didn't used to be so morose. Something must have happened, but how could she broach any kind of personal

59

question when she'd only just arrived at the school? Well, there was one question she could ask.

'Janice, will you tell me the truth?'

Janice looked up, her eyes wide. 'What do you mean?'

'Are you all right about sharing the cottage with me?'

'Not really, if you must know, but I don't have any say in it.'

'Well, at least you've been honest,' Lana said. *This is going to be even more difficult than I thought.* 'Any particular reason?'

'As you can see, I like to spread my things around. And I don't like being nagged about it.'

'Sounds like you've shared the cottage with someone else and it didn't work out.'

'It was a disaster,' came the swift reply. 'And I don't want to repeat it.'

'Was it another teacher?'

'Yes. And the teacher happened to be my husband.'

Lana put her knife and fork neatly together and waited for her to continue.

'Not unusual in normal circumstances,' Janice said, her lip curling, 'but unbeknown to me, he was carrying on with someone else – one of the school cleaners. Can you believe it?' She threw Lana a fierce look.

Lana's hand flew to her mouth. 'Oh, my goodness. When was this?'

'Two Christmases ago. I threw him out. He'd

have to have joined up anyway, so it was no real hardship. And I've been quite happy on my own, thank you very much. My divorce should be through any day now.'

'I admit that what happened to you was pretty awful,' Lana said, rising from the table and taking the plates over to the sink to wash. 'But you'll meet someone else one day. Until then, you mustn't allow yourself to be bitter or it will ruin your life.'

Isn't that what Mum and Dad and my friends keep telling me? And do I take any notice?

'How dare you talk to me about bitter!' Janice sounded so raw and angry that Lana immediately returned to her seat at the table. 'How could I expect you, or anyone, to understand?' Janice continued through gritted teeth. 'He was living a lie.' Her voice rose. 'It'd been going on nearly a year – right under my nose.' She paused, and Lana saw the dark eyes flash with fury. 'So just when I'm enjoying a bit of peace and trying to come to terms with a divorce, *you* turn up, and I'm told to welcome someone I don't know – never set eyes on. I'm used to living on my own . . . having things the way I want.' She shot up from her chair. 'And as far as meeting anyone else, you can forget it. I've had it up to here with men.' She drew a finger across her throat. 'And I don't intend making *that* mistake again.'

Lana washed the dishes on her own, and then excused herself, saying she was tired from the journey. It was a relief to read her book, and then settle in for an early night. It was quite true. She was exhausted, physically and mentally. Bingham school was certainly giving her plenty to think about.

CHAPTER 7

Lana awoke early. Where was she? Peeling flowered wallpaper surrounded her. And the cheap furniture with bubbling grain wasn't hers. Light was filtering through from somewhere behind her head and what seemed only a few feet away she could hear loud snoring. And then she remembered. She was in one of the bedrooms in the cottage in the grounds of Bingham school. And the snorer across the landing was Janice.

She jerked upright and swung her long legs out of bed. Her watch showed half past five. She could easily have another hour but she was going to be first into the bathroom to beat Janice.

By the time Lana had washed and dressed and discovered some porridge oats, she heard footsteps above, pacing up and down. Perhaps Janice was desperately trying to work out how she was going to accept sharing. Lana struck a match and lit the gas ring, then stirred the thickening mixture with a battered wooden spoon. When it was ready she popped the lid on and called up the stairs.

'Janice. I've made some porridge.'

Silence. After a few seconds a voice answered, 'Don't eat the stuff.' Janice's dark head appeared. 'I don't have anything to eat until dinnertime.'

'Well, at least have a cup of tea.' Lana bit back her irritation.

'All right. Be down in a minute.'

Lana had finished her porridge by the time Janice appeared. She did at least sit down and drink her tea.

'I wanted to ask something,' Lana said.

'Long as it's not personal,' Janice answered immediately.

'No, it's not. It's about Priscilla. Do you teach her?'

'Yes. History and geography, but it's hard going,' Janice said, gulping the rest of her tea.

'In what way?'

'She can't concentrate.'

'I'm not surprised when she's lost her parents so suddenly.'

'I think the best way is to ignore the fact,' Janice said, without a scrap of emotion. Lana's eyes went wide. 'Oh, I know that sounds harsh,' Janice went on hurriedly, 'but I think the more she's reminded by people feeling sorry for her, the longer she'll take to get over it.'

Lana didn't agree at all, but she could see it wasn't worth arguing with the woman.

'I understand she's now living at Dr Barnardo's.'

'That's right,' Janice said. 'She used to be very good at most subjects at her grammar school, but now she doesn't bother to finish her homework – sometimes doesn't do any at all – and won't take part when we ask questions. But give it time.' Janice looked directly at Lana and gave one of her mocking smiles. 'As you told me yesterday – time is the great healer.'

Lana flushed. 'I didn't actually use those words.'

'Maybe not, but the sentiment's the same.'

Lana bit her lip. No, she couldn't live with Janice, hearing her chipping away with bitterness day after day. Couldn't she see she wasn't the only one who'd suffered in this bloody awful war? The woman hadn't asked her one thing about herself or why she'd moved from York to Liverpool. Janice obviously wasn't at all interested in anyone except Janice. Janice, the hard-done-by; Janice who couldn't see how well off she was, living in a sweet little cottage – well, it would be if she'd clean and tidy it up now and again – and having one of the most rewarding jobs in the world. Well, she couldn't stop here for the sake of one child and be at the mercy of Janice Parkes.

'Anyway, you'll have your house back to yourself in a couple of hours,' Lana said.

'What do you mean?'

She had Janice's full attention now.

'I'm not going to stay here.'

'What?'

Lana met Janice's dark eyes, wide now with curiosity. 'I'm not going to take up the position of headmistress.'

'Why ever not? You've presumably got the experience.'

'But not the desire,' Lana said. 'I haven't felt comfortable right from the start. Even on my interview, I wasn't made welcome by the woman in the office.'

'Mrs Danvers?' Janice raised an eyebrow.

'Is that her real name?'

'No, it's Dayton. But we call her Danvers. Mr Benton was a pain in the neck at the best of times, but he couldn't do anything wrong in Mrs Dayton's eyes – she doted on him. Just like Mrs Danvers with that spoilt brat, Rebecca.' Janice curled her lip. 'Did you see that film?'

Lana nodded.

'I can't believe you took any notice of a *secretary*,' Janice droned on. '*She* couldn't have changed your mind.'

Best not to say anything, Lana decided.

'You don't mean *me*?' Janice practically thumped herself in the chest. 'Oh, for God's sake.' She shot to her feet. 'Next thing you'll be telling me is that you can't live in the cottage because it's a bit untidy.'

'A *bit*?' Lana exclaimed, thoroughly annoyed. 'I can't move two steps before I'm tripping over all your rubbish. This would be my home too, like it or not, so it's best I go now than drag out the misery.' She frowned. 'You know, I could probably accept the state of the place and even help get it shipshape, but I'm not prepared to share a house with such a bitter woman.' She met Janice's neutral expression with her own glare. 'Funnily enough, Janice, I've got my own problems – not that you'd be interested.' She stuck out her hand. 'So we'll call it a day, shall we?'

'Fine by me,' Janice said, ignoring the hand, and making for the door. 'I'm sure Mrs Danvers will order you a taxi.' She turned to face Lana before leaving, two bright spots of colour appearing high on her cheeks. 'At least I'm not a quitter. At least I'm still here trying to help the children and come to terms with my own rotten stinking existence. So good luck to you.'

With that, Janice marched out.

Raising her eyes to the ceiling, Lana went upstairs. Her suitcase was only half unpacked. If she was honest, she was disappointed in herself for not giving it a chance, but Janice was impossible, and the cottage was not only overflowing with Janice's clutter but it was also dingy to the point of being downright dirty. It would never have worked. She flung her book on the top of her clothes, pulled the lid down firmly to shut the two catches, and looked round to make sure she hadn't left anything. Breathing a sigh of relief she walked down the stairs and out of the door.

Back at the school, quiet now the pupils were in class, she glimpsed 'Mrs Danvers' behind the glass screen in the office, clattering away on her typewriter. Lana set down her suitcase and was just about to tap on the window when she recognised Priscilla rushing through the entrance, a look of determination on her face.

'I need to speak to Mrs Dayton.' Priscilla panted as she practically pushed in front of Lana.

Lana nodded, pleased the woman hadn't spotted her. It might be interesting to stay and watch how the secretary dealt with whatever was on the young girl's mind.

Priscilla rapped on the screen and Lana saw there was blood on her hands. She was about to step forward and ask her what had happened when Mrs Danvers – Lana couldn't think of her by any other name since Janice had named her so – appeared at the other side and lifted the hatch.

'I'm sorry I'm late,' Priscilla said, her breath coming in gasps, 'but there was a cat. It'd been hit by a car and I had to go and fetch the vet.'

'You always find some excuse or another,' Mrs Danvers said in a cross tone. 'The other children manage to get here on time.'

'They live in the village,' the girl protested. 'I come further . . . and I would've been here on time if it hadn't been for the cat.'

Mrs Danvers pursed her lips that had turned white round the edges. 'You disrupt the class every morning with your late arrival. We're having too many complaints about you. I'm going to have to speak to—'

'To *me*?' Lana gently put Priscilla aside as she bent

through the opening and put on her professional smile. 'Miss Ashwin . . . the new headmistress.'

Mrs Danvers' eyes widened and Lana saw her neck redden with annoyance. 'Er, yes, I suppose so.'

'Well, there's no need to worry any further. I'll have a word with her.' Lana turned to Priscilla. 'Can you show me an empty room?'

Priscilla's grey eyes gleamed. She nodded.

'But first you need to wash your hands.'

Priscilla led her along a corridor to the end where there was a gym. Lana looked at the climbing rope, remembering how she'd fallen once as a child and broken her ankle. There was a 'horse' in the middle of the room and a pole ready for netball practice at one side. Metal chairs were lined up against one wall.

'No one will be here until after break,' Priscilla said, as they each took a chair.

'Good.' Lana gave the girl an encouraging smile. 'Now tell me what's going on. You seem to have a problem getting to school on time.'

Priscilla reached for one of her long blonde pigtails and brought it to the front, twisting the end round and round.

'It's not my fault,' she said eventually. 'And this morning I had to stop and help the cat.'

'Did you pick it up?'

'He was bleeding ever so much from his back leg. I wanted to get him onto the side away from any traffic, but he kept growling. I think he was

69

just frightened, so I ran straight to the vet's and he came back with me with a towel and picked him up with no trouble at all. He said I'd saved his life.' She looked up at Lana, her eyes anxious.

'An emergency disrupts the normal routine, but you did the right thing.' She briefly touched Priscilla's arm in sympathy. 'But let's start at the beginning,' she said. 'You're living at Bingham Hall at the moment, aren't you?'

Priscilla hung her head.

'Priscilla?'

'Yes, but it's not my proper home.'

Lana raised her eyebrows.

'It's just for the time being,' Priscilla explained. 'Mum and Dad are away at the moment.' She looked at Lana through misty eyes. 'But they're coming back for me soon.'

Lana didn't know what to say. Priscilla was perfectly old enough to know how her parents had been killed. But the child was denying the truth.

'Sometimes I start off late because I help some of the younger ones to dress,' Priscilla went on. 'And then I get into trouble for going into class when it's already started. Miss Booth is always understanding, but Mrs Dayton used to report me to the headmaster.' She burst into tears. 'I'm glad he's gone. He was horrible.' She pulled a handkerchief from her pocket and blew her nose.

She began to cry again and Lana put her arm around the child's slender shoulders. This was worse than she'd imagined. Priscilla really thought her parents were coming back for her. Her mind raced, wondering how to deal with the situation. Was it too soon to remind Priscilla that her parents were never coming back? It wasn't doing her any good living in a dream when there was no possibility of it coming true.

'Well, you're safe at Bingham Hall for now,' Lana said feebly.

'But when we win the war they'll come and fetch me, won't they?' Priscilla's eyes were anxious. She put her finger to her mouth and chewed a nail.

'I don't know the full story,' Lana said, noticing all Priscilla's nails were bitten to the quick. She'd have to do something about that, but first things first. 'For now I'm going to take you back to class. Which one are you in?'

'Geography.'

Lana's heart sank. Janice's.

'Let's put the chairs back then,' Lana said, undoing her raincoat. 'I'll leave my things here for the moment.' She eased her case into a corner with her foot and threw her coat over the top.

Janice's mouth fell open as Lana strode in to the geography class without her raincoat or suitcase, Priscilla a step behind. The teacher quickly recovered herself and gestured to the children to remain seated, then silently pointed to Priscilla's desk at the side. The child hurried over and slid behind it as Lana went over to Janice.

'Sorry to disturb you,' she said quietly, 'but Priscilla rescued an injured cat.'

'I'll speak to her after class.'

'There's no need,' Lana said, ignoring the flash of anger in Janice's piercing brown eyes. 'I already have. But we've disturbed you enough.' She smiled encouragingly at Priscilla who didn't meet her eye.

Lana returned to the gym and collected her raincoat and case, then walked back to the cottage. Mr Shepherd had given her today to settle in, so she didn't have to be anywhere particular until tomorrow. She smiled to herself. She knew how she was going to spend the rest of her day.

CHAPTER 8

Lana was exhausted but very satisfied. The cottage gleamed. She hadn't known what to do with some of the piles, but half of the stuff was now in Janice's bedroom, stacked as neatly as she could. She'd just finished laying the table for supper when she heard the front door open.

Janice must have gone in the sitting room to dump her coat as usual. All was deathly quiet. After a couple of minutes Lana heard the dining room door close. Then a shadow fell at the kitchen door.

'You decided to come back, then?' Janice came in slamming the door behind her and sat down at the kitchen table.

'I think it was the word "quitter" that annoyed me,' Lana retorted.

'Nothing to do with Priscilla, then?'

'Oh, yes, Priscilla was partly to blame because she needs help . . . anyway, here I am.'

'Mmm.' Janice cast her eyes round the kitchen. 'I see you've tidied up a bit.'

'I wouldn't say "tidied" was accurate. More like

a Herculean effort. But I had nothing else on the list for today.'

'Just as long as you don't throw your weight around,' Janice said, 'and start nagging.'

'I shall do just that if you don't blooming well keep it straight – and clean it sometimes.'

'Oh, I couldn't possibly compete with you. You've done it so well.' There was a sarcastic edge to Janice's tone, which Lana ignored.

'I hate cleaning, but I hate living in a mess more,' Lana said. 'And by the way, I can cook but I refuse to do all of it.'

'I'm not that interested in food, but I'll give it a try.'

'Don't force yourself,' Lana said lightly.

The two women ate their meal in silence.

'Are you sure Cook didn't make this?' Janice said, soaking up the last of the cheese sauce with a piece of bread, and popping it into her mouth.

'All by my own fair hands.' Lana held them out, palms upward, for Janice to inspect.

'Hm. Those lily-whites don't look as though they've scrubbed down too many front doorsteps.'

'I'm not afraid of hard work,' Lana said, annoyed at Janice's perpetual sarcasm. 'I've certainly done more than my share today on the cottage.'

Janice's tight mouth told her not to pursue the subject.

After they'd finished the macaroni cheese and baked apple, Janice sat back in her chair, a look of satisfaction flitting across her narrow face.

'I think I enjoyed that meal better than any for a long time,' she said.

'You're only saying that to encourage me to continue cooking,' Lana said, relaxing a little. 'I think I'm getting to know you now.'

'What, after only a day?' Janice leaned forward. 'Tell me the truth. What happened to bring you back? The last I heard was that you were leaving.'

'Your Mrs Danvers was quite horrid to Priscilla when she arrived late and she threatened to report her. The child was almost in tears when her only crime was to rescue a cat. The woman didn't see me until I made myself known and said I'd deal with it.' She paused. 'I don't like her.'

'None of us do. But she's been here for donkey's years and thinks she runs it.'

'I'm going to keep a close watch on her and if I find she's being unpleasant to the children I shall take it further.'

'It would serve the old bat right.' She hesitated, then said, 'Just one thing, Lana.'

Lana wondered what was coming. She braced herself.

'Thanks for doing the cottage. It looks a bloody treat.'

Lana gave an exaggerated sigh of relief. 'Long as you keep it looking that way,' she said.

The rest of the evening passed in more or less friendly conversation. Janice told her a bit about Wendy Booth.

'Nice woman. Engaged to be married, poor dear.'

'Have you met him?'

'No, I don't need to. Don't trust any of 'em.' Janice pulled a face. 'He's in the Merchant Navy – that's all I know. She doesn't see him for months on end.'

A cold chill slid down Lana's spine. But this sailor was alive, whoever he was, and Dickie was dead. She felt Janice's curious gaze.

'What about *your* love life? Have you got a bloke hidden somewhere?' Janice asked.

'Not really,' Lana said, her eyes pricking. 'Look, Janice, I've enjoyed the evening and I don't want to sound rude, but it's been quite a day, so I think I'll turn in early. Do you mind?'

'Suits me,' Janice said, her lips tightly pulled.

'I'll say goodnight, then.'

Janice simply nodded.

After cleaning her teeth, Lana drew the blackout curtains. She'd laid out her nightdress earlier so she slipped it on and climbed into bed. It was still only just gone nine but the room was cold. She would read for a few minutes in the dim bedside light. Tomorrow was going to be a day to reckon with.

She sat against the pillow, the iron bedhead digging into her shoulders, her book propped up against her bent knees, but couldn't settle to read. Her mind was too busy thinking about Janice. She'd felt the teacher's resentment loud and clear but had been shocked at what she'd had to go through, hearing her husband tell her to her face he'd fallen in love with another woman. Janice was attractive with her dark hair and dark brown eyes, but she obviously hadn't laughed much lately. Lana had the distinct feeling that Janice didn't normally go into the kind of detail she'd poured out yesterday evening to most people.

But Janice had been better company after she'd disclosed the reason why she'd been so upset to share what she'd thought of as her cottage. Lana wished she'd been brave enough to tell her about Dickie. It would have been a relief to talk to a stranger about him.

To stop herself from wallowing in self-pity she opened her book and bent her head to focus on the print, but the words blurred one into the other and she yawned again. This time she felt herself drifting . . .

Lana was up and dressed and had eaten her breakfast before Janice came downstairs, bleary-eyed.

'There's tea in the pot,' Lana told her.

'I feel as though I've spent the night boozing,' Janice said, rubbing her eyes. 'Don't know what's the matter with me.'

'Maybe if you had something to eat in the mornings you'd feel better,' Lana said briskly. 'There's a little porridge left over. I was going to give it to the birds.'

'They're welcome to it.' Janice pulled a face. 'But tea'd be nice.'

'I'm off then – first day.' Lana tried to keep any

apprehension from her voice, but Janice gave her a sharp look.

'One bit of bad news,' she said. 'Mrs Danvers will have to show you where everything is as Wendy and Joan Ford and I have classes first thing. I don't think you've met Joan. She teaches the younger ones.'

'I can cope with Mrs Danvers,' Lana said. 'You should see the kind of headmaster I came up against at my last school.'

'Do you mean you were a teacher like Wendy and me?' Janice demanded.

Lana nodded, furious with herself for letting that piece of information slip out.

'So you've not had any experience as a headmistress?'

'Not exactly,' Lana admitted. 'But I've been in teaching all my working life and—'

'So've I,' Janice interrupted, 'but they turned down *my* application.' There was deep resentment in her tone.

Oh, not another thing for Janice to get worked up about.

'I'm sorry,' Lana said, meaning it.

'Not your fault,' Janice said, her brow furrowing. 'I bet it's because I'm soon to be a divorced woman bringing shame to the school. I suppose I'm lucky they didn't get rid of me.' Janice gulped down the rest of her tea and rose to her feet. 'Well, I suppose I'd better get ready to face another day. Good luck, Lana. I'll be interested to hear how you get on.'

* * *

78

Mrs Dayton looked up from her typewriter as Lana opened the office door and strode in.

'Oh, it's you.'

Lana fought down the bubble of anger at such rudeness. She pasted a professional smile on her face.

'Good morning, Mrs Danvers.' Lana hesitated for a theatrical moment, then said in a mortified voice, 'Oh, I'm sorry, I mean Mrs Dayton, of course.'

The woman threw her a look that was supposed to have turned her to stone, but Lana didn't bat an eyelid. Instead, she continued in an extra pleasant voice: 'I know you must be busy but I wonder if you can spare me half an hour to show me my office, and where things are generally – keys and such.'

Mrs Dayton gave her a pitying look.

'Your office,' she said, mockingly. 'You will be sharing *my* office.' She jerked her head towards the second desk, pushed tight into a corner.

'Is that where the previous headmaster sat?' Lana asked with an innocent expression.

'Of course not,' the woman snapped. 'His office is through there.' This time she jerked her head towards a closed door. 'And he'll be coming back once this war is over.'

'But until that time it will be *my* office while I'm taking his place,' Lana said firmly, with a smile she was far from feeling. Aware of the woman's malevolent eyes on her, she marched over to the door and tried the handle. It was locked. She turned. 'May I please have the key, Mrs Dayton?'

'Mr Benton specifically asked me to keep it locked at all times.'

'The key.' Lana held out her hand, palm upwards.

Pursing her lips, Mrs Dayton opened a drawer and took her time looking for it. Finally, she handed it to Lana without a word.

'Thank you.' Lana looked towards the files on Mrs Dayton's desk. 'I think I'll find my way round Mr Benton's office and leave you to get on. Perhaps after lunch you'll show me what you're working on – explain exactly what your rôle is.'

'I am his personal secretary,' Mrs Dayton said, leaving a gap between every word.

'That's very good news,' Lana said, smiling. 'I'll be depending upon you to do the same for me.'

One – nil to me, Lana thought, as she unlocked the door with a tremulous hand, thankful Mrs Dayton couldn't see it. She mustn't show any sign of weakness. She shut the door behind her and walked over to Mr Benton's desk. He was a methodical man by the look of it; nothing on it except a telephone, an ashtray, a lined pad and a few pencils in a holder.

She spent the next hour checking the records for the number of children who attended: sixty-three in total, according to the cards in the index card drawer. She made a mental note to read through each one giving brief information on age, date of birth, subjects studied, et cetera before the week was out. Their school reports must be kept in a separate file, she thought, searching in another drawer. Yes, here they were. She removed half a dozen files and opened one. It was Priscilla's, from her previous school, The Liverpool College for Girls, dated 10th January 1943.

Priscilla Morgan, b. 21st March 1931.

The Liverpool address had been crossed out and a new one inserted: Bingham Hall, Bingham, Liverpool.

Subjects: Arithmetic, English, Scripture, Geography, History, Art, Needlework.

Priscilla can speak a little German, taught to her by her aunt whose husband was German. Both subsequently lost their lives in the Liverpool Blitz in August 1940. Priscilla particularly enjoys literature and has played the lead twice in school plays with great aplomb.

Priscilla understandably has difficulty with her school work since her parents sadly were killed in January 1943. It is recommended that she attends Bingham school to sit the last year again, now that she will be living at Dr Barnardo's orphanage, Bingham Hall.

Once she is able to come to terms with her bereavement, and with her determination, I am sure she will do very well in the future.

Freda Daunton (Miss)

Headmistress

Poor Priscilla. How humiliating for her. Lana skimmed the report again and grimaced when she read that Priscilla could speak some German. She hated the idea of British children learning that language. But it would be useful if Britain lost the war— She brought herself up sharply. How could she possibly think like that? Of course they were going to win. The alternative was too horrible to contemplate.

There was a knock at the door and Mrs Dayton walked straight in and handed her a sheet of paper.

'You'll be needing this,' she said. 'Your timetable for the term.' With that, she spun on her heel and was about to leave when Lana stopped her.

'Mrs Dayton? One moment, please.'

'Yes.' The woman still had her back to her.

'It might be easier if you could face me.'

Mrs Dayton turned, a scowl on her heavy features.

'In future, would you please knock and wait for me to tell you to enter,' Lana said crisply, but her heart was beating hard. It was going to take all her grit to be a match for the woman and show her right away who was boss, however nervous she felt inside. She pulled herself up straighter in Mr Benton's black leather swivel chair. Somehow sitting at his desk gave her a modicum of confidence, and she couldn't help a wry smile as she looked directly in Mrs Dayton's eyes. 'You see, Mrs Dayton, it might not always be convenient for you to walk straight in.'

'Very well.'

Lana was rewarded by a hard stare from cold dark eyes, but at least this time the woman marched out, slamming the door behind her.

Lana shrugged. No wonder the teachers called

her Mrs Danvers. If there was any trouble she was sure it would come from her direction. Sighing, she glanced at the teachers' timetable. Good. Her first class in English would be the first period after dinner – two o'clock.

She busied herself in the office, studying the curriculum and preparing for her English class. It seemed they were mostly ten- and eleven-year-olds, and as Mr Shepherd had warned her, Priscilla would also attend. They were reading *Great Expectations*. From what she now knew of the child, at least Priscilla would shine in *that* class.

Lana was at her desk in the class well before the children filed in at two o'clock. Mentally she counted them. Thirty-two. She smiled.

'Good afternoon, children. I'm your new English teacher, Miss Ashwin.'

'Good afternoon, Miss Ash-win,' they chimed.

Lana noticed Priscilla was in her place at the side, mouthing the words.

'You may be seated.' There was a scrambling and scraping of chairs. Lana waited until they were still. 'What I'd like you to do is to stand up, one at a time, and tell me your name and I'll repeat it, so I can get to know you all.' She glanced at a child on the end of the first row, and nodded.

A thin girl got to her feet. 'Jennifer Sands.'

The child had difficulty saying her "s's" and a boy sitting close to her sniggered. She'd have a word with him later.

One by one they stood up and stated their names. Priscilla, sitting on the side, was last.

'Priscilla Morgan.' She looked round the class silently, warning anyone not to disagree. 'And I *don't* like being called "Pris" or "Prissy".'

'Thank you, Priscilla, and thank you to the rest of the class. Now turn to your books. I believe you're reading *Great Expectations*.'

'*We're* not reading it.' A tall boy with challenging eyes shot his hand up. 'Mr Benton used to read it to us as if we're all babies.'

'I see.' Lana drew in a breath. She was on home ground now. 'Gregory?'

'I'm Greg, Miss.'

Lana nodded. 'Greg, would you tell us where you've got to?'

Greg flipped over the pages and ran his finger along one of the paragraphs, miming the words.

'Page twenty-eight.'

'Good.' Lana looked at him. 'You can have the part of the convict. Now who would like to play Pip?'

She quickly gave out a half-dozen parts to the children who volunteered by raising their hands. Lana noted Priscilla sat as though in a world of her own, but she was sure the girl was taking everything in.

'I'll read the narrative,' Lana said. 'Any questions before we start?

'What's "narrative" mean?' a child from the back of the class called out.

'Anybody know?' Lana scaled the room. To her delight Priscilla raised her arm.

'The bits in between people talking,' she said.

Lana smiled. 'Well put.' She paused, taking in the children's response. 'Do you all understand?'

'Yes, Miss,' they chorused.

'I don't mind reading the narrative,' Paul, a tall, red-headed boy volunteered.

'Excellent. Perhaps you'd like to start us off, then.'

On the whole they were fairly capable readers, though most of them put little expression in their voices. Except one child who read his part as though he was acting on the stage. She couldn't help but hide a smile. She remembered his name was Robin. His reading was excellent. When she came to write a school play for the children to act, he'd be a good choice for one of the main parts.

She was absorbed in the children's contributions but kept her eye open for anyone not taking a speaking part who wasn't following the story. There was always one. To her disappointment it was Priscilla. She was looking towards the window, then must have caught Lana looking at her, as she turned back with that same expression of despair Lana had noticed when she'd first set eyes on the girl during the interview with Mr Shepherd. She was suddenly anxious for the child. There was no time to lose. She had to talk to her after the lesson.

By the end of the hour the children had become far more enthusiastic about Charles Dickens's novel and if it hadn't been for Priscilla looking so sad, Lana felt her first teaching hour in the new school was a success.

'Priscilla, can you please wait behind?'

The girl looked startled, but nodded. She came up to Lana's desk as the children filed out of the room, one or two looking back to see what 'Miss' wanted with the strange older child in their class.

'What is your next class?' Lana asked.

'Needlework.'

'With Miss Booth?'

'Yes,' Priscilla replied, her lower lip trembling. 'I hate needlework.'

'So do I,' Lana said with feeling. 'We'll go to an empty classroom, but stay here and wait for me while I tell Miss Booth where you are.'

'Do you really hate needlework?' Priscilla asked when they were back in the empty classroom. She looked at Lana, doubt in her eyes.

'Yes. I once had to make an apron. I was no good at it and the teacher told me my stitches were too big and that I'd never make a seamstress.' She looked at Priscilla and grinned. 'I never told her it was the last thing I wanted to do. But I wish I could tell her now that I've improved a lot since the war started.'

Priscilla rewarded her with a slight smile.

'Sometimes we have to do things we don't want to,' Lana continued, hearing her grandmother's voice, 'because when we grow up there'll be all kinds of things we don't like. But in order to get on in the world we have to grit our teeth and do them anyway.' Should she go on? Priscilla seemed to be listening. 'I noticed you weren't really enjoying the English class today.'

'I can't think of anything except when Mummy and Daddy are coming for me.' Priscilla eyes were wet as she pulled her pigtail. 'I try to learn everything in class but I can't. When they take me home, I promise to get better marks.'

Lana had to make a start.

'Priscilla, dear,' she said gently, 'they were killed by a motorcar in the blackout. The driver couldn't put his lights on because of the regulations. It was an accident. Nobody's fault, but they're not coming back. Not ever. I'm so very sorry.'

Dear God, she'd said it.

Priscilla gave her a pained look, her eyes bright with unshed tears.

'Of course they are, Miss Ashwin. I don't know the exact date – that's all.'

'Priscilla, listen to me.' Lana took the trembling child in her arms. 'It's terribly difficult to take in, but you must believe me.'

Priscilla sniffed hard, but firmly extricated herself.

'May I please be excused?' she asked, jumping up. She was out of the door before Lana could open her mouth.

Lana followed, walking slowly, the gap widening between her and the hurrying child, as she returned to her office, wondering what step she should take next.

CHAPTER 9

Back in her office the telephone interrupted her train of thought. She picked up the receiver and Mrs Dayton's voice said, 'Will you take a call from Mrs Taylor, the matron at Bingham Hall?'

'Oh, yes, of course. Please put her through.' There was a pause. 'Lana Ashwin speaking,' she said.

'Ah, good. I've got you,' a pleasant female voice came on. 'It's Maxine Taylor, the matron just up the road from you. You've probably been told about Bingham Hall, the Dr Barnardo's orphanage. The woman in the office said as it was your first day she didn't want to disturb you. But I rarely take no for an answer.'

That damnable woman. Lana bit her lip in annoyance.

'It *is* my first day,' she said, 'but I expect it to be a normal day, and I certainly don't consider anyone an interruption if they need to speak to me. What can I do for you, Mrs Taylor?'

'We're planning to have a maypole dance on May Day for the children, and I wondered if you and the teachers and any of your pupils would like to come along. I thought it would be easier to speak to you first.'

Lana glanced at the desk calendar and flipped the page over to May. 'Ah, it's a Saturday,' she said, 'so no school.' She paused. 'It's very kind of you.'

'Not at all,' came the brisk but friendly tones. 'I don't think the children here have mixed much with the village school children but I think they should. Otherwise, they're going to view themselves as "different" for the rest of their lives – which isn't healthy, in my opinion.'

'I think it's a marvellous idea,' Lana said with sincerity. 'I'd like to talk it over with the teachers first, so may I come back to you in a few days?'

'Yes, of course.'

Lana hesitated. 'Before you go, Mrs Taylor, there's something I'd like to ask you. It's about Priscilla Morgan.'

There was a pause at the other end. 'Ah, Priscilla. She hasn't been with us long. A very sad case.'

'Yes. The worrying thing is that she can't come to terms with the accident. Both parents gone at once and she's lost her home as well. She told me she's waiting for them to come and fetch her. I tried to tell her as gently as I could that they were never coming back, but she was terribly upset and rushed off. It must be dreadful for her and I'm not sure how I can help. I wondered how she was coping at the orphanage.'

'She's very quiet and very good,' Mrs Taylor said. 'Too good. It's not natural. I've tried to talk to her – we all have – but she won't listen. We're hoping time will be the healer.'

Lana bit her lip. It was well over a year since she'd lost Dickie and the ache was as strong as ever. But they were discussing Priscilla.

'It might be a good idea for us to have a proper chat after the maypole dance,' Mrs Taylor said. 'Another month will have passed and we can assess the situation. How does she seem with the other children in class?'

'She sits away from the others in her own world, mostly staring out of the window. Neither she nor the rest of the children take any notice of one another.'

'I wonder if she should see a doctor,' the matron said in a thoughtful tone. 'I must admit I'm as worried as you, especially as she's still eating very little at supper. What about dinnertime at the school? Does she—'

There was a loud crackling on the line and Lana couldn't hear the matron's next words.

'I'm sorry, I didn't catch—'

The line went dead. Lana thought of asking Mrs Danvers to reconnect her but couldn't face the secretary's sneering tone, as though she couldn't even take a simple telephone call.

She spent the next two hours sick with guilt, wishing with all her heart she hadn't upset Priscilla. She should have got to know her better, gained her trust. Suddenly it had become unbearably stuffy in her office. She switched off the two electric bars of the heater and threw on her jacket. A brisk walk would clear her head.

Before the week was out Lana felt at home at Bingham school. In the main, the children were good, though the boys were somewhat raucous when they thought they could get away with it, which had the effect of making the girls quieter. Except Josephine, a cheeky ten-year-old. She interrupted whenever she felt like it. More than once Lana noticed Priscilla frowning at yet another interruption.

'Please put your hand up if you want to ask or answer a question,' Lana said to Josephine. 'Other children want to ask questions besides you.'

The girl immediately swung both arms in the air. Another child who craved attention.

'Only one hand is necessary,' Lana said. 'Keep the question in your head and I'll come back to you. I believe Martin put his hand up before you.'

She nodded to Martin, but before he could open his mouth, Josephine said, 'No, I put my hand up first, Miss . . .'

'You will await your turn, Jennifer. And you will address me by my name.'

'I've forgotten it.' Jennifer's tone was triumphant as she looked round at the class for approbation.

Fuming, Lana beckoned Josephine up to her desk to a class of sniggering children. She turned to the child.

'Now, Josephine. Perhaps you would like to tell

the class that you have a very poor memory and have already forgotten my name. And after class you will write my name out fifty times on your slate before you go home. And I have two more slates you can use as extras so there is no excuse the lines won't all fit.'

Josephine tapped her shoe up and down as she boldly surveyed Lana.

'Shall I remind you of my name?' Lana said evenly.

The child hesitated as though about to say something insolent, but decided against it. 'No, Miss.'

'Then would you like to remind the class in case anyone else has forgotten?'

'It's Miss Ashwin.' Josephine's chest rose with her breath. 'MISS ASHWIN!' Her voice rose to a shout as she faced the class.

Giggles from the girls and more sniggers from the boys.

'Very well,' Lana said, putting a piece of chalk down by the blackboard. 'That's enough. You may go back to your seat. And I don't want to hear another word from you until class tomorrow.'

Josephine made her way to her desk, then glared at Lana.

'You never tell *her* off.' The child pointed to Priscilla. '*Prissy* gets away with everything. She doesn't do her homework and she can't keep up with us in class even though she's older than us. No one likes her here.'

There was a deathly hush. And then a loud scraping of a chair by the window. Before she had time to stop her, Priscilla had sprung up, grabbed her satchel and rushed out of the room.

'I hope you're satisfied now, Josephine,' Lana said. 'You will stay behind and explain yourself before you do your lines.' She threw a glance around the room. 'We're finished for the day, children. You may go.' She waited until the children had disappeared and only Josephine was left, standing sulkily beside the desk.

'Sit down in one of the front seats,' Lana said, taking her chair and moving it nearer to Josephine. It was easier not having a desk as a barrier between them, she thought.

'Now, then. What made you speak in such an unkind way about another pupil?'

Josephine sniffed.

'Have you a handkerchief?'

'No, Miss.'

Lana dug in her bag and handed the girl a neatly folded one. She waited patiently. 'Well, Josephine?'

'No one likes Prissy, only no one's brave enough to say it 'cept me.'

'You mean Priscilla?'

'We all call her Prissy because she's such a fusspot. She tidies her desk after every lesson. We all know she's stupid because she's always bottom.'

'No, she's not stupid. She's just a very sad little girl. And she needs help. I think you might be just the person.'

'What do you mean? I don't even like her.'

'Why not?'

'Because she thinks she's better than us so she doesn't speak to us. So we do the same.'

'It's not that at all,' Lana said. 'It's because she's embarrassed and angry with herself.'

'Because she's stupid.'

'Don't say that word again, please,' Lana said sharply. 'She's *not* stupid.' She looked at the girl. 'Do you have a mother and father, Josephine?'

'Course I do.'

'Then you're very lucky. One day Priscilla had her own bedroom at home and a loving mother and father. The next she was told they'd been killed in the blackout and she had to go and live at the orphanage down the road. It's extremely difficult for her, and you and the others are making it worse by not speaking to her, or including her in your games. I want this to change.' All this time Lana kept her focus on Josephine who looked shocked and upset at the same time. 'Can you understand what I'm saying, Josephine?'

The girl hung her head.

'Josephine?'

Josephine looked up, her eyes flashing. For a moment Lana thought she was going to rebel against her.

'I didn't know, Miss, about her mother and father.'

'There's a war on, Josephine,' Lana said gently. 'Anything can happen at any time to those we love. Do you think you can be kinder to her?'

Josephine nodded.

'And Priscilla's far from stupid. She's a clever girl and I'm sure she would help you with your homework if you got stuck – especially your reading. Then maybe you can put your hand up for a part next time.'

Josephine's face visibly brightened.

'In the meantime,' Lana continued, 'tell her you will be her friend. Try to understand how she feels. Imagine it had happened to you and you'd lost your parents. You'd want to have a friend to talk to, wouldn't you?' Josephine nodded, keeping her eyes averted. 'And the first way to show her you mean it is to tell her you're very sorry for speaking the way you did.'

There was a silence. Lana could almost see Josephine weighing everything up. Finally, she said, 'All right, Miss Ashwin. I'll tell her I'm sorry.'

'Just one more thing, Josephine. We'll forget about writing out my name fifty times, but I'd like you to stand up in class tomorrow morning and tell the children what happened to Priscilla. I'll make sure she's not there. But tell them they must *not* mention it to her afterwards. She'd hate that. Just ask the others to include her – make friends with her. And above all, be kind.' She paused to give time for her words to sink in. 'What do you think?'

Josephine was looking at the floor. 'I'll do my best, Miss Ashwin,' she muttered.

'Your best is exactly what I'm looking for,' Lana said softly.

CHAPTER 10

Josephine carried out Lana's instructions but it only resolved the problem in that particular class. Lana could see Priscilla's mouth set as she went from one lesson to the next, not turning her head to look at anyone.

When Lana spoke to Janice about it one evening she realised the teacher hadn't changed her mind at all.

'Of course I won't tolerate rudeness,' Janice said, 'but I just think we must give it time.'

'I disagree,' Lana said. 'If we don't come out in the open so Priscilla knows we all know and can feel our concern, I can't see how she's ever going to overcome this tragedy.'

'Children are quite resilient,' Janice said. 'Priscilla's quite strong underneath.'

'Let's hope so.' She looked at Janice. 'Oh, I had a telephone call from Mrs Taylor, the matron at the orphanage. She's invited our children to join in with their May Day celebrations. They're having a maypole and it sounded fun.'

'It's the first time we've been invited,' Janice said, sounding surprised. 'I suppose it's because they had that awful matron who hated everyone. But they sacked her and employed a much younger one a while ago. I was told she's having a baby so this Mrs Taylor must be taking over.'

'She sounded awfully nice,' Lana ventured. 'What do you think?'

'You'll find most of the children will be at home with their families as it's a Saturday,' Janice said. 'And I can't see Wendy – or me, come to that – wanting to spend the day at Bingham Hall on our day off. One of us would have to be there to supervise our kids. And I'm not sure it's a good idea anyway, suddenly mixing the two lots of children. It would be far better to let the orphans have their celebration on their own without any added strain of strange children they're forced to play games with, particularly when it's on their special day.'

'You're probably right,' Lana said. 'I didn't think of it that way.'

In bed that night Lana mulled over what Janice had said. She had to admit there was a good deal of sense in it, yet she still felt it was a good idea to get both sets of children talking to one another, that it was more natural than to keep them separated all day, every day. But there was no harm in *her* wandering over to Bingham Hall on May Day. It would give her the chance to see how Priscilla was faring at the weekends. She would form a better picture of the child, and maybe Mrs Taylor might have some suggestions as to how to help the young girl.

Lana changed her mind once or twice as to whether she should venture over to Dr Barnardo's on May Day. It would look strange turning up with no children in tow. She decided to write Maxine Taylor a letter explaining some of her concerns but that she'd be pleased to meet her if it was convenient on that day.

She received an answer two days later.

Dear Miss Ashwin,

Thank you for your letter and I perfectly understand. You may well be right about mixing the children together on May Day. Perhaps some other time when we have a concert or a play and we can invite some of the children from the school to be part of the audience.

That said, I would be delighted to meet you. As you said, it could be useful where Priscilla Morgan is concerned. So why don't you wander over on May Day and see us in the afternoon, say 4 p.m. We should be packing up by then and more than ready for a tea break!

If it's not convenient, give me a ring during the week and we'll make a firm arrangement. No need to reply. We'll see you when we see you.

Yours sincerely,
Maxine Taylor (Matron)

CHAPTER 11

Lana opened her bedroom curtains to a dull, drizzling first day of May. Not the best weather for dancing round the maypole. She quickly got ready and dressed in a dark pleated skirt and cream twinset. Gazing at her reflexion she wondered if it was too severe for a walk over to the orphanage to introduce herself to Maxine Taylor. The skirt swung around her knees as she turned this way and then the other. Oh, dear. She wasn't sure. Did it make her look old before her time? With the rationing, her wardrobe was limited to clothes appropriate for a teacher, together with a couple of summer frocks and a Sunday best outfit. She shrugged. Most women were in the same boat.

She spent the morning marking children's compositions, noting that Priscilla's was a couple of pages of short, jerky sentences, with an occasional description of sudden brilliance. She was a child worth nurturing back to her full potential, Lana decided. She made herself a sandwich in the cottage, unusually quiet since Janice had gone to see her aunt for a couple of days. It was heaven to have the place to herself. She wouldn't stay at the orphanage for long this afternoon. Time on her own was too precious and she wanted to make the most of every minute. Janice would be back tomorrow evening ready for school again on Monday, and then there'd be no more peace.

She sat and read a few chapters of her book, then looked at the clock. Quarter past three. Much too early. But she could start slowly walking, maybe having a wander round the gardens – see how Priscilla was getting on. It would be good to get some air. She rose to her feet and washed her cup and saucer, then collected her raincoat from the peg in the hall.

Lana enjoyed walking along the country lane admiring the trees now in leaf. In spite of the dull sky her heart lifted because she was actually here, beginning her new life. Yes, it was without Dickie, but she knew she'd be doing something important for the future – making sure the children were continuing their education no matter what Jerry threw at them. Dickie would have approved.

She came to a small neat sign: Bingham Hall. The orphanage.

Strolling up the drive, she passed a cottage on the left, which looked as though it was going through some major repairs, and a little further on she saw several tall chimneys cutting through the clouds. She blinked. Built of red brick the house had a turret to one side and a crenellated front, reminding her of a castle. She had to admit it was an imposing house – well, more of a mansion – probably built in early Victorian times, the same as the village school.

What would it be like to work there? Grim, she supposed. All those children, some of whose parents had probably been killed in the war, thrown together with no blood ties, maybe losing brothers and sisters as well. Lana was suddenly grateful to teach at a normal school. An orphanage could never represent 'home' to her.

She could hear an accordion playing and smiled. The children were obviously not letting the dreary rain put a dampener on their day. Screams of laughter became louder as she got nearer.

Another sound. The purr of an expensive-sounding engine behind her. She pressed her back into one of the lime trees to give room to a large black motorcar. It was moving slowly, crackling the gravel. Out of habit, as it drew parallel, she glanced inside. She was vaguely aware of two men in the back seat, but it was the blond-haired man in the front passenger seat, masking the driver, that caught her gaze. He was only a few feet away and she couldn't help looking at him. His eyes were fixed firmly ahead, his profile rigid. But she was struck by the power of his features: the well-shaped nose, the firm set of his jaw, and what she could see of his solemn mouth.

As though he felt her eyes upon him he turned to his left, and for long seconds he looked directly at her. Through her. His eyes were deep-set and she thought they were blue but she couldn't be sure. A quiver ran along her spine. It was as though there was no rain-spotted window forming a barrier between them. He was more handsome than any man had a right to be. Telling herself not to be so silly, but more than a little embarrassed, she swung her gaze from his and fixed her eyes on the rear of the car. Yes, she was right. It was a Rolls. Her brothers hadn't wasted their time teaching her to recognise all the makes and models for nothing. Oh, what she would give to be behind its wheel. But what was a top-class motorcar like that doing at an orphanage?

She shrugged. It was none of her business. She saw the two men emerge from the back of the Rolls-Royce and walk towards the entrance of the house, leaving the driver and his front passenger in the car.

Who were these men arriving in such a grand car? More specifically, who was the blond man? He must be someone important to have his own driver. Maybe he was a local dignitary, yet he didn't look like a local man. Ah, perhaps he was a Dr Barnardo's inspector, though surely either position wouldn't warrant a driver and a Rolls.

Two young women appeared at the front door of the orphanage, the taller woman wearing a smart navy dress. Lana wondered if she might be Maxine Taylor. One of the men said something and the taller woman answered but Lana was too far away to hear the words. The man loped off and in the space of two minutes returned with the front passenger.

The blond man was exceptionally tall, even by her standards, and unusually he was hatless. The sun, out for the first time that day, glinted on his hair. He looked like someone in command with his confident stride. He glanced once towards the children dancing round the maypole. The accompanying man almost had to run to keep up. It would have been amusing at any other time, but there was something unnerving in the scene unfolding in front of her. After several moments the two women and three men disappeared into the house.

Lana strolled over to where the children were playing, trying to shake off the image of the man who looked different from anyone around here, thinking she might ask where Priscilla was. She watched the children for a few minutes. They certainly looked well cared for, but their expressions wore a kind of resilience – she couldn't quite explain it, but it was as though they'd had to face more than most children, which of course was true. Maybe she was being fanciful, but she didn't think so.

Two of the boys were watching her with open curiosity.

'Are you a new teacher, Miss?' one of them piped up. He looked to be about nine or ten with ginger hair.

Lana smiled. 'I'm the new headmistress at the

village school. I've come to meet some of you and Matron.'

'She's gone inside,' the other boy said. 'Some men came in that motor.' He pointed. 'It's a Rolls-Royce,' he added, the awe in his voice unmistakable. 'Isn't it smashing?'

'Yes, it certainly is a beauty,' Lana said with feeling. One day she'd have her own car, though maybe not a Rolls to start with, she thought, smiling to herself.

'I'm having one of them when I'm grown up,' the ginger-haired boy said, a determined expression fixed on his freckled face.

'I'm sure you will if you want it badly enough.' He nodded.

'Have you seen Priscilla?'

'No. She's too toffee-nosed to play with us.'

'I'm sure she doesn't mean to be,' Lana said, surprised. 'I think she's shy.'

The boy grunted. 'She was helping Cook last time I saw her.' He and his friend shot her another look, then dashed off.

So long as Priscilla was well cared for, Lana thought, though it was a pity she hadn't mixed with the others.

It was only a tentative arrangement to see Maxine Taylor at four o'clock, but already it was coming up to that time. The matron would be busy at the moment. She'd have to wait until the meeting, or whatever it was, was over and until then she'd wander round the gardens. No one seemed to be

104

taking any notice as she walked over to the vegetable garden where the gardener had erected wigwams of beanpoles ready for planting runner beans. A boy, bent nearly in two, struggled with a tough-looking weed. A little brown dog watched the boy's every move. The dog cocked his ear, then ran towards her, giving little whines of delight, his tail wagging excitedly. The boy stood up.

'Freddie! Here, boy! Come here!'

Freddie stopped in his tracks and looked round, uncertain as to what he should do – welcome the newcomer or obey his master?

'He's all right,' Lana called, swiftly closing the gap between them. 'Good boy.' She patted the dog's silky head.

'I have to keep watch on him,' the boy said importantly. 'He's only allowed here if he behaves. He used to live here but he only comes to visit now.'

'He's just like most dogs when someone new comes along. He wants to be friends.'

The boy looked at her directly with very blue eyes. Lana took in a quick breath. There was something about him. As though she'd seen him before. But that was ridiculous. She didn't know any of these children.

'Well, I know Freddie's name now, but I don't know yours.'

The boy hesitated, and Lana had the feeling he didn't want to answer. But finally he said, 'Peter – Peter Best.'

'That's a good manly name.' Lana smiled again, but the boy didn't smile back.

He looked much too serious for a child who couldn't be more than nine or ten years old. Dear oh dear, these children must all have the most awful stories to tell – the way they lost their parents. The very idea made her feel sick at heart.

'I'll leave you to the weeding,' she said. 'I do hope I'll see you and Freddie again.'

Peter nodded but his expression was one of indifference.

Lana decided it would be better if she saw the matron at a quieter moment. But when she noticed a group of small girls playing ring-a-ring-o'roses on the lawn, and a dark-haired woman who she guessed was a teacher keeping an eye on them, she thought she'd wander over and say hello.

The woman turned her head at Lana's approach.

'Hello. I'm Lana Ashwin, the new headmistress at the village school.' Lana extended her hand.

'Dolores Honeywell. I'm fairly new here, too, and pleased to meet you.' She smiled at Lana. 'I saw you and wondered who you were.'

'Mrs Taylor invited me over to meet some of the children,' Lana said. 'I was looking for Priscilla really.'

'Well, there's Matron.' Miss Honeywell motioned towards the front door. 'She's with Mrs Andrews – or June, as she was known – who used to be the matron before she married, but I don't know who that tall fair-haired man is.' She paused. 'Oh, he's going over to the greenhouses. Wonder why. He doesn't strike me as a gardener.' Dolores Honeywell turned her attention back to the children.

Lana watched as the blond man walked slowly over to the vegetable plots where she'd left Peter and Freddie just a short while ago. She thought she heard someone whistling. From where she stood she couldn't see the boy clearly, but she saw him standing very still, his back to the man. Then to her astonishment he whirled round and she heard him shout, 'Papa!' and hurl himself into the stranger's arms.

Peter's father?

The tall man held the boy tightly and kissed the top of his head. Lana couldn't take her eyes off the two of them. Bingham Hall was an orphanage, yet it seemed as though Peter had unexpectedly been reunited with his father. She felt the tears prick and turned away, not wanting to encroach on their private moment.

This wasn't at all the right time to speak to Maxine Taylor who'd probably had no idea at all that these gentlemen would be turning up when she'd suggested Lana go over to introduce herself around teatime. She'd leave quietly and telephone the matron in the morning to apologise and make a firm appointment next time.

She slipped amongst the trees lining the drive, the children's shouts and squeals of laughter sounding far away now, and made her way back to the school, the image of the tall blond man gathering his son close to his chest still sharp in her mind. She wiped a tear away with the back of her hand and smiled to herself for being so sentimental, but somehow it was comforting to know that in this interminable cruel war, the scene that had unfolded in front of her looked as though it had all the elements of a happy ending.

But there was no happy ending for Priscilla, Lana thought sadly, as she turned the key to open the cottage door, imagining the young girl in her mind's eye watching such a reunion.

Lana put the kettle on, feeling a little light-headed as she remembered the way the blond man's eyes had held hers. Why had he made such an impact?

She drank her tea without tasting it.

CHAPTER 12

May Day – that night

'**P**ut the torch out!' she hissed.

'That's no good. I can't see a bleedin' thing now.' The youth switched the torch back on.

'Well, put your hand over it.'

'To hear you, you'd think Jerry was flyin' overhead lookin' down at us.'

'You never know.' The girl gave a nervous giggle.

The two of them crept up the drive, the gravel crackling underfoot at every step.

'Go on, then, I dare you.' She dug the youth in the ribs. 'I'll keep watch but they'll all be asleep.'

The youth stretched his neck to assess the open window on the first floor of Bingham Hall. Then he twisted round to her. 'Whadya bet?'

'A shilling.'

'Nah, it's not werf it.' He sniffed and wiped his sleeve across his nose. 'I dunno, though. Maybe it is. It'd buy a packet of fags.'

'Go on, then.' The girl's eyes blazed with the

intensity of her bet. 'There's a drainpipe next to the window.'

The youth nodded and shinned up it without making a sound. He stuck his hand in the gap and pushed the sash up to make enough space to crawl through.

'You coming?' His harsh voice reverberated around the walls of the building.

'Shhhhhh!' The girl put a finger to her lips. 'Go in and unbolt the kitchen door near where I'm standing.'

The youth raised his thumb and disappeared through the opening. Two minutes later he had the door open and the girl slipped through like a shadow.

They were in.

'Look at the size of this kitchen.'

'That's nothing,' the girl said, taking his arm and leading him along a short corridor into the Great Hall.

'Cor, this is something.'

The youth's eyes almost swivelled in their sockets as he took in the vaulted ceiling, the massive stone fireplace, and the chandeliers and sconces, unlit now because of the blackout as well as the late hour. His eyes roamed the walls of oil paintings, mostly portraits, and what looked like hundreds of coats of arms, and the solid oak furniture. He turned to her and gave a low whistle.

'The nobs know how to live, don't they?'

The girl pulled a face. 'They might've been nobs

in them days but Lord Bingham and his family did a runner when the war started.'

'Who told you that?' The youth narrowed his eyes at her.

'I used to work here, didn't I?' the girl said. 'I got ears. You hear things when you work here.'

He threw a look of disbelief that she could have landed such a job.

'Wot did you do?'

'I looked after the special children,' the girl said proudly as she led him along the corridor to the magnificent library. 'Well, I did until that bitch nurse reported me.'

'You weren't crafty enough. You shouldda hung on to yer job.' He stared at her. 'Chance to pinch all kinds of stuff and they'd never notice.' He stared at her. 'What she report you about, anyways?'

'I told them we got a Nazi kid amongst us and we should get rid of him.'

'How d'ya know that?'

'I saw a photo of his German pa in his uniform, didn't I?' A satisfied smirk curled her lips. 'I might not be a clever clogs but I know a swastika when I see one. His jacket was full of 'em. I was the only one who dared speak out and got the sack for me trouble.'

'Phew!' The youth blew his cheeks out. 'You never know what goes on in these places, do you?'

The pair padded up the main staircase in their rubber-soled shoes.

'Wot's that room?' He nodded towards an open door.

'Where the kids paint.'

He pushed it open with his foot and looked around at the childish paintings pinned on the walls.

'I always fancied doing a bit of paintin' meself,' he said, 'but never got the chance.'

'Maybe you would if you hadn't been expelled so many times.'

He grinned, then took a piece of thin paper from his pocket and poked some tobacco into it. With a practised movement he rolled it and licked the ends together with a large red tongue, and stuck it between his heavy lips.

'I don't think you ought to do that,' the girl said, her expression suddenly anxious. 'Someone might smell it and think the place is on fire. And we'll be caught and punished.'

'Don't be daft.' He struck a match and lit it.

'I mean it, Billy. Put it out. It's too dangerous.' She blinked and waved the smoke away from her face.

'Oh, awright. Just give me a few puffs.' He inhaled deeply and blew out a long stream of smoke.

'Billy . . .'

'Stop nagging, Hil, for Chrissakes.' He took one more drag, gave the roll-up a cursory stub on the edge of the Belfast sink, and tossed the still-glowing stub into the wastepaper basket.

CHAPTER 13

Lana struggled to wake up. Bells. The village church bells. She cocked her head to listen, then threw back the covers and leapt out of bed.

There it was again. Impossible. Mr Churchill had ordered all church bells to stop unless . . . dear God, not the invasion! She flew to the window and saw two fire engines screaming past in the opposite direction to the village – they were headed for Bingham Hall. Dear Lord, had the Germans bombed an orphanage this time? Innocent sleeping children and those who looked after them? Priscilla, Peter, that nice-sounding Maxine Taylor.

Feeling sick she swiftly dressed and hammered on Janice's door. No answer. She opened it. Janice was snoring away as usual. Should she wake her? They would need all the help they could get. She shook the woman's shoulder.

'Janice! Wake up! There's a fire at the orphanage. I've just seen the fire engines.'

The sleeping figure moved a fraction.

'Janice! There's a fire at Bingham Hall.'

'What? What are you . . .?' Janice sat up, her eyes wide.

'I'm going to see if I can help. Will you come with me?'

'You're ready. You go and I'll follow.'

Lana ran, her long legs flying as she drew level with others who must have heard the alarm. A dull pain already throbbed in her side. By the time she reached the drive of Bingham Hall she had to stop and catch her breath or she'd never make it up the slope. She looked towards the house and saw flames shooting into the night sky.

But there'd been no siren. No explosion. No bomb. She was sure she'd have heard it if there had.

Eyes watering from the smoke already wafting towards her, Lana hurried up the hill to where a crowd of people and children had already gathered, their faces lifted towards the sky, which was an eerie red. She was near enough now to hear the snapping and cracking of the blaze. Children screamed and cried over shouting adults. Her eyes began to sting badly and her nose filled with smoke. Firemen were pointing their hoses onto the east side of the building where the flames had taken hold, the water pouring in jets onto the building.

She spotted a woman who was urging a group of youngsters further away. Lana stumbled towards her in the dark, and tapped her on the shoulder.

The woman whirled round and Lana saw it was the teacher she'd spoken to at the May Day event.

'What a disaster.' Dolores Honeywell's face was blotchy and her eyes were running from the smoke.

'What can I do?'

'Keep an eye on these kids while I try to find out if the children are all here.'

Before Lana could answer, Dolores had rushed towards the group of firemen.

'Do you know if everyone's out of the building?' Lana asked an older boy.

'No telling,' he answered, his streaming eyes fixed on Bingham Hall.

She couldn't blame him. He was watching his home go up in smoke.

'What's your name?'

He turned. 'Alan.'

'Alan, can I trust you to keep these boys in check? I'm the new headmistress at the village school.'

The boy nodded.

The boys, eight of them, she counted, were all talking and pointing. One was crying.

'Alan's going to look after you for a few minutes,' she told them. 'Please wait here with him until I or one of the other grown-ups come back. Do *not* leave this spot. You'll be in the way of the firemen who are trying to do their job.' She gave as stern a look as she dared without frightening them any further. 'Do you understand?'

'Yes, Miss,' they chorused.

The little boy who was crying stopped and looked at her with fearful eyes.

These innocent children. As if the war and bombing wasn't bad enough. She put her arm around him.

'It's all right,' she said. 'Alan is here to look after you.' The others began talking and she stopped them with her hand in the air. 'And if Alan tells you to move somewhere else for safety, you are to obey him. Is that clear?'

They nodded. She could only pray that Alan would keep them in order as she made her way, running and stumbling over the uneven grass towards Bingham Hall.

She had to speak to one of the firemen. Find out what was happening. If anyone . . . Dear God, don't let there be anyone still trapped.

'Excuse me,' she said to the nearest fireman who was concentrating on pointing his hose on another fire that had taken hold in a different spot.

'Stand back, Miss.'

'Is anyone still in the building?'

'We don't know. One of our chaps has gone in. The matron's trying to get all the names.'

He jerked his head over his right shoulder and she saw a tallish woman with a large group of children around her.

Lana sped over in the direction the fireman pointed.

'Mrs Taylor . . . Matron,' she called in the distance between them.

The woman glanced in her direction.

'I'm Lana Ashwin from the school,' Lana breathed harshly as she rushed up. The matron nodded as though in a trance. 'Can I do anything? Is everyone safe?'

Maxine Taylor's voice was shaking as she answered. 'All the boys are out,' she said, 'and the girls . . . except one – Priscilla Morgan. No one's seen her.'

Oh, no. Not Priscilla. Lana's heart clenched in fear.

'The firemen barred my way,' Maxine said thickly. 'They refused to let me go in.' She seemed to gather her wits as she shouted to someone. 'Charlie! Please help with these children. I must make sure everyone's out.'

Maxine rushed off, Lana running behind. Moments later she saw the matron trip on a fallen branch. A moan of pain sliced through the air. Lana flew over the grass.

'My ankle.' Maxine screwed up her eyes in pain. 'It's not broken but it hurts like mad. Just a bad twist.'

'Let me see.' Another figure ran to the matron's side.

'Oh, Dolores, thank goodness it's you. I've gone and sprained my ankle.'

'See if you can get up,' Dolores said. 'Here, give me your hand.'

'Priscilla—' Maxine began.

'Don't worry, I'll find her,' Lana said, touching

Maxine briefly on the shoulder before dashing over to the home.

'You're not allowed to go in there, Miss,' one of the fireman shouted. 'It's not safe. You're not properly equipped . . .'

Without answering, Lana heaved the front door open and shot inside, her only thought for the young girl. The heat made her reel back, choking. Pulling her scarf over her nose, which immediately made her feel she was suffocating, she pushed further inside and shouted up the stairs. Flames were already crackling from the first-floor landing.

'Is anyone there?' A silence. 'Priscilla! Are you there?' She waited seconds, then bellowed, 'PRISCILLA!'

'Help!'

It was barely a whimper but she heard it. She raced up the stairs, hardly aware of the fire as she shouted, 'I'm coming.' Her head snapped this way and that. 'Where are you, Priscilla?'

'Up here!'

Heart in her mouth, Lana started up the second flight but the flames were bursting around her. She'd be trapped. She'd have to turn back. But she couldn't. There was a child . . . She coughed and a slick of black spittle burst from her mouth.

'Priscilla!'

To her joy she saw a white face over the banister of the second floor – and then it disappeared. A scream made her blood run cold. Within seconds she'd reached the girl who'd crumpled into a heap.

'Priscilla, it's me – Miss Ashwin from the school. Can you get up?'

'No.'

'Please try. We have to get out of the building. The fire is spreading.'

She put her arms around the child's waist and hoisted her to her feet. 'Come on, love. I'm here. We can do it together. Hold on to me.'

She turned towards the stairs but to her horror the flames had hold of the staircase. She recoiled, banging her hand against one of the doorjambs.

'Where's the fire escape?'

Priscilla jerked her head. Lana grabbed her hand. 'GO!'

Priscilla ran a short distance down a corridor, then froze.

'I can't,' she wailed.

Dear God, the child was in shock. She couldn't remember where it was. Heart feeling as though it were about to burst from her chest, Lana tore her scarf from her neck, wrapped it around her hand and seized the nearest door handle. She pulled Priscilla in, then kicked the door shut behind them. Thank the Lord there were no flames in this room, but it was full of smoke. She tripped over something solid in her path as she rushed to the window in her effort to open the sash. Straining every sinew, she managed to push up the pane of glass, and heard men's voices shouting outside. Thank God for the air. She gulped in a few breaths and bellowed.

'Help! HELP!'

Oh, the relief when one of them looked up in her direction.

'I see you,' a man's voice shouted. 'Anyone else with you?'

'A girl – Priscilla Morgan. Matron's looking for her.'

'Is she all right?'

'I think so.'

He raised a thumb. 'Hold tight, love. Ladder coming. Be up in a jiffy.'

'Come and get some air, Priscilla. One of the fireman is going to get us down.'

For a moment there was no reply. Then a scream pierced her eardrums, making her blood curdle. She swung round in time to see Priscilla, only a few feet away.

'Priscilla, what—?'

The girl turned to her and pointed. 'Miss, it's . . .' She broke off. Her eyes were wide. 'There's a m-m—'

'Let me see.'

Priscilla stood aside, her hand covering her mouth as though to stifle another scream.

Lana recoiled. What she'd almost tripped up on was a figure, lying on his back, his bloodied eyes staring at the ceiling. He must have been trying to open the window but collapsed from the smoke. She put her face to his chest. Nothing. She felt for his hand, turned it so the inside of his wrist was towards her. She put her three fingers on his pulse as she'd been taught at one of her St John Ambulance training classes. There was no flicker of life. A youth, too young to be called up. Smoke and tears stung her eyes.

'Is he dead?'

'I'm afraid he is, Priscilla. Don't look any more. It was an accident.'

Smoke was curling under the crack of the door. Her heart beat hard. *Please hurry. Oh, please hurry.*

'We're going to be all right, Priscilla,' she said, as she pulled the silent child into her arms. Priscilla's eyes were unfocused, wide with terror. 'The fireman has seen us and he's going to rescue us. He'll be here very soon.'

She heard more shouts – more like orders – and hardly before she'd finished speaking, a man's face appeared at the window, his fireman's helmet glinting in the moonlight. She pulled Priscilla away, allowing him to haul himself through the gap.

'Thank God you've got the child. We knew there was one missing.' He looked at the terrified girl. 'You Priscilla, love?'

Priscilla nodded.

'Either of you hurt?'

'She needs to be checked for burns – she's been in the building longer than anyone,' Lana said, trying not to show how worried she was in front of Priscilla who was clinging on to her arm and crying softly. More smoke was seeping under the door.

'I'm afraid you'll have to go out the way I came in,' the fireman said. 'But don't worry . . . you'll be all right.'

Lana couldn't look at him. If she had, he would have seen in an instant how terrified she was. 'There's a body over there.' She pointed. 'He's— I'm pretty certain he's dead.'

The fireman felt for the youth's pulse and nodded.

'I'm afraid you're right. Let's get you out first before the fire bursts in. I'll take care of the lad. You go first, love, then the girl. I'll follow behind. There'll be a fireman at the bottom of the ladder holding it steady and one who'll come up the ladder right behind you – and the girl when it's her turn – so we don't have any accidents. Turn round and go down backwards. Don't look down. It'll be all right. We're only two storeys up.'

Lana's stomach turned over with fright. She was petrified of heights. It was no good the fireman telling her they weren't very high up. But she had to keep level-headed in front of Priscilla. She mustn't show any fear.

She nodded. Get it over with – the sooner the better.

'Priscilla, I'm going first down the ladder. Then you, and then a fireman who'll be close behind you and our nice fireman in front. They'll make sure you're safe. Is that clear?'

'Yes.' A whimper.

'There'll be another firemen at the bottom of

the ladder. Just take your time – don't rush. Just watch me and then you follow.'

Lana peered out of the window and could make out two figures at the bottom of the ladder. The fireman took her arm and helped her through the window into the cold night air. Gingerly she put one foot behind her on the ladder. She kept her eyes glued on the brick façade in front of her as her feet almost automatically felt for the next rung. She sensed the figure of a man right behind her. Then before she realised, a fireman's comforting hand was helping her on the final step. She was down.

Anxiously, she tilted her head upwards to see the fireman easing Priscilla through the window. The girl clung on to the ladder with both hands, the fireman, his arms stretched, holding her steady. She put her foot backwards just as Lana had done, but it slipped through the gap between the rungs. Her foot dangling in mid-air, the child let out a piercing scream, but the fireman behind her practically cradled her as he guided her down, step by slow step.

Before she reached the ground he had pulled Priscilla off the ladder and into his arms, then carried her over to a patch of grass and gently set her down. Somebody turned up with a blanket and draped it round Priscilla's huddled form.

'She's in shock,' the fireman said to Lana under his breath. 'Stay with her. The ambulance should be here any minute and she ought to go to hospital.

Have her lungs checked as well as any other burns. She's got a burn on her arm but it doesn't look too bad.' He glanced at Lana. 'Are *you* all right, Miss?'

'I think so.' Lana's voice seemed to her to come from a long way away, as though she were in a dream. She coughed and her throat itself seemed on fire. She looked towards the building. 'Did anyone fetch that poor young man?'

'One of our chaps got him out but it was too late. You knew that, didn't you?'

Lana bit her lip and nodded. 'Is the fire out now?'

'More or less,' he said. 'We're just checking. It's the far wing with the most damage.' He looked at her. 'Are you one of the teachers?'

'Not here,' Lana said. 'I'm the new head-mistress of the village school, but I heard the fire engines so I thought I'd run over and see if there was anything I could do to help.'

'Well, although you ignored our instructions to steer clear, I have to admit you've certainly done your bit, young lady,' he said, grinning. 'This young'un might not have been in quite such good shape without your actions.'

'It was nothing anyone else wouldn't have done,' Lana said, shivering now it was over. She put her arms round Priscilla who was visibly shaking.

'Well done, Priscilla.'

There was no response.

'Are you all right, love?'

Wordlessly, the girl nodded, her face as pale as the moon.

'They're going to take you to hospital to have a look at your arm.' She hesitated. 'Priscilla, why were you the last one to leave? All the other children were out except you.'

Priscilla's mouth tightened as though she was afraid of what she might say. Why? Lana wondered. Had the child slept through it? If so, why hadn't one of the other children woken her? It didn't make sense. And how had the others escaped? Some of them were so young they wouldn't know how to use the fire escape. Someone must have shown them where it was and what to do. And then it dawned on her.

'Priscilla, love, were you helping the others get out?'

Priscilla blinked.

'Miss Ashwin, is that you?'

Lana turned to see Maxine Taylor half running, half hopping across the grass towards them. *Thank goodness the matron was back on her feet.*

'Oh, thank heavens you're safe, Priscilla.' She bent and touched the girl's shoulder but Priscilla stayed rigid. The woman stood and held out her hand to Lana.

'Not the best timing for our meeting but I can't thank you enough.' She lowered her voice. 'We were worried out of our minds that Priscilla had fallen or hadn't got out, but the firemen wouldn't let us through. They said one of them was going

125

to check in case anyone was still there. How did you get in?'

'When no one was looking,' Lana said. 'Is everyone accounted for now?'

'Yes. Every child and staff member. We're just waiting for the ambulance.'

Lana turned her back to Priscilla and gestured for the matron to come round to the other side so they wouldn't be overheard.

'There was someone else in the same dormitory where Priscilla and I were,' she said.

'Oh, no.' Maxine Taylor put her hands to her face. 'Who? We've counted everyone.'

'A man. Hardly more than a boy, really.'

'Is he injured?'

'I'm afraid he's dead.'

Maxine Taylor put her hand to her face. 'Oh, God, how awful.'

'He must have been overcome with the smoke. Another horrible shock for Priscilla, poor girl, as she discovered him. She needs to be checked over because she was in the building the longest.'

'Yes, of course.' Maxine Taylor cocked her head. 'Thank heavens – the ambulance. We've got two other children who need checking as well as Priscilla.' She looked at Lana. 'It wouldn't hurt you to go as well, Miss Ashwin. It must have been awful in there feeling you were trapped.'

Lana shook her head to discourage the matron from saying any more in front of Priscilla who had started to cry again.

'Don't leave me, Miss Ashwin,' she sobbed. 'I thought we were going to burn to death.'

'Of course we weren't, love,' Lana said, stroking the girl's hair. 'We had that nice fireman helping us. And I'm not leaving you – I'm coming with you to the hospital. And then you'll be in your bed before you know it. Sleep will be the best thing for you.'

'I'm not going back inside that place – ever!' Priscilla said, jerking her head towards the house, her eyes wet with tears.

'Shhhh!' Lana turned to Maxine. 'Mrs Taylor—'

'Do call me Maxine. And you're Lana.'

'Maxine, is it all right with you if I take Priscilla to the hospital?'

'That's probably a sensible solution,' Maxine said, sounding relieved.

'As soon as Priscilla has been looked at we'll come straight back.'

But Dr Jason had other ideas.

'She's got a burn on her arm I want to keep an eye on, and a couple of smaller ones – nothing too serious,' he said to Lana after he'd thoroughly examined Priscilla. 'Her lungs are fine but she's still in shock and I'd like to keep her in tonight – give her a mild sedative. She should feel a lot better in the morning and then I'm sure you'll be able to take her home.'

'I'm not staying here!' Priscilla cried out. 'I want to go with Miss Ashwin. I don't want to stay in hospital. I just w-want . . .'

Suddenly, Priscilla slipped from her chair to the floor before Lana or the doctor could reach her. He was beside her in seconds and put his hand under her head to prop her up.

'Priscilla! Priscilla, wake up. It's all right. You're going to be fine.'

She opened her eyes, wide now with terror.

'Where am I?'

'You're in hospital, love, and I'm here with you,' Lana said, taking her hand. 'And Dr Jason is looking after you.'

Priscilla began to struggle. 'I'm not staying in hospital.' She suddenly went white and put her hand up to her forehead. 'I feel dizzy.'

Quickly Lana set her on the chair and Dr Jason put his hand to the back of Priscilla's neck and gently pushed her head towards the floor. After a few seconds he brought her head back up.

'I've got a headache.' Priscilla's voice was small and shaky.

Dr Jason went to a cabinet on the wall and drew out a bottle. He shook a tablet into a cup.

'Take this, my dear. It will help your headache and you'll have a good sleep.'

Priscilla looked at the white tablet and Lana willed her to take it. After a long pause Priscilla slowly put the pill in her mouth and Dr Jason handed her a glass of water.

'I'm going to fetch a nurse who will give you a hot drink and tuck you up in bed, young lady,' he said, going to the door. 'Nurse!'

A plain-looking girl with a kind smile came into the consulting room.

'Can you take young Priscilla? I've given her a pill to help her sleep. I'd like you to keep an eye on her through the night and then the doctor on duty will see her in the morning to have a look at that burn on her arm, and if he's satisfied, she can go home.'

'No! No! I'm going back with Miss Ashwin.'

Priscilla's voice had risen to a pitch and Lana felt helpless.

'Leave her with me, Miss Ashwin,' the young nurse said. 'I promise I'll look after her. She'll be quite safe with me.'

The last thing Lana heard was Priscilla sobbing her heart out.

CHAPTER 14

It hadn't been easy to leave Priscilla at the hospital, even though Lana was sure the nurse would do everything in her power to make sure the young girl was comfortable and able to sleep for a few hours after such a terrible ordeal.

Back in her bed, and trying to justify the feeling of guilt that she'd left her charge with strangers, Lana realised Dr Jason had made the right decision. A nurse would keep an eye on Priscilla all through the night, and in the morning the doctor on duty would check her to make sure she was fit to go home. She would never have forgiven herself if she'd taken Priscilla to the cottage and something had gone wrong in the night. It was just that Priscilla's eyes had beseeched Lana to allow her to go with her. And then that terrible look of despair, then resignation, which had settled over Priscilla's features when Lana had said goodbye – as though she were leaving forever.

Lana woke up late in the morning with a throbbing headache in a head stuffed with straw. For a few moments she forgot about the fire and was only thankful it was Sunday and she didn't have to work. She rarely had a headache and knew she didn't have any Aspros with her. She wondered if Janice had a couple.

Then it came back to her. The fire! Priscilla! She shot up in bed. Where *was* Janice? She hadn't seen her at the orphanage at all, now she came to think of it. She wrapped her dressing gown around herself and crept towards Janice's bedroom. She put her ear to the door. She couldn't hear anything. Normally, Janice's snoring was loud enough to wake her but there was an eerie silence.

Please don't let something awful have happened to Janice when she followed me to Bingham Hall last night. Then she heard footsteps downstairs.

'Janice, is that you?'

'Oh, I thought you were still asleep,' Janice called up. 'I'm making tea.'

'I'm coming down now.'

'You look like you've been dragged through a hedge backwards,' Janice said, scrutinising her with a frown when Lana appeared.

'That's more or less what happened,' Lana said grimly. 'But where did *you* get to? I only realised after all the chaos that I hadn't seen you.'

'I never got there.' Janice rubbed her hand round her back. 'Because I was rushing and probably still half asleep, I fell down the last four stairs.'

'Oh, no.'

'Oh, yes,' Janice said, with a shrug. 'Stupid, as I was carrying my shoes in one hand and a glass of water in the other. For goodness' sake don't go around barefoot as I've still found slivers of glass even though I've spent ages trying to clear it up.'

Lana glanced down at her bare feet. Too late. She curled her toes under as if that would help.

'Janice, you could have broken a bone.'

'I know. I managed to crawl back up the stairs but my back is killing me. I must have badly bruised something.'

'You should go to the doctor's.'

'No. It can't be that serious or I wouldn't be able to walk. But I must say it's hard to stand up straight.' She grunted as she bent to pour the tea and handed Lana a cup. 'But more important than my stupid back, what happened with the fire? Did it do much damage?'

Lana quickly told her about Priscilla.

'I think she'd had a hand in helping to rescue the young ones,' Lana finished. 'I asked her and she didn't seem to want to answer. And then Maxine Taylor came up so I had to explain to her what Priscilla had just gone through.'

'What's she like? Mrs Taylor, I mean.'

'She seems nice. But Priscilla refused to go back into the home, which you can't blame her for. She found a young man dead in the dormitory where the fireman rescued us.'

'Oh, God.' Janice shuddered.

'It was dreadful. The man who rescued us said Priscilla was in shock and should go to the hospital, so I went with her.'

'Sorry I missed all the drama,' Janice said.

'It wasn't exactly a barrel of laughs,' Lana said, feeling annoyed.

'No, of course not,' Janice put in quickly. 'Sorry. You must think me an unfeeling devil. It's just that I'm drained of emotion these days.'

It was probably wiser not to make any comment. Lana set her cup down. 'Why don't you come with me to the hospital this morning? I'm going to collect Priscilla, if she's well enough. You could then have someone examine you – just to make sure.'

'Too much to do. I'll see the doc next week if it gets worse. You go and let me know how she is. Good job today's Sunday. She should be right as rain tomorrow for school.'

Yes, you are unfeeling, Lana thought. There was no possibility that Priscilla would be as right as rain by tomorrow after her traumatic night. But it was impossible to argue with Janice.

Even though it was Sunday Lana was at her desk to work. It would take her mind off things, Priscilla in particular, and besides, she'd told the hospital to ring her at work as there was no telephone in the cottage.

She was glancing through some of the children's school reports when the phone rang.

The hospital.

'Is that you, Lana?'

She recognised the voice. Maxine Taylor.

'Did you manage to get any sleep?'

133

'Not much,' Lana admitted. 'It was late when I got back from the hospital.'

'That's what I was ringing for – well, to see how you were, of course, but to find out how Priscilla was. They rang me last night to say they were keeping her in.'

'I haven't heard yet,' Lana said. 'I told them I'd fetch her when she was ready to be discharged.'

'That would help tremendously, as I'm filling in for one of the nurses today. But there's more.' Even over the wire Lana heard Maxine exhale. 'There's substantial fire damage to two of the classrooms, especially the art room and the girls' dormitory. I'm going to have to ask a huge favour. Do you think you could put seven girls up in the school and take some of the older children into your classes until we get the repairs done? It could be a few weeks – I hope not longer – but it's difficult to get these sorts of repairs done with the war . . .' She trailed off. 'I've been ringing round but most of the tradesmen have joined the forces – or the Home Front.'

Lana didn't hesitate. 'I'm sure we can find some space for sleeping them. It might be a bit rough and ready, though. We'll find extra chairs but they'll have to share the books.'

'That'd be marvellous. I'm so sorry to land this on you when you've barely got here,' Maxine said.

'Don't worry about that. We all have to muck in. I'm more than happy to help.' She paused.

134

'Do they know how the fire started and who the young lad was?'

'Not yet,' Maxine said. 'I hope to know more tomorrow.'

Lana swallowed. Another young life extinguished. But a flicker of relief rushed through her head. She didn't know him. But she knew Priscilla. And she thanked God that the young girl with those soft grey eyes, full of terror last night, was safe.

As if Maxine read her thoughts she heard her say, 'Yes, it's dreadful, but at least our children and all the live-in staff managed to escape – though I was desperate to find Priscilla. She was the only child we couldn't account for.'

'It was a miracle she wasn't seriously burned,' Lana said fervently.

'I know. I can't thank you enough.' Another pause. 'If you ring to tell me when you expect to collect her I'll send Harold in the motorcar for you.'

'I was going on the bus.'

'No. It will take too long. We have enough petrol to cover these emergencies and she'll be feeling a bit fragile.'

At least Maxine has some heart.

'All right. Thank you. I'll let you know.'

Priscilla, her arm now bandaged, seemed grateful that Lana had come to take her back to Bingham Hall, but although Harold asked if she was comfortable, Priscilla just said yes and sat rigidly, staring out of the window, her mouth tight. But as soon as Harold steered the car up the drive Priscilla began to shake uncontrollably.

'What is it, love?' Lana asked, a sinking sensation in her stomach as she put an arm around the trembling shoulders. Priscilla was staring at the front door.

'I can't go in. I'm not ever going into that horrible place ever again.'

Lana thought quickly. Priscilla had only been at the orphanage a short while and had never adjusted to living with so many children, and no longer having a loving mother and father and her home. Maxine had asked her if she could sleep all the girls at the school. But it wouldn't be any different from Bingham Hall for Priscilla. What if she offered Priscilla to share her own room at the cottage. Put up a small bed for the girl. Gave her some extra loving care. Lana was positive the child had been instrumental in getting many of the other children to safety. She wouldn't be surprised if Priscilla had nightmares from such a disaster.

She'd need to discuss it with Janice. It was only polite. And Janice herself had admitted that Priscilla had been through a lot, and that was *before* the fire.

'Please, Miss Ashwin, let me come back to the school with you.' Tears were pouring down her cheeks although she was making no sound of crying. It couldn't hurt, Lana thought, to let the child stay the night, and then ask Janice if she would mind if it became a few weeks longer.

'Harold, could you just wait with Priscilla for a few minutes while I speak to Matron?'

'Certainly, Miss.'

Lana hopped out of the car and pulled the bell cord outside the great oak door. She heard the bell chime faintly within. After a few moments the door juddered open to reveal a maid dressed in neat apron and cap.

'Yes, Miss?'

'I have an appointment with Matron – Mrs Taylor.'

'She's expecting you, Miss. Please come in.'

Lana stepped into the magnificent hall.

'Would you take a seat, Miss, and I'll tell Matron you're here.'

'Thank you.'

Instead of sitting, Lana wandered around the vast space, her shoes clicking on the flagstone floor, taking in the huge stone fireplace where a log fire crackled warmly. It should have felt welcoming, but the very sound sent a shiver down her spine. Thankfully there was no sign of any fire damage in this part of the house. She glanced at the hundreds of coats of arms and was peering at an oil painting of a man in a plumed hat redolent of the seventeenth century – probably one of the previous owners of Bingham Hall – when the maid returned.

'Will you follow me, Miss?' She led Lana to a door a few steps down a passage and knocked.

'Please enter,' said a voice she recognised.

Lana turned the handle and Maxine rose to meet her.

'It's lovely to see you properly this time,' she smiled, giving Lana a warm handshake.

Lana couldn't tell in the dark last night, but she saw now that Maxine was a few years younger than she'd thought, not quite so tall as herself, with striking turquoise eyes that seemed to miss nothing.

'Do sit down.' She looked beyond Lana and frowned. 'Where's Priscilla?'

'I can't stay long,' Lana said, sitting on the edge of the visitor's chair. 'Priscilla's still in the car with Harold – she's in rather a bad state. Oh, not physically, though she's got one nasty burn—'

'But not bad enough to keep her in?' Maxine's eyes filled with concern.

'Oh, no.'

'That's good. I'm a nurse so I can easily look after her.'

This was embarrassing. She liked Maxine on sight but it was going to be difficult to explain. The matron's smile was encouraging.

'She's shaking like a leaf and doesn't want to come inside,' Lana said. There was no time to pick her words to be tactful. 'She's still in shock and all she sees is a building she never wanted to come to, and finds it impossible to call home, and then the fire . . .' She looked at Maxine. 'She won't talk about it but I believe she helped several children out of the building before she thought of herself. She was last, and then trapped.'

Maxine's mouth fell open. 'Oh, my goodness! What a brave girl. Of course I understand. Poor child.'

Lana plunged in. 'She's asked if she can come back with me. I share a cottage with one of the teachers. It's only two bedrooms but my room is big enough to put another bed in. It may only be for a few nights until she gets over her ordeal in the fire.'

'That's very kind of you,' Maxine said. 'As long as it's not too much trouble.' She paused. 'Especially when we're asking a lot of you for our other girls. But if I know Priscilla is with you, I shan't worry. I, or Dolores – that's our new nurse – will come over every day to check on her.'

'I've met Dolores,' Lana said, relieved. 'Well, I'd better get back to the school so we can finish preparing one of the rooms for the temporary dormitory.'

'We'll come over later with the girls and the bed linens and pillows, and whatever we can salvage.' Maxine rose to her feet. 'And you probably need a mattress for Priscilla.'

Lana nodded. 'It would be useful.' She hesitated. 'You haven't found out yet who that poor young man was?'

Maxine's face immediately dropped. 'No. The ambulance took him away. The police assured me they'll let me know if they find out who he is. It's very worrying if he was an intruder, though, with all the children . . .'

'We'll all feel better when we know.' Lana glanced at her watch. 'I must go,' she said. 'Harold will be wondering what's happened.'

CHAPTER 15

'We'll probably see you later on,' Lana told Harold when he dropped her and Priscilla off at the school.

Harold nodded. 'Very good, Miss.' He raised his cap.

'Right, Priscilla,' Lana said briskly. 'I think we'd better go and see Mrs Parkes who I share the cottage with.'

Priscilla's mouth immediately turned down. 'I don't like Mrs Parkes. She's too strict.'

'I'm sure she doesn't mean to be,' Lana said. 'But she has a large class of children to teach. We need the older children like you to help make it easier for her.'

Priscilla didn't look convinced.

'You know all the girls from the orphanage will be sleeping here at the school until their dormitory is repaired?' Lana said.

Priscilla shrugged. 'They're all such babies. But it's probably better to have them than the boys. They're always trouble.'

She sounded a little spoilt, Lana thought. Used to getting her own way. And no wonder, as there was never any mention of a brother or sister or else Maxine would have told her. And then she berated herself for thinking anything the slightest bit bad about Priscilla. The young girl had lost everything in her world, and although she didn't appear to believe it was a permanent situation, Lana knew one day soon she was going to have to talk to her again. It was downright unhealthy for her to have such faith that her parents were coming back for her. It wasn't as though she was a little girl, where it would be understandable if she couldn't take it in.

'It's because you're not used to boys, I expect,' Lana said, smiling, 'but they're not all trouble. Some of them are really interesting. You have to give them a chance.'

'I prefer to be on my own. I never wanted brothers and sisters. Mummy and Daddy are happy just to have *me*.' She looked straight at Lana. 'Our little joke is that they say, "You're our favourite daughter," and I say, "I must be because I'm your *only* daughter."' She gave a mirthless giggle.

Lana's heart plummeted. Poor child. Whenever Priscilla mentioned her mother and father it was always in the present.

'Let's go and speak to Mrs Parkes. It's only good manners as you're going to share the cottage, though you might only be on a mattress to start with.'

'It won't be for long,' Priscilla said. 'Mummy

141

and Daddy will be here any day now to fetch me home.'

Lana felt a stinging behind her eyes. She had to think of something to make Priscilla's parents' death a reality. She'd think about it later, but for now she needed help with the emergency preparations, although Janice would probably not be much help after her fall. Lana unlocked the cottage door and saw Janice asleep on the sofa in the little sitting room. She put her finger to her lips for Priscilla to be quiet.

'Can I have some water, please?' Priscilla asked, her voice shaking.

Lana nodded and went into the kitchen, Priscilla following, then held a glass under the cold-water tap. But just as Priscilla was about to take it, she suddenly slumped to the floor. Lana slammed the glass on the draining board and rushed to her.

'Priscilla, love.' Priscilla's eyes fluttered open. Lana waited a few seconds, then put her hand under the back of the girl's neck and very gently pulled her to a sitting position.

Priscilla's face was so pale Lana could see the faint blue lines of her veins in her forehead.

'Where am I?' Priscilla's eyes rolled in her head. She blinked and tried to focus.

'You're in the cottage at the school . . . with me – Miss Ashwin.'

'What's happening?' Janice appeared at the kitchen door. She glanced down at Priscilla. 'What's going on? Why is Priscilla here on a Sunday? She looks like death.' Her tone was almost accusing.

Lana shook her head to warn Janice not to say anything more. Hesitating, she wondered how to broach the subject of Priscilla staying at the cottage. But Janice was tapping a foot, impatiently waiting for an answer.

'She's going to stay in my room for a few nights until . . .' Lana was about to say 'until the repairs are finished', but Priscilla beat her to it.

'Until my parents come back for me,' the girl said with a tremor, 'which will be any day now.'

Janice looked at Lana, her lips drawn together in a tight line. 'Did you think to discuss this with me first?'

'Yes, of course,' Lana said, feeling more like a teacher still in training than a headmistress, 'but you weren't around and I had to make a decision.' She drew in a deep breath and said very softly so only Janice could hear the words. 'Listen, Janice, Priscilla's still in shock and just now fainted, so I don't want to argue in front of her. She's had enough to put up with, poor kid. And I don't have a lot of time to devote to the problems at Bingham Hall. But we should be good neighbours after what they've just gone through. And Maxine Taylor is a really nice woman. You can tell she loves the children. She's also a qualified nurse and—'

Janice threw her hands in the air in resignation and rolled her eyes. 'All right, all right, I get the message.'

'Good.' Lana felt on firmer ground. 'Then we'd better get started or the staff at the orphanage will be here any minute with the bedclothes for the girls. They're staying, too!'

Despite Janice's painful back and grumpy mood, she and Lana, with Priscilla, managed to find seven small tables in the schoolhouse where the girls could put their few personal bits and pieces, and the two women spaced them out in one of the classrooms designated for a makeshift dormitory.

They were just about to stop for a cup of tea when there was a loud knocking on the school-house front door. Lana ran to open it. Dolores and another woman, her strawberry-blonde hair styled in a perfect Victory Roll, were standing outside, their arms full of linens and pillows. Harold followed carrying more bedclothes.

'We're going to have to make several trips before the girls come this afternoon,' he said, cheerfully. 'Matron's trying to sort out some mattresses that weren't damaged.' He glanced at Lana. 'Where should we put these?'

She led them to the emergency dormitory where the three of them dropped everything in a pile on a large table.

'I'll be off, then,' Harold said, 'to pick up the next load.'

Dolores introduced Lana to the beautifully turned-out woman – a teacher by the name of Athena Graham.

Lana raised her eyebrows.

'I know,' Athena said, smiling. 'Parents were Greek nuts.'

'I like it,' Lana said, smiling back. 'What do you teach?'

'English and Mathematics. But you have to turn your hand to anything these days.'

Although Athena was smiling, Lana saw sadness in her eyes and wondered why.

'Ah, I teach English as well, and you're right – we have to be prepared to teach any subject when there are so few of us.' Lana paused. 'Has the fire done a lot of damage?'

'Not so much as we first thought,' Athena said. 'The hospital sick bay's unscathed, which is a relief. And thank God the library miraculously escaped. Those books could never be replaced, and the room would have cost a fortune to restore. No, the fire caught the girls' dorm on the second floor, the art studio and a couple of classrooms. It seemed to be contained on that side of the home and the firemen came almost immediately.' She sighed. 'It's just that nearly all the builders and plumbers are working flat out in Liverpool patching up people's houses and shops. But Maxine's doing her best to get some workmen, so we hope it won't be too long with this arrangement. Although it's very kind of you to help,' she added quickly.

'Not at all,' Lana said. 'I'm looking forward to meeting the girls and, of course, the older boys you're sending over to join the classroom.' She eyed the bed linen and pillows. 'What about their personal bits and pieces – toys and things?'

'They don't have much,' Athena said. 'Lucky if they have more than one toy. And they will probably be donated from the villagers. But it's things like losing little mementos and photographs of their families that's the most upsetting.'

'Poor little kids,' Lana said. Her heart ached for them. 'We'll make them as welcome as we possibly can. I'm hoping Priscilla will help me settle them in. She was marvellous last night helping them escape the fire. She made sure they were all rescued before she tried to escape herself.' She turned to the girl and smiled.

Priscilla said nothing.

'I heard about it. It was very brave of you,' Athena said, smiling at her.

Priscilla shrugged and touched her bandaged arm with her fingertips.

'When did the doctor say you had to have it looked at again, Priscilla?' Dolores asked her.

'I don't know.'

Lana gave a small shake of her head at Dolores. 'I'll speak to you later about it,' she said. 'She really was a brave girl. I don't think any of us have properly taken it all in yet, least of all Priscilla.'

'Quite the little heroine.'

The four women swung round to see Mrs Dayton masking the doorway, a sneer on her lips.

Anger rolled through Lana. How dare the bloody woman sneak up and say something so sarcastic to a child who'd lost everything? Where was the woman's heart? She obviously knew nothing about children.

'And now the school's been landed with even more of the little devils to deal with.' Mrs Dayton curled her lip. 'As if we don't have enough of them already.'

'Excuse *me*,' Lana said, 'I would prefer you to keep those kinds of opinions to yourself. And they're not devils, Mrs Dayton, they happen to be children who've been entrusted to us to educate and look after until they can go safely back to Bingham Hall.'

'Sooner the better, I say. And I always say it how it is,' Mrs Dayton returned. 'Then everyone knows where they stand. Mr Benton always appreciated my candour.'

Lana glared at the secretary. Who on earth did she think she was? She was talking as if she owned the place.

'In case you haven't noticed, I'm *not* Mr Benton,' Lana said, her eyes flashing, 'and I do *not* appreciate what you call *candour*, especially in front of the children. I'm not sure why you're here on a Sunday, so perhaps you'd step into my office and explain. I'll see you now!' She turned to Janice. 'Mrs Parkes, will you take Priscilla back to the cottage while the others collect some more stuff from the home?'

'I'm going with Miss Graham and Miss Honeywell,' Priscilla burst out. 'I can still carry things with one arm.'

Lana's heart sank. The child must dislike Janice intensely to prefer going over to the orphanage, which she hated, than being with Mrs Parkes.

'No,' Janice said briskly. 'You'll be in the way over there, and you need to look after that arm, so come back with me. We'll make a pot of tea. By the looks of you, you could do with one.'

Lana gave an inward sigh of relief. Janice wasn't really an unkind person – she just liked to be in control. It was just her way. She must remember that in future.

Lana's heart was thudding as she strode in front of Mrs Dayton to her office, but for once she was trembling with fury, not nerves. She wondered what she was going to say to the woman. Why did she hate Priscilla so much? Or was it any child? Lana momentarily closed her eyes. The next ten minutes would be crucial for her to assert herself as the headmistress.

Mrs Dayton showed no fear or concern that she was being brought to heel. She sat down perfectly composed on one of the visitor's chairs.

'There's a lot goes on in this place you'd never know unless I care to enlighten you,' she told Lana, her mouth hard.

'Really?' Lana said.

'I'm only acting in everyone's best interest – by saying we can't take on any more children.'

'I'm not interested in your opinion, Mrs Dan . . . Mrs Dayton. I say we *are* going to have these girls.

148

They have nowhere else to lay their heads. And that's the end of it.'

Mrs Dayton's nose wrinkled. 'The situation won't work.'

'You may be right,' Lana said, 'but we have to try. So may I count on your help? Or is it beyond you and would you prefer to give in your notice?'

Mrs Dayton's face turned bright red.

'Well, Mrs Dayton?'

Mrs Dayton rose to her feet. 'Will that be all, *Miss* Ashwin? I've used up too much of my precious day off already.'

'I don't believe I requested you to come in on a Sunday,' Lana returned coolly.

'Someone told me the school was on fire so I thought I'd better come and see for myself. Thank goodness it wasn't us.'

'Children were involved whether it was at the school or the orphanage,' Lana said, shocked at how unfeeling the woman was. She gave her a level stare. 'It was terrible for them. But I'm looking for people to help in a practical way, not just come and gawk. There *is* a war on, we mustn't forget, and we have to all do our bit to help one another, as well as the country . . . don't you think, Mrs Danvers?'

She'd tried so hard to use Mrs Dayton's real name, but Rebecca's housekeeper was always uppermost in Lana's mind whenever she spoke to the secretary. She bit her tongue so as not to say anything about the slip-up. She wouldn't apologise to the woman.

'It's Mrs *Dayton*, I'll have you know.' Mrs Dayton's face flushed again with annoyance.

'I do beg your pardon, Mrs Dayton. Purely a slip of the tongue.'

She wondered if the woman was aware of the reference.

Mrs Dayton snorted.

'That will be all, Mrs Dayton. You may go.'

Lana stretched up and caught her breath. She'd been lugging mattresses and sheets and pillows for ages. Were the others on their way back yet? Then she heard them. A group of girls rushed through the door, their voices reaching a pitch as they carried in an assortment of clothes and shoes, the younger ones clutching a doll or teddy bear each. A child with skin the colour of coffee and a halo of black curls hung back with Athena and Dolores who were endeavouring to keep them all in order. Lana wondered what the child had been through. What any of them had. She noticed they weren't dressed as well as many of the children who attended the village school, and their sandals and shoes were badly scuffed and worn, but with the rationing, Lana thought gloomily, shoes were one of the most difficult items to come by.

'Quieten down, please,' Athena said loudly, clapping her hands. Seven pairs of eyes swivelled round. 'I want you all to meet Miss Ashwin who is the headmistress of the school. You are to do exactly what she tells you while you're staying

150

here.' She paused, her eyes flicking over each child before continuing. 'Say hello to Miss Ashwin.'

'Hello, Miss Ashwin,' they chorused in piping voices.

Lana beamed at them.

'Hello to you all. You must tell me your names.'

They all began to shout at once.

'Line up and tell Miss Ashwin one at a time,' Athena said. 'Just your Christian names for now. Miss Ashwin will learn your surnames when she gets to know you.'

'I'm Pamela,' a girl with brown pigtails called out.

'And your name?' Athena asked the little girl with the halo of black curls.

'Betsy.'

'How old are you, Betsy?' Lana asked gently.

'Seven, Miss.'

Two identical little girls holding hands were next. 'Daisy and Doris,' said one of them. 'We're twins,' she added unnecessarily.

'Can you tell me which one is which?' Lana said.

'I'm Daisy and she's Doris,' the same child said as she pointed to her twin.

'Can Doris tell me her own name?'

'Course she can, but she doesn't need to 'cos I've already told you.'

Some of the children giggled.

Lana hid a smile. Daisy was obviously the bossy one.

The other girls were Megan with a Scottish accent, Janet, a plump little girl wearing spectacles that

151

emphasised her serious demeanour, and Nora, a child who simply stared unblinkingly.

'Thank you, children,' Lana said. 'I'll do my best to remember you all, but if I forget or make a mistake you'll have to tell me. Now, why don't you all choose where you'd like to sleep.'

Several children made a beeline for the mattress nearest the window and there were a few tears before Athena and Dolores agreed that the twins could sleep together on that one.

By the end of the afternoon Lana felt quite drained, but pleased every child now had a make-shift bed and a small table.

'Why don't you come over to Bingham Hall for supper tonight?' Athena said, as the girls prepared to walk back to the orphanage. 'Then Harold will bring all of you back as the children will be tired out, I should think.'

Immediately Lana thought of Janice. She should ask if it would be all right to bring her as well. But a tiny part of her felt she would so love to have an hour or two away from the teacher, especially as she knew Janice was not at all happy with the new arrangements. Her conscience won.

'Would you mind if I brought Janice?' she said.

'Of course not. Do ask her.'

But Janice said "no, thanks" in a terse voice and that she would be perfectly happy to have a quiet meal on her own and the cottage to herself.

★   ★   ★

In the dining room Maxine gestured for Lana to take the chair next to her at one of the three long refectory tables. When everyone was seated the matron folded her hands together and the children's clatter died down as they chanted:

'Thank you for the world so sweet,
Thank you for the food we eat . . .'

The moment they finished grace the level of noise rose.

Maxine turned to Lana. 'The last but one matron, Mrs McPherson – we renamed her "The Fierce One" – wouldn't allow the children to speak at all. Not utter a word. June Lavender, who took over when the woman was sacked, changed all that. And I agree with her. It's not healthy. But I do try to keep the noise down as much as I can.'

But even Maxine couldn't stop forty chairs scraping, the giggling, the rattling cutlery, the noisy slurping, thought Lana. Nor stop an argument taking place between a boy and a girl on the next table.

'I didn't steal nothing,' one of the little girls shouted back.

'You must've done. Wasn't no one else near. Why d'ya keep so close to me, then, if you wasn't after it?'

'I just wanted to look at it,' she said.

Lana wondered what they were talking about.

Maxine stood up and walked over to the two of them.

'What is Pamela supposed to have taken, Thomas? And don't use the word "stolen" – we don't say that here.'

'*I* do,' Thomas said in a belligerent tone. 'She stole my *Beano* and I want it back.'

'*Did* you, Pamela? Please tell me the truth.'

'I wouldn't read such a baby comic,' Pamela said scornfully.

Lana wondered how Maxine and the teachers managed to deal with them all, twenty-four hours a day. And then she remembered she was going to have a taste of it herself with the seven extra girls until the repairs at Bingham Hall were completed. She and Janice and Wendy would have to take turns keeping an eye on them through the night. Oh, well, there was a war on, after all.

CHAPTER 16

For some reason, the blond-haired man crept into Lana's head on more than one occasion. It had happened again when she'd woken this morning and a whole fortnight had already passed. Ridiculous. It was one of those split-second moments when you encounter someone and feel you know them, and have always known them. She hadn't admitted this to herself at the time, but now she knew this was exactly what had happened. And she was as convinced as her heart was beating faster that the man had felt the same stab of recognition.

She dug her toes further down in the bed until her feet stuck out at the end. She wished they would make beds a few inches longer. A double bed would be the just the ticket as she could lie diagonally. She smiled to herself. If there'd been one that size there wouldn't have been room to bring the other mattress in for Priscilla.

Now, she listened to Priscilla's agitated breathing. Lana had taken a long time to fall asleep last night because of the girl's jerky movements and small moans. Sadly, they were becoming a normal pattern. She turned her thoughts to the blond man again.

He appeared to be the father of the little boy who she'd been talking to in the vegetable garden – Peter Best. But who were the two men with him? Acting almost like policemen. And if Peter had a father then he wouldn't be an orphan – wouldn't be at Bingham Hall. It didn't make sense.

Maybe his father *had* committed a crime and was in prison. Maybe those two men with him really *were* policemen.

Yes, that was it.

A stab of disappointment raced through her. She shook herself. She was imagining things. Maybe he'd been away abroad, fighting – perhaps been injured and had needed to recuperate after an operation. He couldn't have a wife or surely Peter would be with her. She must have died young. And now he'd recovered he'd returned to fetch his son. Why did it bother her so much that she didn't know for sure? She smacked the back of her hand for letting her imagination run wild, and threw back the covers. If she was so curious she could easily pump Maxine for information. She was seeing her that day to give her the orphans' reports on their progress at Bingham school during their first week.

'They've found out who the youth was who died in the fire,' Maxine said, when Lana was taken by

156

one of the maids to the matron's office a few hours later.

'Oh.' A feeling of dread swept through Lana. He'd looked so young. She'd never forget those staring wide-open eyes.

'It was Billy Barber. Aged seventeen – from the next village. They say he had a drunken mother and a father who was never there. Only a few curious neighbours turned up at the funeral.'

'Poor boy.' Lana momentarily closed her eyes. 'He didn't deserve an ending like that.'

Maxine grimaced. 'Apparently, he's been had up for burglary several times – probably what he was doing breaking into the home – and I remember he put an old lady in hospital last year when he stole her handbag. It just shows how these youngsters go off the rails when they don't have a stable home life.' She shook her head. 'Let's change the subject to something more pleasant. We're planning a fair in July. Stalls selling second-hand kiddies' clothes and books, craft stuff and a tombola . . . oh, and a raffle. We've told our kids we want to invite the children from Bingham school to join in and they seemed to like the idea. Well, all except one,' she finished, 'but he doesn't join in playing with the others here anyway. He's nearly always by himself. I think he prefers it.'

'Do you mean Peter Best?' Lana said.

She saw Maxine give a start.

'Yes. How did you know?'

'I spoke to him on May Day. He was weeding

the vegetable garden and he introduced me to the little dog, Freddie, and then he told me his name. I thought he was a dear little lad, but his lovely blue eyes were so sad. Then I realised *all* the orphans must have a terribly sad story to tell.'

'They do,' Maxine said with feeling. 'Shocking, some of them. I'm afraid it will have affected them for life, but it's our job to give them as normal a life as possible.' She looked directly at Lana. 'So you came over on May Day?' Lana nodded. 'I know we arranged to meet at four o'clock but some visitors unexpectedly arrived, and I'm sorry to say our meeting went straight out of my head.'

'Yes, I guessed it might have when I saw a Rolls-Royce turn up the drive. It was odd seeing such a grand car parking outside an orphanage.'

'Why do you say that?'

'Well, with the petrol rationing. Those large engines guzzle up the petrol. I suppose I notice these things because I'm a driver. My brothers taught me.' She paused. 'Sorry, you must think me very nosy, but it did strike me at the time.'

'What else did you see?' Maxine's voice sounded a little guarded.

Lana was immediately on the alert.

'Nothing, really. I saw you in the distance with another lady . . . would it be June Lavender who you said used to be the matron?' Maxine nodded. 'And you looked as though you were going to be busy when I saw the passengers go with you into the house.' She wouldn't mention the blond man and how she saw him embrace the little boy, Peter Best, who'd called him Papa. 'So I decided to leave our meeting for another day. I meant to telephone you the next day to apologise but it slipped my mind with the fire and everything.'

Maxine was quiet for a few moments. Then she seemed to come to a decision.

'It's probably only fair to put you in the picture, as Peter will be one of the boys joining your class.'

Lana held her breath. Was Maxine going to tell her about Peter's father?

'It's not very straightforward with Peter,' Maxine said, putting her cup down. 'In fact, if you've finished your coffee I'd prefer us to have a chat in the library where we can be undisturbed.'

What on earth was Maxine going to tell her?

'I'd like that,' Lana said, rising up and trying not to show her curiosity. 'I've wanted to see the library. Athena mentioned how beautiful it is.'

She followed Maxine along the corridor, almost to the end. Maxine pushed the oak door to reveal the grand interior.

Lana couldn't help a gasp of surprise. She'd only just got over her amazement at the magnificent hall, but now she gazed up at the timber-vaulted ceiling, the fluted pine columns, the old tiled fireplace. For a private house it was impressive. And packed solid with books.

Maxine followed her gaze and chuckled. 'You're thinking exactly what I thought,' she said. 'I'd never seen such a large collection of books. June, the previous matron, told me it was Lord Bingham's private collection.'

'What happened to him?'

'We don't know. He fled with his family at the beginning of the war, and Dr Barnardo's took over the house. That happened quite often, apparently.'

'What if he ever comes back to reclaim his property?' Lana said. 'The war's got to end sometime and it must surely still be rightfully his.'

'I don't know what the terms are when Barnardo's took it over,' Maxine said. 'I hope he wouldn't turn us out. It's so important for these children to have stability.' She led the way into a small room off the main library. It was shelved with more books and a large round table was placed in the middle with several metal chairs. 'Let's sit down here.' She closed the door.

Lana sat, grateful for the cushion on the hard seat. Her attention was focused on Maxine who sent a sharp glance towards her as though trying to weigh her up and deciding how much to tell her.

'One of the passengers in the motorcar was Peter's father,' Maxine began. 'We've been trying to find him to tell him about Peter. A few months after the boy was sent to his grandmother's, here in Liverpool, her house was bombed. He came home from school to find no home and no grandmother. The lucky thing for him was that he was found wandering the streets – in shock, no doubt – and was picked up by a Dr Barnardo's inspector.'

'I don't understand,' Lana said. 'Was his father away fighting?'

'Not exactly,' Maxine said. 'You see, Peter's father was in Germany.'

'Oh, no,' Lana whispered. 'A prisoner of war.'

'No. He was . . . is German.'

For a moment Lana's heart stopped. And then she breathed out.

'Oh, poor man. So he's a Jew. A refugee.' She said it as a statement and was shocked at Maxine's next words.

'No, Lana, that's the trouble.'

A cold chill stole through her. If he wasn't a Jew, there could only be one explanation. Dear God. That poor little boy had a *Nazi* for a father. How would you ever explain that to a child? She remembered how he'd embraced his son. Well, she supposed even Nazis loved their children. But how could she have ever thought there was even the slightest connection between the blond man and herself? A man whose people had killed Dickie. She should have known instinctively that all was not right. Yet Peter had no trace of a German accent.

Lana managed to find her voice. 'So how did you find out?'

'Let me tell you from the beginning.' Maxine rubbed the back of her neck as though to ease a pain. 'Peter said he'd had a photograph of his father but he lost it. To cut a long story short I found out that Hilda had taken it and shown it to her mother.'

'Hilda?'

'She used to work here,' Maxine explained, 'but we had to sack her as she was such a troublemaker and called Peter a Nazi in front of the other children. Anyway, when Hilda finally returned the photograph, I was horrified to see that the father was dressed in a Nazi uniform, and was a high-ranking officer.'

Lana gasped. She kept her eyes fixed on Maxine, unable to believe the words the matron was telling her.

'The mystery began to unravel from the time Mrs Brown – that's Hilda's mother – came to the orphanage when June Lavender was the matron. She brought with her a metal box that contained a pile of letters from Carl Best to his wife in England. She was English and had taken Peter to England a few months before the Germans invaded Poland.'

Carl. The blond man's name was Carl. The man whose gaze has distracted me too many times. And all the while he was a German. A Nazi. Fighting against us. Responsible, however indirectly, for murdering my darling Dickie.

It was as though someone had walked over her grave. She shuddered. Forced herself to stay calm, but she could feel the hairs rise on the back of her neck.

'How did this Mrs Brown get hold of the box?' Her voice was thick. She felt she needed to keep clearing her throat where a lump had lodged.

Maxine frowned at her as though wondering why she was taking this so much to heart. Lana hoped it was her own imagination. It was the last thing she wanted to confess – that she blamed every single German for Dickie's premature death and that she would never forgive them. If she poured out her past to Maxine she knew she wouldn't be able to stem the flood of tears she'd lately managed to keep bottled up.

'Mrs Brown was Peter's grandmother's next-door neighbour,' Maxine continued. 'When Peter's mother became ill she took the box to her mother, Peter's grandmother. When Peter's mother died, the grandmother thought she wouldn't survive her own cancer, so she told Mrs Brown if anything should happen to her she was to make sure the box was put in the hands of whoever was looking after Peter at the time.

'Crofton – that's my fiancé, though he was only a good friend at the time – spoke German and translated a couple of the letters—'

Maxine broke off, as though she'd said too much. It was obviously a complicated story as well as being particularly shocking. Lana was just about to ask Maxine why Carl Best hadn't been locked up when there was a sudden knock at the door. Maxine sprang up to open it, and a plump young nurse stood there.

'Matron, I'm sorry to interrupt but can you come right away? Bit of a ding-dong—'

'Please go, Maxine. I can see myself out.' Lana

jumped to her feet and retrieved her bag and file of the children's reports.

'If you're sure . . .'

One of the maids held open the heavy oak door and Lana slipped through. All she could think of was getting back to the school. She had a class to teach in an hour and needed a cup of tea and a lump of sugar first to settle her nerves. She had to be calm and in control when she faced her class. Especially now she had the extra children from Bingham Hall. And Peter Best, the little German boy.

Lana couldn't believe she'd been at the school for a whole two months and it was already June. She'd put in her report to George Shepherd who occasionally telephoned to find out how she was getting along. He seemed pleased with the attendance and the results of an English Literature test she'd set the classroom last week. She felt especially proud that Priscilla had come second. Priscilla had even given a slight smile when the class clapped, but it had soon slipped back to her expression of despair when Lana told her the decorations were now being done since the structural repair work on Bingham Hall was finished. That it wouldn't be long before she and the other girls could go back to the orphanage and sleep the night.

'But I don't want to,' Priscilla had said. 'It's too noisy in the dormitory. I like it here with you.'

Lana couldn't help being sympathetic. The

young girl's life had been turned upside down. But it was time for Priscilla accept the truth – that her parents were truly dead and Bingham Hall would be her home for the foreseeable future.

She suddenly remembered Billy Barber and told Janice he'd been the boy who was found dead in the fire.

Janice tutted. 'What can you expect with parents like that?'

Lana spread her hands. 'Janice, Meg told me there was never a church service for Priscilla's parents.'

'That's right. If there had been I would've gone, as she's one of our pupils.'

'I think I'll suggest to Maxine that we have one either at Bingham Hall or in the village church. Somewhere safe where Priscilla can say goodbye to them.'

CHAPTER 17

July 1943

The fair was in full swing by the time Lana arrived with half a dozen children from the school. She'd been disappointed with the lack of enthusiasm from most of the parents who had said in no uncertain terms that they didn't want their children mixing with orphans.

They're not lepers, Lana thought angrily, when she'd read yet another letter from a parent saying their child would not be attending the fair at Bingham Hall. Perhaps the parents thought the orphans would be an unruly lot and be a bad influence on their child. Yet Maxine was keen for both 'sides' to play together and learn from one another. Lana had agreed but it wasn't working out quite the way they'd hoped.

The children whose parents were willing to let them attend the fair were all boys who, Lana had to admit, were more difficult than most of the children at the school. She only hoped they would behave themselves and not let the school down.

She was herding them towards the various stalls,

166

thinking they'd enjoy competing to win a prize, when her heart practically stopped. It couldn't be. She looked again, wishing she'd worn her spectacles. She shouldn't be so vain, she thought crossly. The tall man half turned. There was no mistake. Carl Best! He was obviously here to see his son, but he was a prisoner. Why was he given such freedom?

As though he felt her eyes on him, the man turned fully, and for the second time his eyes held hers.

Furious with herself for being caught staring at him, she dragged her gaze away and grabbed hold of the two smallest boys.

'Come on, you two. Let's go and see if you can ring a prize in the tombola.'

The other four boys, too old for hand-holding, raced off before she had a chance to remind them that this was not their property and they must respect it.

'Behave yourselves,' she called after them, but she knew her words would fall on deaf ears. At least they were older and didn't need watching every minute. It might be best to leave them to mix with the others naturally without any teacher's interference.

It took all her willpower not to look in the direction of Carl Best. She wished she hadn't come. Why hadn't it crossed her mind that he might be here to see Peter? She suddenly saw the tall German on the periphery of her vision heading for the bookstall close to where some children were on the slides and swings. One of the boys, Edward, pulled her hand.

'Miss, I want to go on the slide.'

'So do I,' Joe on the other side piped up.

'You can go later,' Lana said, 'after you throw a rubber ring around a prize you like the look of.' She pointed in the opposite direction of the slides and swings – and the bookstall. 'Look, the tombola is just over there. It'll be fun. I'll have a go as well.'

'I don't want to.'

'Nor do I.'

She looked down at each determined face. She saw Carl Best pick up a book and leaf through it, only a dozen yards away. He seemed to be wandering about on his own this time but surely if he was a prisoner he ought to be accompanied. He could easily escape at any time. No one would notice if he suddenly disappeared into the copse. For goodness' sake. She was being dramatic and anyway it was none of her business. The boys tugged at her hands, reminding her she hadn't given them permission to play on the slides. Could she leave them on their own? They couldn't get into mischief having a slide, surely. Then she noticed Dolores watching over three little girls on the roundabout only a few yards away from the slides. Yes, they'd be perfectly safe.

'All right,' she said. 'Miss Honeywell will be there keeping an eye on you. I'll go and check on the other boys.'

No sooner had she said the words than Edward and Joe tore their hands away from hers and dashed off, shouting with delight. She'd have to go over and speak to Dolores and ask if it was all right to leave the two boys in her care for ten minutes. She squeezed her eyes tightly for a second or two and took in a deep breath, reluctant to admit she was nervous at the thought of running into Carl Best. The last thing she wanted was to see some German close up.

'You go on,' Dolores said. She was sitting on one of the benches fanning herself with a programme leaflet. 'I'll watch them – don't worry.'

Lana decided to stroll over to a stall she'd noticed selling all kinds of craft goods. She was just admiring an embroidered felt case, especially for holding a powder compact and lipstick, and wondering if she should treat herself when there was a sudden scream from behind her and boys' shouts. She whirled round and saw Peter Best in a fight with Luke, one of the boys she'd brought from the school.

'You don't know anything,' Peter was shouting. 'I've got a father.'

'You can't have,' Luke kicked him on the shin. 'This is an orphanage – for *orphans*! And that's what you are.'

'I'm *not* an orphan. My father's here.'

'Tell me another porkie,' Luke goaded.

Peter suddenly thumped him and Lana rushed towards the pair as they fell to the ground, rolling on top of one another, over and over. She managed to grab Luke under his arms and pull him off Peter who was crying.

'The orphan pulled my ear,' Luke whined.

'Don't call him that,' Lana admonished. 'He has a name – Peter. I'm ashamed of you both. You've been very naughty boys. You're supposed to be playing nicely together. Get up, Peter – this minute.'

'He started it,' Peter said, tears furrowing a path down his cheeks. He bent to rescue his cap.

A shadow fell over her. She turned and looked up into the angry blue eyes of Carl Best.

'I do not know who you are,' he said, his voice dripping ice. 'Perhaps one of the teachers. But I would prefer that you do not speak to my son in such a tone. He is not to blame.'

'I'm Lana Ashwin, headmistress of the village school,' Lana said coolly, her heart pumping so loudly he must hear it.

'Papa,' Peter said, flinging his arms round his father. His father bent and hugged him briefly.

'Run and play, Peter. I would like to speak to this lady.'

'I don't want to play with them,' Peter said sulkily. 'I hate all of them. I'm going to find Freddie and take him for a walk.' He looked beseechingly up at his father. 'Can I?'

Carl Best hesitated. 'All right, but only ten minutes. Don't go along the drive. Keep in the gardens as I will have to leave soon and I want to be sure to say goodbye.'

He turned his attention back to Lana who desperately tried to put on a calm exterior although she was fuming inside.

'If you are from the school,' Carl Best said, 'why do you interfere with my child? It should be for the teachers who work *here* to see he obeys – not for you to do.'

How dare he be so rude? She'd only tried to break up the fight before the boys got seriously hurt.

'Mr . . .' She broke off. She wasn't supposed to know his surname, let alone his Christian name. Embarrassment flooded her cheeks at her near slip-up.

'Herr Best,' he cut in.

'Mr Best,' she said, deliberately using the English form, and thankful she was tall so she didn't have to tilt her neck too far, 'I was invited to bring some of our children at the school to the fair. It's my responsibility to keep an eye on them, and if they misbehave, to intervene. Most children who get into fights, no matter who starts, are equally to blame.'

'Not Peter,' Carl Best said firmly. 'I have taught him he must walk away when someone tries to make him angry. He must not fight.'

'Well, he didn't this time,' Lana flared, 'but I can't say I blame him. When anyone is being horrible it makes you want to hit them back. Peter was only being a normal boy. He has to learn to stick up for himself in situations like that.'

'You are encouraging my boy to be a bully.'

'Of course I'm not,' Lana flashed. 'He was just giving as good as he was getting. I just didn't want either of them to get hurt – that's all – and that's why I reprimanded both of them. Whatever school I teach at makes no difference.'

Carl Best studied her for a long minute. Then he shrugged.

'I apologise, Madam.' He gave an almost imperceptible bow and she couldn't tell whether he was being sarcastic or whether it was simply his German-ness coming out.

She watched him walk away, his shoulders square, his head high, not looking at all subdued as a German prisoner of war ought to look.

The rest of the afternoon passed peacefully enough, but Lana wasn't able to concentrate. She barely listened to Dolores when she began telling her about her boyfriend who'd been sent somewhere in Scotland. Her mind was in turmoil. Why did Carl Best appear to have such freedom? She still hadn't spotted anyone this time who looked like a policeman keeping an eye on him, but she supposed they must be about and wouldn't be letting him out of their sight in a hurry. What was it about the man that was so special to the British?

But whatever the reason, he was a German. And she must never forget it.

She didn't see Herr Best, as she'd decided to call him from now on to remind herself exactly who he was, for the rest of the afternoon. She didn't know whether to be relieved or disappointed. He was such an enigma. She wanted to get to the heart of him – not for any personal reason, she quickly assured herself, but out of sheer curiosity. And wanting the best for Peter, of course.

Lana was disappointed Maxine was not anywhere in sight. She'd hoped they might continue their conversation from before the young nurse had called the matron away. She spent most of the rest of the afternoon making sure the six boys were occupied, though they were only playing with each other – except Luke. This time it was Athena who broke up another skirmish between him and one of her Bingham Hall boys. Lana was embarrassed to conclude that Luke was deliberately picking fights. Maybe mixing the two sets of children was a bad idea after all, but then how would the orphans make their way in the outside world if they were always kept separate? And how would the more privileged children learn to be kind to those not so well off? Maxine must be aware of the problem as well, which is why the matron so badly wanted today to be a success.

By the time Lana had rounded up her six boys and they were walking back to the school where they would either ride their bikes or walk home, she was exhausted. She couldn't work it out. She was used to handling many children at once, awkward ones as well as the obedient ones. So why had the afternoon proved so dispiriting and draining? It wasn't anything to do with bumping into Carl Best, was it? To notice how handsome he was, and how different, close up, to her idea of a German Nazi? Even though he'd looked and sounded so angry, she knew he was only defending his beloved son. Lana swallowed hard. He was someone she'd had no experience of. She must put him out of her mind.

'How did it all go?' Janice asked as soon as Lana entered the sitting room, now in the same dreadful state as it was when she'd first seen the cottage. She tried to ignore the spurt of anger. What was the point of her trying to keep everything clean and tidy when Janice patently couldn't care less?

'So-so.' Blast. She'd meant to say it all went swimmingly.

'What's that supposed to mean?' Janice gave her a long look. 'Oh, I bet they didn't all get on like nice little kiddies, did they?' Without waiting for an answer, she carried on, 'Well, don't say I didn't warn you. I bet those orphans are an unruly lot when they're let loose.'

'It was *Luke* who was unruly.' Lana rushed to defend the Bingham Hall children. 'Picking fights with kids smaller and younger than himself and encouraging Leonard to do the same. They were little humbugs. I felt so embarrassed. Thank goodness I only had the six to contend with. Don't know what I'd have done if more parents had given permission for their precious offspring to mix with the lowly orphans.'

'So they were right not to let their kids mix after all, then,' Janice said with a smirk.

'It seems so.'

Lana thought that was the end of the conversation about the fair, but she was wrong. Janice's next words made her jump.

'Anyone interesting there?' Janice asked.

Lana hesitated a second too long. 'Er, no, I can't think of anyone.' She was determined not to discuss her encounter with Carl Best to anyone, least of all Janice.

'Took your time to answer.' The smirk was even wider.

Lana gritted her teeth. 'I don't know anyone except Maxine and two of the teachers,' she said.

'Sounds like a dull afternoon to me.'

'Not completely,' Lana said. 'I had to break up a fight with Luke and one of Bingham Hall's children. Luke set about him. The little boy is smaller but wiry and he gave Luke a good thump. I told them both off.'

'Go on.' Janice inspected one of her nails as though she didn't have a care in the world whether Lana continued or not.

'The boy's father came along and told *me* off,' Lana said, keeping her voice light.

'I thought they were orphans.'

'Oh, not Peter,' Lana said, then bit her tongue. She hadn't meant to say his name.

'It wouldn't be little Peter Best you're talking about, would it?' Janice said, watching her closely. 'And his very good-looking and very German papa?'

CHAPTER 18

In class, standing in front of the children, teaching them her beloved Shakespeare by getting them to act the parts as a way of learning, stopped Lana from going over and over the image of Carl Best as he looked down at her from his height of well over six feet. His bright blue eyes had flashed with anger and his mouth was tight, as though he'd been trying to hold himself in check.

The annoying thing was that it really hadn't altered his looks at all. He was simply one of the most handsome men she'd ever set eyes on. And certainly the first man she'd paid any real attention to since Dickie. What a shame he was German, she thought, now thoroughly cross with herself that she was even thinking along such lines. But he looked like a man who was used to getting his own way, dictating to others . . . She shuddered. Yet he obviously adored his son. She couldn't imagine his work beyond being in charge of hundreds of enemy troops. Couldn't see him signing death certificates for thousands of Jews. Condoning the camps. Torturing prisoners.

Or was that still an exaggerated picture? She'd heard various sides of the argument in the newspapers, but her brothers had insisted they were true, even though they were in the Navy and likely heard things third-hand. Lana swallowed hard, trying to dislodge the lump of guilt in her throat as Dickie's image floated in front of her.

'Miss, can I play the Fairy Queen?' Josephine broke into her sinister visions of murderous Nazis and Dickie walking away from her in disgust.

Lana hesitated. Josephine certainly was no angel but she'd vastly improved since Lana had had a serious word with her, particularly towards Priscilla.

'All right, Josephine. I'll let you, but just for this lesson. We want others to have a chance to be the Fairy Queen, too.'

Josephine grinned with delight. 'Thank you, Miss.'

'She's no good at reading,' Oliver called out. 'She can't read any big words.'

'Yes, I can,' Josephine swivelled her head to the side to glare at him.

'That's enough!' Lana rapped on her desk with the blackboard rubber. 'Let's start. You all know what part you're playing, so show me how well you can act.'

The children rose to the occasion and even the ones who didn't have a part followed the story with their fingers or rulers. As usual, Priscilla hadn't volunteered. Lana hadn't forced her. She was still an intense, nervy child.

* * *

Lana hated to admit it, but she was lonely. Wendy Booth was a lovely woman but she didn't see much of her except for a tea break in the afternoon after the last class. She'd begun to get used to Janice's ways but realised they would never be real friends. You just couldn't get close to her no matter how hard you tried; Janice was too eaten up with bitterness. In a way, it hadn't been all bad to meet Janice, Lana thought, as she washed the dishes for the umpteenth time and wiped down the kitchen in the cottage. Janice had taught her one important thing, though the woman hadn't realised it – not to remain bitter as it would ruin the rest of your life. Slowly, Lana was beginning to let go of Dickie in her mind. But where did that leave Carl Best? And why was she even asking that question?

When Janice had dropped her bombshell that she knew about Peter's father being a German, Lana's mouth had fallen open, and without warning her face had blazed red.

'How do you know about Peter and his father?' she'd managed to reply.

Janice tapped her finger on her nose.

'Where did you hear it?'

Janice hunched her shoulders for a second. 'One of the cleaners who does the home as well as here. She told Mrs Danvers one of the children had a German father. What's important is whether it's the truth or not.'

'Yes, it is, if you must know,' Lana said, this

time not able to suppress her intense irritation with the woman.

'Well, don't forget who he is,' Janice said. 'You want to steer clear of him.'

'What on earth are you implying?' Lana said.

'Good-looking man . . . you're a grieving fiancée. I can see it all happening.'

'What? A romantic liaison with a German POW? It's out of the question.' So why did her heart pound at the very idea?

'He seems to have a lot of freedom,' Janice said, watching Lana as she cleaned up around her.

'I'm sure there's a policeman lurking not far away.' Lana banged a plate into the rack above. 'Anyway,' she looked at Janice, 'I really don't want to talk about it.'

'Then we'll talk about Priscilla,' Janice said without pausing. 'How much longer do we have to put up with her?'

'Janice, have you no compassion? She's a damaged child and I'm trying to make things a little easier for her. Please show some patience and kindness . . . if it wouldn't be *too* much trouble,' Lana added.

Janice shrugged. 'Thanks for supper. I think I'll go to my room.' She stood up and went out of the door without another word.

Lana was preparing her next class when the telephone rang.

'Is that Lana?'

'Yes, Maxine. You're just the person I need to speak to.'

'Makes two of us,' Maxine chuckled. Then her tone changed to a more serious note. 'Lana, I was wondering . . . actually I have a favour to ask you. It's rather unusual but I don't want to discuss it on the phone. Could we meet somewhere private?'

'Would you like to come here for a change?' Lana asked, intrigued. Maxine sounded as though she had something on her mind and wasn't sure how it would be taken. 'We'll be completely private in my office.'

If Maxine could get past Mrs Danvers.

'Good idea. Tomorrow afternoon – say, five o'clock.'

'Yes, I'll be free then,' Lana said.

She couldn't wait to find out what favour Maxine wanted from her.

Dead on time, Maxine arrived at Lana's office.

'You managed to get past her then,' Lana said with a welcoming smile.

'Who, the woman behind the glass screen whose looks could kill you stone dead?'

Lana laughed. 'The very one. She does her best to make my life a misery. I've tried really hard with her but it's impossible. She liked the head-master before me and she lets it be known that she resents me.'

'They had someone awful like that with the matron before June,' Maxine said. 'Thankfully, I never met her but June said she was a horror. Quite cruel with the way she treated the children, which was even worse. Things changed for the better the minute June took over.' She caught Lana's eye. 'Anyway, I haven't come to discuss ogres. I need a favour and you're the only person I'd trust.'

'I'll be glad to help,' Lana said. 'What do you want me to do?'

'I've made a promise to one of our boys, but it means someone taking him on a train – rather a long way away, so it will take all day.' She regarded Lana. 'I thought as it's the summer holidays the school will be closed and you might have the time.'

'Where do you want me to take him?'

'Bletchley.'

'I've never heard of it.'

'It's in Buckinghamshire.'

'Who would I be taking?'

'It's Peter, the little chap you've already met – with the German father.'

Lana's stomach lurched. 'I don't see—'

'It's just that his father is allowed to see his son occasionally, even though he's officially interned. But as you can imagine, it's difficult for him to come here – much easier for Peter to be taken to *him*.'

'Yes, I suppose so.' Lana was stumbling for the right words. How could she tell Maxine that she could not . . . would not have anything to do with Carl Best and all he stood for.

'I'm sorry, Maxine,' she began, steeling herself

182

against the look of surprise in the matron's beautiful eyes. 'Anything . . . ask me anything else and I'll do it gladly . . . but not that.'

'I know the children here aren't your responsibility but I'm at my wit's end. I'd take him myself, but I need to be here as Barbara's in the sick bay so we're really short.'

'I'm sorry . . .'

'I understand. It's a long journey and you'd be looking after one child who isn't easy . . . though goodness knows, none of them are really, but you understand more when you look at their backgrounds.'

'It's not the journey.'

'Then what is it?'

'It's because his father is a German. I can't stand them and can't bring myself to do anything to help them.'

'They're not all bad,' Maxine said in a neutral kind of tone.

'Maybe not *all* the civilians, even though most of them appear to go along with Hitler and his mad ambitions to rule the world for a thousand years.'

'Perhaps it seems like it to us, here in England,' Maxine replied, 'but if we were starving with no work and a family to feed we might not be so different. And don't forget, people are only told what the Nazis want them to hear.'

The dreaded word. She gulped. 'The Nazis killed my fiancé.'

Her eyes stung with unshed tears and Maxine's face began to blur.

Maxine jumped up and came to Lana's side of the desk. She laid a hand on her shoulder.

'Oh, Lana, I'm so sorry. I had no idea. No wonder you're so upset. May I ask you what happened?'

'His ship was torpedoed,' she said dully. She looked up at Maxine. 'It wouldn't be quite so bad if Peter's father wasn't a Nazi.' She didn't want to say his name.

Maxine's eyes widened. 'Who said he was a Nazi?'

'*You* did. When you were telling me about the photograph.'

Maxine's expression suddenly relaxed and she smiled. 'Oh, Lana, I remember now. I hadn't finished telling you when Kathleen came in saying she needed me urgently. No, no, Herr Best is not a Nazi.'

'But . . . you saw him in his uniform.'

'Yes, and at the time I thought exactly the same. But when Crofton translated the letters to his wife he said he wouldn't be at all surprised if he turned out not to be a Nazi even though he wore the uniform in the photograph. When I studied Herr Best's face in the photograph I have to say he didn't strike me as a cruel man at all. In fact, the very opposite.' She gave Lana a steady look. 'Anyway, the letters were warm and loving but there was a strange allusion to a poem, and we realised it was a coded message. We put two and

184

two together and came up with the idea that he might well be a resister. And that he was trying to escape to England. The next letter implied he'd been successful. And you remember when you saw him arrive in the Rolls-Royce on May Day, he was accompanied by two gentlemen – well, they were policemen. A detective inspector and a sergeant, sent with Herr Best so he could see his son for the first time in four years. He was only allowed to give us very sketchy details of his escape and that he was working for British Intelligence.'

She couldn't take in what Maxine was telling her. Carl Best wasn't a Nazi after all. And even if he wasn't, what difference did it make? He was still German. The enemy.

But if he was really working for us . . .

'I didn't know there was a German resistance,' Lana said finally, shaking her head.

'Maybe not a formal one as we know with the Free French,' Maxine said, 'but nevertheless, he's working with us. Apparently, he has information the British are very keen to use. Of course, he couldn't hint what this might be – it's all top secret. But you can be sure he's on our side – well and truly.'

Lana's brain whirled. A resister. Not involved in Hitler's frightening regime. Yet even if he wasn't a true Nazi he must have convinced them he was loyal to the cause or he surely would have been kicked out. Probably worse. So he'd have to

185

convince them he was as cruel as they. As intent on invading countries, bombing cities to smithereens and clearing out the Jews as the other Nazis in their despicable regime. She shuddered.

'You're still not convinced, are you?' Maxine broke into her confusion of thoughts. 'If this is the case, then I understand, but look at it like this. Peter's gone through more than any child ever should and it's affected him terribly. He's never really made friends because he feels different. You cannot imagine his joy at being reunited with his father again at the fair. Except it's not the end of the story for the little chap. He'll have to remain at Bingham Hall until the end of the war but at least Herr Best is allowed to see him occasionally, and I want to do everything in my power to see that he does, as who knows how long this blasted war will go on for.'

Lana was silent.

I don't want to do this. I don't want to see Carl Best, Nazi or no Nazi. I don't like him and he made it very clear he doesn't like me. *But how do I explain all that to Maxine, who will think I'm crazy?*

Maxine broke the silence.

'If you think about it, Herr Best put himself in a very dangerous situation pretending to be something he wasn't. There's no doubt if they'd found out he wasn't loyal he'd have been shot. And there could have been ramifications for his wife and son. That's why he sent them to England for their safety. And even that must have aroused some suspicion.' She caught Lana's eye. 'What do you say, Lana? Do you have the courage to overcome your loathing of anyone German? For little Peter's sake?'

CHAPTER 19

Lana couldn't settle. She was thankful to have the cottage to herself after Priscilla had gone to bed. She didn't know where Janice was. The woman never bothered to leave her a note to say when she'd be back. She looked around the kitchen that was strewn again with Janice's rubbish. Lana had tried to make a point, only cleaning and tidying her own things, but it had made no impact on Janice whatsoever.

Priscilla had her own view. She would rather clean the mess in the kitchen than do her homework, despite Lana's discouraging her. It was becoming a problem. The child was falling further behind and in no uncertain terms was blaming Janice.

'We have to realise that not everyone is the same,' Lana told Priscilla. 'Mrs Parkes is perfectly content to live like this. I doubt if she even notices all the rubbish.'

Priscilla looked sceptical. 'She *must* notice.'

'Well, it's not for us to make a judgement,' Lana said, then stopped.

Wasn't that exactly what she was doing with Carl Best? Judging him? Maxine had tried hard to put him in a different light, and to point out not all Germans blindly followed their Führer. Some were even brave enough to work completely in opposition, even if it cost them their lives. Carl Best was apparently one of these people.

Maxine had left Lana's office, obviously disappointed she hadn't said she would take Peter to see his father. Lana sighed heavily. Had she always been so lacking in backbone? She didn't think so. It was Dickie's senseless death that had made her despair so much. But she was still making him the excuse even though a little boy's happiness depended on seeing his father. His mother and grandmother had died. His father was all he had in the world. And it seemed she was the only person at this particular time who could help him.

The next morning after Priscilla had gone to her class, Lana went straight into her office and picked up the telephone.

'Bingham Hall. Maxine Taylor speaking.'

'Maxine, it's Lana. Look, I'm sorry about yesterday. I wasn't thinking straight.' She took in a breath. 'I'm flattered that you asked me if I could take Peter to see his father. Of course I will.'

'Oh, Lana, I'm so pleased . . . and grateful. I felt awful pursuing it after you'd told me about your fiancé, but there was no one else to ask here. So thank you. We'll sort out a date when you're free.'

'School closes at the end of the week, so I could take him Monday or Tuesday. Would that do?'

'I'll make the arrangements and ring you back to confirm the day.' Maxine sounded relieved. 'Thank you, again, Lana. You didn't have to, and I really appreciate it.'

'Well, I've met Peter and he's a nice little lad.' Lana paused. 'But I'd like to ask *you* something, Maxine.'

'Go on.'

'Would you have any objection if I took Priscilla as well?'

'I'm not sure,' Maxine said, and Lana could imagine the matron turning over the idea. 'It would do the child good to be out for the day but how do you think Peter would take it? He'd be sharing his father, which is a bit unfair.'

'No, it wouldn't be like that,' Lana replied. 'If it was just the three of us it'd be *me* who'd be in the way. Mr Best and Peter need time to be together without me hovering around, but if I had Priscilla it would make it less awkward for them.'

She didn't say that it would be less awkward for *her*, having Priscilla.

There was a few seconds' silence. Then Maxine said, 'Actually, I think it's a very good idea.'

Lana breathed out.

'I probably don't need to say this, Lana, but as you can appreciate, this is a delicate situation and I wouldn't want anyone to know any details of where you're going or who you're meeting. As far as the staff here are concerned, you're taking Peter and Priscilla to spend the day with your family. Would you mind telling that small fib?'

'No, I think you're right,' Lana said. 'I won't let it go any further my end. And I'll warn Peter and Priscilla as well. They're both old enough to keep a secret.'

'Then it's settled. You'll need to come over and I'll give you money and directions, et cetera. Shall we say tomorrow? Come for coffee and one of Bertie's famous rock cakes.'

'I'll be there.'

The receiver crackled and she couldn't hear Maxine's next remark.

'Sorry, Maxine, I didn't catch that.'

'I said are you sure you're all right about doing this? I don't want to push you into something you feel uncomfortable about.'

'I'm perfectly happy about it,' Lana assured her.

To her surprise, she realised she meant it.

For the first time since she'd known Priscilla, the child's face lit up at the prospect of an outing and a long train ride.

'Priscilla, it's really important you don't tell anyone where we're going or who we're meeting. I should be in a lot of trouble if anyone finds out, and so would Peter's father. So you must promise to keep this a secret. We're on a secret mission.'

'Like spies,' Priscilla said, screwing up her eyes. 'I'm not a baby. What about Peter? Have you warned him too?'

'Peter's been used to keeping secrets for the last four years,' Lana said. 'And he doesn't say much to the other children. I think Freddie knows more about him than all the children put together, so it will be good for him to have you as a friend.'

'He's too young to be my friend,' Priscilla said, pulling a face.

'Then pretend you're an older sister. He desperately needs someone to talk to nearer his own age who knows about his father.' She looked at the serious child. 'Remember how alone you felt when you first went to Bingham Hall.'

Priscilla's face clouded over. Had she said too much? Lana held her breath. Then Priscilla smiled.

'I have a secret as well, don't I? The others think I'm an orphan like them, but you know my mummy and daddy are coming to fetch me. They may have to wait until the war's over but they'll come for me one day.'

Priscilla looked up at her with pleading eyes, as though willing her to agree.

Lana's stomach turned. This poor child. She still believed she'd see her parents again. It was probably better not to argue with her at this precise moment, but she must talk to Maxine soon about having a special service in the chapel for Priscilla's parents. And have the Reverend speak to Priscilla in private beforehand.

'Where are you off to, all dolled up this morning?' Janice asked as she stood by Lana's bedroom door

192

and watched Lana put the finishing touches of lipstick on.

Lana turned and laughed a little self-consciously. She might have known Janice would be curious as to why she was wearing make-up and her new summer frock. She'd spent some time wondering if it should be a skirt and blouse, but in the end had decided on the turquoise-flowered cotton dress with short puffed sleeves and a sweetheart neckline. She needed to look her very best with the extraordinary day she was facing.

'It suits that lovely red hair of yours,' her mother had said when Lana had shown her the dress.

Today Lana just wanted to be herself rather than a teacher, simply giving two children some kind of normality in this topsy-turvy world.

'Just going to see my parents,' she said, after a few seconds' pause. 'Taking Priscilla. I thought it would do her good to have an outing. Let's hope she's ready.'

'Let's hope,' Janice repeated, her eyes narrowing as if she didn't believe a word Lana was uttering.

Lana wasn't going to mention taking Peter as well – that would definitely have aroused Janice's suspicions.

'Well, have a nice time with your *parents*,' Janice said, and now her tone was slightly mocking.

'Thanks, I will.'

'Are you catching the bus?'

'No, Harold over at Bingham Hall is going into town so he's offered us a lift to the railway station.'

Janice raised her eyebrows.

'You're getting very pally with them at the orphanage, aren't you?'

'I like it there,' Lana said defensively. 'And I like Maxine very much.'

'She's okay, I suppose, the little I know her. Not sure about that Judith woman.'

'I've not met her, so I can't say.'

Lana could feel this conversation was going to go on if she didn't bring it to a halt. She picked up her handbag and gloves. It was such a beautiful morning that she decided not to wear a hat. It would be good to feel the sun and air on her face and in her hair. She tucked a cardigan in her soft open bag.

Lana practically had to brush past Janice who backed away so she could shut the bedroom door behind her. Now where was the child?

'Priscilla!' she called as she stepped outside. 'We're leaving right now!'

Maxine and Peter were waiting for Lana and Priscilla in the Great Hall, Maxine with a wide smile of welcome.

'Goodness, Lana, I don't believe I've ever seen you with your hair down. It looks positively Pre-Raphaelite.' She turned her gaze to Priscilla. 'And you've left yours loose today as well. It suits you.'

Priscilla made not the slightest acknowledgement.

'Well, Peter,' Lana said, looking at the boy who

194

was tapping his foot, his body looking tense with impatience, 'today's a special day for you, so shall we go?'

'Yes, Miss Ashwin.' Peter pulled on his cap and said goodbye to Maxine as he bolted towards the front door.

Harrold dropped the three of them at Lime Street station where they had to wait half an hour for their train, amongst crowds of soldiers saying goodbye to their sweethearts. Lana's eyes pricked with tears, and she focused on a poster demanding: *Is your journey really necessary?*

Both children were quiet for almost the whole two-hour journey, buried in their books, although Peter looked up once and asked when they'd be there.

'It depends on how long we have to wait in Northampton,' Lana told him. She hesitated. 'Peter,' she began, in almost a whisper, 'you know we still have to be very careful to keep it a secret that you're meeting your father today, don't you? You must never tell anyone about the journey or where we get off, or about your father, because—'

'Yes, Miss Ashwin, I know,' Peter interrupted. 'I don't talk to the others about anything like that.' He glanced up at her. 'I might whisper to Freddie about it when I get home, though,' he said with a grin, his blue eyes shining with mischief.

It so completely transformed his usual serious expression that Lana wanted to laugh out loud with delight. It was the first time Peter had shown he had a lovely sense of humour. She caught Priscilla looking at him, a smile tugging at the corners of her mouth. Maybe the day would turn out better than she'd expected.

All the stations had had their signs removed to confuse the Germans should there be an invasion, so Lana kept her ears pricked for the guard. When she thought they were never going to arrive his sudden announcement made her jump.

'Bletchley! Anyone for Bletchley!'

Only one nervous-looking young woman with a suitcase stepped on to the platform besides Lana and the two children. The young woman looked around her and Lana saw a man approach and say something to her. The young woman nodded and the man took her suitcase. They disappeared. Odd, Lana thought. The young woman didn't look as though she'd ever set eyes on the man and yet they'd gone off together. She shrugged. She needed to look out for Carl Best. But he was nowhere to be seen. She looked up and down the platform. Maybe they hadn't allowed him to come after all. She felt a twinge of disappointment and told herself she was disappointed for Peter's sake.

They walked the length of the platform and back, Peter's mouth drooping further as the minutes on the station clock ticked by. The three of them passed the ticket office for the third time. A fair-haired man appeared through the barrier. Lana's heart leapt. But it wasn't Carl Best. Then Peter suddenly gave a whoop of delight as he rushed off to throw himself into the arms of a tall blond man who emerged behind the first one. The next moment Carl was hugging his son, just as he had at Bingham Hall.

'Papa, I thought you wouldn't come.'

'I told you I would,' Carl said. 'Only something very important would keep me away if I'd promised.' His eyes met Lana's over the top of Peter's head, lingering for a few seconds before he gave her a small nod, then acknowledged Priscilla. 'I see you have brought a friend with you, Peter. That is nice. What is her name?'

'It's Prissy, and she's not a friend,' Peter immediately said, as he pulled away to look up at his father. 'She's come to keep Miss Ashwin company so *I* can have you to myself.'

How on earth had the child worked that one out? Lana thought. It happened to be the truth, but she certainly hadn't dreamed he would come out with such a statement, especially in front of Priscilla, who threw him a contemptuous gaze.

'I'm Priscilla,' she said to no one in particular. '*Not* Prissy.'

'But that's what everyone calls you,' Peter argued.

'That's enough, Peter,' Lana said sharply, then flushed with embarrassment. She was doing it again. Telling off his son. Interfering. She braced herself. Carl remained silent, watching her. 'And it's not true,' she continued, not daring to look at Carl. 'I wanted to give Priscilla a treat as well. I think she deserves it after her bravery.'

'What did she do?' Carl demanded.

How was it possible for eyes to be that blue?

'Later.' She shot him a warning glance.

He seemed to understand because he said, 'I think we should go or it will look as though I am up to no good.' He looked at Lana. 'Is that how you say it?'

'Yes.' What a strange thing to say. She glanced over at the tall fair-haired man who for an instant she'd mistaken for Carl Best. She'd felt him looking their way more than once.

Carl followed her line of vision. 'That's who will be keeping his eye on me for the rest of the day,' he said in a calm voice.

She stared at him. 'You mean he'll be with us all day?' She felt embarrassed again. 'To make sure you, er—' she stammered.

'Yes.' He lowered his head a little so their eyes were on the same level. 'To make sure I do not try to run away.' He shrugged. 'Why would I do that? I am here because I want to help.' He touched her on the arm and she felt the tension of him transfer to her. 'Come. Let us walk into the town and have something to eat. You must all be hungry.'

'I'm hungry, Papa.'

'And you, Priscilla?' His eyes fell on the child who was standing silently.

She just shook her head and deliberately stepped to Lana's other side. Lana reached out her hand but Priscilla appeared not to have noticed it. The four of them made their way out of the station, forming such an awkward group, Lana decided ruefully, that no one could possibly mistake them for a proper family.

Lana realised Carl Best knew his way around the town as he headed straight for a café that was crowded, unusually with more women than men. She noticed several of the women, some in uniform, turn the moment Carl stepped through the door in his light-coloured trousers, white shirt and navy blazer, an appreciative smile on their lips, watching as he made his way to the counter. Peter clung to his father's hand as though he never wanted to let him go. Poor little chap. But at least they were together at this moment. Lana blamed the smoke for the sudden stinging of her eyes, as she pushed her way through the tables, looking for a vacant one.

'Miss Ashwin, those people are just leaving.' Priscilla pointed to a table in a darkened corner where the woman was reaching for her handbag and the man was throwing some coins on the table.

'Well spotted, Priscilla,' Lana said. Carl Best had his back to her. She moved to touch him on the arm to alert him as to where they would be sitting. A soft tingle ran through her when he turned and looked at her, his blue eyes delving deep, the same way he had when she'd seen him on the drive at Bingham Hall.

He nodded and moments later they were all squashed round a table only meant for two, a waiter kindly bringing two more chairs for Priscilla and Peter. Lana sat opposite Carl so his son could sit next to him, but wished she hadn't as it was difficult to stop glancing at him. He was unnervingly handsome but she'd never seen him give a spontaneous smile. Was he always this serious? She turned to concentrate on Priscilla, glad she'd thought to bring the child, although by the look on Priscilla's face she didn't seem as though she was enjoying the unexpected outing that much, now they were actually here.

Carl passed the menu to Lana, and she suddenly felt acutely embarrassed. He was a prisoner of war so he wouldn't have any money on him. But if she paid for everyone she might not have enough for any emergency on the journey back to Liverpool. She swallowed. It was no good. She had to come out with it.

'There is no need for worry, Miss Ashwin. You may choose what you desire on the menu. And also the children. I am able to pay for everyone.'

Lana looked at Carl, shocked to think he had known what she was thinking. She mustn't blush. She wasn't a schoolgirl, for heaven's sake. But she couldn't help the warmth stealing into her cheeks.

'If you're sure . . .'

'I'm very sure.'

And then he looked across at her and smiled. It was the same smile she'd seen on Peter earlier that day, and it lit up his face. His eyes shone, and she couldn't help a tiny fizz of delight that he was human, after all, as she gave him a grateful smile in return. But it wasn't only delight that caught her at that moment.

Lana was thankful when their food came and she didn't have to make conversation. It wasn't that Carl was so difficult, or that Peter and Priscilla were acting as though the other didn't exist, but it was the awful feeling of being watched. And of course that was exactly it. The man on the platform had joined an elderly gentleman who was sitting alone only a couple of tables away. No matter how she vowed to ignore him, she could see him out of the corner of her eye, pretending to be occupied with his meal. But she knew different. How must Carl feel having a pair of eyes on him constantly? She shivered inwardly.

Peter was tackling his rabbit stew with enthusiasm even though Maxine had mentioned what a difficult child he was to feed. How only yesterday he'd complained that the food in the home was goat's food – all those greens and mustard and cress. The boy was obviously bent on being on his best behaviour in front of his father who looked far more relaxed now he was sitting with his son.

'Thank you for my dinner,' Priscilla said politely to Carl as she put her knife and fork together.

'It was a pleasure for me,' Carl said, looking at her plate, barely touched, 'although I do not think you enjoyed it very much. Would you like something more?'

Priscilla shook her head.

'Thank you, Papa, for *my* dinner.' Peter was not to be outdone on good manners.

Lana watched as Carl gave his son that lovely smile again and her heart squeezed. What must it be like to have a son . . . or a daughter? The bond between the two of them was evident and she caught a look of pure envy in Priscilla's eyes before the child looked away. This terrible war. Lana gave a start. It was the Germans who'd caused all the misery they were going through, and yet here she was, having a pleasant lunch with a German who used to be a Nazi – there was no getting away from it – no matter that he was now working for the British. She realised he looked different from every single man in the café with his way of conducting himself in such an assured manner; his height, his blond hair and even his expression was so different from an Englishman's. He was younger than most of them, for a start, and as well built as any serving soldier. The women in the café had thought the same. Even the waitress had given him a second look. But was it because he was such a good-looking man – or had they suspected he was German?

She tried to brush the thought away. As if he knew what she was thinking again he said, 'Do you want to ask me anything, Miss Ashwin? You know I cannot say any details, but it must be strange for you to sit with me, knowing so little of my situation.'

Peter had excused himself to go to the lavatory and Priscilla was entertaining herself by watching the other diners.

'I've never heard of Bletchley,' Lana said, then in a low tone she added, 'Do you work in the town?'

'Not far from here,' he said, just as quietly.

Lana was aware that the minder had his ear cocked as though he might pounce at any moment and take Carl Best by the scruff of his neck and remove him from the café. She shook herself from thinking such an absurdity.

'Are there other people like you working there?' she said tentatively so as not to draw attention to the fact that he was a prisoner.

'No – I am the only German. But there are people from other countries as well as British.'

She suddenly had a thought. If the British got hold of any German papers, Carl would be useful in deciphering them.

'Are you able to use your excellent command of English? Translating for the British, perhaps?'

Carl Best hesitated. 'Something like that,' he said finally. 'This is where I cannot say more.'

'Of course,' Lana said. 'I understand. It's just that it's difficult for me . . .' she broke off.

'Difficult to see how I must fit in?'

'Something like that,' she said, and smiled.

He smiled back. '*Touché.*' He picked up the bill and left a florin on the table, before making his way to the till.

CHAPTER 20

For the next two hours the four of them wandered round the small town, looking in shop windows that had very little on display. But at least there were no signs of any bombing by the *Luftwaffe*, Lana was thankful to note. She'd dreaded seeing Bletchley in case there was more destruction in the streets of houses and rows of shops. The Germans had destroyed so many of their cities and here she was, trotting along by the side of one of them. Granted he was no ordinary German, as she now knew, but nevertheless he'd actually served in Hitler's army.

The thought made her shiver and Carl looked at her as he fell in step beside her, Peter gripping his hand and Priscilla lagging behind them.

'You are not beginning a cold?'

'No, no. I was thinking . . .' She wanted to tell him the truth. How nice it was to wander round a town that appeared untouched but it was too embarrassing. She didn't know him well enough to make such comments, and it might well embarrass him too. If only they could have an honest discussion. But it would never be possible. She stopped and pointedly looked behind her, waiting for Priscilla to catch up.

'What were you thinking that made you so sad?'

She looked up at him, conscious that Peter was listening. 'This awful war. I'm sick of it.'

'Me too. My family is broken, all for the sake of some megalomaniac.'

She felt angry on his behalf. The agony of not knowing what had been happening to his wife and child. When the letters from his wife had suddenly stopped he must have suspected the worst.

'Have you any family still in Germany?' she asked.

'My parents are in Berlin and I worry about them every day.' He paused and she saw his eyes moisten. 'I had a brother.'

Had. That terrible word.

'What happened?'

'He was a pilot.' He looked at her directly. 'He was shot down by one of your boys. Friedrich was only nineteen. My kid brother. He had his whole life in front of him.' He screwed his eyes up as though to prevent the tears.

Unaware of what she was doing, she touched his arm. 'I'm so sorry,' she said, tears choking her throat. It was the first time she'd ever really thought what misery there was on the other side as well. How Germans must feel, losing members of their family, their cities destroyed.

But they started it, a voice whispered. She sighed. It was all so complicated.

'Let us talk of more happy things,' Carl said, and briefly touched her hand, which was still on his arm.

She dropped her hand as though it had been scalded and felt him immediately draw away.

'Miss Ashwin, I'm thirsty,' came a plaintive voice.

'We'll stop and have a cup of tea soon, Priscilla,' Lana said, thankful for once that the child had interrupted.

It seemed to Lana hardly any time at all before they were back on the platform at Bletchley, waiting for the return train.

Lana stepped to the side while Peter flung himself into his father's arms, tears streaming down his cheeks. Carl said something to him in German and took out a handkerchief and wiped his tears away.

'Come, Peter, you are nearly a man now,' Carl said gently in English, glancing at Lana and shaking his head.

She saw a tear steal down his own cheek and for a crazy moment she wanted to brush it away.

'I don't want to leave,' Peter said, sniffing as he took the handkerchief from his father's hand. 'Why can't I stay with you. I'm not an orphan,' he gave Priscilla a sly glance, 'like the others.'

Lana saw Priscilla stiffen.

'Priscilla—'

But Priscilla was already marching towards the

other end of the platform as though she couldn't bear to be with them. Lana hesitated.

'It might be kinder to let her be for a few moments.' Carl's voice came from behind.

How close he was. Close enough to smell the clean maleness of him. She stepped back in confusion, almost forgetting what she wanted to say. Gathering her wits she turned to face him.

'The terrible thing is, she won't admit she's lost both parents. They were killed in the blackout and she was brought to Dr Barnardo's a few months ago. She has nightmares and since the fire she's been sleeping in my room at the cottage by the school.'

'It is too much for a young girl to bear,' Carl said. He bent to give Peter a kiss. 'Go and find Priscilla and when the train comes you can save Miss Ashwin a seat. And be kind to Priscilla. She is very sad at the moment.'

Peter nodded, his face tear-stained.

Carl cocked his head. 'I think I hear the train coming.' Peter turned an anxious face towards Lana, then back to his father. 'Off you go, son. Miss Ashwin will follow in two minutes.'

Peter shot off, his thin legs flying along the platform. All of a sudden Lana felt shy. It was the first time she'd found herself alone with him and she couldn't think what to say.

'Miss Ashwin – Lana?' Carl's tone was grave. 'May I please call you Lana?'

He looked at her with his deep-set eyes and it

was though something had shifted between them. She said the first thing that sprang to her mind.

'Only if I'm allowed to call you Carl.'

His face broke into a warm smile, showing his creamy white teeth. 'I would like that very much.' He suddenly became serious again. 'And may I write to you?'

The train puffed its way into the station, the steam enclosing them as though there was no one else in the world.

Lana swallowed. 'If you would like to.'

'I would also like that very much.' He hesitated and ran his hand over his short blond hair. 'And will you write back to me?'

A quiver ran across Lana's shoulders. He was standing there, waiting for her reply. Out of the corner of her eye she saw the man who was watching them take a few steps in their direction.

'If you would like me to.'

'I would like it more than very much.'

And then he laughed, breaking the mood in an instant. 'You must go or you will miss the train.'

It was only when she was in the carriage, wrapped in her jumble of thoughts of all that had happened, did she realise she had told a German she would write to him. But by doing so, was she betraying Dickie?

Both children were silent on the journey home. Lana knew Peter would be thinking of his father and wishing he could have stayed longer with him, but she had no idea what was going through Priscilla's head. She was reading a book so Lana tried to engage Peter in looking at the scenery, but for the most part it was gloomy. Neither child gave any response, and in the end Lana gave up.

She leaned her head back on the cloth headrest, thankful Maxine had given her enough money for them all to go second class. Her eyes began to droop with the rhythm of the train's wheels over the rails.

It was nearly midnight when they arrived back in Liverpool. It had been another gruelling journey, stopping once for nearly an hour, and this time they had to change twice, each with another long wait. Peter was fractious and Priscilla threw him contemptuous looks. It had started to drizzle and Lana's cardigan was becoming soggy, clinging to her summer dress. She worried that the children would get colds if they stayed in damp clothes waiting for the bus. As they stepped out of the railway station Lana's eye went to the taxi rank. Would she have enough cash to take a taxi all the way to Bingham? She could tell both children were exhausted and it would be wonderful to sit in the back of a comfortable cab.

Gripping Peter's reluctant hand, she stepped over to the front taxi and the driver rolled down his window.

'Where're you going, love?' he asked.

'Could you please tell me your charge to go to Bingham Hall – it's the orphanage.'

'I know it.' He furrowed his brow. 'I could make it a straight pound.'

It was too expensive. She thanked him and backed away.

'Tell you what, love, I'll do it for ten bob, seeing as you've got the nippers.' Before she could reply, he'd sprung out of his cab and opened the rear door.

Oh, the relief to be whisked to Bingham after all the changes and delays they'd gone through that day.

'I can't thank you enough,' she said, when they arrived at the orphanage. She handed him a ten-shilling note and an extra coin.

'That's all right, love.' He pressed the shilling back in her hand. 'You just get in the warm. And get those kiddies dried off.' His tyres crunched on the gravel as he drove away.

She pulled the bell cord and one of the maids – she couldn't remember her name – ushered her in.

'I would like to go with you, Miss Ashwin,' Peter said, looking at her with his father's blue eyes.

'I'm sorry, Peter, but there is no spare bedroom where I live.'

'Priscilla stays there,' Peter said sulkily.

Lana felt Priscilla at her side stiffen.

'It's only until the decorators have finished the girls' dormitory,' she said. 'Which will be soon.'

She was relieved to see Athena come down the staircase.

'Sorry Maxine wasn't here to let you in,' she

said, 'but she was needed in the sick ward and asked me if I'd look after Peter.'

'I don't need anyone looking after me,' Peter said firmly.

'No, but you're probably hungry,' Athena said, smiling. 'Bertie's left some supper for you all.'

'I don't want anything,' Peter said.

Athena caught Lana's eye, then turned to Peter. 'Cook will be upset if you don't eat it. She's made you a nice Spam sandwich.'

'I *hate* Spam and I can get ready for bed on my own.'

Before Lana could speak Athena shook her head as Peter ignored her and trudged up the stairs without looking back.

'He's tired out,' she said. 'But you and Priscilla come and get yours.'

'Would it be too rude if we take it with us?' Lana said. 'Priscilla's tired – we all are, and we could have it back at the cottage.'

'I'll pack it up for you.'

Athena returned in five minutes with the sandwiches packed in greaseproof paper.

'Would you let Maxine know I'll telephone her tomorrow?'

'Yes, of course. I'm going home in the morning for a few days so I'll leave her a note.'

Priscilla padded along by her side without speaking. Every so often Lana glanced at her but the rigid profile told her nothing. Twice she tried to say something but Priscilla refused to respond.

As soon as they reached the cottage Priscilla ran upstairs and flung herself on her bed and sobbed. Lana followed.

'Priscilla, love, what is it?'

'Leave me alone.'

'I'm not going to leave you alone. Don't forget I live here too.' She tried to make a joke but Priscilla remained on her stomach, crying her heart out into the pillow.

'Priscilla, you're going to make *me* cry in a minute. Here, take my handkerchief.'

Priscilla reached an arm out and snatched it. After plenty of sniffing she finally sat up, her eyes red-rimmed and her face flushed.

'Please talk to me, love. You know I'll understand.'

'How can you understand?' Priscilla shouted. 'Peter's got his father and I don't know where my mother and father even are. Maybe the house got bombed and that's why they haven't received my letters.'

This was terrible. Perhaps there was another way for Priscilla to understand what had happened. Keeping her arm firmly round the child, she said: 'Priscilla, I'm going to tell you a story. One day a lady met a man who was in the Navy. He was everything she ever dreamed of – dark-haired, very handsome, with a lovely smile, and he made her laugh. When the war started they knew they would be separated for long periods while he was out at sea on his ship, but they decided to become engaged. He gave her his grandmother's engagement ring but she wouldn't wear it on her finger. She always wore it round her neck because he was about to go away and fight and she wanted them both to tell her parents they were going to be married the next time he was on shore leave.

'He wrote as often as he could and soon it was time for him to come home for a few days. He said he'd be docking in Liverpool in October. She was so excited. But he never came. His ship was blown up by the Germans. She never saw him again. She was broken-hearted. The future they'd dreamed of was in ruins.' Lana gulped. She noticed Priscilla was actually listening. 'She didn't know how she could bear to go on,' Lana continued. 'But she had to. It was happening to thousands of families up and down the country. She thought she would get her revenge and join one of the services, but in her heart she wanted to go on doing what she was good at. Teaching. So she changed her teaching job in Yorkshire and went to Liverpool to make a fresh start, knowing it was what her fiancé would have wanted. He was always so proud of her.

'At first the lady kept pretending he was still alive. That he'd come back and they would get married. But her head told her it would never happen. She had to face it or she would suffer for the rest of her life.'

Lana stopped. Had she gone too far? Would Priscilla think she was off her head? But Priscilla

214

was watching her, chewing her bottom lip, another tear falling down her cheek. She could hear Priscilla's jerky breaths and saw the girl's eyes flick to Dickie's engagement ring.

'The lady was you, wasn't it?'

Lana gulped. 'Yes, it was. I'll never forget him, but I have to carry on. And it's the same with you. We must both make new friends and they'll help us. And you and I will help one another.'

Priscilla screwed her face up as though hardly daring to utter her next words. Lana heard her gulp as she asked, 'Are Mummy and Daddy really dead?'

'Yes, darling, they are. But they're still watching over you, just as Dickie is watching over me.'

'I don't know what to do.' Priscilla brushed her arm across her face.

'I've been thinking about asking Mrs Taylor if she could arrange a service in the chapel especially for your mother and father. You could invite the children and pick out any music you think your parents would like. It would be a way of saying how much you love them and to say goodbye.'

There was another silence. Then in a small voice Priscilla said, 'Would you come with me?'

'Yes, love, of course I will.' She looked at Priscilla. 'Why don't you clean your teeth and hop into bed. I'll be up shortly. All right?'

To her huge relief Priscilla nodded.

Janice had propped a letter for her on the mantelpiece. The envelope was typed with a county council rubber stamp. Lana unfolded the sheet of paper and glanced at the signature. It was from Mr Shepherd.

> Dear Miss Ashwin,
>   I should be grateful if you would be so kind as to come to the council offices (address above) on Monday morning at 9.30.
>   There is something important I wish to discuss.
>   I look forward to seeing you then.
>   Yours sincerely,
>   George Shepherd

Frowning, Lana skimmed the note again in case she'd missed something. She couldn't make out the tone. Was he going to tell her off or was he going to praise her? It was impossible to guess. She shrugged. Monday would come soon enough, no doubt.

CHAPTER 21

Living in Bingham village, Lana realised, as she looked at the devastation around her in the centre of Liverpool, meant they were cocooned from much of the war itself. Yes, they would sometimes hear the sirens go off in Albert Dock, and the noise of explosions, and occasionally feel the vibrations, but thankfully the bombing didn't impair much on the children's daily lives. Maxine had told her two bombs had dropped in the grounds of the orphanage in the last two years, causing three adults and two children's deaths, which was tragic, but thankfully lessons, the daily routine and Bertie's delicious meals made from generous rations by the government, were the staples of life at Bingham Hall.

Lana had never been a great one for shopping so an outing in the city didn't appeal at the best of times, but maybe today she should take the opportunity to visit one of the art galleries – Athena had mentioned the Walker Gallery, saying it was Liverpool's finest. She'd wander over after seeing Mr Shepherd.

At a quarter to ten Lana stood outside the town

hall. Dominating the surrounding buildings in Castle Street with its classical portico and dome, it had taken a hit during the Blitz, but appeared to be open. She gasped as she stepped inside. She wasn't expecting such a sumptuous interior. A massive chandelier hung from an ornate ceiling and marble pilasters formed a rhythmic pattern to the walls of the foyer.

Before she had time to admire such a room, a woman dressed from head to foot in black ushered her into a small waiting area and at exactly ten o'clock she took Lana down a wide corridor and knocked on the third door along.

'Enter.'

'Miss Ashwin to see you, Sir.' The woman made a small bob with her head.

'Would you bring us tea?' George Shepherd asked her. She nodded and disappeared.

Mr Shepherd rose from his chair and removed his spectacles before taking Lana's proffered hand.

'Thank you for coming, Miss Ashwin. Do take a seat.'

He gestured to one of the visitor's chairs with a jerky movement. Lana was sure he was uncomfortable – nervous, even. What was going on? He certainly didn't look as though he was about to sing her praises. She waited while he cleared his throat.

'Miss Ashwin.' He cleared his throat again. 'Miss Ashwin, how are you finding the job?'

She gave a small start. She sent him a report

each week and always received an answer back straightaway saying how delighted he was.

'Um, very well, I believe. The children seem to have accepted me. They're making excellent progress with their reading and writing, and I'm very keen that they do so. We're writing a play with some made-up songs telling the story of *Oliver Twist*, and Priscilla Morgan, the child you said needs the most attention, has taken a major rôle. Already she's improving and actually joining in a little with the others in her class. She's—'

'Quite, quite,' Mr Shepherd interrupted. 'Most interesting. However, I . . . Now let me see.' He picked up a file on his desk and flipped through it, then frowned. 'Now where's that letter gone?'

He adjusted his spectacles and put his hand on an envelope, which had already been opened. Unfolding the paper, he put it down and removed his spectacles again, before he looked her in the eye.

Lana began to feel quite concerned. She wished he'd get it over with, whatever it was he wanted to tell her.

'Now where was I? Oh, yes, the letter from Mr Benton.'

Mr Benton? The previous headmaster? Why was he writing to Mr Shepherd?

'Miss Ashwin—'

There was a knock at the door and the same woman came in with a tray of tea. She set a cup down in front of Lana and the other in

Mr Shepherd's line of vision. Lana noticed he seemed almost grateful for the interruption by the way he smiled at the woman and didn't dismiss her right away.

'Will that be all, Sir?'

He seemed to come to his senses. 'Yes, indeed, Mrs Lidbetter. Thank you.' He hesitated again. 'Take your time with your tea, Miss Ashwin.' He put his own cup to his lips and took a few gulps.

'Please, Mr Shepherd, tell me why you need to speak to me. It must be something important.'

'Ah, yes, of course.' He sent her a grave look. 'I have had some rather disturbing news.'

Lana's heart plummeted.

'You remember my telling you Mr Benton was the headmaster, but joined up to fight our worthy battle. Well, I'm afraid he's been injured.'

It was awful to feel such relief, but obviously Mr Shepherd was sounding her out. He wanted her to continue in her position on a permanent basis. That's why he wanted to know how she personally felt about the position, not just the reports she sent off to him. Her heart sang. It was the best news he could have given her.

Although she was delighted she made herself look serious. 'Oh, that's awful. Poor Mr Benton. But of course I'll stay on permanently.'

Mr Shepherd drummed his fingers together. 'I'm not sure you understand,' he said. 'He's been injured too badly to continue fighting but he's not at death's door.'

'Oh, thank goodness.'

'He's asked to have his old job back.'

Cold shock waves poured down Lana's spine. No.

'But if he's injured surely he—'

'He's lost an arm. But he's not ill. Just can't hold a gun. He assures me he can do the job just as well with one arm.' He looked beseechingly at Lana and shook his head. 'What can I do? I have to let him have it. He's entitled to it.'

'But that's most unfair on me,' Lana burst out. 'I'm so happy there and doing good work with the children.'

'The thing is, Miss Ashwin, it was only a temporary position. I did make it clear at our interview.'

'Yes, but I thought it was going to last longer than a few weeks,' Lana said, a spurt of anger threatening to rise to the surface. 'I wouldn't have accepted the job if I'd known.'

'I don't suppose Mr Benton wanted to lose an arm,' Mr Shepherd said calmly.

Trying to gather her thoughts she took a few sips of her tea, which was now lukewarm, but she felt she was choking.

'When will he be coming back?' she asked finally, her voice cracking.

'In a fortnight.'

'It doesn't give me much time to make another big change to my life.'

She looked at the man facing her. There was a light sheen of sweat over his top lip as though he couldn't wait to get this meeting over with. She couldn't feel sorry. It was all very well for him. He probably lived in Liverpool, or close by, and apart from The Merchant Navy, had been sitting at this same desk for the last twenty years. She'd moved all the way down here from Yorkshire – some two hundred miles – to start a new job. It was her chance to try to come to terms with losing Dickie. Now her new job, which she was growing to love, had been cut short by one ex-soldier's request.

She suddenly felt ashamed. Poor man had lost an arm. It must be devastating for him. Regaining his old position would likely make him feel more normal again after what he'd been through. He had no idea who'd taken his place. Mr Shepherd was right. He'd made it clear from the advertisement as well as at the interview that it was not a permanent position.

Lana sighed and finished her tea, then rose to her feet. She extended her hand.

'I'm sorry, Mr Shepherd. You must think me awfully churlish when I'm only thinking about myself and there's a war on. It's just that—'

'Don't give it another thought,' he said, shaking her hand. 'It's a shame as you were doing an excellent job.'

'I'll have everything packed up by Friday week.' Lana gulped as she felt the telltale prick of tears. She would not let him see her cry.

Mr Shepherd rushed to open the door for her.

'I'll send you your last month's salary,' he said,

'and see if there's a chance they can put in an extra week for your trouble.'

'I'd be very grateful.' It took all her effort to smile at him as she told him goodbye.

Outside, she felt someone had punched her in the stomach. That weak cup of cold tea hadn't helped at all. But she didn't care to linger in Liverpool. It was just too depressing. She couldn't bear the idea of going back home with another failure, even though Mr Shepherd had made it patently clear this was nothing to do with her performance at work. She felt her eyes brim and told herself off.

Come on, Lana. It's not the end of the world. You'll just have to rethink this whole teaching lark.

But it was far from any lark. She took it seriously but at the same time she loved it.

And then it hit her. Priscilla. The child was just beginning to trust her. To open up a little. How could she leave such a bruised young girl? That awful look of despair in Priscilla's eyes would be back. And she hadn't yet told Maxine her idea of having a service in the chapel for Priscilla's parents. She'd better do it right away before she had to pack up her things and say goodbye.

CHAPTER 22

Two hours later Lana was sitting in Maxine's office.

'I'm looking forward to hearing how everything went yesterday,' Maxine said, leaning forward, eager for news.

'Carl – I mean Mr Best—'

'Oh, it's Carl now, is it?' Maxine teased, her eyes twinkling with mischief.

Lana could have bitten her tongue out as warmth stole to her cheeks.

'I do believe you're blushing,' Maxine said.

'He asked me to call him Carl,' Lana said, wishing she was anywhere but under Maxine's amused gaze.

'I'm not going to tease you any more,' Maxine said, chuckling, 'but it doesn't sound as though you found him to be quite the enemy you thought.'

'It's true,' Lana said, 'now I know he wasn't a supporter of Hitler – quite the opposite. I have a feeling there's a big story behind his escape but of course he can't say anything, especially with the minder's eyes fixed on him all the time.'

'Yes, that must be horrible.' Maxine paused. 'So what did you talk about?'

'Mostly I left Peter to have as much time as possible with his father,' Lana said. 'That was the important thing.'

'What about Priscilla? Was she all right?'

'She was quiet, which is what I expected. It was rather an unnatural meeting for everyone really. But she was okay – that is, until we got home. Then she sobbed her heart out. I guessed what was coming. She was envious that Peter had seen his father and she didn't even know where her parents were.'

'She's still set on that track,' Maxine murmured, writing a few notes on a pad.

'Not exactly.' Lana quickly told Maxine the story she'd related to Priscilla.

'So she accepts that her parents are never coming back for her?' Maxine said, scribbling away.

'I think so, but she's in a state now, as you can imagine. I've been thinking. Would it be possible for you to arrange a service in the chapel here especially for her parents, with some hymns, so Priscilla can say goodbye to them? Not to close the door on them – I don't mean that,' she added hastily, 'but to let them go.'

'I think that's a really good idea,' Maxine said. 'Would you help the child to pick out some hymns and prepare her for the service? She trusts you.'

Lana was silent. This was exactly what she wanted to do – help Priscilla in any way she could. But she'd be home in a week. There was no point in staying any longer. Maxine was looking at her directly, waiting for an answer.

'Sorry, that sounded a bit rude of me,' Maxine said, smiling. 'I didn't mean it to come out quite like that. I'm sure you've got plenty to do preparing for next term, and marking papers and, of course, there'll be Sports Day, which the kiddies love.'

'No, no, it's not that,' Lana said unhappily. 'You see, I'm only here for a few more days.'

'What do you mean?'

'The previous headmaster's been injured – lost an arm – but wants his old job back.' She told Maxine about her meeting with Mr Shepherd earlier on that morning, and her eyes swam with tears. 'I don't want to go home. It'll be as though I haven't achieved what I set out to do – to be the best headmistress I can possibly be. I wanted so much to help Priscilla. She's such a damaged child. And now I won't have the opportunity—' She reached in her handbag for a handkerchief and blew her nose. 'Sorry, Maxine, but it's all been rather a shock.'

'Oh, Lana, it's me who's sorry.' Maxine came round from her desk and bent to put an arm round her. 'Just as we've become friends. There must be something we can do so you don't have to leave.'

'Well, there isn't. And I know two people who will be delighted.' She gave Maxine a watery smile. 'Janice will be over the moon to have the cottage back to herself, and Mrs Danvers will be thrilled to have Mr Benton back. She always sounds as though she's in love with him, the way her face takes on this reverent expression.'

Maxine chuckled. 'I don't know her but if she lives up to the name of Rebecca's housekeeper, then she must be awful. But I *have* heard the reputation of the headmaster and wasn't very impressed. Priscilla says he was very strict with the children.' She looked thoughtful for a few moments, then said, 'There is one rather remote possibility but I hardly like to mention it for fear of offending you.'

Lana felt a flash of hope. 'You won't offend me in the least – not how I'm feeling at the moment.'

Maxine rose from her desk. 'I was just about to have a cup of coffee, so let's go into the library. I'll get Beth to bring it through.' She sent Lana a stern glance. 'You look like you need it. You go on – you know where the library is, and I'll be with you in a couple of minutes.'

Lana would have loved more time to browse in the library. It made the one at the school pale. Running her eyes over the titles in the English Literature section gave her something to occupy her mind and calm her upset nerves. A few minutes later Maxine returned and ushered Lana into the small side room they'd used before.

Intrigued, Lana sat at the large round table and Maxine took the adjacent seat, turning the chair so she was facing her.

'I suddenly had a thought, but you might not think it at all suitable.'

'Go on.'

'We're going to have a vacancy here soon.'

Lana's heart leapt. 'Oh, Maxine, how wonderful. And if you're worried that I'd be offended to be offered a teaching position after being a headmistress, don't be. I'd accept it in an instant . . . In fact,' she smiled happily, 'I wasn't keen on keeping tabs on the other teachers. If I'm honest, I'd prefer to spend more time in class with the children. That's where I belong.' She held her breath.

Maxine shook her head. 'I'm afraid it's not a teaching position. I wish it was as I know you'd be ideal.'

It was the second blow of the morning. 'But . . . what is it then? I can cook a bit but I'm no professional.' She tried to laugh but it fell flat.

'Didn't you once mention you could drive?'

'Yes.' What was Maxine getting at? What did that have to do with a vacancy at Bingham Hall?

'Harold, our chauffeur, is going into hospital for an operation next month. He'll be off work at least six, maybe eight weeks, so it's another temporary situation, I'm afraid, but at least it would give you time to think what you wanted to do, and maybe apply to one of the schools in Liverpool. It's not a full-time job, though, so the pay would be pro rata.'

'I'd be happy to stand in for him,' Lana said. Anything to stay longer, she thought. 'But I'd love to teach in the times I'm not needed, or fill in when anyone's not well or on holiday.'

'The trouble with Harold's job is that we never know. Most of it is routine stuff like going into Liverpool for supplies, or helping Charlie on any heavy jobs, but if there's an emergency you'd have to drop tools and rush off. And that could be in the middle of a class.'

There was a knock at the door and Beth came in with a tray of coffee and Bertie's warm scones, straight from the oven. The comforting smell reminded Lana of her mother when she would have a baking day once a week before she became ill.

Maxine poured the coffee and handed her a cup. 'Sugar?'

Lana shook her head. 'I gave it up when the war started. Dad said we were bound to have sugar rationing along with many other basic ingredients, so I decided I could do without it.'

Maxine nodded. 'Your parents own a grocery shop, don't they?'

'Yes. But the trouble nowadays is that the customers think we can take what we like from the shop and don't have to worry about coupons. They don't believe we do exactly the same as everyone else, even though it's tempting sometimes.'

'It must be,' Maxine smiled. 'We're so lucky here, and Bertie's a marvel. Don't know what we'd do without her . . . but back to you.'

'I've just had a thought,' Lana said. 'Priscilla. Because of all that's happened to her and how she finds it difficult to concentrate. You mentioned she's slipping behind so I could give her extra coaching in the evenings – on a volunteer basis, of course,' she added hastily.

'Getting Priscilla up to scratch would be marvellous,' Maxine said thoughtfully. 'Maybe it's worked out for the best. She can pack her bits and pieces and come back with you. The other girls have settled with us again.' She looked directly at Lana. 'Could you manage on a part-time wage?'

'I could and would,' Lana immediately said, smiling confidently, trying not to show how desperate she felt. She mustn't let this opportunity slip by. Besides, it would be driving, which she adored.

'Well, everything is all found,' Maxine said, tapping her pen on her notepad, 'so I suppose it's not out of the question. You wouldn't have a cottage, unfortunately. Would that present a problem?'

'I wouldn't expect separate accommodation,' Lana said quickly. 'I don't have it now. I share it with the messiest person I've ever come across. I'll be quite happy with a room in the house if that's on offer.'

Maxine nodded. 'Yes, but first let me speak to Mr Clarke at Dr Barnardo's headquarters. I'm sure he'll be relieved that I've fixed something up satisfactorily.' She looked up. 'I have to ask this. Have you a driving licence?'

Lana breathed out. 'Oh, yes.' Some of the tension left her body for the first time that morning, even though nothing definite was settled. Dr Barnardo's might not agree to her taking over the driving.

'I'll let you know as soon as—'

Maxine was interrupted by a frantic knocking at the door. She sprang up and opened it and a maid stood there, her eyes wide.

'Beth, what on earth is the matter?'

'Miss, come quick. Bertie needs you.'

'Is someone hurt?'

'No, it's a mouse!'

'Oh, no.' Turning to Lana, her face a shade paler, she said, 'How are you with mice?'

'I'm not scared of them, if that's what you mean,' Lana said, grinning. 'Do you want me to come with you to offer moral support?'

'Yes, please.'

'It's gone behind the dresser,' Bertie said when the two women appeared in the kitchen. Lana closed the door behind her.

Ethel, the kitchen maid, was standing on a chair squealing with fright.

'Let me have a look.' Lana bent right down, almost on her stomach, and looked under the enormous pine dresser holding dozens of utility plates and bowls. Peering out at her was a quivering little brown creature with bright eyes. 'Poor little thing,' she said as she scrambled up. 'It's terrified.'

'Not as terrified as *me*,' Ethel said, clinging on to the chair.

'Why don't you all leave the kitchen for ten minutes while I try to catch it?' Lana said.

As soon as Bertie and the maid disappeared, followed by a sheepish Maxine, Lana located the larder and found the cheese. She crumbled a tiny piece onto a saucer, then put it by the back door. She opened it and kept it ajar with a milk bottle. Then she waited. After a few minutes the mouse poked his head out. Lana hardly breathed. It emerged and sniffed at the slight breeze from the open door, then ran towards it. It stopped when it discovered the cheese crumbs. It grabbed one and scampered across the stone threshold and straight out of the back door. Immediately, Lana closed it and went to call the cook.

'It's all safe,' she said as Bertie came in with the terrified maid. 'Where's Maxine?'

'Gone back to her office, no doubt,' Bertie said. 'What did you do?'

'I just let it out,' Lana said, laughing. 'It was only a little field mouse. It wouldn't have done anyone any harm.'

'Och, I wouldn't kill it,' Bertie said emphatically. 'I don't kill anything. But they're not right in the kitchen. We have regular inspections and we don't want to be closed down.'

'Then the perfect solution is a cat,' Lana said. 'If you had a cat, I guarantee you wouldn't have any more problems.'

CHAPTER 23

Lana's optimistic mood dwindled over the next few hours. She was sure the powers that be at Dr Barnardo's headquarters would never allow a woman to take over Harold's position. Before the war had started she'd had several drivers wind down their windows and tell her she should be at home looking after her husband and not be a danger to everyone on the roads. She'd always ignored their rude comments, tossing her red hair and staring ahead, but now she began to falter. And she hadn't driven for several months. Well, there was nothing she could do until she heard from Maxine.

She wished the new term had started so she could keep occupied in class, but they wouldn't be returning for another ten days, and by that time she'd be gone – either home, or with luck, to Bingham Hall. As it was, she'd finished marking their end-of-term tests, but it was pointless to prepare the new term as Mr Benton would likely have different ideas.

She dictated a brief letter to all the parents to

explain that Mr Benton would be returning, ready for the new term.

'Oh, that's the best news I've heard for a long time,' Mrs Dayton said, her eyes gleaming with triumph, as though she alone had brought back the headmaster. 'The children will be delighted.'

Lana said nothing.

The woman stopped clacking her typewriter and looked Lana in the eye. 'Bit of a shock for you, I expect, Miss Ashwin,' she said.

'Not at all,' Lana returned coolly. 'I knew from the start it was only a temporary position.'

Why should she explain anything to this awful woman?

'I don't expect you imagined it would come to an end *quite* this soon.' Mrs Dayton tapped a few keys, then with a flourish she banged the carriage return.

'I'll leave you to it, then, Mrs Danvers,' Lana said, calling her by the nickname on purpose this time. 'I believe there'll be sixty or so letters to type. And I don't want carbon copy letters going out – the parents must all have an original. When you've finished you may leave them on my desk for signature.'

With that, Lana swept out of the room and back to her office. Putting Mrs Danvers in her place had only given her a few moments' pleasure. She sighed. She might as well go back to her room and start packing.

⋆   ⋆   ⋆

Janice was in the sitting room reading when Lana entered the cottage.

'You'll be pleased to hear Priscilla and I are leaving the cottage,' Lana threw over her shoulder, as she was about to go up to her bedroom.

'What?' Janice looked up, startled.

'You'll soon have the cottage to yourself.' Lana managed to stop an irritable note in her voice.

As she expected, Janice didn't bother to hide her expression of delight.

'Really? What's up?'

'My time is what's up. Mr Benton is coming back as headmaster.'

And that's all I'm telling her, Lana thought, not waiting for Janice's response as she leapt up the stairs.

She looked around her room. Not only the cottage itself, but even her bedroom had never felt like home, particularly with Janice around, and she'd almost welcomed the arrival of Priscilla to take some of the heat out of their awkward relationship.

She began a letter to her parents, determined not to mention her job had come to an end until she'd heard from Maxine. She was just signing off the letter when Janice came running up the stairs saying Mrs Danvers had an urgent telephone call for her.

Please not one of her brothers.

Lana flew over to the school, heart banging as a feeling of dread landed in the pit of her stomach.

'Take it in Mr Benton's office,' Mrs Danvers said, pasting a smile on her thin lips.

She grabbed the receiver. 'Hello. It's Lana Ashwin.'

'Maxine here.'

'Oh.' Lana sat down with a thump.

'Lana, you'd only just gone two minutes when I had a call from the hospital. Harold collapsed in the town. Nothing to do with his forthcoming operation, apparently. They think he's had a mild heart attack. Thank goodness someone from one of the cafés helped him and called the ambulance. He's all right but they've given him strict orders to rest before his operation. I was wondering . . . any chance of you clearing out of the cottage right away and maybe starting here tomorrow? You wouldn't be letting anyone down at the school, seeing as it's still closed for the summer.'

'What about head office?'

'I've phoned and explained. They're absolutely delighted. I told them I would send all the details to them tomorrow so they can get the official paperwork out to us.'

'Oh, Maxine, I'm so sorry for poor Harold, but yes, we'll be over tomorrow with our things. I can't thank you enough.'

'No need,' Maxine said firmly, but Lana detected the relief in her voice. 'You've got me out of a difficulty. I know it's only for the time being, but something else might turn up in the meantime.'

'I hope so.' Lana paused. 'Oh, will I be driving Harold's car – the Rover?'

'There isn't another one,' Maxine said, chuckling. 'Is that all right?'

A good reliable motor.

'More than all right,' Lana said happily.

'Sorry I can't send someone over with the car but no one else drives, so you're going to be really popular around here.'

'That'll make a nice change.' Lana laughed. This was a new phase in her life. Something good was going to come from her dismissal from the school. She could feel it in her bones.

It was bright and sunny late morning when the taxi passed through the colonnade of lime trees and the driver dropped Lana and Priscilla outside the orphanage. Lana had telephoned Mr Shepherd to explain she'd be leaving right away, but she'd had to leave a message with his secretary, along with her forwarding address at Bingham Hall. She hadn't bothered to say goodbye to Mrs 'Danvers' – just made sure she'd left the office tidy for Mr Benton's return. Janice had merely wished her good luck; that she'd need it looking after all those difficult kids. Hearing that had made Lana even more sure that her natural place would be at Bingham Hall.

'Does the architecture remind you of anything?' she asked Priscilla.

Priscilla shrugged, then said, 'I suppose it looks a bit like a castle with that turret and everything.'

'Yes, it does,' Lana agreed. 'What's inside the turret – do you know?'

'It's the chapel,' Priscilla said shortly, as she pulled the bell cord beside the massive oak door.

Ah. Where we can hold the service.

Charlie answered the door and immediately took their cases. 'You'll be on the third floor. And, Miss Priscilla, you'll be back in the dormitory. I'll take these to the rooms.'

Priscilla pressed her lips together, but Lana touched her arm and the girl gave her a small smile.

'Good morning, Miss Ashwin,' Maxine said, appearing in the Great Hall. 'Welcome back, Priscilla. Why don't you come with me and leave Miss Ashwin to unpack.'

Lana followed Charlie up the wide curving oak staircase, her breath a little short by the time she set foot on the third-floor landing. She grimaced and made a vow to do more walking while she was here.

'There we are, Miss.' Charlie set her case in Lana's room. It smelled of polish and there was a vase of fresh flowers on the windowsill. Just that small gesture made her feel as though she was welcome. Everyone working here was trying to do their best to help these little souls and she would now be one of them. She felt content for the first time since she'd arrived in Liverpool.

It didn't take long to unpack. Lana looked out of the window that was at the front of the house, looking down the sweeping drive. She took in the clear view of the colonnade of lime trees, which formed a beautiful arcade, and her heart lifted. This would be her peaceful place to renew her energy, to help her feel she belonged. She refused to remind herself that it would only last for a few weeks. She'd face that when the time came.

'You're just in time for coffee,' Maxine said, smiling as she met Lana in the Great Hall. There was a rush of feet. 'Here they all come for their milk and biscuits.'

They poured into the hall from all directions, talking, pushing, shouting.

'Children,' Maxine said, clapping her hands. 'Stop this noise immediately. I have something to tell you. Mr Harold is not very well at the moment and the doctor has ordered him to rest before his operation. So he'll be away for a few weeks. But we have a new lady who'll be taking his place – Miss Ashwin. Some of you already know her from the village school. Please make her welcome, and don't make a nuisance of yourselves, you boys, begging for rides. You know there's a petrol shortage.'

'Ladies can't drive,' a freckle-faced young lad called out scornfully.

'That's all you know,' chimed Betsy who Lana recognised.

'You don't know nofink,' the boy rounded on

the child. 'You're only a girl with a funny brown face.'

Betsy burst into tears.

'Enough!' Maxine clapped her hands together. 'That was extremely rude and hurtful, Jack, and you will apologise to Betsy immediately.'

'I'm not going to. She *does* look funny. She don't look like any of us.'

'Immediately after you've had your break, you will come to my office,' Maxine said, and Lana saw the flash of anger in the matron's eyes. 'Now, go and have your milk and biscuits, all of you. And no more of this nonsense. Betsy, if you stop crying you can come and sit with me and Miss Ashwin.' She paused. 'Those who don't believe ladies can drive will not ever be offered a ride in the car. And that includes you, Jack, so pay attention! Betsy was perfectly right. Ladies can drive just as well as gentlemen can. And don't you forget it. Is that clear?'

There was a chorus of 'Yes, Matron.'

'They won't be as good as men drivers,' Lana heard Jack mumble to one of the other children as they pushed one another into the dining room.

'Jack's a bit of a handful,' Maxine said. 'Always has to have the last word. But another one with a sad story, as they all do.'

'I think you're all marvellous,' Lana said. 'I know even with spending time with Priscilla how different children are when they've gone through something dreadful. You can't let them get away with

240

everything and yet you have to be very patient and understanding. Talking about Priscilla, I didn't see her go into the dining room.'

'She said she wasn't feeling very well so I've put her in the sick ward. Dolores is keeping an eye on her.'

'Oh, she didn't mention not feeling well,' Lana said. 'I'll pop down and see her later.'

CHAPTER 24

Lana couldn't wait for Charlie to take her to the coach house, now used as a garage where Harold kept his precious motorcar.

'It belonged to Lady Greenway from the village,' Charlie told her. 'Her husband bought it brand new several years ago, but he died fairly recently. They had a chauffeur, but her Ladyship's now gone to live with her daughter and son-in-law, so she gave it to Bingham Hall as a very generous gift. Harold was over the moon as it was a much better motor than he used to drive.' He paused to open the garage doors. 'There it is. What do you think?'

'Oh, a Rover 14,' Lana exclaimed, clapping her hands at the sleek black motorcar. 'I'd say it's a '36 or 7.'

'I don't know about that,' Charlie said, stroking his chin. 'Only know Harold was chuffed when it was delivered a few weeks ago.' He paused. 'Can't believe the chap's had a heart attack. He's a good bit younger than me. You never know what's round the corner, do you?'

'No, you don't,' Lana said, 'but that doesn't

mean it's all going to be bad.' She ran her hand gently over the boot. 'Is there a key?'

'Yes, he keeps it on this shelf.' He reached upwards and felt along a shelf, then handed her the key.

'It's the only one we've got, so be careful with it.'

'I will, but it doesn't seem very sensible to have only one key. What if it got lost?'

'I'll let you work that one out, Miss,' Charlie grinned. 'Anyway, there should be some petrol in the tank. Mrs Taylor has the ration card and the log book of the journeys, so I'll leave you to it, then.' He doffed his cap and disappeared.

Lana opened the door and sank into the leather seat behind the steering wheel. She sniffed the leather, giving a sigh of satisfaction, feeling completely at home. If only the job was permanent she'd be more than content. But she mustn't think such things when poor Harold was still in hospital. She was simply helping him out, that was all.

She pulled the choke halfway, turned the key and pressed the starter button. She let it run for a minute then put the gear into reverse. Slowly, she eased the car out of its home. She'd drive into the village to see if there was anywhere she could have another key cut. It would be a good excuse to get the feel of the motor, which was much bigger than she was used to. That didn't worry her, but she needed to understand the way it handled.

The tyres crackled down the drive, tossing the shingle, immediately bringing back the scene when she'd first walked up to Bingham Hall and the Rolls-Royce with Carl Best had passed her. He had caught her eye and it was as though he'd looked into her soul. She'd felt then he was someone of importance. Someone special. Strange how she now knew his name and that he was Peter's father, and had spent several hours in his company, but she hardly knew anything else about him. But that was the war. No one was allowed to say what they were doing. And it was far worse because this man was German, and had been a member of that odious regime, even if he wasn't a Nazi any longer. She mentally shook herself. She had to get rid of such an unpleasant train of thought. The image didn't fit Carl Best.

She turned right out of the drive and headed for the village, enjoying the feel of being in control of such a wonderful piece of machinery. She couldn't help breaking into a smile at the surprising turn of events when her attention was caught by someone running ahead, holding a cloth bag. Someone not much more than a child. Someone with blonde pigtails. The girl turned when she heard the car behind her. Priscilla!

Where the blazes was she going? She was supposed to be in the sick ward. Surely she wasn't running away.

Lana slowed right down and pulled over in the lane a hundred yards in front of the child. Priscilla had obviously not seen who it was in the car as she kept up her running speed. Lana wound down the window.

'Priscilla!'

The girl froze in her tracks. 'Miss Ashwin!'

'Get in the car, Priscilla. We can't talk through a window.'

Priscilla hesitated, and for a moment Lana thought she was going to bolt off. Instead, she opened the door and climbed in, pulling it shut behind her.

'What's all this about? Matron said you didn't feel very well today, so she sent you to the sick ward.'

Priscilla looked ahead, her face set like stone. 'It was an excuse. I feel trapped in that place. It's like a prison.'

'That's a terrible thing to say,' Lana said, 'when everyone is trying to be so kind.'

'I hate it there,' Priscilla burst out. 'It wasn't so bad when I was with you, even though the cottage was really Mrs Parkes's – she hates children. And I hate Mrs Dayton. She's always trying to get me into trouble.'

'I'm sure she isn't,' Lana said, but she knew Priscilla was right. 'Where were you going?'

'I wanted to see how that cat was.'

'The cat?' For a moment Lana couldn't think what Priscilla was talking about.

'You know. The one that got hit by a motor or something that morning when I was late.'

245

'Ah, yes. You rescued him. Well, I'm sure he's recovered.'

'I thought if no one has claimed him we could give him a home.'

'Sorry, love, animals aren't allowed.'

'Cook could probably persuade Matron. She's terrified the inspector will find mouse droppings in her kitchen and close it down.'

Lana's lips curled in amusement. Priscilla wasn't going to be fobbed off. And they did need a cat at Bingham Hall not only for the mice – it would be wonderful for the children as well.

'I could come with you to the vet's.'

'Would you, Miss Ashwin? I keep wondering if the vet saved his life.'

'I expect he did, love.'

Priscilla bit her lip. Then she said, 'Miss Ashwin, if you're now at Bingham Hall, who will be in place of you at the school?'

'Mr Benton's coming back.'

Priscilla instantly pulled a face. 'I hate that man. He was horrible to me when Mummy and Daddy were l-l-lost.' She broke into sobs.

Lana put her arms around the shaking child. 'Come on, love. You've been very brave, and you have to go on being brave. But you have me as a friend.'

'I'll have to go to the school for my classes and you won't even be there. Only that horrible Mrs Dayton, and horrible Mrs Parkes and the horrible headmaster.'

'Try not to be too harsh with Mr Benton. He's come back from helping to fight the war for England because he was shot in the arm. He had to have it amputated.'

'Oh.' Priscilla looked shocked. 'How will he be able to teach with only one arm?'

'He'll just get used to it,' Lana said. 'It must be awful for him, so he'll need everyone's support.'

'It still doesn't make me like him,' Priscilla said vehemently.

'Let's forget about him for the moment.' Lana gently pulled back and started the engine. 'I was going into the village to have another key cut for the motorcar, but we'll go to the vet's instead, and you can be my first passenger. We'll check and see what's happened to the cat, and then go straight back to Bingham Hall, or Matron will be raising the roof, wondering where you are. So tell me where I have to go.'

'All right.' Priscilla lowered her gaze, then glanced up at Lana. 'It's lovely that you've come to Bingham Hall, Miss Ashwin. I shan't mind it quite so much.'

'I'm glad,' Lana said, smiling at the child.

She couldn't tell Priscilla that Maxine had only given her a couple of months at the most.

Priscilla led her down a side street of large houses, which had mostly been divided into flats, except the vet's. Lana parked the motor where Priscilla suggested. The two of them walked up the drive to a substantial Edwardian house, painted white with decorative timbers. An open porch ran across the front and looked as though it continued around the side of the ground floor. The house was set in a fair-sized garden, and although both the house and garden had an air of neglect, Lana loved it on sight.

Priscilla knocked loudly on the front door and a woman in a white coat ushered them in and led them to a waiting room where a large black dog was barking loudly. His owner, a stout lady, was trying to quieten him down.

'My little friend here brought in an injured cat a few weeks ago and we wondered how he was,' Lana told the nurse.

'He was a big black and white cat.' Priscilla opened her arms to indicate the size, a worried expression crossing her face. 'Do you remember me?'

'Oh, yes, of course.' The nurse hesitated. 'Mr Drummond unfortunately had to remove his back leg. But he's all right,' she added quickly. 'We found his owner who was very relieved and happy to have him back.'

Lana looked at the nurse. 'I don't suppose we could have a quick word with the vet, could we? Priscilla would like to thank him in person.'

'Let me see if he's free. Just one moment.' She was back. 'Come with me.'

Lana and Priscilla followed her down a short passage and knocked on the first door. A voice told them to come in.

'Just a couple of minutes,' the nurse said, 'as Mr Drummond has a busy afternoon in front of him.' She clicked the door behind her.

'Ah, the young lady who saved Blackie's life.' A well-built man of about Lana's height, somewhere in his early forties, with twinkling eyes and unruly brown hair rose from his desk and extended his hand first to Priscilla and then to Lana. 'Do sit down.'

'You took his back leg off,' Priscilla said, almost accusingly. 'How will he walk and run with only three legs?'

'He will,' Mr Drummond smiled. 'It will become second nature very soon. His owner is overjoyed to have him back. She was beside herself when he didn't turn up for his supper that night.' He turned to Lana. 'Your daughter is an exceptional young lady. Most people would have left the cat where it was – probably frightened they'd get bitten.'

'Priscilla's not my daughter,' Lana said, smiling at her, 'but I'd be very proud if she was.' She was gratified to see Priscilla give a half smile back. 'We've come from Bingham Hall.'

'Ah, Dr Barnardo's.'

'That's right. We have mice in the kitchen and wondered if you know of a cat that needs a home – one that doesn't mind a lot of children and noise and is a good mouser.'

'I might have just the one,' Mr Drummond said. 'An elderly lady came in two days ago in tears because she's going to live with her daughter who unfortunately lives on a main road with very little garden. She was terrified that if she took her cat with her he'd get killed on the road. She's left him with me hoping I could find a loving home for him.'

'How old is he?' Lana asked, thinking it was not much use taking in a cat in its last years who probably wouldn't be swift enough to catch any mouse.

'Oh, still young. Only three. A fine cat.' He got to his feet. 'Stay there a moment and I'll bring him in. Name's Rupert.' He grinned. 'The cat, not me. I'm Frank.'

Priscilla giggled. It was such a sweet sound to Lana's ears. And what a nice man Mr Drummond was.

Frank Drummond came back with an enormous ginger and white cat in his arms. He put him on the desk, and the cat blinked at Lana and Priscilla with beautiful golden eyes. Priscilla put her hand out to stroke his head and Rupert began a purr like a sewing machine.

'He's gorgeous,' Lana said.

'He needs a good home,' Mr Drummond said, then added, 'Don't we all?'

Lana detected a flicker of sadness in the vet's eyes, even though he was smiling. She wondered briefly what had led him to make such a remark. He sounded as though he'd been badly hurt by someone. Or was she imagining things?

'Oh, can we take him, Miss Ashwin?' Priscilla said, patting Lana's arm. 'Please.'

It was the first gesture she'd made towards Lana, and her heart turned over. Rupert would be Priscilla's cat, she was certain.

'We need to speak to Matron first, love,' she said.

'Would you like to telephone her from here?' Mr Drummond said. 'The thing is, we can only keep a healthy animal for a week, and then I'm afraid . . .'

Lana shook her head and shot a warning glance in Priscilla's direction. But the girl was completely absorbed with tickling Rupert under his chin.

'Well, you know what I mean,' Mr Drummond said softly, catching Lana's eye.

'I'd better speak to the matron myself,' Lana said, looking at her watch. 'I think she'll agree, but for now she'll be wondering where we are.'

Priscilla opened her mouth to protest but Lana stopped her by gently taking her arm.

'Thank you for seeing us, Mr Drummond, and I hope we'll be back shortly to collect him.'

'I do hope so,' the vet said, shaking Lana's hand. 'He's a lovely boy and apparently gets on well with children.' He turned to Priscilla. 'Oh, I almost forgot, young Miss. That cat you rescued. The lady left me something to give to whoever had rescued her beloved Blackie.' He went to his desk drawer and picked up a brown envelope, then handed it to Priscilla.

Back in the car, Priscilla tore open the envelope. She read out the note. '*For the kind person who found my darling Blackie and took him to the vet. This is a little something to show my appreciation. Grace Martin.*' Priscilla retrieved a slip of paper. 'It's a pound note,' she said, looking at it with wonder in her voice, and turning it over. 'I would have done it for nothing.'

'I know you would, love,' Lana said, smiling, 'but Mrs Martin obviously wanted you to have it. We'll tell Matron so she can keep it safely for you.'

'I want to keep it myself,' Priscilla said tightly.

'It's a lot of money. And you've nowhere you can lock it up. Matron has a safe in her room.'

'No. Please don't tell her about it. It's mine and I shall hide it.'

Lana hesitated. The child was old enough to look after and be responsible for her own things, but it wasn't the same as living in a house with your mother and father. There was no privacy in the dormitories. She drove up to Bingham Hall and switched the engine off. 'All right,' she said, turning to Priscilla. 'It'll be our little secret.'

She was rewarded with a rare smile.

When Lana and Priscilla stepped into the Great Hall there was pandemonium. Children were flying in all directions, the girls screaming, the boys chasing them, and calling out that they were babies; Ethel was standing on a chair again, and Maxine was trying to gain control. Lana knew at once what had happened.

'Two mice this time,' Maxine said as she saw

Lana. 'Bertie's going bananas. I think we'll have to get a cat.' She clapped her hands loudly and roared to the children who immediately stopped in their tracks. 'It's more frightened of you than you are of it,' she said. Lowering her voice she turned to Lana. 'Animals are against the rules at Bingham Hall, but I suppose having a cat who's earning its keep could be seen as part of the workforce.'

Lana grinned. 'And I know just the very one!'

CHAPTER 25

'I'm just going to collect the cat,' Lana told Bertie the next morning. She'd arranged to pick up Rupert at nine o'clock, before the surgery opened.

'Not before time, hen,' Bertie said, raising her flushed face from the oven and taking out a huge pie for the day's dinner. 'I've seen one of the little rascals again this morning. Cheeky as they come – just sitting looking at me, nose twitching.' She set the pie on the vast pine table and studied it critically. A little gravy was seeping out at one of the corners. 'Hmm. Not bad.'

'It smells lovely,' Lana said, sniffing the air. 'Rupert is going to love living here with these sorts of aromas.'

'Och, and we'll be pleased with *him* when he keeps these rodents out of my kitchen,' Bertie said, pulling a face.

'I'm sure he will. What I need is something to put him in. Have we got a big basket?'

'Let me see.' Bertie straightened up. 'I'll have a look in the scullery. I think there's something that will do the job.

She came back with a large flattish basket. 'This should do the trick.'

'If he's well behaved, it will. If he doesn't like the idea of coming back with me there's nothing to stop him jumping out,' Lana said, taking it. 'Well, wish me luck.'

Priscilla had wanted to go with her to collect Rupert, but Maxine had told her to go with Athena to help look after some of the younger children she was taking swimming. They'd already left on an early bus for Liverpool.

'He'll be here when you get back,' Lana had assured her. 'He'll need to be quiet anyway at first so he can settle in.'

She and Priscilla had decided that the best place for him at night was a bed in the scullery, but to leave the door open to the kitchen, as that's where the mice were first seen.

She pulled up outside the surgery and grinned to herself. It was the first time she'd seen Priscilla so excited, and all because Rupert was going to make Bingham Hall his home. Lana had to admit she was just as delighted.

'Mr Drummond's expecting you,' the same nurse said as she opened the door. 'First door down.'

Before she'd raised her hand to knock, Frank Drummond had opened the door, a happy smile on his face.

'Do come in, Miss Ashwin.' He peered round. 'Where's that young lady of yours?'

'Gone swimming, but she can't wait to get back and see him.'

The vet nodded. 'I just want to go through a couple of details with you. Have you ever had a cat?'

'Yes, we've always had cats at home. My mother loves them – Dad, too, even though he pretends otherwise.'

'That's good.' He caught her eye and looked as though he was about to say something but thought better of it. 'Give him any leftovers, twice a day. Be careful to remove fish bones. Plenty of fresh water – not too much milk. I never think it's that good for them. He's a lovely cat who I think will settle in well. Don't let him out for a few days – he'll have to have a dirt box to start with. But you've got all the garden he could ever want, so when he's used to the home let him come and go as he pleases.' He took his glasses off and looked directly at her. 'Any questions.'

'I don't think so. Oh, one. Has he been doctored?'

'Yes. He shouldn't stray far now.' He grinned at her. 'No more chasing after the lady cats. All he'll be chasing is mice.' He got up. 'I'll go and fetch him. Is that his basket?'

'Yes, but I'm a bit worried he'll jump out.'

'I'll carry him to the car. Put the basket on the front seat and I'll drop him in, then shut the door quickly. Once you get there he won't be near any roads so he should be fine.'

He came back holding Rupert who was yawning from being woken up.

'Hold him for a minute so he gets used to the smell of you,' he said, handing the cat to her.

She put him over her shoulder like she used to her old cat, Binkie, and Rupert allowed her to stroke him for about two seconds before he struggled and leapt down.

'He needs to get used to you.' The vet bent and picked him up again. 'Come on, boy. You're going to a lovely new home with Miss Ashwin.' He smiled at her and she liked the way his eyes crinkled at the corners. 'Actually, I could pop over to the orphanage with you. I start a bit later today and go on an extra hour this evening . . . if that would help,' he added.

She hesitated. Maybe she was wrong, but she had the feeling he liked her. She didn't want to encourage him – he was probably married anyway – but she was anxious that Rupert would run off.

'Are you sure you want the bother?'

'We always go and look at the place when someone offers to have one of the strays,' Frank Drummond said seriously. 'Just to make sure they're going to a good home – not that I'm at all concerned about his home at Bingham Hall with his own cook.' He grinned, and she couldn't help smiling back.

Once the vet had settled Rupert into the basket in the back seat, the cat sniffed the cushion and turned round a few times until he was satisfied, then settled down, though his eyes were alert.

'There's a good boy.' Frank Drummond stroked

257

Rupert's head, then turned to Lana. 'He won't like the car – none of them do.' He twinkled at her. 'Count this as an official visit – though I won't bother to make notes,' he said, chuckling.

During the short journey with Rupert plaintively meowing, they chatted about the animals he'd recently attended. Then as they approached Bingham Hall he asked about the orphans.

'I've only been at Bingham Hall a couple of days,' Lana explained, 'so I haven't even met all of them as I'm not teaching as I was at the village school. I'm taking over the driving while Harold's in hospital. He had a mild heart attack recently but was already down for an operation in a fortnight's time. He'll have to rest for several weeks afterwards.'

'I'm sorry to hear about Harold,' Frank Drummond said. 'Nice chap. I hope he makes a complete recovery – just not too soon.'

Lana kept her eyes fixed on the road, but out of the corner of her eye she could see him smile as she turned into the drive. He was flirting with her! She didn't want to encourage him but it *was* rather nice to be noticed. For some reason Carl Best popped into her head, but she shook the thought of him away.

'It's very kind of you, Mr Drummond, to help me with Rupert—'

'Oh, call me Frank, please. This is a village. We don't stand on ceremony in Bingham.'

'Frank, then. And I'm Lana.' She parked outside

the house, and switched off the engine. Frank leapt out and went round her side to open the door.

'Thank you,' she said, but as she moved to climb out, her skirt somehow got caught in the seat mechanism and the material rode up her legs several inches. Impatiently, she unhooked it and smoothed down her skirt, but not before she noticed the appreciative glint in Frank's eyes. She dipped her chin so he couldn't see the telltale warmth stealing across her cheeks.

He lifted Rupert and the basket from the back seat and followed her into the house.

'I've never been inside Bingham Hall,' Frank said as he stood in the Great Hall and looked around. 'What a superb room – based on the baronial style.' He turned to Lana. 'Here, you'd better have him.'

Lana took the basket and stroked Rupert's back. He was taut as a bow, sitting upright, and twisting his head this way and that. Suddenly he pricked his ears. A bell rang and children began streaming from one of the classrooms, some of them with voices raised. Before she realised, the cat wriggled under her hand and jumped free of the basket. With not a second's hesitation he flew up the grand staircase – a ginger blur.

'Oh, a cat,' Bobby whooped with glee. 'C'mon, Alan, let's go and find it.' He made to rush after Rupert.

'You'll do no such thing, young man.' Frank grabbed his arm and pulled him back. 'He's terrified.

Just leave him. He'll get used to it after a week or two, but you must give him time to settle in.'

Bobby shook Frank's hand off. 'I don't have to take orders from you, Mister. I've never even seen you before.'

'But you'll take orders from *me*.' Maxine appeared from her office. 'Your next class will start in exactly three minutes, Bobby, and you will go in now. But first, you will apologise for your rudeness to the gentleman.'

I'm glad she can be firm, Lana thought, hiding a smile.

'Sorry, Sir. Didn't mean it, Sir.'

There was not a scrap of sincerity in his tone, Lana thought with some amusement, but Frank merely raised his hand and said, 'Best get to your class, young man.'

Bobby dashed off.

'Maxine,' Lana said, aware of the matron's curious eyes, 'may I introduce you to Frank Drummond, the local vet. Frank, this is Mrs Taylor, the matron.'

'Please call me Maxine,' Maxine said, extending her hand. 'It's very nice to meet you . . .' Her eyes fell on the empty basket. 'But I thought you were bringing the cat.'

'We are, but he bolted up the stairs,' Lana said. 'He was scared when he heard the children shouting. I couldn't hold him.'

'He'll be hiding in a cupboard somewhere,' Frank said, 'but he'll settle in a few hours.' He turned to Lana. 'Leave him until about five o'clock and rattle his dish, and I can assure you he'll be down like a shot.' He glanced at his watch. 'I suppose I'd better be off for my first appointment.' He turned to Maxine. 'I'm sure Rupert will do an excellent job, but any problems,' his eyes lingered on Lana, 'let me know.' He disappeared.

'Well, Lana, you don't waste any time,' Maxine teased.

'What on earth are you talking about?' Lana assumed an innocent expression.

'You know jolly well what I'm talking about. Calling him Frank, of course.'

'He asked me to,' Lana said, grinning.

'He's nice. *Very* nice. In fact, I'd say he's rather dishy.' She looked at Lana in a pointed fashion.

'Don't start matchmaking,' Lana chuckled. 'I've got enough to do to sort out our new man in the home – Rupert.'

Athena and the children returned from swimming in time for dinner, each child boasting to the others how good a swimmer they were. All but Priscilla. Lana noticed as usual she didn't join in but as soon as the child spotted her she rushed up.

'Miss Ashwin, did you fetch Rupert?'

'Yes, love, I did.'

'Where is he?'

'He's hiding somewhere upstairs.'

'I'm going to find him.' Priscilla put her foot on the bottom step.

'Mr Drummond said to leave him in peace for a few hours,' Lana warned.

'He's probably frightened,' Priscilla said. 'I'm going to talk to him. Tell him he'll be safe here.'

'You won't find him.'

Priscilla ignored her and ran up the stairs two at a time.

'We'll be eating dinner in ten minutes' time,' Lana called after her, but Priscilla was too intent on her mission to reply.

Lana washed her hands in the cloakroom, noticing her face in the mirror. She was sure there were one or two lines she hadn't noticed before. Thirty-one. She glanced at her ring finger, Dickie's engagement ring winking up at her. She was supposed to be married – maybe even have a baby by now. She pulled a face in the mirror, then smiled. Life at Bingham Hall was going to be a challenge – but this time she was sure it would be a worthwhile one, even if it was only temporary.

She dried her hands on the roller towel and stepped through to the Great Hall just in time to see Priscilla coming down the stairs, making little comforting noises to the large ginger cat who was lying on his back in her arms, his paws in the air, looking the picture of contentment. And the little girl's face was full of softness and love.

CHAPTER 26

Four days later Lana collected Mr Clarke from the railway station as Maxine had arranged for him to come and meet Lana and stay for lunch.

The three of them adjourned to the library after lunch and Ethel had brought them in a tray of tea.

'I hope you understand my concern,' Mr Clarke said, his bony hand stirring a teaspoon of sugar in his cup. 'We've never had a lady driver before and there were questions at headquarters as to whether you were fully experienced – capable – that sort of thing.' He gave Lana an apologetic smile. 'But I trust Mrs Taylor implicitly in her recommendations,' he added, turning his attention to Maxine, still smiling, 'and told them so.'

'I won't let either of you down,' Lana said quietly. 'It's a big responsibility and I'm very aware of it, especially where children are involved.'

'Quite.' Mr Clarke brought out his pipe. 'Do either of you ladies mind if I smoke?'

'Not at all,' Maxine said. 'I prefer it to a cigarette.'

'Can't abide by *them*,' Mr Clarke said, lighting

the bowl and giving several little popping noises. He leaned back a little in one of the leather seats and looked around. 'This certainly is a fine library,' he commented. 'I could spend a day wandering around these shelves.'

'You're welcome to do so any time,' Maxine said, laughing.

Lana felt the meeting had gone well when she delivered him back to the station a few hours later, his compliment on her driving still sounding in her ears. She allowed herself a small triumphant smile as she switched off the engine. Closing the garage door, she thought how wonderful it would be if she could take the Rover for a good long run. What motors needed every once in a while, but with the strict petrol rationing that was impossible.

Yes, the meeting had gone well, but no one had brought up the subject of her wages. The list of driving duties Maxine had given her definitely didn't require someone full-time and she wondered how Dr Barnardo's could afford to pay Harold. She shrugged. It was none of her business what arrangement they had with the chauffeur, but she'd go potty if she had to wait around for hours, or even a day or two, to be given the next driving job. She needed to contribute towards the teachers' workload. She would speak to Maxine at the first opportunity.

★   ★   ★

Those first few days the noise level at Bingham Hall after classes were finished had exhausted her and she was beginning to feel lonely in the evenings when she went up to her room. This evening, after supper, she'd find Maxine or one of the teachers to have a cup of tea with in the common room.

The idea flickered across her mind that she might one day be able to give Peter a ride in the car to visit his father. But it would take quite a lot of petrol and she had no idea what the coupon allowance was at Bingham Hall. She must remember to ask Maxine. It would be so much easier than taking the train with those interminable waits on platforms for the changes. Thinking of this brought Carl Best's face to her mind, imagining how he must have felt as he glimpsed his son at Bletchley station. She sighed. There'd been no word at all from him, and Maxine said Peter had begun to wet the bed again. He'd lost his mother and grandmother, and although the miracle had happened and his father had been found, it must feel to Peter that he'd been snatched away from him once more.

Lana entered the common room and immediately relaxed when she saw that Maxine was the only person there. She liked the other teachers, although she had reservations about Judith Wright, but Maxine was her favourite. Even though the matron was probably several years younger than herself, Lana felt she could say anything to her of her fears and worries and Maxine would understand. She was sure there was something unresolved in Maxine's life.

Maxine looked up from her book and her face lit up in a welcoming smile.

'Come on in. There's cocoa in the thermos.'

'I'm all right at the moment, thanks,' Lana said. 'I just wanted to talk to you about something.'

'I'm listening.'

She plunged in. 'Mr Clarke didn't mention my wages, so I'm hoping he's told you what I'll be paid.' If it was less than four pounds a week she'd be disappointed.

'Oh, I'm sorry, Lana, he should have discussed it. Dr Barnardo's have offered three pounds five shillings a week, all found.' She looked across at Lana. 'Would that be acceptable?'

'I realise I'm working shorter hours than teaching,' Lana said, 'but I was hoping for at least four pounds.' She gave Maxine a direct look. 'This may sound very rude, but are they offering the same as they pay Harold?'

Lana held her breath. Had she gone too far? Was it her imagination or was Maxine a little flushed.

'Not exactly,' Maxine admitted. 'I did check when Mr Clarke wrote to confirm your pay and although I'm not permitted to tell you the amount, I will say on the q.t. that he was earning more.'

'It doesn't seem right, does it, for doing the same job?' Lana tried to control the spurt of resentment. It was what she'd expected. 'The Suffragettes won us the vote, but they didn't make much progress for women to be paid the same as men for doing an equal job.'

'I know.' Maxine sighed. 'One day, perhaps, things will change.' She looked thoughtful for a few moments, then appeared to make a decision. 'I'll telephone him tomorrow and ask if it could be raised to four pounds. How would that be?'

'I'd very much appreciate it,' Lana said. 'And I'd like to start coaching Priscilla – not to get paid anything for it,' she added quickly, 'but to keep me busy. I think she'd quickly improve but at the moment some of the children can sometimes be cruel, calling her stupid for not keeping up. I think her main failing is lack of concentration as she's an extremely bright child. Wendy Booth at the school told me she's above average at maths, but her grasp of history and geography has deteriorated since her parents died. She doesn't volunteer to take part in English classes, which I want to change, as her school report said she was very good at literature and starred in school plays.'

'You've obviously taken to the child,' Maxine said, smiling.

'I have. She's a difficult girl and I think her parents spoilt her rotten. But there's a flash of humour sometimes – and she adores Rupert.'

'I'm glad,' Maxine said. 'If Rupert never catches a mouse it will be worth having him.'

The two women chuckled.

'By the way,' Maxine said, 'I've spoken to the

Reverend about the service for Priscilla's parents and we've set the date for Sunday 19th September . . . here in the chapel.'

'Oh, that's marvellous. I do think it will help.' Lana hesitated. Was she asking too many things when she'd only been at the home a week? But she trusted Maxine to understand. 'Then there's Peter. You told me he's started wetting the bed.'

'Poor little chap,' Maxine said, frowning. 'You've not told me much about the meeting with his father.'

'There isn't much to tell,' Lana said, trying to ignore her heart beating faster than it should. 'It's plain to see that Herr Best adores his son but knows it's going to be difficult to see him very often while there's a war on.' She wouldn't mention Carl asked her if she would write to him. 'I would love to know how he is helping the British, but of course I do understand he can't say or even hint what he's doing. And then there's the minder chap who has his eye on him at all times. It's a frightful situation.'

'I feel sorry for him,' Maxine said. Then with a wicked twinkle in her eyes she said, 'Do you think he's good-looking?'

The question took Lana so much by surprise she almost gasped. 'Um, yes, I suppose so. I haven't thought about it.'

'Really? Are you sure about that?'

'Not *absolutely* sure. Any more than I'm *absolutely*

sure that Frank is rather dishy, as you so succinctly put it.'

The two women looked at each other for a second or two, then broke into peals of laughter. What a relief, Lana thought, to have such a nice friend with a sense of humour.

'Letter for you.' Maxine caught Lana as the children were going into the dining room for breakfast the next morning. She looked at the envelope before handing it over. 'Oh, it's postmarked Bletchley.' She gave Lana a knowing wink. 'I wonder who it could possibly be from.' She grinned at Lana as she gave it to her.

'He asked if I'd write to tell him how Peter is getting along, and I told him I would. Nothing more, so no need to make anything of it.'

Lana tucked the envelope in her skirt pocket without even glancing at it, determined not to seem flustered in front of Maxine who was still smiling at her. But he'd written – just as he said he would. Her heart gave a little leap. Of course, it would be about Peter and his concern as his father.

The letter was burning a hole in her pocket. Every movement she made she could hear it rustle. But she'd offered to help with the children's breakfast and then Athena had tottered off to the sick ward with a bilious attack, so Maxine asked if Lana would be kind enough to step in. Only several hours later could she escape to her room and rip open the envelope. She'd know in seconds what kind of a letter he'd written. But why was she placing so much importance on it? It would be all about Peter.

All this buzzed through Lana's mind as she pulled the folded sheet from the envelope and smoothed out the creases. Her eye raked down the page to see how he'd signed off. *Sincere wishes.* She shrugged. Why should he have ended with anything different? She began to read.

15th August 1943

Dear Lana (as we agreed),

I hope the journey back went well. For me, I had work to do immediately, but it was very nice to have two hours with my son, and I want to thank you deeply for bringing him to me. I only wish it could have been longer.

Peter has changed very much from the little boy I remember. Yes, he is older, and it shows, but it is mainly because of his mother and grandmother leaving him to face the world alone, and knowing Papa is too far away. It must be a shock for him to arrive in an orphanage when he knows he still has a father but had to keep him a secret. Too much for a young boy, you would think, but he is strong inside and I know I can rely on you to be a friend to him. I can see he trusts you.

And now I turn to you, Lana. It was difficult for me to say much when we met. My new life is so different here. I know you understand. For now, I can only thank you for looking after my boy, and I hope you may bring him to me again very soon. Please see that he writes to his papa to tell me about the things he is learning, and tell him I will write back. I would like him to keep up with his German before he forgets it, as one day, God willing, we will have a peaceful country once more. But maybe that is something to hope for the future.

I look forward to your letter more than I can say. My address is at the top of the page.

Sincere wishes,

Carl Best

Lana read the letter three times in quick succession, her stomach fluttering as she tried to work out what Carl seemed so hesitant to put into words. She had the strangest feeling he wanted to say more than the words she could see on the page. And that he knew she would see these invisible words and understand. Or was she simply putting more into the letter than Carl ever intended? If that was the case, then she was being ridiculous. Thoroughly annoyed with herself, she still couldn't resist another reading.

His love for his son shone through the letter and she wished she could somehow help Peter more. She needed to think of something that would make him feel important. Give him confidence. A sudden thought struck her. Carl seemed to be worried that Peter would forget his German, and on Priscilla's report it mentioned she knew a little German.

But Peter might be a problem. Maxine said he'd been told never to speak German here in Britain, but surely that wasn't fair to the child. He'd forget it if he never spoke it. He shouldn't be made to feel ashamed of being half German. And maybe he would come out of his shell if she suggested to him that he could teach Priscilla. By doing so he would gain that much-needed confidence, which should have a beneficial effect on Priscilla as well. Lana's face broke into a smile.

She couldn't wait to discuss her plan with Maxine.

But before she went downstairs to see whether Maxine had any driving jobs for her, she read Carl's letter one more time. No, there was nothing in the letter that was anything personal whatsoever.

'Could you collect these from the chemist's?' Maxine asked her, handing Lana a short list of items. Lana ran her eyes down it. Camomile lotion, TCP, 2 x Mum deodorant and 3 x Kotex. 'You have to buy your own sanitary towels but if you ever get stuck I keep a couple of packets of Kotex in all the time. They always remind me of when I was at St Thomas's Hospital in London as a second-year nurse and used to have to teach the probationers how to stitch the damned things.'

She grinned at Lana. 'That kind of job could send you cuckoo.'

'I didn't know you were a nurse in London.'

'Oh, yes. I was right in the thick of things. That poor building got struck so many times.' She briefly closed her eyes. 'My dear friend, Anna, died in one of the explosions.'

'How dreadful.'

'It was. I still miss her.'

'Did you leave to get away from all the bombing?' Lana asked.

A shadow passed across Maxine's face, and she saw tears gather in the matron's eyes.

This had happened before, Lana remembered. She seemed to be touching on a raw nerve.

'No-no, it wasn't that. I—'

'I'm sorry. I didn't mean to pry,' Lana said gently.

'It's all right. I fell in love with one of the surgeons when I was there.' Maxine's voice was shaky.

'Then you're well out of it.'

'Yes. That's it. He was the wrong person but—' Maxine broke off again. 'It isn't quite that simple. One day, when we have time, maybe I'll tell you the story, and how this place began to help me to come to terms with what happened. It was the children really. They need us, Lana, but they don't realise how much *we* need *them*.'

It was true, Lana thought. Even being here such a short time, she was settling in, feeling part of the team, being useful. But she mustn't rely on it too much. Her weeks were numbered.

'I'm beginning to get to know them,' Lana said, smiling. 'And you're right. They help enormously.' She paused. 'I've had an idea about Priscilla and Peter.'

She swiftly told Maxine about the idea of Peter speaking to Priscilla in German.

'It seems an opportunity for the two of them to help one another gain confidence,' Lana finished.

'I think it's a very good idea,' Maxine said. 'I know Judith Wright has a degree in languages, and one of them is German, but she flatly refuses to teach it.'

'Do you think we should ask her first?' Lana said, anxiously. 'I don't want to cross wires with her.'

'No, it won't be necessary. I'll leave it to you to fix it up with the kids.'

CHAPTER 27

Rupert the cat took a whole three days before he gained full control of Bingham Hall. He was an instant success with almost every child who wanted to play with him. He allowed the girls a minute or two of playing games, but was much more wary of the boys with their loud voices and rougher actions. No one was allowed to pick him up except Lana and Priscilla. But it was Priscilla he followed, purring his engine purr, and nuzzling her face. To top it all, he regularly sneaked onto her bed when no one was looking.

'She's a different girl,' Maxine commented when she and Lana were having a cup of cocoa one evening in the common room.

'It's all down to Rupert,' Lana said. 'He's reached her where no one else could. And the other children give her more attention because they want to be popular with Rupert as well. But he's found his heroine and he's going to stay close to her.'

'It's wonderful to see them together,' Maxine said. 'A match made in heaven, I would say.' She looked across at Lana. 'By the way, have you replied to your Herr Best?'

Lana flushed. 'Not yet. I will do. And a slight correction – he's not *my* Herr Best. And even if I liked him like that – which I don't – he's not exactly the ideal man to develop any relationship with.'

'Because he's German?'

'Yes, if I'm honest.'

'But you know he loves this country. He was married to an Englishwoman. She wouldn't have had him if he hadn't been a *good* German.'

'It's that Nazi uniform you said he wore in the photograph. That's hard to forget.'

'Yes, it was a shock until we uncovered the truth that all the time he wanted to work for us. It's very difficult for him to explain when he's under oath not to tell anyone anything outside British Intelligence. I feel sorry for him.'

A picture of Carl flashed in front of Lana. His intense blue eyes, not steely, not unnerving, but with a sadness there for the loss of his wife. He probably felt a deep sense of loss for how his own country and its people had changed. She wondered if he had seen the sadness in her own eyes.

She forced herself to wait a full week before she replied to Carl's letter. It had been a difficult one to write. She'd made two attempts, then berated herself for wasting paper when it was in such short supply.

Just write it, she told herself, and don't think too much while you're at it.

She read her reply again, to make certain it struck the right note. Not too formal; friendly, but not overly so. She took a few deep breaths to steady her nerves, trying to put herself in Carl's head, as though he were reading it.

Dear Carl,

Thank you for your letter, which I was pleased to receive. I hope work is going well for you.

First I want to reassure you that Peter is well and is doing much better in his lessons. I'm sure this is because he knows you are not so far away now. I've told him we will come again as soon as possible to see you, and he seemed content with this. So please try not to worry about him.

I have spoken to the matron about Peter's German and come up with an idea. I found out that Priscilla already knows a little German and thought it would help both of them if Peter was to talk with her for half an hour a few times a week in German. That way, Peter keeps up with his language and Priscilla continues to learn it. They will be helping each other to succeed. If you don't have any objection then I will arrange it, so long as both of them like the idea.

You know I will always be a friend to your son. He is a lovely little chap.

I went for a walk along the drive this morning. It was as hot as the day in Bletchley. The lime trees were such a bright green, overlapping on either side and forming an arc. It was very beautiful. I hope there are trees where you live. Nothing seems so bad when you realise some of them are hundreds of years old – that nature will continue, no matter what.

I hope he doesn't think I'm completely soppy, Lana thought, frowning. Then her brow softened and she smiled. So what if he did.

Well, I have to go to Liverpool for some items, so will post this off today.

Sincerely,

Lana Ashwin

It would have to do. She found an envelope and peered at the address again on the letter Carl had sent: 2 Blackthorne Cottages, Station Road, Bletchley, Bucks. She carefully copied it, then tucked the letter in and licked the seal.

After picking up her bag and the letter she went downstairs to ask Bertie if she needed anything bringing back.

When Lana returned from Liverpool Athena stopped her as she was on her way to the dining room.

'A chap came when you were out this morning,' Athena said.

Lana's heart jumped. Surely he would not be allowed here so soon.

'Peter's father?' she enquired.

Athena looked at her with a raised eyebrow. 'No, this one was very English. About your height, untidy dark hair and twinkling eyes.'

Frank Drummond.

'The vet,' Athena finished triumphantly. 'He asked especially for you.'

'Oh.'

'He wanted to know how Rupert was getting along. I told him he runs the place now, but Priscilla is his special one. He seemed pleased about that, but deeply disappointed you weren't around.' She gave Lana a knowing look.

What was it with these women who seemed determined to match her up with some man? Lana was about to speak when Athena burst out laughing.

'He was rather nice,' she said. 'Quite fancy him myself.'

'I don't have any claim on him,' Lana said, 'so he's all yours.'

Athena smiled. 'I'll remember that, next time he comes calling.' She smoothed her already smooth hairdo. 'I've never particularly got on with cats – more of a dog person really – but I believe I ought to get to know Rupert better!' She was still chuckling as she made for her classroom.

Lana watched the disappearing figure, Athena's words ringing in her ears. She wasn't a bit perturbed about Athena's announcement that she was prepared to make a deliberate friendship with Rupert. She had no romantic notions about Frank. He was just a lovely man, that was all.

'Look what's all over the front page of the *Daily Express*!' Maxine's voice was excited as she shoved the newspaper into Lana's hands one September morning before breakfast and stood over her shoulder as Lana read it out.

ITALY SURRENDERS TO THE ALLIES
'It's all over now'

'I can't believe it.' Lana looked up at Maxine, feeling dazed by such headlines.

'Mind you,' Maxine went on, 'it sounds as though they were forced into it, but nevertheless, they're now fighting on our side. Bit of a blow to the Germans, I should think.'

Immediately, Carl's image swam into Lana's vision. He must be feeling relieved that this could prove to be a big step towards an end of the madness. One day when the war was finally over he'd want to take Peter back and be amongst his own people. For some reason the idea depressed her. By then, if the bombing continued at this rate, many German cities would be unrecognisable. But she couldn't stop thinking about it, trying to grapple with her imagination. Peter hadn't lived in Berlin for a long time. His dream may not match the reality after the war. His friends would likely be the sons of Nazis from Carl's circle whom Carl would presumably have to ban Peter from seeing. Their lives could be in danger, even though the war had ended, if one of the Nazis learned Carl had been a spy for the British.

Lana shuddered at the thought. At least for now, Carl and Peter were safe in England.

She'd never really put these notions into words, and it quite shocked her. It seemed an age since she'd talked to him in Bletchley, but it had been so awkward and rushed at the end. And even if she could talk to him this minute she knew she wouldn't be able to discuss such concerns about Peter. It would be far too painful for Carl. Once again she wondered what work he was doing. He'd responded evasively to her suggestion that he was translating. 'Something like that,' he'd said.

As though she'd conjured him up, there was a letter from him propped up on the table they used for the post in the Great Hall. Her heart made a strange little thud as she picked it up, wondering how he had answered her letter. She immediately took it upstairs to her room and ripped it open.

Dear Lana,

You cannot know how happy I was to receive your letter and to hear that my dear son is safe and well. I imagine you talking to him, smiling with him, and not letting him forget his papa. I cannot thank you enough for all you are doing.

I felt I too was walking with you along the drive, looking up at the canopy of trees, breathing the air. I could almost forget the war and dream of being free. That is what I miss most of all – except for Peter, naturally.

Everyone is working hard and sometimes someone gives me a kind word, but I know it is hard for them.

When is it possible you may come to Bletchley again with Peter, and of course, Priscilla? We might go on a long walk in the country instead of being in a town, which I do not like so much. What do you think?

I don't have any objection to Peter and Priscilla speaking German. I think it a wonderful idea and want to thank you for being so thoughtful.

Yesterday I had a nice (although short) letter from Peter. I know he misses me. I will write to him very soon. Sometimes it is difficult to know what to say to him. It is difficult to put into words what I want to say these days.

Please write back soon.

I send you kind wishes and thoughts,

Carl

This was a different tone from the first letter he wrote, Lana thought. It was as though he'd dared to put a little of his feelings in writing, even though he said it was difficult for him. She felt a spurt of pleasure that he'd enjoyed reading about her walk along the drive, admiring the trees. And that he'd rather be in the country than wandering round shops that had little to offer, reminding both of them that this was one of the effects of war. What on earth would he think if he saw Liverpool and the devastation? But then, he would have seen Berlin. She knew that city had taken a beating early on in the war by Allied bombing. She sighed. All he was suggesting was going for a walk in the country next time. And yet because he was German it raised all kinds of complications.

CHAPTER 28

The service for Priscilla's parents was to take place the following Sunday. On the Thursday before, Priscilla had become very morose, sinking her nose into Rupert's thick fur, and talking softly to him when she came back from the village school. She hardly spoke to Lana. Wendy Booth had mentioned she was almost totally silent in class and Lana was sure it was because of the impending service. She'd have to have a word with her at the first opportunity.

It came on Friday after supper when Priscilla was about to slip upstairs to find comfort with Rupert who would normally be on her bed.

'Priscilla, I need to talk to you for a few minutes in the library.'

Priscilla turned to her with solemn grey eyes. 'I'm just going to say hello to Rupert.'

'No, leave him for a while. He'll still be there when you come back. This is important.'

Priscilla followed Lana to the library, her mouth drooping. Lana pulled up a chair for her and sat on one close by. She took one of Priscilla's hands, and for once the child didn't snatch it away.

'Priscilla, love, what's wrong?'

'Nothing.'

'There is. Everyone says you're not speaking to anyone. I thought you were much happier now you've got Rupert.'

'I am,' Priscilla said, her eyes anxious. 'You're not going to take him away from me, are you?'

'No, of course not. He's like your shadow. He'd be terribly upset. Besides, he's enjoying his rôle of chief mouse catcher.'

There was a small smile in response.

'Please tell me, love. Is it Sunday that's worrying you?'

Priscilla shook her head, then burst into tears. 'I don't want to say goodbye to them,' she sobbed.

'You don't have to say goodbye. This is to give us all a chance to remember them.'

'No one here knew them. Why should they want to remember people they've never met?' Patricia took the handkerchief Lana pressed into her hand and dabbed her eyes. 'I don't want to go into the church.'

'It's just the chapel, Priscilla, with those beautiful stained-glass windows. I think the Reverend would be disappointed if you don't come. You've already told him the hymns your mum and dad liked.'

Priscilla was silent, tears still rolling down her cheeks. She put her middle finger in her mouth and began to bite the nail.

'You can sit by me,' Lana said, gently removing Priscilla's finger. 'But if you're really unhappy about it, then I'll telephone the Reverend tomorrow. How about that?'

Priscilla turned her head to meet Lana's eyes. 'Will you promise you'll sit next to me?' she said.

'I promise, love.' She put her arms around the trembling child.

The children had just sung the last line of 'All things bright and beautiful' and had sat down when Priscilla suddenly shot to her feet and pushed past Lana, then Maxine who was at the end of the pew.

'I'm not an orphan!' she shouted, her eyes wild as she twisted her neck this way and that to make sure everyone heard her. 'And my parents will come and fetch me as soon as they can.' With that, she dashed along the nave towards the entrance.

All the children craned their necks to see Priscilla disappear out of the door. They all started talking at once and Maxine got up to hush them. Lana made to go after her, but Maxine put a restraining hand on her arm.

'Let her be,' she whispered. 'The child is terribly upset. She'll have gone to find Rupert. He's the only one who can give her some comfort.'

Lana sat down again, defeated. She'd hoped that having a service would finally be the point where Priscilla could put an end to the delusion that her parents were still alive. She bit her lip. It had turned out to be a bad idea. What else could she do? Priscilla was too young to realise this was going to ruin her life if she couldn't come to terms with their death.

The Reverend's voice broke into her worried thoughts.

'I know we're all very sorry that Priscilla is so upset,' he said to the congregation. 'Children, you must all be kind to her. So say your prayers tonight. Say a special prayer for Priscilla, for her to be strong.' He looked at the gathering of mostly children. 'Do you think you can do that?'

'Yes, Sir,' several children called out.

'Course she's an orphan – like the rest of us,' Thomas chimed in. 'Why don't she admit it? Seems daft to me.'

'Everyone has to cope in their own way,' the Reverend pointed out. 'Priscilla needs patience and understanding – and friendship.'

'She don't want to be friends,' Thomas answered back.

'That's enough,' Maxine said. She gave a nod to the Reverend.

'Then I think it's time we can all leave quietly.' He gestured to Athena who was at the piano.

Athena began to play Elgar's 'Funeral March', not very well. Maxine headed for the back of the chapel and Lana stood where she was, making sure the front rows filed out in an orderly fashion, though she couldn't stop them talking.

In the dining room Bertie had laid out some biscuits she'd made that morning to go with their milk. When Lana briefly told her what had happened, she shook her head in dismay.

'Poor lass,' Bertie said. 'Only time will heal.'

CHAPTER 29

One early morning, a few days later, when Lana came downstairs to make a cup of tea to try to pull herself round from a sleepless night, she heard Rupert outside the back door asking to come in.

Sounds like he's got another mouse and wants to show it to someone, she thought a little irritably, longing for that first cup of tea as she put the kettle on. She opened the back door.

No sign of Rupert. What was he playing at? She stepped out and shivered a little in the early autumn air, the chill passing straight through her dressing gown. She cocked her head. Yes, there he was again. Rupert had a habit of catching a mouse, and with it still in his mouth making an awful choking mewing noise.

'Rupert, come on out,' she called. He sometimes obeyed her when he heard her call, but not this morning. 'You'll come when you want your breakfast,' she muttered, turning to go back to the warmth of the kitchen. She stopped. She hadn't noticed it when she'd stepped out, but now she spotted a delivery box which the grocer's boy must have left very early this morning. If it wasn't too heavy she'd take it in for Bertie to deal with.

But it wasn't full of groceries. She saw what looked like an old army blanket and then something moved. What was Rupert playing at? She smiled, wondering why cats loved cardboard boxes so much. Gingerly, she pulled the blanket back in case she surprised him and he panicked and clawed her.

It wasn't Rupert.

Two tiny identical babies with wisps of dark hair looked back at her with wet unfocused eyes.

Lana sat back on her haunches, heart beating madly, dizzy with shock. Two babies! Where had they come from? Who had left them? How could anyone leave them outside in this damp? Thank God the weather was still mild. Had it been winter they surely would have perished. They looked so small, so fragile. She picked the box up, placing one arm underneath to stop it from giving way, and went into the kitchen. By this time both babies were whimpering, their sound so similar to Rupert's when he was hungry.

She set the box on Bertie's huge pine table, but before she had time to think what to do next, Beth came into the room.

'Morning, Miss. Is there a cuppa still in the pot? I need to take one to Cook.'

The whimpering started again, much weaker now.

'Goodness, Miss. What's in that box?' Beth went

over and peered in. 'Oh, my goodness gracious.' She looked up at Lana, her eyes wide with disbelief. 'Where've they come from? What are we going to do with them?'

'They'll have to go to the Maternity Hospital in Liverpool,' Lana said. She stuck her finger out and one of them clutched hold of it with an icy hand.

Lana picked the little mite up. 'Oh, it's soaking wet. And smelly. Poor little soul.' She planted a kiss on top if its dark head. 'You'll be all right, love, now we've found you and your sister . . . or brother. Yes, I know you're hungry and you've got a full nappy and I expect your twin's the same.' She glanced at the maid. 'As far as I know, Bingham Hall's never taken in babies, so they won't have any kind of baby formula. They need a mother's milk, Beth, and right away. I don't suppose you know of anyone in the village who's just had a baby, do you?'

Beth's face lit up. 'I do, Miss. The woman opposite me mam. She's had a little girl but told Mam the other day she's got enough milk to feed another.'

'Let's hope she's got enough to feed *two* more,' Lana said wryly, 'although the weight of these mites is probably no more than one normal-sized baby.'

'Shall I go and fetch her, Miss?'

'We'll both go. I'll drive you.' Lana looked at her watch. It was only half past six. She hoped the new mother would be up by now and able to come over quickly. 'Can you keep an eye on the babies while I get dressed, Beth? I'll only be ten minutes.'

'All right, Miss.'

Lana was about to put the baby back into the cardboard box when she noticed a slip of paper poking out of the folded blanket. She took it out, then laid the baby on its side to curl against its sibling. She glanced at the slip of paper.

Patricia and Jean are twins. I cant look after them.

At that moment Maxine wandered into the kitchen, smothering a yawn.

'Was that Rupert yowling?' The young matron suddenly froze, her eyes fixed on the box where the two babies had begun to cry again. 'What on earth—?'

'Twins left outside the back door,' Lana explained. 'Whoever left them must have reckoned on someone being up really early. Poor little mites. Whatever must the state of the mother's mind be to leave her babies, not knowing who would find them and take care of them? She must have been desperate—' Lana broke off, watching in alarm as the blood drained from Maxine's face as she sat down.

She shot over and rested her hand on the back of Maxine's neck, gently pressing her head between her knees.

'Just stay there a few moments,' Lana said, keeping her hand on Maxine, 'then come up slowly.'

Maxine did as she was told, and when she was

sitting up Lana wiped the perspiration from her forehead. Beth handed her a glass of water, just as Bertie came into the kitchen.

'My goodness – is this a party? What's going on?' She caught sight of the box and hurried over. 'Och, if it's not two bairns.' She looked at Maxine. 'What's the matter, hen? You look like death.'

'I'm all right,' Maxine said weakly, her eyes moist. 'It was the shock of seeing those two little mites – the way they'd been abandoned. We need to telephone the midwife.' She tried to struggle to her feet, then put a hand to her head.

'I'll telephone the midwife, don't you worry. I have her number in my address book,' Bertie said, firmly setting Maxine back in the chair. 'Beth, make another large pot of tea. Matron looks like she could do with one, and so could all of us. And those bairns will need feeding.'

'Beth knows a woman in the village who's just had a baby who might be prepared to give them some of her milk,' Lana said. 'I was about to go and get dressed and fetch her over here.'

'I'll watch them while you go,' Maxine said.

'You'll do nothing of the kind,' Bertie said. 'Beth, before you go, take Matron to the common room and I'll bring a tray of tea and biscuits in two shakes of a lamb's tail. She'll soon be as right as rain.'

'Bertie, can I leave you to keep watch on the babies until Beth and I come back?' Lana said. 'I'm hoping this woman might have some spare nappies we can buy from her as well.'

'You go off and fetch her, hen,' Bertie said. 'I'll get on to Mrs Daniels. She's a bit of a dragon but she knows her job. Until she gets here I'll keep an eye on them, don't you worry. But don't forget I've got some cooking to do today as well.' She gave Lana a wink.

Lana smiled. Nothing put Bertie off of her stride for long.

Beth pointed out the terraced house; it was the one with the grimy net curtains and a dustbin in the centre of the little front garden as though it were a prized ornament. Lana drew up outside.

'I expect she's up by now with *her* new baby,' Beth said, 'but it might be best if she sees me first, seeing as she knows me mam.'

'Good idea.' Lana watched as Beth ran up the path and knocked on the door.

It immediately opened and a tired-looking woman, too old from where Lana sat to be a new mother, stood there, her baby screaming in her arms.

'It's Beth, isn't it?' she said. 'Edna Butcher's daughter?'

'That's right.'

'Aren't you working at the orphanage?'

'Yes,' Beth said. 'I've just come from there with our driver.' She jerked her head towards where Lana was sitting in the car. 'Mrs Lewis, we found two babies left out on the doorstep an hour ago. They're crying like billy-o and are soaking wet and smelly . . . and they're hungry. Matron wondered if you might be able to give them some milk.'

'From these?' Mrs Lewis put her hands under her generous breasts and jiggled them.

'Yes,' Beth grinned.

'Well, I'm always bragging I've got enough for two, but whether they'll stretch to three, God knows.' She narrowed her eyes at Beth. 'Well, I've been wanting to see inside the orphanage, so p'raps this is my chance.' The baby let out a loud squawk and Mrs Lewis hushed it. 'I'd better get my coat and put something on this new'un.' She disappeared inside.

'Well, if this isn't something grand to ride in,' Mrs Lewis said as Lana opened the front door of the Rover for her. 'And fancy – a *lady* driver.' She bent low so the baby didn't hit its head, as Beth climbed in the back.

Lana was worried as she drove back to Bingham Hall. Mrs Lewis didn't smell too good, and neither did the baby. But at least she'd brought a basket with a couple of dingy-looking nappies. She mustn't judge her. Nothing seemed normal these days and if Mrs Lewis had an abundance of milk, it would be the answer to their prayers.

Five minutes later Lana, Beth and Mrs Lewis, carrying her baby, had gathered in the kitchen. Bertie was cutting up carrots and turnips for soup. She turned round when they came in.

'The bairns fell asleep soon after you'd gone.'

'Thank you for keeping an eye on them,' Lana said, going over to the kitchen table.

Mrs Lewis followed her and peered in the cardboard box. 'What little beauties. But they need changing.' She put the nappies that had obviously been cut from an old towel onto the pine table and delved into the basket. 'There they are,' she said triumphantly as she laid two large safety pins on top of the nappies. 'That's all I could find spare, so you'll have to do the triangle method.'

'Shall I do it, Miss?' Beth said. 'I'm used to babies with Mam having one every year after I was born.'

'Be better if they're cleaned up before I put them on my titties,' Mrs Lewis said in a practical manner.

Lana nodded to Beth who picked one of the babies up. The baby immediately started to cry, very weakly.

'Not in *my* kitchen, you don't,' Bertie said firmly. 'You go out into the scullery for that job.'

In fifteen minutes Beth had got both babies' bottoms washed and dried, and their nappies fixed in place.

'I can't put them back in that,' the maid said, pointing to the box. 'It's damp with wee and the box isn't that strong-looking. I'll go up to the nursery and see if we have anything more suitable.'

Beth came back to the kitchen carrying a cot. 'I think they'll be quite snug in here.'

'Did you telephone the midwife?' Lana asked Bertie.

'I did.' The cook glanced at Beth. 'Take Mrs Lewis into the common room, Beth, so she can have some privacy. No one will be there now. Matron's back in her office and the kiddies are only just surfacing.'

'Can I leave the little'un in here?' Mrs Lewis said. 'He might get jealous seeing another baby on his mam's tittie.' She laughed and Lana cringed inside.

'Of course, my dear,' Bertie said, looking amused at Lana's expression. 'He'll be perfectly safe.'

'Let's go and do the deed then,' Mrs Lewis said as Beth carefully picked up the cot with the babies.

'I don't know what came over me.' Maxine gave a pensive smile from behind her desk when Lana stepped into her office.

She was still looking pale, Lana thought. What could have upset her so much? It was a shock for all of them to see the babies in a cardboard box, but Maxine was a nurse and surely would have seen far worse.

'Is there anything you want to talk about?' Lana said. She saw Maxine stiffen. 'I'm not meaning to be nosy,' Lana hurried on, 'but I *am* older than you so I might be able to help in some way.'

'The voice of experience.' Maxine tried to smile but to Lana's alarm, the young matron broke down into heart-rending sobs.

'Maxine, love, what is it?'

For a full minute there was no answer. Finally, Maxine stopped crying and looked up at Lana, her eyes red and her nose blotchy.

'Do you remember . . .?' she started, then blew her nose. 'I'm sorry. You must think I'm the most ridiculous person to be a matron. I'm not normally like this.'

Lana put a hand on her shoulder. 'I don't think anything of the kind. I only want to help.'

'You see, I had to give away my baby . . . little Teddy.' She began to cry again, this time almost without making a sound.

'Oh, Maxine.' Lana remembered Maxine telling her she'd fallen in love with one of the surgeons at St Thomas's. Was he the father of the baby? She wouldn't ask. Maxine would tell her in her own time – if ever.

'What happened to Teddy?' Lana asked softly. 'Did you have him adopted?

'Yes.' Maxine's voice shook. 'But I don't know who. They said it was a very nice couple who'd been thoroughly vetted. But how do I know if it's true?'

'You must believe them,' Lana said unhesitatingly. 'By law they have to be extremely careful who they give a child or a baby to.'

'I only hope you're right. I have nightmares thinking about it.'

Maxine sounded weary, Lana thought. As though she'd gone over and over the same questions, and hadn't found any new answers, let alone been able to draw any comfort.

'It was the surgeon I told you about.' Maxine's tone was flat.

'I thought it probably was,' Lana said. 'Well, your secret is perfectly safe with me.'

'Thank you, Lana,' Maxine said. She gave a deep sigh. 'It's comforting to have a friend.'

'That goes for me too,' Lana said, smiling. 'Are you feeling a little better?'

'Yes, much.' Maxine's eyes grew anxious. 'Did you telephone the midwife? It'll be Mrs Daniels, though I've never met her.'

'Bertie telephoned while I went to fetch Mrs Lewis in the village. She's just had a baby and has already given them some milk. So you're not to worry about anything.'

'Poor little dears,' Maxine said, with tears in her eyes. 'I do hope they survive. They're very small – prem, by the size of them. They'll need a lot of care – and luck.'

'Any idea who might have left them?' Mrs Daniels, the midwife practically barked, after she'd inspected the twins.

'None whatsoever,' Lana said. 'Only clue is this note.' She handed it to the woman.

They had gathered in the common room, which Maxine had suggested was the safest place where they'd have the fewest interruptions. The teachers would all be in the classrooms at this time of the day. The babies were tucked away from any draught, and now they'd taken some of Mrs Lewis's milk they were both fast asleep.

Mrs Daniels glanced at the note and frowned. She raised her head. 'That's it. No apology. No name. And no apostrophe in "can't", so I doubt the girl comes from a good family. If she's from the village I'd know about it. But if she lives in town, she'd have gone to one of the hospitals, I would've thought.' She looked at the note again. 'I'll make some enquiries.' She threw a glance at Maxine. 'Do you mind if I keep this, Mrs Taylor?' She gestured at the note. 'At least it's a clue of sorts, which the police might be interested in.' She stood up. 'Well, thanks for the tea. I'd better get the twins to hospital.' She made a tutting noise as she jerked her eyes towards the ceiling. 'Lucky I've got the car today.'

'I would have driven you,' Lana murmured.

The midwife dropped the last of her equipment into her bag before looking up. 'Oh, yes, of course. I forgot. You're standing in for Harold. Frank happened to mention it the other evening – he's our vet, you know. Frank Drummond.' She gave Lana a studied look with sharp brown eyes. 'I don't expect you've met him yet.'

'I have, as a matter of fact,' Lana said, not knowing whether to be amused or irritated that word had got around the village already that she was the temporary driver. She wondered idly if Mrs Daniels had designs on him, calling him

Frank and mentioning she saw him the other evening. She wasn't an unattractive woman, with her shiny dark hair in a smooth coil at her neck, her slim figure clad in a navy blue uniform with crisp white collar and cuffs. But it was her strident voice – the tone bossy and arrogant. She'd be about Frank's age, Lana guessed. She shrugged. It was none of her business who Frank liked or who liked him, or what they talked about of an evening.

'Well, thank you for everything,' Maxine said.

'Only doing my job.' The midwife smiled somewhat smugly, Lana thought. 'And do call me Celia.'

'I didn't really take to her,' Lana said, when Celia Daniels' car vanished down the drive, the babies safely in the cot on the back seat.

'Nor me,' Maxine said. 'I thought she had an extreme sense of her own importance.'

'And I thought it was just me,' Lana chuckled.

'And what was all that about Frank Drummond?' Maxine said. 'She spoke as though she wanted to let us know they were very friendly.'

'She certainly sounded quite possessive,' Lana said. 'I'm not sure why she had to bring him into the conversation. Anyway, isn't she married?'

'Divorced,' Maxine said, a glint in her eye.

CHAPTER 30

'Priscilla, I'd like to discuss something with you,' Lana said one day after dinner. It was a few days after the twin babies had been left at Bingham Hall, but with all the drama they caused, her idea to try to help Priscilla had gone clear out of her mind. Lana looked at Priscilla, upset to see the dark circles under her eyes had deepened – a sure sign of not sleeping properly.

Priscilla gave her an old-fashioned look for one so young. 'What about?'

'Shall we go to the library? We shouldn't be disturbed there.'

Lana took Priscilla into the small room off the main library and gestured for her to sit at the table.

'I read your file when I was the headmistress of the school,' Lana said, 'and noticed your aunt taught you some German. Is that right?'

Priscilla nodded.

'How well can you speak it?'

'Not much,' Priscilla said in a sulky tone. 'My uncle was from Germany. He wouldn't speak in

302

German except sometimes to Auntie Elspeth. But now we're at war with the Germans I'm glad I don't have to do it any more.' She pulled one of her pigtails.

'The war has to come to an end one day,' Lana said. 'And I think German would be a very useful language to know.' She wasn't quite sure why she was actually saying this, but she badly wanted to encourage Priscilla.

'I didn't like it that much. All that grammar. *Der, die, das.* It's too difficult.'

'What if you had someone German to help you, and you could have a proper conversation?'

'What, Peter's father?' Priscilla's grey eyes widened.

'No, Peter himself.'

Priscilla looked even more surprised. 'He wouldn't want to teach me. He doesn't even like me.'

'Not teach. Just talk. And I think when you got to know each other you'd get on together. His father is worried that he'll forget all his German. You started to learn, and if you don't do some regularly, you'll forget what *you've* learned as well.' She gave Priscilla a smile. 'What do you think?'

'If you say so.'

'Try not to sound *quite* so excited, love,' Lana said with a straight face.

Priscilla actually broke into a smile. 'I'll try not to.'

It wasn't the first time she'd noticed Priscilla

had a sense of humour. Lana was determined to see Priscilla's smile – hear her laugh – much more often. But for now she had to tackle Peter.

Peter was less compliant. At first he shook his head.

'I don't want to speak German. Matron kept saying when I first came here that I must never speak German.'

'There was a reason,' Lana said. 'She didn't want the other children to be nasty to you when we're at war with Germany.'

'Priscilla doesn't like me.'

'Of course she does. You just don't know her. And she's not been so lucky as you. You've found your papa. She's lost both her parents.' Peter bowed his head. 'She needs a friend,' Lana went on, 'and I think you could help. You'll be doing her a kindness and you'll practise your German. Your father is anxious you don't forget it.'

As soon as Lana uttered the words Peter's face changed.

'Papa said that?'

'Yes, he did. One day you'll go with him back to Germany and it would be a great shame if you'd forgotten how to speak it.'

'All right, then. I'll do it with Priscilla.'

'It's a two-way thing, Peter. You must tell her when she pronounces something wrong, or says the wrong word, or can't find the right word, and it will remind you of words you thought you'd forgotten. Do you think you can do that?'

'I suppose so.'

'You sound nearly as enthusiastic as Priscilla,' Lana smiled. 'Why don't you both have the sessions in the library after supper. Twenty minutes to start with. Then build up to half an hour once or twice a week. I think you'll be amazed at the progress you'll make. But this is yours and Priscilla's secret. The other children don't need to know.'

'Yes, she's actually standing right here,' Maxine said, smiling and handing the receiver to Lana. Both women were in Maxine's office that afternoon.

'Who is it?' Lana mouthed the words.

'Our lovely local vet.' Maxine winked as she left her office, quietly shutting the door behind her.

A warm feeling stole over Lana as she spoke into the receiver. 'Frank?'

'Hello, Lana.'

She liked the tone of his voice. It was always so cheerful. She wondered whether it was a cover-up, or how he genuinely felt.

'I just wondered how Rupert was.'

She could picture his grin at the end of the telephone, certain she would know the real reason why he was ringing.

'Rupert is just about paying for his board and lodgings,' she said. 'I reckon he catches about two mice a week – the ones we see, anyway, though it's probably a lot more. The children adore him, especially Priscilla. He's really her cat.'

'That's marvellous. A happy ending.' He paused. 'And how are *you*, Miss Ashwin?'

She detected a chuckle in his voice. 'Very well, thank you, *Mr Drummond.*'

'I was wondering, Miss Ashwin, if you'd care to go to the pictures with me to see "Woman of the Year". It's a Katharine Hepburn–Spencer Tracy film. Thought it might be right up your street.'

She'd known this would happen – that he'd ask her out sooner or later. She'd tried to prepare what she would say to him so as not to hurt him. That it wasn't fair to him. Because she liked someone else. Someone whom she had to remind herself she could never have. But Frank was such a genuinely nice man. It would be an honour to have him as a friend.

'I would like that very much, Mr Drummond,' she found herself saying, then laughed. 'And why do you think it would be right up my street?'

'Well, you're an independent woman and so is Katharine Hepburn – in real life as well as on the big screen apparently.'

'I'm flattered you spotted the connection.'

He laughed. 'And it's wonderful you've accepted my modest invitation, Miss Ashwin. May I pick you up tomorrow evening? I'm afraid my old banger isn't quite up to the standard of the Rover.'

'I'd be honoured to ride in your old banger, Mr Drummond.'

'Six o'clock tomorrow then.'

It was only when she replaced the receiver that Lana remembered the formidable Mrs Celia Daniels and her comments about her close friendship with Frank.

'It's strange I haven't seen Rupert since noon,' Bertie said, as Lana went into the kitchen to make a cup of tea for her and Maxine before the children finished classes. 'He usually comes in several times to see if there's any titbits coming his way.'

'Well, he's probably found something more interesting outside,' Lana said. 'He does stay away a few hours sometimes.'

'Hmm.' Bertie pressed her lips together. 'I know that cat. I should do. And it's not like him.'

'I'll have a word with Priscilla,' Lana said. 'He might be upstairs on her bed. You know that's where he likes to be.'

When Priscilla returned from school she told Lana Rupert had been on her bed at night as usual, then gone off to the kitchen to have his breakfast. 'I was just about to go and find where he'd got to,' she said, agitatedly pulling one of her pigtails. 'He normally comes down the path to greet me. He knows what time I get back in the afternoon.'

'Yes, I've seen him do that,' Lana said. 'We mustn't worry just yet.' She glanced at the anxious child. 'Cats do wander off sometimes when they find something interesting. But if he's not in for his supper I think we'll have to go out and look for him.'

'But that's ages,' Priscilla said in protest. 'I want to start looking now. He might have had an accident. Maybe a fox—'

'I doubt it,' Lana said, trying to keep her voice calm so as not to alarm Priscilla further.

The children at Bingham Hall had finished classes for the day, and Lana spotted Peter in one of the groups, but not really part of it. He always seemed happier on his own. Her heart went out to him. No matter what she and Maxine hoped, Peter had never really fitted in, but at least the others weren't tormenting him any more.

'Peter,' she called. He spun round. 'Come here a moment.'

He rushed over. 'Are we going to see Papa again?' His eyes lit up with hope.

Lana put her hand on his arm. 'No, love, not yet anyway. Nothing's been fixed yet, but I'll talk to Matron and maybe we can arrange something soon.'

She hated the way Peter's face fell.

'Peter, have you seen Rupert today? Cook said he hasn't appeared since noon.'

'No. He's probably chasing mice.'

'Maybe,' Lana said, 'but Priscilla and I are going out to look for him.'

'I'll help, if you like.'

It was just what Lana hoped the little boy would say.

'All right. Go and get your coats on, both of you,' she said.

Immediately they were outside Priscilla dashed off one way and Peter the other, ignoring Lana's shouts to keep together, and both calling Rupert's name.

Lana decided to search along the drive. She'd seen Rupert go this way many a time, her heart in her throat as he disappeared from sight, too close to the road. She searched in the under-growth between the lime trees, dreading what she might find. She could still hear the children calling him as she reached the road. She'd have a quick look in case he'd got run over and someone had put his body into the hedge at the side. But there was nothing and now she was too far away to hear the children.

Reluctantly she made her way back up the drive, searching the opposite side but there was no sign of him. Utterly miserable, and knowing how Priscilla adored her beloved cat and would be devastated, she reached the house when she heard Peter's shout.

'Miss! Miss Ashwin, I've found him!'

Lana's heart thudded.

'Where are you?' she shouted back.

'At the greenhouse.'

She rushed behind the house to the vegetable garden, past the first greenhouse, which was a pile of glass from a bomb the previous year, to the one standing intact. Priscilla raced behind her.

Peter was on his knees, stroking the animal who was lying on his side, his eyes closed, his muscles twitching, saliva frothing at his mouth. Lana noticed a pile of vomit a couple of feet away.

Peter jumped to his feet at their approach. 'I don't know if he's still alive.' There were tears in his eyes.

'Please let me see him,' Priscilla almost pushed Peter aside in her anxiety. He made no comment as he brushed down his short trousers.

The young girl knelt down by her cat's side and stroked one of his paws. 'Rupert,' she whispered. 'What's the matter?' Rupert opened one eye and looked in her direction, then closed it again. 'He's alive,' she whispered, looking round at Lana.

'Let me see.' Lana crouched down and gently felt along his fur to see whether he'd been wounded. There didn't seem to be any sign of blood or that he'd been in a fight. When she felt his stomach he let out a moan. 'What's the matter, old boy?'

'What do you think's wrong with him?' Priscilla said, her voice shaking.

'I think he's been poisoned.'

'Oh, Miss Ashwin, please do something,' Priscilla begged, the tears streaming down her face. 'Please don't let him die.'

'He needs help quickly. We'll have to go in and get an old towel and put him in his basket. Then get him to the vet's right away.'

'I'll come too.'

'No, Priscilla,' Lana said firmly. 'Supper will soon be ready and you and Peter need to have your meal. It's quicker if I take him over myself. I promise I'll do everything I can to save him. Just run in and get an old towel from Cook. And Peter, could you ask Cook if she has an empty jam jar and an old spoon. We need to take some of this sick to show Mr Drummond and he might be able to tell what he's eaten.'

The children shot off and two minutes later they came back with a towel and jam jar, and Rupert's basket.

'I'll do the sick,' Peter said, and proceeded to scoop up some spoonfuls into the jar.

Priscilla handed the towel to Lana.

'We'll get him into his basket,' Lana said, 'and then you stay with him in the scullery while I go and get the car out of the garage.'

'All right, Miss Ashwin, but you will hurry, won't you?'

'Yes, love, I will.'

'You're right,' Frank said, when he'd gently examined Rupert. 'It's probably rat poison.' He took the thermometer from Rupert's bottom and held it up. 'Mmm. Too high, as expected.'

'But no one at the home would put poison down, or anything like that,' Lana said. 'That's why we got Rupert in the first place.'

'They wander off,' Frank said, looking at her,

his expression concerned. 'He could easily have eaten something from one of the neighbouring properties. Just because there're several acres around Bingham Hall doesn't mean he won't go further afield.' He softly pressed Rupert's stomach and the cat gave a whimper of protest. 'He's in some pain, poor old boy. I'm going to drip some milk and water into his mouth to neutralise any traces of poison and give him an injection to relax him and stop the pain. It's good that he's already vomited. I'll keep him here overnight and see how he does. He's still a young cat and strong, so let's cross our fingers.'

'He's such a dear cat,' Lana said, tears pricking her eyes. She ran her hand gently over Rupert's head but he didn't stir. 'We joke that he has to earn his keep, but we'd love him even if he never caught one mouse.'

'That's probably it,' Frank said. 'The last mouse or rat he caught could have eaten something poisonous. How much sick was there?'

'At least a cupful,' Lana said. 'I've brought you a sample.' She took the jar from Rupert's basket and set it down on the table.

'Good. Very good.' Frank nodded. He unscrewed the jar and sniffed. 'I don't want to have to pump his stomach if I don't have to. Did you notice any diarrhoea?'

'No, but I didn't really look. I should have done.'

'Don't worry. I'll let him sleep and keep an eye on him. In the meantime,' he gave her apologetic glance, 'it looks like our evening at the cinema is off.'

'I know. But Rupert needs your attention now.' She caught his eye. 'There'll be another time.'

'I hope so,' Frank said. 'In fact, I'm banking on it.' He smiled. 'Try not to worry too much about Rupert. I'll ring you in the morning to let you know how he is.'

'Thank you, Frank. And let me know the bill.'

He shook his head. 'No bill,' he said. 'It's the least I can do for poor Rupert.'

'You're very kind.' Lana smiled warmly at him. It was the sort of gesture Dickie would have made. She remembered how he'd found someone's purse and taken it to the police station and refused the reward. She'd thought at the time how lucky she was to be in love with such a darling man. She swallowed. There was something about Frank's manner that reminded her of Dickie.

Frank laid his hand on her arm. 'Lana . . .?'

She jumped. 'Yes?'

Frank dropped his hand. 'No, nothing. It doesn't matter.'

Driving back to Bingham Hall, still worried about poor Rupert, Lana wondered what Frank had been about to say. She didn't know whether she was disappointed or relieved that he'd decided not to say anything after all.

CHAPTER 31

Priscilla opened the front door when Lana jumped out of the car. She'd put it in the garage later.

'Where is he?' Priscilla's words sounded as though they were being torn from her.

'I've had to leave him with Mr Drummond for the night.'

'Is he going to die?'

'I hope not.' She saw the alarm flare into Priscilla's eyes. 'I don't think so,' she tempered it, praying she wasn't giving the child false hope.

Most of the children were gathered in the Great Hall, clamouring to hear how Rupert was.

'Is he dead, Miss?' several of them shouted.

'Good riddance if he is,' Reggie, a tall, well-built lad whose trousers no longer reached his ankles, said in a loud voice. 'Horrible animal.'

Alan, standing near him, gave Reggie a quick kick in the shin.

'Ouch! What was that for?'

'That's for saying what you did about Rupert. You should be his biggest fan the way you scream out every time you see a poor little mouse.'

Reggie turned bright red. 'Course I don't.'

'Yes, you do. It's *you* who's the scaredy cat, the stupid one, not Rupert.'

In an instant a fight broke out, various voices cheering them on. Lana rushed towards the two boys.

'Break it up this minute, both of you!'

'He started it,' Reggie said, rubbing his arm. 'He kicked me.'

'And this is another one from me.'

To Lana's horror she saw Priscilla kick the back of one of Reggie's legs. He gave a howl of pain.

'You little beast,' he said, glaring at the girl. 'Teacher's favourite orphan,' he added sarcastically, 'even though you say you aren't one, we all know you bloody are. Mummy and Daddy got bashed to pieces in town.'

There was a deathly hush. All eyes were on Reggie.

'You will *not* swear at Priscilla, and say such hateful things.' Lana got hold of Reggie's arm, thankful she was taller than him. 'Apologise to Priscilla *at once*!'

Reggie shrugged her off in one easy movement. 'Why should I? She kicked me.'

'Say you're sorry, say you're sorry,' Betsy said, hopping up and down. Doris and Daisy took their cue and several more children joined in.

Reggie threw them a contemptuous look.

'I'm giving you one more chance to apologise,' Lana said.

'You can't make me.'

'Well, then, you can go into the kitchen and tell Bertie you're doing the washing up this evening, then drying the dishes and putting them away. If you don't, I assure you there will be trouble. And I shall be reporting you to Matron.'

'What's going on?' Maxine appeared in the hall.

'Reggie's just going to tell Cook he's clearing up the kitchen this evening.'

Maxine nodded to him. 'Off you go, then.'

Reggie threw her a scornful glance and mumbled under his breath as he slouched out of the hall.

'Come into the office, Lana,' Maxine said, 'and bring Priscilla. I want to hear how Rupert is.'

'Mr Drummond thinks like me that he's been poisoned,' Lana began, when they'd all sat down, 'but he's given him an injection to help him sleep and wants to keep an eye on him overnight.'

'*I* could have done that,' Priscilla said, her grey eyes flashing steel. 'Why did you have to leave him with someone he doesn't know?'

'He *does* know Fr–Mr Drummond.' Lana caught herself in time. 'He's the one who his owner took him to. And you know yourself how kind he is.'

'I suppose so.' She chewed her nail. 'Miss Ashwin, Reggie said—'

'Forget it, Priscilla. He's in an angry mood at the moment.'

'Not about the orphan bit, or the swearing,' Priscilla said, slowly. 'No, I mean when he said it would be good riddance if Rupert died.' She turned her eyes on Lana. 'I think *he* poisoned Rupert!'

'We can't say that, Priscilla,' Lana warned. 'You must keep those thoughts to yourself because we have no evidence. Mr Drummond is sure that Rupert ate a poisoned rat which one of the farmers may have put down.'

Frank Drummond rang her first thing the following morning.

'Rupert's had a good night's sleep,' he said, his tone so cheery that Lana was certain the news was good. 'He's had a little bread and warm milk for his breakfast and kept it down. And he jumped out of his box. So no need to worry. You can come and collect him any time. He'll do better at the orphanage, if you put him somewhere quiet, than listening to the barking dogs in the surgery.'

'Oh, thank goodness he's better.' Lana breathed out her relief. 'I'll come in about an hour if that's all right.'

'Fine. And don't forget we've got a date tonight.'

'Ah! I was going to tell you when I saw you later that Athena, one of the teachers, asked me if I would fit in another rehearsal for the children. She and I are writing a comedy for them.'

'Sounds fun,' Frank said. 'Well, what about tomorrow evening? We said we'd see that Katharine Hepburn film.'

'We did,' Lana said, smiling, even though he couldn't see her. 'It'll be a real treat as I haven't been to the cinema since I came here.'

Lana put down the receiver, a thoughtful expression on her face. If she'd never met someone else, Frank would be— She cut herself off sharply. It was no good at all thinking like that.

But she did owe Carl a letter.

Priscilla begged Lana to let her go with her to collect Rupert.

'I would, if it wasn't term time, love, but you need to be in class. I don't want you to miss any more lessons. But at break time you can come and see how he's getting on. Mr Drummond recommends that Rupert has a quiet place to sleep and recover from his ordeal. He's a bit subdued at the moment but he'll recover.'

As Lana drove to Frank's surgery she tried to work out how she should act with Frank. It wasn't fair to him to pretend anything more than she felt – which was friendship. But she was certain he wanted more than that. Oh, well, she'd have to play it by ear.

She hadn't needed to worry after all. The nurse opened the door and smiled when she saw who it was.

'I've got him ready,' she said. 'Come in. Mr Drummond is out on an emergency. One of the horses in the village has had an accident.'

A flicker of disappointment chased through her. She'd wanted to thank him in person.

Rupert was in his basket, only this time Lana could see she didn't need to worry that he'd jump out. He managed to struggle up when she said his name, and when she stroked him she heard a faint purr.

'He needs to be kept quiet for a day or two,' the nurse said, 'but Mr Drummond said he'd be right as rain in a few days. Just give him a little bland food like chicken or fish – maybe mix it with a spoonful of mashed potato, and plain water to drink. If he doesn't respond then you'll have to bring him back. But I don't think you'll have any problems with him. He's definitely on the mend.'

'Thank you very much, Nurse,' Lana said, smiling, as she took the basket with Rupert who was now fast asleep.

'Good luck with Rupert,' the nurse called out as Lana opened the front passenger door and set the basket on the seat.

Lana turned and waved. She shut the car door and went round to the driver's side. 'You're going home, Rupert,' she told him.

'Rupert!' Priscilla was the first to come flying from the house as Lana lifted out the basket with Rupert curled into a ball on the cushion. He pricked his ears when he heard his true mistress.

'Be very quiet and gentle around him for a few days,' Lana warned her. 'He needs time to fully recover. I'm taking him to Bertie. She'll keep an eye on him while you're having lessons.'

'Can we see him?' Doris and Daisy, with Betsy not far behind, rushed up, excited to see Rupert.

'He has to be kept quiet,' Priscilla said, repeating Lana's words. Immediately the twins quietened down but Betsy was determined to stroke him.

'I love Rupert,' she said. 'He's not going to die, is he?'

'Of course he isn't. Listen to that purr. He's already getting better,' Lana smiled. 'Let's go inside and settle him in.'

After she'd had a word with Bertie and put Rupert and his basket in the scullery, she knocked on Maxine's door and went in.

'Good – you're back,' Maxine said. 'How is he?'

'He's going to be fine, so Frank said. Just needs rest. I was wondering if you have any other driving jobs for me today?'

Maxine glanced at her diary open on the desk. 'No, nothing vital at the moment.' She looked directly at Lana, twiddling her pencil. 'But I'd like you to take Peter to see his father again – sometime soon. It's been a few months now. Would you mind?'

It was difficult to answer. All kinds of thoughts and confusions rushed through Lana's head. There was something between her and Carl – she was sure of it – and she didn't want to put herself into an embarrassing position, especially in front of Peter. What was Maxine saying?

'And I think you should take Peter on your own,' Maxine said, without waiting for a reply. 'From what you told me, Priscilla wasn't exactly happy last time.'

'It's true,' Lana said. 'She feels Peter has found his father, but she's lost hers and her mother, for good. She still doesn't want to believe that she'll never see them again. I feel so sorry for her. But I think you're right. I won't take her again.'

'Lana, is there something wrong? If you'd rather not go, please tell me.'

Lana bit her lip. 'I feel in the way, as far as Peter is concerned. He wants his beloved papa to himself, and I understand completely. But it's an awkward position to be in, even though Carl does his best to include me. But Peter resents it.'

She couldn't say any more to Maxine or she'd reveal something she didn't even want to admit to herself. That she found him devastatingly attractive. A German. The enemy. How could she? She brought herself up sharply. No, he wasn't the enemy – he was working for the British. But to anyone over here, she knew he'd be classed as the enemy. She suddenly had a thought.

'It'll be Christmas in a few weeks' time. Wouldn't it be better if he could come *here* to see Peter? They might let him come without the minder as he'll be making straight for his son at Bingham Hall. That's what's so awful. It keeps reminding us that he's still under observation.'

'That's probably a good idea,' Maxine said. 'I'll put it to the powers that be. See what they say. It's probably better for Peter on his own home ground than mooching around Bletchley. They can have some privacy in the library and go for walks.' She looked directly at Lana, and to Lana it seemed deliberate. 'He could stay a couple of days as it's a long way to come and the trains will be up the creek, no doubt. I'll see what they say.'

Staying a couple of nights. Lana felt a warmth rush to her cheeks. Her voice shook a little as she replied. 'I owe him a letter, so shall I mention it?'

'By all means.' Maxine gave her another of her sharp looks. 'Lana, are you *sure* you're all right?'

'Of course I am. Why on earth shouldn't I be?' She caught Maxine's surprised expression and lowered her head, her face flushing with shame. 'I'm sorry, Maxine,' she mumbled. 'I didn't mean to sound rude. I'm a bit on edge lately – expect it was all the worry about Rupert.'

She was grateful Maxine made no further comment, except to nod and say how pleased she was that Rupert was on the mend.

She had no driving duties for the moment so it was a good time to answer Carl's letter, Lana decided. In her room she opened the chest of drawers and took out his last letter to remind herself, though she knew it by heart.

She laid a fresh piece of notepaper on her lap, resting it on a magazine, picked up the fountain pen Dickie had given her and started to write.

Dear Carl,

    I'm so sorry not to have answered your letter before now. It's been busy here, yet no actual news except that Peter and Priscilla have agreed to speak German a couple of times a week in the library. I've suggested no more than half an hour to start with. Their first session will be tomorrow after supper. I'm not going to attend. I thought it best to leave them to it – they're old enough. I'll keep you posted as to progress!

I have spoken to Maxine today and we wondered if you might be allowed to come to Bingham Hall at Christmas. It's only a few weeks away and Peter would love it. Maxine suggested they might even let you stay a night or two as it's such a long way to come in one day.

She paused. Again, that warm feeling flooded her cheeks. Desire prickled and her thoughts raced back to Dickie. The way he used to hold her, make love to her, tell her that if it hadn't been for the damned war he'd have whisked her down the aisle long ago. She pushed the thoughts away. What was the good? It was a different world and now it seemed all anyone ever talked about was the war. She was glad she was at the orphanage, listening and talking to the children, the staff's only concerns being to protect, nourish and educate them for the future. She sighed and reread what she'd written so far, then continued.

Maxine is going to have a word with your superior, and I obviously won't breathe any of this to Peter, but if you can manage it and it's confirmed, then he will have something wonderful to look forward to. I will also be pleased to see you again.

Shocked, she read the last sentence. She'd hardly realised she'd written such a sentiment. She was going into realms she shouldn't. He'd probably be embarrassed. Yet she knew in her heart he wouldn't be. Telling herself she couldn't cross it out or he'd demand to know what she'd said, and starting again would be a waste of paper, she chewed her lip as she finished the letter.

The weather is turning cold (always a safe subject, she thought) and leaves have started to fall with a vengeance. It does look beautiful in our gardens. It always gives me hope that there are better things to come.

Peter is writing to you, so you should hear from him shortly.

With very best wishes,
Lana

The ending looked a little cold. She frowned. She couldn't think of how to alter it. Just for a crazy moment she wished she could say more. That she was thinking of him. Or should she tear the whole thing up and start again, and to hell with the new sheet of paper? She hesitated a few moments, then quickly folded the letter and sealed it in an envelope. She'd walk to the village and post it before she changed her mind.

When she arrived back she found Maxine in her office, her face creased in a frown.

'Oh, there you are, Lana. I wonder if you could do me a favour and fill in for Judith Wright this morning? Her class will be starting in,' she looked at her watch, 'twenty minutes. It's history. Henry VIII. Would that be all right?'

Lana took a mental breath. She had nothing prepared and her own study of the Tudors seemed a long time ago.

'Yes, of course. But is she ill?'

'Read this.' Maxine handed her a letter.

Dear Mrs Taylor,

I am sorry to leave you in the lurch but I have not been happy at Bingham Hall for some time. You might remember when Miss Lavender was matron, I was only filling in on a temporary basis. That's all I wanted but she persuaded me to stay on, which was not what I'd planned.

I have now made up my mind to go and by the time you read this my taxi will have arrived to take me to the railway station, where I'll be catching a train to Cambridge, my home town.

I would prefer to have told you in person but you were not in your office. I prepared this letter anyway so it was official.

I'm sure Miss Ashwin will be able to fill my place admirably.

Yours sincerely,
Judith Wright

'Isn't it a cheek?' Maxine said, when Lana put the letter on the desk.

'On several accounts,' Lana returned. 'She's putting you in an awkward position.' She caught Maxine's eye. 'Please don't think you have to offer me Judith's job, Maxine. You've been more than kind to me.'

'Trouble is, Harold's due back in two weeks' time,' Maxine said, glancing at her diary. She looked at Lana and smiled. 'Are you telling me you'd turn it down?'

'Oh, no,' Lana said hurriedly. 'It's just that—'

'It's just nothing,' Maxine said. 'I was trying to think of a way to bring Mrs Wright's job to an end. She's never been happy here and the children don't much like her. I think I'll ask the children how they'd feel to have Miss Ashwin as their permanent teacher. I'm sure they'd hate it.' She grinned.

'You're incorrigible,' Lana said, laughing. 'And if you're offering me the job, then yes, please. But until Harold returns I'll do any necessary driving first thing or after classes – unless there's an emergency, of course.'

'That would be wonderful, as no one else here drives. You've taken a weight off my mind.'

'I just need to get down to some history and geography so I stay at least one lesson ahead of them,' Lana grinned.

When Lana announced that Mrs Wright wasn't coming back and she would now be their teacher the children whooped with joy. Alan and Bobby whistled, and the little girls clapped their hands and Betsy called out 'Hurray'. Lana was touched by their enthusiasm.

'Are we still going to do the play, Miss?' Bobby called out.

'Yes, we are,' Lana said. 'We'll go through the whole thing this evening in the library instead of doing just a piece of it. Then we'll see who's getting to know their lines and who isn't. I don't expect you to be word perfect yet so don't look so alarmed, Megan. We still have over a month before Christmas Eve.'

When Carl might be here.

The rehearsal was a disaster. The girls were better than the boys but that wasn't much consolation.

'It's no good the girls at least knowing where they come in if you boys don't,' Lana said, her eyes sweeping over them. 'You'll let them down – and us. It appears that only Peter knows where and when he enters and leaves.'

'He would,' Reggie said, making a rude sign. 'Goody-two-shoes Peter, teacher's pet.'

'Reggie!' It was Athena. 'You will refrain from

making that sign. It's quite disgusting.' Gordon and Jack giggled. 'Not sure what's so funny, you two.' Athena glared at them. 'You won't find it funny when you come on the stage in front of everyone and look right ninnies.'

'What stage?' Reggie said belligerently. 'I've never seen no stage.'

'Any stage,' Lana corrected automatically.

'You don't need to concern yourself about it,' Athena said. 'Just concentrate on learning your part.'

'It's stupid.'

'All right, Reggie,' Athena said sharply. 'It's obviously too stupid for you. From now on you're out of it. Alan has very little to do. He'll do your part as well.' She turned to the boy. 'Are you happy with that, Alan?'

'I suppose so.' Alan didn't sound particularly enthusiastic.

Reggie flushed with annoyance but the two teachers took no more notice of him. They gave the rehearsal another half an hour but if anything, it grew worse.

'Right,' Lana said. 'You're obviously all tired so we'll have another session on Thursday. That will give you time to learn your lines. None of you, except Priscilla and Peter and now Alan, have a big part, so you should easily do that. Any difficulties, come and see me or Miss Graham. Boys, off you go.' She clapped her hands and they scraped back their chairs, flung them to the side and disappeared. 'Girls, why don't we ask Matron to come and talk to us about your costumes? She and Mrs Steen will be making them.'

The girls broke into delighted squeals and Lana smiled. Maxine and Barbara Steen had been eager to help with the sewing.

But when Athena returned she was on her own. 'Mrs Steen's already gone home and Matron was having a quiet cup of tea in the common room. I told her not to worry . . . it was time to pack up anyway. She said she'll come on Thursday to talk to us about clothes.'

'Never mind.' Lana glanced at the little group. 'Anyone eight or younger, it's time for bed, but well done, girls. You put the boys to shame.'

The girls beamed and clapped. As they scrambled to leave the library, pushing and shoving in their usual hurry to escape, Lana heard Betsy say, 'I hope the boys don't spoil things again at the next rehearsal.'

'They'd better not,' Athena said to Lana, 'or they'll get a clip round the ear from me.'

CHAPTER 32

'I daren't ask if you're comfortable, Lana, when you've been used to that superb motor you've been driving.'

Lana gave him a sideways look. Frank Drummond wasn't the best driver in the world, she'd realised after the first three minutes. He was too cautious, then he would grind the gears and the car would leap forward. But she liked the shape of his hands on the wheel. His fingers weren't long, but they looked strong and capable. She liked his profile. He couldn't be described as classically good-looking; his nose with a slight hook to it reminded her of a Roman emperor. She told herself not to be so ridiculous and stole another glance. This time he caught her and grinned, his smile a little lopsided.

'What is it, Miss Ashwin? Is it that you can't believe your luck that you're out with the most handsome chap in Bingham?'

Really, the man didn't know how attractive he was, Lana thought with a start. That smile was so infectious she couldn't help grinning back.

'How did you read my mind, Mr Drummond?'

'One of my many talents, so be careful what you think when you're with me.'

'Oh, I will.' She gave an exaggerated shudder. 'Thanks for the warning.' She paused. 'And for your information I'm perfectly comfortable.' She wouldn't tell him that the interior smelled strongly of animals, though it was hard to differentiate the particular species. She was grateful she hadn't worn anything good. Her brown winter coat was bound to be covered in dog hairs at the very least by the time they arrived at the cinema.

'Really? You honestly don't mind such a drop in status?' He twisted his neck to look at her and she wished he would keep his eyes on the road, especially now they were out of the village and heading towards Liverpool.

'The Rover's a pure joy to drive, but this one reflects your character. It's a Morris 8, isn't it?'

'No idea.' He suddenly swerved to avoid a cyclist and sounded the horn. 'Silly devil.' He turned to her again. 'Not you, Lana. That cyclist. Why doesn't he get over? Idiot.'

Just as he finished grumbling the Morris gave a loud bang, jolting her forward so she had to put her hand on the dashboard to stop herself going through the windscreen.

'Sorry about that,' Frank said, as though this was a normal part of his trips in the car. She thought of all the animals that had to suffer his driving. 'Are you okay?'

'Yes, but I don't think your car is,' Lana said,

as it was now jerking in hops and leaps. 'You'd better pull over and find out what's happened.'

'Oh, all right. Probably just a bump in the road.'

He jumped out and slammed the door shut.

'Bad news,' he said as he got back into the driving seat. 'The rear tyre's flat as a pancake. I'm afraid we'll have to limp back to Bingham.'

'Whatever for? You've got a spare on the back.'

He didn't answer except to frown. Puzzled, she said, 'Well, it won't take more than a few minutes to change.'

This time he looked sheepish. 'Trouble is, I never learned how.'

'What?' Lana's jaw dropped. 'How can you drive without knowing how to change a wheel?'

'I cross my fingers when I get into the car,' he said carelessly. 'So far I've been all right – or within walking distance of a garage, at any rate.'

'Well, we're at least a couple of miles away from any garage,' Lana said. 'And I don't fancy walking that far so I'd better have a look at it.'

'It's definitely flat,' Frank told her.

'I'm not disputing your diagnosis,' Lana said, hiding a smile. 'I'm going to cure it – just like you cure the animals that come to you.'

'What are you talking about?'

'I'm going to change the damn wheel.'

'*You?*'

His tone was so incredulous she didn't know whether to laugh or be cross.

'Yes, Frank. Me. *I* will change it. And you can jolly well help me!'

'I can't let you do that. Getting your hands oily – dripping onto your clothes.'

'Don't be daft. Someone's got to do it and you've told me you don't know how. Good job for you I *do*!'

He opened his mouth in protest, then shut it again when she glared at him and opened the car door. Removing the spare from the rear of the motor she turned to him.

'Right, do you know how to jack it up?'

'More or less.'

It was mostly 'less', Lana decided, as she watched Frank fumbling.

'Here, give it to me.'

He handed over the jack, looking crestfallen.

'No wonder it burst,' Lana said, ten minutes later, as she rolled the tyre between her hands. 'It's as bald as a baby's bottom, and here's the culprit.' With a triumphant flourish she held it up to him. 'Look – a stupid nail.'

'Actually, it's a *horseshoe* nail,' Frank said, with a smirk of satisfaction.

'Whatever nail you want to call it, you need to buy another tyre,' she snapped, 'and soon, because the spare is almost as bad.'

'Don't you know there's a war on?' Frank said. 'You can't just go out and buy a tyre any more.'

'Well, get a decent second-hand one then,' Lana shot back. 'You need your car for your work. And it needs to be safe.'

'Are you really that worried about me?' He cocked an eyebrow.

'Not you in particular – but I *am* worried about the innocent animals who don't have a say as to whether they want to ride with you or not.'

He grinned. 'All right, Miss Bossyboots, I'll do it straightaway.'

'See that you do.' Lana stretched up and set the ruined wheel on the back of the car. 'Right. All done. We can go now.'

Frank handed her an old towel to wipe her hands. It stunk of animals. She hid her distaste so as not to hurt his feelings.

'Never known a woman who knows so much about cars and can even change a wheel.'

Lana gave him a swift glance. Was he being sarcastic?

'It comes from having two car-mad older brothers,' she said, matter of factly. 'Women are perfectly capable of doing anything they put their minds to, Frank, so don't you forget it.'

He threw back his head and roared with laughter. 'Oh, I wouldn't. Not now I've seen *you* in action.'

His laugh was so contagious she couldn't help joining in.

There was a long queue at the Woolton Picture House, but eventually they took their seats.

'Not the best ones, I'm afraid,' Frank whispered as the lights dimmed.

'They're absolutely fine,' she said as Frank took

her hand warmly in his. There was no quiver, no tingling, as she'd felt whenever Carl's fingers had accidentally brushed against hers – yet unexpectedly she felt perfectly content.

But the Pathé Newsreel sent shivers across her shoulders. Night images of Berlin, filmed from above by RAF cameramen, showed bombs raining down on the city like huge tumbling stars, exploding on impact in bright flares. How many men, women and children would be killed on such a night? Lana swallowed the bile in her throat.

The newsreader spoke with urgency:

'The expected blow at the heart of Nazi Germany might be said to open the Battle of Berlin. This crushing attack was four times greater than the biggest the *Luftwaffe* ever delivered on London. It created terror, devastation and chaos by its stupendous intensity . . .

'You travel over the blazing and shaking city below . . .

'Flying there, too, is a young Flight Sergeant listening on his intercom to the rest of the crew wishing him twenty-first birthday greetings . . .'

Lana thought she would be sick. A young man who might not make it back. She couldn't listen any longer. She was about to jump up when Frank put his arm around her and whispered, 'It's all right, Lana. The film's about to start.'

'I think the film was quite the wrong one to take you to,' Frank said, as they walked back to where he'd parked the car. 'Katharine Hepburn was certainly more than a match for Spence. Reminded me of you,' he added, his eyes twinkling mischievously.

She laughed. 'I'm taking that as the ultimate compliment.'

He took her hand and gave it a gentle squeeze.

The drive home was fortunately without any more mishaps, though Frank's driving hadn't improved. Lana was sure he had no idea how bad some of his habits were. He constantly ground the gears and didn't always remember to signal when he turned until the last second. Once a driver behind them screeched his brakes and wound the window down, shaking his fist and shouting a few ripe words.

'Cheeky beggar,' was all Frank said.

Lana couldn't help feeling relieved when they reached Bingham Hall, wondering if there was any way she could tactfully offer him a couple of driving lessons.

Frank switched off the engine and got out to open Lana's door.

It was very dark now. The orphanage still abided by the rules of the blackout even though the bombing of the docklands had not been nearly so fierce in the last months. But she could see Frank's eyes gleaming as he looked at her.

'That was one of the best evenings I've had in a long time,' he said.

'Me, too,' she said, and with a start of surprise she realised she meant it.

'Really?'

She nodded. 'I've not been out much since – well, since Dickie died.' There was the familiar pricking behind her eyes. 'But everyone's in the same boat. Not just me.'

Frank caught her hand. 'Can we do this again . . . soon?'

'Yes, I'd love to.'

'Lana?'

Before she could answer he'd taken her into his arms. His mouth was warm and firm on hers and for a wonderful few seconds she found herself responding. Then she pulled back in panic, her blood rushing. This wasn't right. What *was* she doing responding to another man's kiss? The first man since Dickie. But she didn't want to give Frank any false hopes. Not when she was beginning to think about another man in an entirely different way.

'I'm sorry. I shouldn't have done that.'

His expression was so contrite she had to say something.

'It's all right, Frank. You haven't offended me or anything. It's just that—'

'You love someone else,' he finished.

'I'm not sure,' she said, looking away from the hurt in his eyes.

Swiftly she kissed his cheek and ran the few yards to the oak front door. Athena must have heard her because she opened the door and Lana slipped in. Seconds later she heard Frank's old

Morris skid on the gravel, stones flying up in the air, as he swung the motor down the drive.

The next morning there was no time to dwell on her evening with Frank. Lana threw herself into her old rôle as teacher, trying to instil a sense of history into some of the boys who had little interest. The only time they sat up was when she told them more about Henry VIII and all his wives.

'He was some king,' Alan said admiringly.

'Do you think he had a right to ruin so many queens' lives?'

'If they weren't no good.'

'Any good,' Lana corrected. 'What do you mean – if they weren't any good?'

'If they didn't give him sons to grow up and be king,' Bobby put in. 'You couldn't have girls – they weren't clever enough to rule the country.'

Lana looked at the girls in the class who sat in silence.

'Boys, don't answer this question. I want one of the girls to answer.' Her eyes swept over the small group of girls who always sat together. 'Do you think girls are as clever as boys?'

'I do,' Betsy piped up, 'but they always shout over us and don't give us a chance to say nothing.'

'Don't give us a chance to say *anything*.' It was Megan.

'That's correct, Megan. And have you any thoughts on the subject?'

'Course we're as clever as the boys.' Megan

looked round the class as though to warn the others not to disagree.

'Prove it,' Bobby said.

The girls were silent. Pamela's forehead was creased in thought.

'What about Cleopatra?' Lana suggested. '*She* was much more clever than Mark Antony.'

'She weren't that clever,' Bobby put in. 'She had to put a snake on her tittie to kill herself.'

There were snorts of laughter from the boys.

'Pamela?' Lana said.

'The easy one is Queen Victoria,' Pamela came back in a flash. 'She was Queen longer than anyone, so she must have been more clever to beat the men who wanted to get rid of her.'

'Well, she was the rightful heir to the throne,' Lana said, hiding a smile. 'And Princess Elizabeth will one day be Queen.' She clapped her hands. 'Right, children – time to open your history books. I believe we were on page 88.'

CHAPTER 33

Lana hesitated about asking Maxine if she'd been able to find out if Carl could come to Bingham Hall to visit his son. So many times it had been on the tip of her tongue to say something, but she'd always held her words in.

Why was she reluctant? she wondered. If it was any other father wanting to see his child there wouldn't be any problem. So why was Peter's father any different? Or was it because there was a thread as fine as spider's silk forming between them; so new it could easily be broken just by mentioning his name?

Frank had telephoned her twice to ask her out, and both times she turned him down, making a feeble excuse that the home was busy with Barbara away with a heavy cold.

Days turned into a fortnight and rehearsals were going a little better. The boys seemed to be getting into the spirit of it, and it amused her to hear Bobby and Alan clipping along the corridor practising their lines, and Alan even hummed his big song. She'd noticed there wasn't nearly so much fighting breaking out since they'd become engrossed in the play, though Reggie still worried her. He was now a strapping lad, getting on for fifteen, and ought to be doing an apprenticeship of some sort. Something using his hands – like carpentry, perhaps.

One morning, in Maxine's office, she mentioned her concerns.

'What do you suggest?' Maxine said.

'I'd like to talk to him – find out his interests.'

'Please do,' Maxine said immediately, 'because I've been seriously thinking of reporting him to head office. He's not interested in his lessons and is often quite disruptive.'

'Let me speak to him first,' Lana said. She hesitated. It wasn't really her place to comment but this was important for Reggie's welfare. She plunged ahead. 'Maxine, he's almost a man. Is it possible for him to have a new pair of trousers? The ones he's wearing are several inches above the ankles. And he desperately needs a larger-sized jacket.'

'You're right,' Maxine said. 'I should have noticed before now that he's growing fast. Alan is another one. Leave it to me and I'll find some coupons.'

'One other thing,' Lana said. 'I don't mean to talk out of turn but I think he's old enough to have his own room now. The boys he shares with are quite a bit younger . . .' She hesitated, hoping Maxine wouldn't be offended. 'It's just that I have two older brothers,' she added quickly, 'and I know that's how *they* were at Reggie's age.'

Maxine smiled. 'I'm not a bit upset if you point

out any child's needs. And I'm sure I can find Reggie something.' She picked up a couple of envelopes on her desk and handed them to Lana. 'These are for you.'

Lana glanced at the top one – Geoff, her beloved older brother. She couldn't wait to hear his news and if he'd heard from Nick lately. Then her heart leapt. The second letter was from Carl. She wanted to rush upstairs straightaway and read it. Devour it. *Steady. Keep calm.* She was aware Maxine was watching her.

'Herr Best, I presume,' Maxine said, with a knowing grin.

'Oh, um, yes,' Lana stuttered, determined not to let her face go red like some young girl. 'And one from my brother,' she added, trying to take the attention off Carl's.

'Herr Best seems to be keeping up quite a correspondence.' Maxine was still smiling.

'I've told you before – it's only to find out how Peter's getting along.'

'I'm beginning to wonder.'

'Don't make something out of nothing,' Lana said, irritated. Her nerves felt on edge these days, but she couldn't put into words the reasons why.

'Sorry, Lana. You know I'm only teasing.'

Immediately, Lana felt contrite. 'I didn't mean to snap at you,' she said. 'It's just that . . .'

'Just what?' Maxine raised her eyes to Lana. 'You're not falling in love with him, are you?'

Lana's heart did a cartwheel. 'No, of course not. Don't be so silly. He would be the last person I'd choose to fall in love with.'

'We don't always have the choice,' Maxine said softly. She looked up. 'Lana, are you sure you're all right?'

'I'm sure . . . honestly.'

'You just seem like you've got something on your mind.'

'No, really.'

'I know I'm younger than you,' Maxine persisted, 'but I'm a trained nurse and I know there's something bothering you.' She gave Lana a mock-severe look. 'Are you getting enough sleep? If not, I can give you something to help.'

'Yes, Nurse Maxine, I'm sleeping perfectly well.' Lana sent her a smile, trying to make light of it, but in truth, Maxine was right – she'd had two or three bad nights lately.

'Then go and read your letters in peace.'

Lana rose to her feet as Maxine returned her smile. Before either of them could say anything further there was a knock at the door and Lana opened it. Peter stood there, a solemn expression on his face.

'Hello, Peter. Did you want me or Matron?'

'Matron.' His eyes shifted to Maxine. 'Is there a letter from my father today?'

Lana was aware the lad knew as well as the other children that they were not allowed to bother Matron unless there was an emergency.

'Come in for a few moments,' Maxine told him. 'Lana, you stay too.'

'No, I'll leave you to it,' Lana answered. She was about to close the door when she heard Peter say, 'Is Papa – I mean my father – is he coming at Christmas? He said he would try. He promised.'

Lana longed to hear the matron's answer, which was probably why Maxine had invited her to stay while she spoke to Peter. Poor little chap. He was so desperate to see his papa again. She felt a prickling under her eyelids and fled to her room. Once there she sat on her bed. Her brother's letter first. She had to know he was safe. She read it quickly, thankful Geoff sounded cheerful and that Nick hoped to get some shore leave very soon. Her mother would be so happy to see one of her boys. Lana swallowed. This terrible war – shattering people's lives, pulling loved ones apart. How much longer . . .?

She slit Carl's letter open with trembling fingers. This time she pulled out two sheets of paper.

My dear Lana,

You cannot know how welcome your letters are. And I hope to tell you good news! You mentioned in your last letter that your nice matron was to see if I might come to the home a day or two over Christmas. She has succeeded! My superior has said yes, and even better news – I might be able to come <u>alone</u>.

I believe they have already written to Mrs Taylor and merely await her confirmation that it would not inconvenience her in any way.

Of course I am longing to see my son – but I am also happy that I will see you too, if you do not go home for Christmas. Please tell me you will stay at the orphanage.

I hope you do not mind that I say such things, but you have been on my mind lately when I am given a short break from work. I am so happy you are doing everything you can for Peter, but I fear you have had a difficult time yourself in this terrible war. There is a deep sadness to your eyes which I know very well. You will tell me if I am wrong – but I don't think so.

Please tell Peter the good news that I will see him on Christmas Eve. In Germany it is a more important occasion than Christmas Day. Before the war it was magical. Now it is a nightmare. But I am here in England so I am one of the lucky people.

Lana, my dear, I don't know how I should sign this, so I will just say,

Carl

With shaking hands Lana put the letter back in the envelope, then pulled it out and read it again. What was Carl trying to say? He'd made it plain he wanted to see her again; he felt instinctively that she was sad underneath her confident manner, and he'd called her his dear. She didn't know what to make of it. But there was a definite shift in the way he expressed himself in this last letter.

What should she do? She'd never hinted she was seeing someone else as it hadn't seemed necessary. But if he knew she was seeing Frank she was convinced he would be hurt, even though Frank was only a friend. As she was to him.

Who was she fooling? What about that kiss? Frank wasn't being merely friendly then. Her face warmed as she remembered how she'd responded to him for a few seconds. His lips had somehow felt right. But seconds later she'd pulled away, as though she was betraying Carl. It was ridiculous. Carl had never voiced anything to her that could possibly be construed as having any serious intent. She was sure any commitment was the last thing Carl would be thinking about. And she couldn't blame him. He was just lonely, that was all. Missing his wife and probably feeling just as guilty that he found another woman attractive.

She shook her head to clear the knots she was tying in her mind. And failed. Maxine hadn't said anything about Carl coming. Was that what she wanted to tell Peter? He'd be so thrilled. She would have loved to have been the one to tell him – to bring the gleam of excitement into Peter's bright blue eyes – eyes the exact colour of his father's.

Stop thinking like this.

But no matter how hard she tried, she couldn't

stop a delicious frisson that Carl would soon be here for more than a couple of hours, and that he was looking forward to seeing her.

She needed to answer his letter immediately. He'd be pleased to know she wasn't going anywhere else for Christmas.

Dear Carl,

I've just received your letter with the good news, and I believe Maxine is at this very minute telling Peter so he will be very happy. I'm here over Christmas but hope to be going home to see my parents early in the New Year, all being well.

I am sure your visit here will be easier than meeting in Bletchley. You will have more time to see your son in a more comfortable setting!

I look forward to seeing you on Christmas Eve. Are you coming by train?

With best wishes,

Lana

She read it through, knowing she'd deliberately asked a question at the end so he would be sure to reply. She admitted to herself that she longed for his letters, even though each one churned up her emotions. Deliberately breaking up such a dangerous line of thought, she went to look for an envelope, then folded the letter and slid it in. She'd post it at lunchtime. He'd get it tomorrow so he'd know she was thinking of him.

She pressed her lips together to stop any more of this nonsense, and reread Geoff's letter.

She caught Reggie as he was pushing his way through the younger children to be first in the dining room for their mid-morning break.

'Reggie!'

He turned, a frown immediately forming.

'Please collect your drink and come to the library. I need to talk to you.'

All heads turned to Reggie.

'What about?' Reggie's tone was, as usual, challenging.

'Just do as I ask,' Lana said. She picked up her own cup and took it to the library, wondering if he would follow.

A couple of minutes later she heard his heavy footsteps as he opened the library door.

'We'll go into the small room,' she said. 'Come and sit down.'

Reggie drank his milk in one go. She thought he was just showing off so didn't make any comment.

'Milk's for babies,' he said when he'd drained the mug noisily and put it back on the table. 'I'd rather have coffee.'

'Milk is better for you – you're still a growing lad.'

'I'm as tall as any man,' Reggie shot back, 'but I've outgrown these clothes.' He stuck a leg forward to show Lana. 'I look ridiculous.'

'Matron is going to sort that out,' Lana said, 'and get you a larger jacket. And I'm going to show you how to tie your tie properly.'

'What's wrong with it?' Reggie's tone had become belligerent.

'You haven't started from the beginning. I can tell you just pulled it over your head exactly as you took it off yesterday – already knotted.'

Reggie narrowed his eyes but said nothing.

'I have two brothers,' Lana said. 'I know about these things.' She looked directly at him. Might as well plunge straight in as was her usual way. 'Reggie, what do you enjoy here?'

'Are you talking about lessons?' He gave a smirk.

'Yes.' Lana ignored the hint of an innuendo.

'Nothing,' Reggie said triumphantly. 'I'm not interested in nothing here.'

She decided now was not the time to correct his grammar. She waited.

'Most kids my age are out working and making money,' he went on.

'This is what I want to talk about. But it would be nice to know what you might like to do in order to *make* the money.'

'I don't care. I just want to earn money and get out of the home. Be with kids my own age. I feel trapped here.'

'But wouldn't it be better if you enjoyed what you were doing to earn the money, instead of being bored stiff and watching the clock all day?'

Reggie shrugged.

'There must be something you really like,' Lana persisted.

Reggie fingered his chin, which showed the first hint of a beard. 'Yeah, there is one thing.'

She looked at him expectantly.

'I've never done nothing like it but I want to learn to cook. I did ask Cook once if I could have a go, but she told me to get out of her kitchen – she was too busy to talk to me.'

'Would you like me to have a word with her?'

'Nah. She made it clear she don't want me.'

'I'm not so sure. If she thought you were serious . . . Not that I'm advocating you do an apprenticeship with her – ideally, you need to be away from the home and out in the world – but it might be a good place to start . . . so you get a little experience, which would hold you in good stead.'

She caught his eye. If he wasn't so belligerent all the time, his expression perpetually surly, he didn't have a bad face. His hair was dark and thick, though he wore far too much Brylcreem, and he had lovely dark brown eyes, although they were narrowed with suspicion at this moment. She made up her mind.

'I'll have a word with Cook.'

'Do what you like, Miss,' Reggie said. He gave her a twisted kind of smile. 'I suppose if she said I could help, she'd at least let me have a cup of coffee.'

Lana told Maxine about her conversation with Reggie.

'I didn't get anywhere when I tried to talk to him once,' Maxine said. She gave Lana a rueful smile. 'I suppose it takes a teacher to understand the more difficult children.'

'The thing is, Maxine, he's no longer a child,' Lana said. 'He has a lot of anger in him, and pent-up energy he needs to release. If he can get really interested in cooking he could get a job in one of the hotels or restaurants in Liverpool. And live in. He's getting to the point where he needs to make his own way. Know he has a future outside these walls.'

'I totally agree,' Maxine said. 'We'll have a word with Bertie.' She looked up. 'Will you or shall I?'

'Maybe best from you as you've known her a lot longer than me.'

'I'll talk to her straightaway.' Maxine paused. 'Actually, why don't I ask her if she's free for ten minutes or so and have her come to the office while you're here, as you were the one who suggested it.'

Five minutes later Bertie was in the office, looking a little flustered.

'Is something the matter, Matron?' she said.

'No, no,' Maxine answered, 'but Lana has a suggestion to make to you and we wondered how you'd feel about it.'

'It's about Reggie,' Lana started.

'What about him?' Bertie said, her ready smile disappearing. 'He's trouble, that one.'

'It's because he's at a loose end,' Lana said. 'He

should be out working by now. He's not interested in his lessons and what he'd really like to do is learn to cook. But when he mentioned it to you once, he said you weren't too happy about it.'

'Not with *his* reputation, I wasn't,' Bertie said firmly. 'He's too familiar by far with the maids, always putting his arm round them when he thinks no one's looking, making them giggle and squeal. I'm not having any nonsense like that going on in my kitchen.'

'What if we tell him you'll give him a chance, but if he gets out of line – cheeks you, or interferes in any way with the maids – he won't be given a second chance? He'll be out.'

'Hmm.' Bertie looked thoughtful. She turned to Lana. 'What would you be expecting from him – and from me, for that matter?'

Lana hid a smile.

'I'd want him to start as a trainee. Everything from the bottom job upwards, but not moving up to the next stage until you are completely satisfied. Maybe learn how to prepare breakfast . . . the porridge and suchlike, so you have an extra half-hour to yourself in the mornings. Help to clean the kitchen after supper. You're always saying you don't have enough help cooking for all of us, so you might find he turns out to be an asset.'

'Maybe.' Bertie didn't look very convinced. 'I can see him trying to take over.'

'If he does, then I give you full permission to deal with him as you wish. But any real problems you know you can come straight to me,' Lana said. 'It might take him a little while to settle in, so there's sure to be a few sparks at the beginning, but I've a feeling he'll end up making the most of the opportunity,' she added. 'And you're always very calm and in control.'

'You don't know what I'm like, hen, when things go haywire,' Bertie said. 'I can lose my temper quick as anyone. I certainly don't need more sparks flying from the likes of Reggie.' She paused and rose to her feet. 'Let me think about it over a cup of tea.' She suddenly smiled her usual cheerful smile. 'That always helps me think straight.'

CHAPTER 34

It was five days to Christmas Eve and the children were in a permanent state of excitement. Lana and the teachers had given them various jobs to keep them occupied and calm them down. The older boys would help Charlie to choose the main tree and carry it into the Great Hall, and anyone who volunteered would make the paper chains and table decorations. This year Maxine decided only children of eight years and younger would be allowed to decorate the second smaller tree, and Lana asked Priscilla if she would supervise them. Everyone would have a turn in Barbara's class to make Christmas cards for Cook, Matron and the teachers – and if they had a special friend.

Lana was concerned that all these preparations would take precedence over the play. The children definitely needed more practice. She decided to have a word with Maxine after breakfast.

'Maxine, do you think we can break up a day before, so we can spend time on the play? We're still not ready, and we need a dress rehearsal so they're used to their costumes on the night.'

'Yes, of course. I'll tell them at break time there'll be

no more classes until the first of January. You'll be the most popular teacher here,' Maxine laughed.

'Can you believe it will be 1944 and still no sign of the war ending?' Lana said soberly. 'Every time there's a piece of good news you think it might be coming to an end, but it never is.'

She brushed away the thought of Carl still having to work as a prisoner of war, even though the British were apparently pleased to have him on their side. What must it be like for him? She tried to imagine it the other way round. That she was in another country doing her best, yet knowing she wasn't really accepted, and longing to get back to where she felt she belonged.

'Doesn't seem possible, does it?' Maxine agreed.

'Do you think you'll see Crofton over Christmas?'

Maxine shook her head and her eyes were moist when she looked at Lana.

'I've no idea. He hopes so, but there's never any guarantee of anything.' She suddenly smiled. 'We're getting maudlin and it's Christmas, and I'm determined the children are going to have the best Christmas ever.'

'Did you know Reggie has made the Christmas puddings?'

'Really.' Maxine's eyes were wide. 'I thought Bertie did them months ago.'

'No, she couldn't. She said dried fruit was in really short supply so she's had to leave it more or less until the last minute so she could save enough coupons.'

'Well, well.' Maxine grinned. 'Seems you might have been instrumental in changing the lad after all.'

'More Bertie than me,' Lana chuckled. 'I certainly noticed a difference when I put my head in the kitchen door the other day when he was making them. He barely looked up, he was so engrossed. And Bertie was busy, seeming to let him get on with it, though I'm sure she has her usual beady eye open at all times.'

'What about Ethel and Beth?'

'They were just getting on with peeling the vegetables and washing up. All was humming.'

'That's incredible.' Maxine wrote a few lines on her pad. 'I shall be sending in my monthly report to Mr Clarke telling him this latest. I think he'll be as astonished as I am.' She looked up. 'By the way, how's Priscilla these days?'

'We make sure we keep her busy,' Lana answered. 'And I know she's enjoying her part of Nancy in the play. Did you know she has the most beautiful singing voice?'

'No, I didn't,' Maxine said. 'How wonderful.'

'The other children actually stop muttering in the background when she starts to sing. I can't wait for you to hear her.'

'I'm looking forward to it,' Maxine said. 'It will make a lovely change for Christmas Eve.' She caught Lana's eye. 'I keep meaning to tell you, Lana, that the powers that be are allowing Carl to come and see us over Christmas.'

'Yes, I had a note from him telling me.' Lana somehow managed to keep her voice steady.

'They must really trust him,' Maxine remarked.

'I think they must.'

Lana quickly made an excuse to leave Maxine's office. She thought she might give herself away if she stayed a moment longer.

Bingham Hall was buzzing with children's chatter and giggles as they decorated the two trees or sat at tables making paper chains, handing the streamers one by one to Lana and Athena, who were balancing on ladders, to decorate the ceilings. Meanwhile, Barbara was busy with last-minute touches to the props and costumes for the play.

The dress rehearsal on the twenty-third, the day before they were to perform, was another disaster. Even some of the girls forgot their lines, too busy admiring their own and each other's costumes and giggling. The boys, who'd finally been improving, had dropped right back and Lana and Athena were beside themselves trying to instil in them how important it was not to muck about, but to concentrate.

Lana banged loudly on the small table where she and Athena, joined by Barbara at the last minute, were watching. Priscilla and Pamela jumped.

'We're on the stage tomorrow evening, Christmas Eve,' Lana said when they finally fell silent. 'Some of you are consistently good, and I want to say a very big thank you, but others have slipped backwards. This is the last chance we'll get to make this right. So I want to run it one more time. And concentrate – *all* of you. Some of you are leaving it too long between one child's lines and your own. So then I think you've forgotten to come in.' There was some muttering and Lana clapped her hands. 'No more talking,' she said, 'unless you have any questions.' Her eyes swept round the group. 'Anyone?'

'Please, Miss, I want to go to the lav.'

'Betsy, you must remember tomorrow night – and all of you – that you go to the lavatory half an hour before the performance. You can't suddenly break off in the middle of the play or the audience will think you're a proper baby. And I know you're not,' she added hurriedly when she saw Betsy's mouth turn down at the corners. She looked at her watch. 'Let's have a break for ten minutes and then be back here promptly.'

The second run-through was better, but Alan and Bobby were still muddling their lines, and Doris and Daisy got the giggles at a poignant moment when Peter had to ask for more porridge. Lana sighed. They were tired. She must remember they were only children with difficult backgrounds. None of them was going home to a warm and loving family, no matter how hard Maxine and the others tried to give them affection. It wasn't the same as having a loving mother and father as she herself had. She must always remember how lucky she was and not be hard on the children.

'Much *much* better,'she smiled, after she and Athena and Barbara had finished clapping. Most of the children grinned back. 'Thank you, everyone. Cook has cocoa for you as a special treat in the kitchen. Change out of your costumes and then run along and we'll see you tomorrow. Be here in your costumes at four o'clock. If anyone needs help, the three of us will be close by.'

Later that evening in bed, Lana admitted she'd wanted to impress Carl at the play she and Athena had written, and show him how they'd coached his son as the star of the show. She felt a flicker of shame that she'd been mostly upset for her own sake – her own vanity – which was making the children fractious. What did it really matter if they weren't word perfect? But she couldn't help thinking that Peter wouldn't let her down.

But as she snuggled under the covers, she admitted something else. It wasn't just Peter she was thinking of.

Lana slept fitfully. Every time she awoke only another hour had passed. Her mind buzzed. What time would he arrive? He knew the play was starting at five o'clock. Maybe he'd be here for dinner. If so, where would Maxine seat him? Telling herself not to be such a fool she closed her eyes again, willing sleep.

Then Frank popped into her head. She'd not meant to say anything to him about the play when they last met, but somehow it had slipped out. 'It sounds wonderful,' he'd said. 'Do you think your matron would allow me to come and watch it?' How mean she'd felt when she'd quickly replied that it wouldn't be allowed – it was only for the inhabitants of Bingham Hall. He'd looked so hurt she'd felt a stab of guilt. Still did.

When the hands on her bedside clock showed twenty-five past five, Lana gave up. It was Christmas Eve after all. Throwing back the bedcovers she rushed to the mottled mirror over the washbasin. Yes, just as she thought. Her eyes, feeling full of grit, were pink. What a picture she would present. Heart sinking, she ran her hands through her wavy red hair. To her critical eyes it appeared lank and dull.

She sighed and went downstairs.

After breakfast, as the children were spilling out of the dining room, Priscilla came up to her.

'Miss Ashwin, I wanted to ask you something – did you invite Mr Drummond to our play this afternoon?'

Lana was so taken aback she could hardly look at Priscilla's upturned anxious face.

'I don't think he'd be interested,' she said.

'Oh, he would, I know he would,' Priscilla persisted. 'And he'd like to see Rupert. And Rupert would be pleased to see him.'

'Maybe not,' Lana said, desperate to put the child off. 'Rupert might very well think Mr Drummond had come to take him back to the clinic.'

'Oh, I hadn't thought of that.' Priscilla fiddled

with one of her plaits. 'It would have been nice to see him, that's all . . .' She gave Lana a sly look. 'Besides, I think he likes you . . . in fact, *more* than likes you,' she added, tossing the pigtail back in position and sending Lana a mischievous grin.

'He's a very nice man and I like him too, but don't start any matchmaking, Priscilla,' Lana said in a firm voice, though her heart was thumping uncomfortably. Who else thought the same? Was there no privacy to be had at Bingham Hall? 'No more of that nonsense, do you hear?'

'If you say so, Miss Ashwin,' Priscilla said, looking contrite, but Lana could tell the child didn't believe a word.

Then something struck her. She'd never seen the usually solemn girl give such a wicked-looking grin. Lana couldn't help smiling. If Priscilla thought that Frank more than liked her, and even teased her about it, then Lana wasn't going to argue. Priscilla was behaving much more like a normal girl of her age. And that was a miracle.

Later that day, she came across Priscilla in the playroom reading when she was meant to be keeping an eye on the younger ones.

'What are you reading, Priscilla?'

Priscilla snapped the book shut. 'Nothing,' she mumbled, her face flushed. 'Just something one of the maids left lying around.'

Lana stretched out her hand and Priscilla

361

wordlessly gave it to her. The paper jacket showed a painted picture of a woman with long blonde hair in a fashionable roll at the front, and a man's dark head behind her. *The Heart Remembers*.

'All the library has are books written by people who've been dead hundreds of years,' Priscilla said defensively.

Priscilla was growing up, Lana mused, and needed to be treated less like one of the children. She'd take her to the library in Liverpool next time she went in.

Lana had asked Maxine if they could lay the tables up for dinner first thing in the morning so the Christmas table decorations would make a festive splash throughout the day.

'Good idea,' Maxine said. 'It's never too soon to start Christmas.' She looked at Lana with a glint in her eye. 'And if Herr Best arrives early I'm sure he'd appreciate the trouble you've gone to.' She gave Lana a saucy wink.

'Maxine, stop it!' Lana gave the young matron a mock glare. 'It's bad enough with Priscilla trying to match me with Frank Drummond.'

'Oh? Do tell.' Maxine's smile was wide.

'Nothing really. She wanted to know if we'd invited him. I told her we hadn't, and she was disappointed. Then she said, "I think he likes you." Then added, "*More* than likes you."'

'It must be a good feeling to be so much in demand.' Maxine grinned. 'Seriously, we should have invited Frank. He's such a nice chap. And he'd probably liked to have seen if Rupert was settled in.'

'That was Priscilla's argument.'

Oh, what had she started? She'd now have to explain to Maxine that it would be a bad idea with Carl in the audience. But why should it be? He was a father wanting to see his son in a play. Nothing unusual about that. But she knew in her heart he was also coming to see *her*.

The front doorbell rang and Lana's pulse began to race. It was him. How wonderful he was early. He must have started out at dawn. It rang again.

'Doesn't sound as though anyone's around,' she said, her voice shaking. 'I'd better answer it.'

She sprang to her feet and hurried to the Great Hall. Heaving the door open she was about to greet him when the smile of welcome died on her lips.

'May I come in?'

For a few seconds, Lana couldn't think who the woman was.

'Celia Daniels, the midwife, if you remember.'

'Oh, of course.' Somehow Lana remembered her manners. 'Do come in.' A flood of disappointment enveloped her as she held the door wide.

Celia Daniels stepped, or rather tottered, into the Great Hall on high heels – not the most practical in the heavy rain. She shook out her umbrella and Lana pointed to the umbrella stand.

'Have you come to see Matron?' Lana asked.

'You *and* Matron,' Celia Daniels said unexpectedly.

'Do take a seat,' Lana said, 'and I'll see if she's free.'

Lana put her head in the door of Maxine's office. 'Maxine, it's Celia Daniels – you know, the midwife who came when the twins were left here.'

Maxine rolled her eyes. 'What on earth does she want?'

'She'd like to see both of us for a few minutes.'

Celia Daniels was impatiently tapping her stiletto on the stone slab floor. She looked up with raised eyebrow as Lana approached her.

'Yes, Matron can see you. Would you like to follow me?'

'Do take that wet raincoat off, Mrs Daniels,' Maxine said as they entered the office.

'Celia, please,' the midwife said, a false note sounding in her apparent friendly request. She removed her coat and handed it to Lana without even looking at her.

'I expect you're wondering why I'm here,' she said, 'but I thought I should update you on the twins.' Without waiting for their reply, she went on, 'They were obviously taken care of in the babies' ward, but it was touch and go for a few weeks – they were so tiny. Premature, of course, but they can do so much more these days for prem babies. And I'm pleased to tell you that they have now put on a little weight and are out of the incubators.'

'That's marvellous news,' Lana said, watching her friend. Maxine had suddenly gone quiet. 'It was very kind of you to come and tell us.'

Celia gave an imperious nod. 'They should be ready for adoption in another month or two,' she said. 'Let's hope someone will take them both. It would be a pity to split them up.'

Lana stole a glance at Maxine whose eyes were brimming with tears.

'Well, thank you again for letting us know,' Lana said. 'We appreciate your trouble—'

'Oh, that's not the only reason I'm here,' Celia interrupted, then opened her handbag and took out a silver cigarette case. She flipped open the lid.

'Cigarette, anyone?' She waved the case vaguely in the air.

Lana shook her head but Maxine spoke firmly.

'I'm sorry, Celia, but I don't allow smoking in my office – only in the common room.'

'Well, we can go to the common room.'

'I'm afraid not. The room is reserved for the staff only.'

'Actually, I wanted to speak to Lana in private.'

Maxine's eyes widened, but she immediately rose to her feet. 'I've plenty to get on with so you can talk here in my office.' She disappeared.

Why did the woman want to talk to her in private, Lana wondered. It didn't make any sense. She gave her a surreptitious glance. There was no way on earth she would ever have guessed Celia

Daniels was a midwife if she hadn't seen her in action a few weeks ago. Today she was wearing a very smart frock, and her hair and make-up made her look more like a mannequin than someone in the nursing profession. She wondered if Maxine thought the same. Then Lana's curiosity waned and she wanted to get this conversation over with and see the woman out of the door before Carl arrived. She swivelled her chair round so she had a better view of Celia.

'What did you want to talk about?' she prompted.

'Actually, it's about Frank.'

Lana gave a start of surprise.

'Frank Drummond, the vet?' she said, feeling her neck grow warm, knowing full well who Celia was referring to.

'The very one.' Celia crossed her legs and gave Lana a pointed look. 'I gather you've been seeing him.'

'Excuse me, but—'

'Oh, no, don't start that about it being none of my business.' Celia folded her arms in front of her. 'He's told me about this play or whatever nonsense you're doing this afternoon—'

'I wouldn't call it nonsense,' Lana said defensively, thanking her stars she was keeping very calm. Why on earth was the woman talking about the play? 'The children are enjoying it immensely and that's what counts, I would have thought.'

'He seems quite put out not to have been invited. I can't understand why, mind you.'

'The play isn't for the general public,' Lana said, now seething. 'It's for the children's own entertainment, and the staff or any parents to attend.'

'I thought they were orphans here.'

'No,' Lana corrected her. 'Not completely. We still have a couple of evacuees, and we have a child with a father in the military.' She brushed Carl's image away. 'I'm sorry but I still don't understand why you're here talking to me about Frank. If he's upset with me he can tell me himself. He doesn't need anyone to stick up for him.'

'Oh, but he does,' Celia said, looking at Lana directly in the eye. 'He wouldn't dream of saying anything to you about how hurt he was. But he did to me. He knows he can tell me anything. I've always been a good friend to him. And it *is* my business how Frank is treated. I don't want to have him upset at all by anyone. You see . . . I love him. And I believe he loves *me*, even though he probably doesn't know it yet and believes he has feelings for someone else . . . *you*.'

Lana swallowed in astonishment. Celia's name had never come up in any of their conversations. She stared back at Celia, whose unusual dark eyes burned into hers.

'You've come all this way for nothing,' Lana said, getting up, 'although it was good to know the babies are doing well, but I realise now that it was just an excuse to tell me to lay off Frank.' She drew in a sharp breath. 'But I believe at thirty-one I'm old enough to choose my own friends, and yes, even to choose whom I fall in love with, without asking anybody's permission. And I also believe Frank is old enough to fend for himself.' She held Celia's surprised gaze. 'I'll see you out, Mrs Daniels.'

As soon as Lana closed the door on Celia Daniels, she breathed out a long sigh. She could feel herself getting hot with the temper she'd fought to control rising again. Who did Celia Daniels think she was, to come here and tell her who and who not to like?

But was there a tiny grain of truth in Celia's words? Lana asked herself when she went upstairs to her room to clean her teeth. If she was absolutely honest, she deliberately hadn't invited Frank to the play because there'd been a possibility that Carl might be able to come. She wasn't in love with Frank, no, but she enjoyed his company very much. Their banter together always lightened her mood when things got difficult at the home with one or more of the children and she always felt perfectly at ease with him – a feeling she had to admit she didn't often have with Carl. Enigmatic was the word she'd use to describe *him*. And his face – his beautifully cut features, the startling blue eyes, full of expression and love when his attention was on his son – that was what entranced her.

But Frank was completely different. He was a wonderful friend. So why hadn't she been candid with Celia? Told her point blank she wasn't in love with the vet?

'It was her whole attitude,' Lana muttered crossly. 'As though she had a right to tell me to back off. If Frank's unhappy with our arrangement he can jolly well tell me himself.'

With the mean thought that she hadn't assured Celia she wasn't in love with Frank because she privately thought he deserved better, Lana hurried down the stairs.

CHAPTER 35

Lana didn't get a chance to tell Maxine what had transpired between her and Celia Daniels because the matron was endeavouring to do the last-minute touches to make the library ready for the play.

Lana looked at her watch. If Carl didn't come soon he'd be in danger of missing the play. The children were to congregate half an hour before it began so Barbara and Maxine could check the outfits and Athena could take her position as 'prompt' in case anyone forgot their lines.

When the doorbell finally went it made Lana jump. She wanted to answer the door herself but Ethel beat her to it.

'Carl Best,' she heard him say in his distinctive voice, making her heart miss a beat. 'I believe I am expected.'

'Do come in, Mr Best. I'll let Matron know you're here. She's arranged your room on the fourth floor,' Ethel said, in a nervous but curious tone. 'Charlie will help with your luggage.'

'Oh, no, I can manage very well,' she heard Carl say.

Lana stepped into the hall and immediately Carl broke into a smile.

'Ah, Miss Ashwin,' he said, coming forward. 'I hope I'm not late.'

'You're exactly on time.' Lana returned his smile, wishing with all her heart that Ethel would disappear – that no children's feet would come pounding down the stairs.

'Shall I show you your room, Mr Best?' Ethel offered.

'That's all right, Ethel,' Lana said swiftly. 'I'll show Mr Best.'

'As you wish, Miss.' Ethel gave a bob of her head as she made towards the kitchen to giggle with one of the maids, no doubt, Lana thought crossly.

'Was it a difficult journey?' Lana asked, desperate to sound normal even though her heart was banging against her ribcage.

'Not so bad,' Carl said, as they walked up the staircase. 'A couple of stops unaccounted for.'

'Have you eaten?'

'Yes, thank you,' he said. 'But I would enjoy an English cup of tea.' He smiled at her and she thought her heart would melt.

'I'll see you have one as soon as you're settled,' she smiled back.

'And how is my son?'

'You'll see him in about three-quarters of an hour. I think . . . I hope you will be surprised at how he's changed.'

'We hope for the better,' Carl said seriously.

'Oh, yes, it's definitely for the better.' She had to turn away from the intensity of his gaze.

She could feel herself making aimless conversation the nearer they got to his room. They were on the last flight to the fourth floor. Maxine said he was to have June's old bedroom, and Lana hadn't seen it, though she could well imagine it would be a little old-fashioned.

This was the room Carl was to have for the next two nights. Lana's pulse raced as she turned the handle. It was locked. She'd forgotten to ask Ethel for the key. He'd think she was stupid.

'I don't have the key,' she said, turning towards him. She was close. She could smell the scent of him. A clean smell, but slightly musky. It made her senses reel.

He looked down at her, his expression serious. 'I will wait for you,' he said.

With flushing cheeks she ran down the stairs.

She was a little breathless by the time she hurried back up the four flights. Her heart almost stopped to see Carl on the top landing – it was like a mirage. Telling herself not to be so stupid she pulled her stomach in tightly to steady her nerves, and brushing past him she turned the key.

With relief she noticed the room was neat and clean. Someone had put a couple of apples and a few walnuts with a nutcracker, and even an orange, in a glass bowl on a crisp white runner on top of the chest of drawers. Beside it stood a jug of water complete with a little beaded crocheted cover. She glanced at the washbasin which was also spotless, though it had a slight crack. But at least the house-maid had taken some trouble for their guest.

'Do you think you'll be comfortable?' she said as he followed her in and set his bag down.

'Quite comfortable, thank you, Lana.'

He made her name sound special and she swallowed.

'The play will be starting very soon,' she said. 'You'll just have time for a cup of tea before you take a seat.'

'Will I be allowed to sit next to you?'

'I-I'm not sure. I think Maxine and Athena are arranging the seats.'

'We will hope so,' Carl said. He seemed to hesitate. Then he stepped forward and held both her arms. 'Lana, I'm so pleased to see you. To be here. I am longing to see my son, but I am so happy you will be here.'

'I'm glad, too,' she said, smiling at him, feeling shaky as he gently pressed his fingers on her arms.

He bent his head down and for a mad moment she thought he would kiss her. She didn't know what to do. She wanted him to kiss her more than anything, but it wasn't right. He'd only found out about his wife a few months ago. And he was a prisoner of war. Besides, Peter needed him. And he was German – no matter whose side he was on, nothing could alter that fact. These jumbled thoughts flew round her head, throwing her into confusion.

She felt his breath on her face.

'Lana . . .'

'I think we should go downstairs,' she said, averting her gaze. If she stood there one moment longer she would fold herself in his arms, hold him to her, feel the warmth of him. She felt the heat rush through her. If he had an inkling as to what she was thinking . . .

She saw the disappointment in his eyes, but only for a fleeting moment. Then he smiled and released her gently. 'You are right. We must go.'

Even by the time they'd reached the Great Hall, she could still feel the imprint of his fingers through her blouse to her skin. 'I'll go and organise that cup of tea,' she said, unable to hide the tremor from her voice.

Without giving him time to answer she rushed to the kitchen. Only Reggie was present, stirring something on the stove.

'Reggie, we have a visitor. Would you mind doing tea for the two of us?'

'I wouldn't do it for anyone else, Miss Ashwin.' Reggie turned and grinned. 'But as it's you . . .'

'Thank you, Reggie,' Lana said firmly.

'Oh, Reggie, make that three cups,' Maxine said, coming into the kitchen. 'In fact, four. Miss Graham's probably dying for one as well.' She looked at Lana and grinned. 'I see our handsome Herr Best has arrived. Why have you left him on his own in the hall?'

'Only until I give him a cup of tea,' Lana said

a little defensively, then saw the twinkle in Maxine's eyes. It was all going to be all right. She was sure.

Maxine turned to Reggie. 'Can you bring the tray into the library, Reggie? We've just got a quarter of an hour before the play starts.'

The boy nodded. 'You go on, Matron. I'll bring everything.'

Lana was glad Maxine was with her when they stepped into the hall. Carl immediately stood up and Maxine extended her hand.

'It's very nice to see you again, Mr Best,' she said. 'Why don't we all go in.'

'I've put you both on the front row,' Maxine told Carl, 'so Peter can see you. Athena and I will sit on the side to make sure everyone is where they're supposed to be and prompt anyone who forgets their lines.'

Lana took her seat beside Carl, hoping Peter wouldn't get so excited to see his father that it would put him off. She hugged herself. He'd be fine. She was sure of it. As though Carl was aware of her thoughts he lightly touched her hand and smiled.

'It is like going to the theatre,' he said.

'Even better,' Lana returned, 'with your son in the starring rôle.'

He pressed her hand.

Maxine came to stand in front of the audience of children, almost all the staff, and a handful of adults Lana didn't recognise.

'I'd like to give a warm welcome to our visitors

today,' Maxine said, dropping her eyes to the front row and smiling at Carl. 'We do hope you enjoy the play with music, which Miss Ashwin and Miss Graham have written especially for the children. You'll recognise where it's taken from, but this version is . . .' She paused. 'Well, you'll soon see. But please keep in mind that this is their very first performance, though we hope it won't be their last.'

The children who were not in the play clapped, and Carl joined in, turning to Lana with a smile. She felt almost too overwhelmed to react but managed to give a few feeble claps.

Peter was the first one to appear. He wasn't dressed any differently from usual, though Athena had dirtied his face and knees and ruffled up his usual beautifully groomed little chestnut-brown head. His face nearly split in two when he spotted his father. Carl held up a cautionary hand and Peter nodded, waiting for the other children to join him. Lana, with the help of Priscilla, had written the words of most of the songs and Athena had set them to music. When the children were all grouped around Peter who held out a bowl, they began to sing:

'Please, sir, he wants some more,
Oliver wants some more,
He'd ask you himself but he's much too
   shy,
For he knows you'll be cross, which will
   make us cry,
Please, sir, give Oliver some more.'

Lana sat quite entranced. The children were all playing their parts beautifully. Betsy did a solo dance with a couple of cartwheels to end her performance and the audience clapped her loudly. The child gave them a big grin, and a hurried bow, and practically bounced off the stage.

Lana straightened up in her seat when an adult-sized person appeared. Where was Alan? He was supposed to have taken over as Fagin when Reggie had acted up that time. But here was Reggie, large as life, grinning from ear to ear, dressed in a long shabby coat and a pointed hat like a witch's, opening his mouth to sing his special song to the children, to keep them under his roof so he could live off them.

She couldn't help smiling as Reggie caught her eye. Then he went into full singing mode, and danced with the children, telling them they had to stay with him as he would always see they had food on the table so long as they brought him a steady supply of stolen goods. When had he managed to rehearse all this? Peter looked as though he was enjoying himself interacting with the others – so different from usual. She stole a sideways glance at Carl. His attention was fixed on the play, on his son. It was so good to see. It was what Peter desperately needed. His father's love and attention. She had to be careful not to allow her feelings to show where Carl was concerned. Peter needed him so much more. She blinked back the tears and Carl touched her hand for the briefest of moments. She took in a shaky breath and allowed herself to become immersed in the play again.

Now Priscilla came to the front of the chalk line, which Lana had drawn to mark the edge of the stage. As Nancy in the play, Priscilla was looking quite grown up with her hair loose and wearing a full skirt Maxine had cut down from a donated one. She stood calmly waiting for her introduction.

Nancy began her song of lost love, sung with such power and emotion in her crystal-clear voice that Lana felt goose pimples crawl up her arms and her eyes fill. Priscilla had endured such sadness in her young life and here she was pouring everything into the song.

When Nancy's final note died the children jumped up, clapping and shouting Priscilla's name. Lana couldn't help noticing how the play had brought out the very best in the young girl, giving her confidence and showing off her angelic voice. As Priscilla stood on the makeshift stage, keeping in character with her eyes downcast, Lana glowed with pride. Then she grinned. The one who had truly broken through Priscilla's shell had just strolled into the library. He padded softly to the front row where, to the amusement of everyone, including the children performing, he jumped straight onto Lana's lap. Carl turned to give her a startled look and frowned, which made Lana want to giggle. Rupert began to purr loudly, digging his claws up and down before he settled, and Lana bit her tongue to stop herself from laughing. Carl obviously didn't approve of Rupert's interruption. It flashed across her mind that Frank would have roared with laughter.

There was another ten minutes where the children pretended to steal from Alan who was dressed in long trousers and a man's jacket like a man on the street, and Charlie who played an old man who had no idea what was happening when the twins, Doris and Daisy, delved into his pockets and brought out an old scarf and a bag of coins.

Cheers and clapping rang in Lana's ears as Rupert jumped from her lap and she and Carl stood to leave. A flying figure ran towards them.

'Papa,' Peter said, for a split second giving his father a hug, then drawing back and extending his hand for a handshake instead. 'I'm so happy you came. Did you like the play?'

'I loved it,' Carl said, smiling. 'And you've become taller since last time I saw you. A real young man.'

Peter's face broke into a grin. 'Rupert enjoyed it, too,' he said. 'Did you see him, Papa?' Carl nodded, his smile fading a little. 'Papa, Matron said you can come and have tea in the dining room with all of us at the end of the play.' He got hold of his father's arm. 'Come with me, Papa, and I'll show you where it is.'

With only the briefest apologetic backwards glance to Lana, Carl allowed himself to be led away.

Which is how it should be, Lana told herself

briskly. She sniffed and opened her bag for a handkerchief when Priscilla came to her side.

'Miss Ashwin,' she said, 'are you quite well?'

'Yes, I am,' Lana said, smiling at the child. 'I'm hoping I haven't got a cold coming.' She put her arm round Priscilla. 'I just want to tell you how proud I am of you, love. You have a wonderful voice and the audience gave you a standing ovation.'

'They did, didn't they?' Priscilla's eyes were shining with excitement.

'They did.' Lana looked at her fondly. 'Shall we go to the dining room and have a cup of tea and a slice of Cook's fruit cake.'

'A perfect end to a nearly perfect day,' Priscilla said.

Lana knew exactly what Priscilla meant.

Maxine had told all the younger children they had to have a nap in the afternoon as they would be allowed to stay up later than usual. Peter grumbled he was too old to go to bed like a baby, but he went off obediently with the others.

'You'll be here when I get up?' he asked his father, anxiety coating the words.

'Yes, Peter, your papa will be here. I am here for two days.'

'All older kids not going for a nap can come with me to the art room,' Barbara announced as she and Lana were in the Great Hall. She glanced at Lana and grinned. 'You can leave me with them,

Lana,' she said, 'so you can entertain our guest.' She sent Lana a huge wink.

Lana nodded as though it were the most natural thing in the world to be given the freedom to entertain a German prisoner of war. Her nerves were beginning to get the better of her. In the old days she had always enjoyed Dickie's teasing, but nowadays she seemed to become embarrassed at the slighted provocation. What on earth was the matter with her? She was behaving like a seventeen-year-old.

She waited while the children followed Barbara, their shouts and giggles fading as they went up the staircase and into the studio. She turned to Carl. The safest thing would be to go for a walk. She needed some fresh air anyway to cool her cheeks.

'May we walk outside?' Carl said.

It was so strange how he often seemed to know what she was thinking.

'I had the same idea,' she said, smiling. 'I'll fetch my coat.'

Carl was standing by the oak door when Lana came down the stairs. Her heart turned over at the image. To think he was waiting for *her*.

'Shall I open the door?'

Lana nodded, wanting to slip through before anyone else spotted them and made a comment.

Outside, the cold made her gasp, and Lana pulled her hat down a little, trying to cover the tips of her ears. They walked a couple of feet apart, but she could feel the vigour of him so strongly, her shoulder might have been touching his. As though he knew, he glanced at her.

'Are you warm enough?'

'I have been warmer,' she said, smiling, the cold wind biting her cheeks.

They were walking down the drive, through the avenue of lime trees, bereft now of their leaves. She tripped over a root and would have fallen if he hadn't shot out his arm to steady her. A quiver ran along her spine and she wondered if he thought she'd tripped on purpose. She wanted to tell him she would never play silly little games like that, but she didn't say anything because it would give it more attention than it deserved.

They came to the road in silence. His hand was still under her elbow. It felt strange cupped in his hand. How she longed to simply put her hand in his. Before she could think what she was doing she stepped off the main drive and into the light woodland at one side, then stopped. Carl stopped abruptly with her, and with one movement had pulled her into his arms. His lips found hers – gently at first, then he was holding her tight to his chest, his mouth firm now, pressing deeper. She felt the tip of his tongue and moaned.

'Lana. Oh, my darling. I want you so.'

'I want you, too.' She could hardly speak. She was a woman who had fought against loving this man, but now it was too late. He'd kissed her. And she wanted more of his kisses. She looked up at him. There were no words to tell him she was crazily, madly in love with him.

'I love you,' he said.

Lana drew back, startled. He'd said the words she'd been about to say. Everything had changed now. Nothing would ever be the same. She stared up at his face, so alive with passion. She suddenly felt ashamed of the anger she'd nursed for so long against anyone or anything German, but thank goodness this man had shown her that there were still honest, decent Germans.

'Lana, please say something – even if it's something I do not want to hear.'

'I love you, too.'

'That is all I need.' He bent his head down and kissed her again and she clung to him, ripples of pleasure coursing through her body.

Breathless, she finally pulled away and tried to smile but the muscles in her face seemed to have frozen. She felt something trickle down her cheek. Carl kissed her eyelids.

'Do not cry, my darling,' he whispered. 'Everything is going to be all right.' He kissed an inch of flesh on her neck where her scarf had come askew, and then his mouth found hers again and she gave herself up to him.

'We must go back,' she said, finally. 'They'll be wondering what has happened to us.'

Carl gave her a wry smile. 'I am wondering the same thing.'

⋆　⋆　⋆

They didn't speak as they made their way back up the drive, yet Lana was sure Carl was feeling the same turmoil she was experiencing. Now and again she glanced at him but he was resolutely staring ahead, as though he needed to focus on something ordinary because of the extraordinary things they had just told one another. She badly wanted to keep in close contact with him, but she knew she mustn't reach for his hand with any prying eyes staring at them through the windows as Bingham Hall came in sight.

Just as she reached for the bell cord, Carl turned to her and said, 'Lana, never forget what I have told you just now. Whatever happens to us – will you always remember?'

His gaze was imploring. He seemed to be uncertain about the outcome of their love. She tried to brush the idea away. She'd thought the same so many times. There were so many obstacles and maybe Carl thought there would just be too many to overcome. She wouldn't think about it now. He was only here for a little longer than a day and she didn't want to spoil the time they had – precious because it was so short. And Peter must be given the attention he craved from his father.

Once inside they'd have to pretend they'd only been discussing Peter. They must never raise any suspicion with the staff, or even Peter, that there was anything more between them.

'I'll never forget,' Lana said, softly, as she looked into those dazzling blue eyes.

He quickly pressed her hand and gave a smile but it was almost perfunctory.

Lana's head buzzed. The war was doing terrible things. Making people act abnormally, leap to unwise decisions, and say things that perhaps were best left unsaid. She sighed and pulled the cord.

'I'm going to see if Bertie needs any help,' she said as they stepped inside. 'Maybe I can lay up the tables for supper.' She turned to him. 'Would you like to take Peter into the library where you can spend some time with him on your own?'

'I would like that very much,' Carl said.

Lana was delighted to see Reggie carrying trays to and fro from the kitchen to the dining room, actually looking as though he was enjoying himself by the wide grin he gave her, his tie for once neatly in place. It had worked out so well. Bertie gave a weekly report to Maxine who kept Lana updated, and it seemed the cook found him invaluable.

'He's even learned to respect Rupert,' Bertie told Lana with a twinkle, when she'd asked if she could do anything to help. 'Well, nobody's going to get the better of Rupert, who's allowed Reggie into *his* kitchen. But I know he's taken to Rupert as I've often caught the lad giving him a sneaky piece of meat.'

Lana chuckled, and picked up the tea towel. 'How's he getting on with learning the main courses?'

'He picks it up as though he's been doing it for

two years instead of two weeks,' Bertie said. 'Quite honestly, I don't know what I'd do without him now.'

'I'm so glad,' Lana said, stacking some plates on the dresser. 'Everyone at some point or another needs a helping hand.'

'And how's that Mr Best?' Bertie asked.

Lana warmed just to hear his name and had to sternly remind herself that she must act like a teacher who had merely been giving information to a parent about one of the children.

'He said he enjoyed the play very much,' she said, as steadily as she could muster.

Bertie shot her a look. 'And I believe you and he had a quiet walk together afterwards when the bairns were having a nap.'

Lana gave a start. 'Not much happens that you don't see, Bertie.'

Bertie laughed. 'Och, I'm just teasing you, hen. But I have to admit, he's a very handsome man. He must have had all the ladies swooning over him in Germany.'

Somehow Lana didn't like that image at all. She needed to change the subject, but before she could think of something to direct Bertie's mind in another direction, the cook said in an unexpectedly serious tone, 'Lana, pet, be careful.'

'I don't know what you mean,' Lana said, not daring to look at Bertie.

'I think you do, hen. I really think you do.'

CHAPTER 36

Bertie's words, which Lana was sure were meant to be a warning not to get too deeply involved with Carl, whirled in her head as she sat at the same table as Carl and Peter, though several feet away on the opposite side. She couldn't help feeling jealous that Athena had placed herself next to him while she was settling the younger children who were shrieking with excitement that Father Christmas would be here in a few hours' time. Disappointment seeped through her. Once, she saw Carl look her way and catch her eye, then, so quickly she wondered if it had really happened, he'd turned to his son again.

Bertie had produced a delicious Christmas Eve supper with ham and egg sandwiches and blanc-mange and jellies with artificial cream, but Lana had difficulty in swallowing, so conscious was she of Carl. When she dared to steal another glance at him he didn't seem to be enjoying his meal any more than she was. She wondered if it was for the same reason. Of course not, she told herself irritably. He was too wrapped up in Peter to take much notice of what he was eating. She tried to swallow a small piece of ham but it felt like a piece of leather sticking in her throat. She didn't know what to do. It wouldn't go down, but she could hardly try to remove it. She began to cough and grabbed her glass of water, feeling Carl's eyes on her. Somehow she managed to swallow the lump of meat.

She couldn't go on like this. Not one thought was clear in her mind. Nothing made sense to her. Only that she loved this man, but in her heart she knew it was a forbidden love. Tears stung the backs of her eyes. If she wasn't careful she would break down. She felt a tear slide from her eye and quickly brushed it away before anyone noticed. She hadn't banked on Carl. He'd seen her action. Even from where she sat she could tell his eyes, too, were shining unnaturally. She told herself it was because he was overcome with the deep pleasure of having his son by his side. But her heart told her it wasn't only that. Her mouth became dry. She swallowed. It made no difference. She couldn't stay at the table a moment longer. She put both her hands on the table to push herself upright.

She saw Carl glance at her again, but she carefully kept her face averted.

'Is everything all right, Lana?' It was Athena, looking concerned.

'I'm feeling a little under the weather. I didn't sleep much last night but I'll be okay.'

'Are you sure? Do you want me to come with you?'

Now Athena and Carl were both staring at her. Her heart began to race. She had to get away.

'No, really, Athena. It's a bit of a headache. I'll have a lie-down for a while.'

'Shall I send for Dolores?'

'No, no,' Lana said. Nurse Dolores was the last person she wanted fussing round. 'Honestly, I'll be all right.'

'If you're sure.' Athena went back to her meal – and Carl.

Feeling she would pass out at any moment, Lana managed to stumble from the dining room. She put her hand out to steady herself on the hall panelling. Her heart was thumping. Maybe she'd take a cup of tea to her room. And Bertie might find her a couple of biscuits.

But only Reggie and Ethel were in the kitchen.

'Have the others already finished?' Reggie asked, with a surprised tone, when she entered the room.

'No. They're still in the middle of eating. I have a headache so I thought I'd make a cup of tea and take an aspirin.'

'You look white as a sheet, Miss,' Ethel said, folding the tea towel over the oven rail and standing in front of her. 'I'll put the kettle on. You go on upstairs and I'll bring it up to you. You look right done in, Miss, if I may say so.'

That was exactly how she felt – right done in.

Lying on the bed, drifting a little, she reprimanded herself for getting worked up. At this rate she'd make herself ill. Pulling herself off the bed she went to the sink and splashed her face with cold water, then grimaced. She looked awful. Her eyes were hazy, her hair awry. She unpinned it and let it loose. It was Christmas Eve after all. Then she dabbed a little powder on her nose and touched her lips with nearly the last of her precious lipstick. Goodness knew when she'd be able to find another one in the shops. Things were becoming scarcer by the day.

She made herself smile in the mirror and breathed out a sigh that steamed up the glass. Just as well. She pulled the bedroom door behind her and walked downstairs, almost bumping into Carl and Peter who were making their way with the other children to the library for Christmas carols.

'You are not well, Lana?' His voice was deliberately low.

'It was just a headache – it's nearly gone now,' she added untruthfully.

'Then will you come and sit by Peter and me?' She nodded.

Charlie and Harold had set the tree in one corner of the library but well away from the walls so the children could walk round it and admire their efforts. It looked magnificent. Lit with dozens of candles and coloured balls the villagers had given them over the years, the tree glowed, throwing a magical light onto everyone in the room.

Athena was at the piano, flipping over the music book propped in front of her. Lana spotted four seats at the back, which she preferred. She led the way over, Carl and Peter following, and Peter talking nineteen to the dozen with his father. A warm feeling stole round Lana's heart. Little Peter was happier and more contented-looking than she had ever seen him. Carl sat down with Peter on his left and Lana took the seat on his right.

Where was Priscilla? Lana stood up and looked round before she saw her in the doorway looking wildly for a seat. She gestured for her to join them and the child gave a relieved smile as she made her way to the last empty seat on Lana's right.

Maxine stood and announced that there would be carols and that if any child would like to sing a carol on their own, to please tell her. No one volunteered.

Lana turned to Priscilla. 'Why don't you sing "Once in Royal David's City", and we'll all join in on the second verse.' Priscilla looked doubtful. 'Come on, Priscilla. We'd love to hear it.'

Priscilla nodded and stood up. As in the play, her voice soared to the top notes effortlessly, like an angel's. The children sang a few more carols with the adults, and Maxine made further announcements about the plans for the following day.

'We shall have Christmas service in our chapel,' she said. 'And then we have the present opening afterwards.'

Doris and Daisy hugged one another in anticipation and Maxine smiled.

To Lana's surprise Carl rose to his feet.

'May I say a word?' he said. His presence was so strong that everyone became silent again. 'I would like to thank Matron for inviting me to Bingham Hall so I could see my son, Peter, this Christmas. You do not know how much it means to me that you have made me feel welcome.' He turned this way and that, smiling. 'And now Peter and I would like to sing for you "O Tannenbaum". The Tannenbaum is a fir tree bringing peace on earth.'

Lana didn't understand the words but the tune was familiar. Carl's voice was rich and confident, giving her goose pimples. As though he knew, Carl brushed his hand against hers when he sat down. It set her pulse racing. There was a silence. And then the children clapped – harder than they ever had. It was just the perfect ending.

'That was wonderful, Mr Best,' Maxine said, smiling, and glancing at Peter. 'And you, Peter. We all enjoyed it very much. And now I would like to wish everyone a very merry Christmas.'

'Merry Christmas,' they all called to one another. 'Merry Christmas.'

Lana noticed that only Priscilla kept her lips firmly pressed together, her hands still clasped in her lap.

'Would you like to come to the common room with us, Carl?' Maxine said, after the children had disappeared to get ready for bed. 'Athena and Barbara are staying on and Kathleen, one of our nurses, who for once isn't on night duty. I thought we'd have a sherry and a chat, if that appeals.'

'Don't turn down the offer of a sherry, Carl.' Athena laughed. 'It happens so rarely at Bingham Hall.'

'I'll drink to that,' Barbara said, chuckling.

'Lana?' Carl turned to her, catching her unawares.

It was the first time he'd said her name in front of others and she desperately hoped no one had noticed. But Maxine had called him Carl. It was Christmas, after all, and it seemed ridiculous with a war on if you had to keep within such boundaries.

'Do you feel well enough?' he asked quietly.

'Yes, that would be lovely.'

Did she mind that the others would be curious about this German and why he was here?

'That is very kind of you,' Carl said, giving the matron a smile. 'I would like that very much if I am not in the way.'

'You're not in the way at all,' Maxine said, smiling back. 'We'll be delighted to have you. I'm afraid you'll be the only man here, but if you can bear it, I'll go and get the sherry and some glasses.'

'Please let me help you with them,' Carl said.

'Thank you,' Maxine said. 'You can come with me to the dining room . . . where we keep anything resembling alcohol under lock and key,' she added, smiling.

Lana's eyes lingered as Carl followed Maxine out of the library. She couldn't believe he'd told her he loved her only a few hours ago. Did she believe him? Of course she did. A serious man like Carl would never give his love lightly.

Her stomach in knots she forced herself to help Athena and Barbara to arrange the chairs in a group, trying to concentrate on their chatter, hoping they didn't expect anything from her. To her ears their words were meaningless and she couldn't have added anything sensible if she'd wanted to.

It wasn't long before Maxine and Carl returned with the sherry and glasses, some crackers and small squares of cheese. Even though she wasn't much of a drinker, Lana couldn't wait to take some sips of the sherry, thinking it would help to dispel her nerves. Carl poured her a glass and handed it to her. She noticed his hand tremble very slightly, which didn't do anything to help calm the turmoil inside her; she couldn't resist gazing up at him. His eyes pierced hers and he seemed to understand though he kept his expression neutral. He turned to finish pouring glasses for the others and soon the six of them were relaxing in their armchairs and savouring the taste.

Lana relished the warmth of the liquid as it slid down the back of her throat.

'Cheers, everyone,' Maxine said, smiling round at the group. 'And a very Happy Christmas.'

'Happy Christmas.' They raised their glasses.

Lana took another sip. She noticed Carl simply hold his glass up and repeat the words but he didn't put it to his lips.

'The last few hours before it becomes a madhouse,' Kathleen said with feeling. She looked at the staff. 'Who's filling the stockings this evening?'

'I've put Lana down for it,' Maxine said with a grin. 'She's not had that pleasure yet.'

'Do you want me to help?' Athena said.

Lana was about to open her mouth and say she'd be delighted when she caught Carl's eye.

'May I help Lana instead?' he said, directing his attention to Maxine. 'It is a long time since I have had my son at Christmas.'

Lana's heart missed a beat. This was becoming a complicated situation and Maxine might read far more into it than she should.

But the matron merely said, 'If it's all right with Lana.'

'It's all right with me,' Lana said, grateful that she managed to get the words out without stuttering. 'Where will I find everything to be given out?'

'All their treats are in boxes in the pantry on one of the back shelves,' Maxine said. 'Give them one of everything. The toys are already wrapped and labelled with their names.'

Lana nodded. 'Okay, what time should we start?'

'Leave it until eleven,' Barbara said, 'to make sure they're well and truly in the land of Nod.' She took the last swallow of her sherry. 'Oh, that was nice,' she said, in a regretful tone. 'I could be tempted with another one but I'm not going to.' She looked at Lana. 'Actually, it's a lot of fun sneaking around, and then when one of the kids wakes up, trying to fool them that you're nothing to do with Father Christmas.' She broke off with a chuckle.

They talked until half past ten when Athena and Kathleen began to yawn.

'I'm calling it a day,' Athena said, rising to her feet.

'Me, too,' Kathleen said, putting her empty glass back on the tray. '*My* day started off with the weekly nits inspection. Not my favourite duty – nor the children's, judging by their shrieks and moans.' She chuckled. 'What about you, Barbara?'

'Yes, I've had enough for one day with all those costume alterations, but I must congratulate the two of you on a great play with very catchy tunes. It went really well and the audience thoroughly enjoyed it.'

'I think they did,' Lana said, happily. 'A few of them were singing along, once they'd caught the melody.'

'I enjoyed it too, very much,' Carl said. 'It was a privilege to see.'

Five minutes later the four women had said their goodnights and Lana and Carl were alone.

'I hope it does not sound rude but I thought they would never go,' he said.

Lana smiled. 'I was thinking exactly the same.'

They chatted a while, mostly about Peter. Then Carl held out his hand.

'Shall we go, then?'

She nodded, and he gently pulled her to her feet.

They found the boxes of treats and toys, and carrying two apiece they made their way to the second floor where the dormitories were.

'Shall we do the girls first?' Lana whispered. 'Give the boys a bit longer to settle.'

Carl nodded and followed her as she carefully turned the handle to the girls' room. Inside, all was silence. The two of them crept round the beds, filling the stockings with the rare treat of an orange, an apple, a soft teddy for Nora, a colouring book and crayons for the twins, Daisy and Doris, a lined notebook and decorated pencil for Pamela, for Betsy a mouth organ (she'd seen one of the boys, Harvey, play one, and had made a loud wish that she'd like one, too), a rag doll with a china face for Megan.

'Last one is Priscilla,' Lana whispered. 'She's got two handkerchiefs from the home, but I've added a bracelet she said she liked when she saw me wearing it once – it was actually when I took her and Peter to meet you that time . . .' She broke off, a little embarrassed as she felt Carl's eyes on her. 'And as she's the eldest I felt she should have something more grown up,' she added, trying to hide her confusion.

'Ah. I think that is good.' Carl tipped a few boiled sweets into the stocking, then went round to place a few in the other girls' stockings.

'I think that's it,' Lana said. 'Let's go and do

the older boys' dorm and finish with the younger ones – where Peter is.'

Twenty minutes later they were filling Peter's stocking. Lana couldn't take her eyes off the way Carl was looking at his son. It seemed to her there was regret, sadness, joy, and a whole range of emotions flitting across his face. As he bent to kiss the sleeping child Peter's eyelids fluttered open and he stared up at his father.

'Papa!'

'Shhhhh.' Carl put a finger to his lips. 'We must not wake the others.'

'Are you Father Christmas?'

'Just this once,' Carl whispered. 'But you must not tell the other children. *Der Weihnachtsmann* had so much to do tonight, I offered to help.'

'You don't need to tell me fairy stories,' Peter whispered back. 'I stopped believing in Father Christmas when I went to stay with Grandma. She told me he wasn't real.'

Carl turned and gave Lana a shrug. She had to bite her lip to stop the giggle that threatened.

'I didn't realise how grown up you are now, Peter,' he said softly. 'And I'm very proud of you. But now it's time for you to close your eyes and go back to sleep.' He kissed him on the forehead, then nodded for Lana to go to the next bed.

What a lovely father he was, Lana thought. He must have been heartbroken having to say goodbye to both his wife and his son, then having to keep his wits about him as he tried to steal information he knew the British would find invaluable. He must be working in a pressured environment, strongly believing that right would prevail. Yet the war was still raging – even worse in the Far East, where she couldn't begin to imagine what conditions the soldiers were living in. She shuddered.

'Lana.' He whispered her name and a quiver zigzagged through her body. 'Is this young man the last?'

'Yes. It's Alan. Let's fill his stocking quickly and go.'

'Don't fall over Rupert,' Lana warned when they were about to climb the next flight. The cat was curled up in a ball on the landing – his favourite sleeping place near Priscilla if he couldn't sneak onto her bed.

'No, I won't.'

On the third-floor landing Lana stopped. They were standing close together now. He was looking at her with a question in his eyes. The brightest blue she'd ever seen. Her own eyes dropped to his mouth. Lips that had kissed her deeply, only hours ago. She wanted to kiss him again. To never stop. Her breath came in short jerky gasps. He drew her into the circle of his arms.

'Lana, how is it possible you are so beautiful?' He held her away from him and his eyes roved over her face.

She tried to laugh it off, but he stopped her.

'You *are* beautiful. I would love to spend the rest of the night with you. But it is not possible here.'

'No, it isn't,' Lana said. 'I think we'd better say goodnight before we regret something.'

She didn't know how she stopped him from kissing her, but she knew if she let him it would be fatal. One kiss and she would allow him to lead her to his bedroom. She fought for control, hating to see the disappointment in his eyes, which only seconds before had held desire.

He hesitated. 'Then I will say goodnight, Lana.'

'Goodnight, Carl.'

She watched as he went up the last flight of stairs and when she heard his door click she unlocked her bedroom door.

Once in bed she could only think of him. Would he be cleaning his teeth at this moment? Folding his clothes neatly? Or would he already be in bed? If so, was he thinking of her as she was of him?

A wave of longing swept over her – a longing so powerful that she was thankful she was lying down. She was thirty-one, for goodness' sake. She'd lived with a man when in her twenties. She'd become engaged to Dickie and they hadn't waited because of the war. So what was the point now to say no to Carl when they loved one another and who knew what was in store with the war going on and on? Who would know if she crept up the last flight of stairs to his room?

CHAPTER 37

She'd forgotten how every step creaked on that last flight of stairs. She forced herself to breathe in slowly to calm her racing heart as she climbed the last few steps to the fourth landing. *His* floor. She was outside his door. Would he be asleep? Or would he at this moment be wondering if she would come to him? She listened for any sounds coming from the maids' rooms.

She thought she could hear him breathing – regularly, as in sleep – but maybe it was her imagination. If one of the maids came out of her room right now, she didn't know what excuse she'd make. Whatever she said, the maid would know differently. She would know exactly what Lana was up to. But all was quiet. She tapped on the door and waited. Biting her lip, she knocked again, a fraction louder.

'Carl, are you awake?' Her voice was barely above a whisper but he'd hear her if he wasn't asleep, she was sure.

She waited a full minute, her heart beating loudly in her ears, still thinking he might come to the door.

But there was no sound within. She tightened her fist and raised it once again. She'd knock much louder this time – he would surely hear it and come to her. But just as her knuckles almost hit the door she let her hand fall, tears springing to her eyes. Carl had made the decision for her. If he hadn't heard her – if he'd been fast asleep – then he'd made it inadvertently. But if he *had* heard her, he was pretending not to have done. He was being the gentleman, protecting her reputation.

She was certain he knew she was standing there.

She was now just as certain that he had made the right decision.

Her knees shook. Her whole body trembled with desire and misery. Gripping hold of the banister to stop herself from pitching forward, Lana crept back down the stairs and into her room. She huddled down into the bed, still warm from the imprint of her body. Gratefully she pulled the blanket up a little further, thankful no one would be any the wiser to her rashness. She lay awake for some minutes, turning one way and then the other, heat rising in her face as she thought how utterly foolish she'd been. Whatever would he think of her? She was finally drifting off when there was a thundering at her door. She shot up in bed, heart hammering. Surely not Carl. Unless there was another fire! Dear God. Jumping out of bed she flung open the door. Priscilla burst in.

'Miss Ashwin! Oh, Miss Ashwin, please help

me.' Tears were pouring down her face, and she was clutching her stomach.

Alarmed, Lana took hold of the trembling girl. 'Come and sit down, love.' She sat her on the edge of the bed. Priscilla's eyes were wide with fear. 'Now tell me what's the matter.'

'I'm dying!'

'Of course you're not. What makes you say that?'

Silently, Priscilla opened her clenched fist to show Lana a bloodied handkerchief.

'I'm bleeding to death,' she choked. 'And my tummy . . . I've got the most awful pains. Please help me.' She began to sob.

Dear God. Hadn't Maxine told the child about her impending monthlies? Or one of the other nurses? She supposed they'd thought Priscilla wasn't old enough yet to learn about the facts of life, but someone should at least have warned her about the changes that would soon occur in her body. Lana sighed and quickly found Priscilla a spare pair of knickers and a Kotex.

'You're not going to die, love. The bleeding is normal and you need to wear this to catch it. Put it in these knickers.' She handed them to Priscilla who looked at the towel with doubt, then turned her back to Lana and did what she was told.

'It happens to me every month,' Lana explained. 'It happens to all women every month.'

Priscilla stopped crying. She was hunched over, holding her stomach. 'I don't understand.'

Lana swallowed. How far should she go in

explaining? Better not go into too much detail, so as not to alarm the girl who, in spite of starting her monthlies, was still a child in many ways.

'Blow your nose, then listen to what I have to tell you. But say nothing to the other girls. They're too young to understand. Their turn will come one day, but tonight, on Christmas Eve, you've become a woman.'

'I'm going downstairs to make you a cup of warm milk and honey,' Lana told Priscilla after she'd explained to the astonished girl about this new development in her body and had given her an aspirin.

It was dark as a dungeon as she gingerly made her way down the stairs. She stood on something soft. There was an angry meow and a loud hiss, then a streak of ginger brushed past her down the stairs with the speed of an arrow.

Poor Rupert! She must have trodden on his tail.

She hurried after him to the kitchen. Switching on the light she found the cat with his back turned to her, licking his front paw and methodically washing his face. Kneeling down she stroked him.

'I'm sorry, Rupert. I didn't see you, it was so dark.'

Rupert allowed her to apologise and stroke him until he began to purr. After pouring some milk into his saucer, she put the rest in a small saucepan and heated it up. When the drink was ready she glanced at Rupert and smiled; he was stretched out on his back in the middle of the kitchen floor fast asleep. But as she turned to switch out the light she banged her thigh hard on the corner of the pine table. Wincing with pain, she almost overbalanced and the milk slopped into the saucer. Cursing under her breath – was this night ever coming to an end? – she grabbed a dishcloth and wiped the saucer dry, then shut the door behind her.

She'd tell Maxine in the morning about Priscilla, and ask if it was possible for her, now she'd started her monthlies, to have her own room for privacy. If Maxine could find somewhere for her, she was sure it would more than make up for Priscilla's scare.

Only when Priscilla was safely tucked up in her own bed and Lana had returned to her bedroom did a terrible thought strike her. What if Carl had answered her knock? What if they'd been in bed together when the terrified girl was trying to reach her for help? She would have gone all over the house searching for her – maybe even raising the alarm. Lana shivered. It was too awful to contemplate. She thanked her lucky stars that Carl had had enough wisdom and common sense for both of them.

The following morning Lana opened her eyes, gritty through lack of sleep. The top of her leg felt sore. Probably the bruise had already come out. She lay there, not wanting to move. Not wanting to face the day – or Carl. A shudder of guilt swept over her as she recalled last night. How she'd sneaked upstairs, the only thing on her mind being to wrap herself in Carl's arms. To spend the night with him.

As Lana talked herself into getting out of bed, she inspected her leg. Yes, there was a big purple bruise. Her punishment.

Carl hadn't shown up for breakfast. Maybe he was taking advantage of not having to get up early to work. Having a lie-in. But she knew that wasn't the reason. He was a man of discipline, routine. Should she go to his room – perfectly legitimately this time – and make sure he was all right? As she was turning to go back upstairs he hurried down the main staircase, a look of concern on his handsome face. Her heart turned over.

'Ah, Lana, there you are.'

'There's still some porridge and toast,' Lana greeted him, desperate to appear normal, 'but it's pretty noisy in there, with the children shouting about the toys they were given and the little extras in their stockings.'

'Have you seen Peter?'

'Yes. He wondered where you were.'

'I was writing you a letter.'

Lana looked at him. He had such a serious expression she felt alarmed.

'Why are you writing to me when you're here?'

He shook his head. 'To explain . . . or try to.'

A small group of children passed between them,

shoving and giggling, clutching their presents tight to their chest as though they would never let them go. Bobby stopped for a moment and turned his head over his shoulder to stare at them. Lana frowned and flicked her hand. The boy sniggered but followed the others into the dining room.

A boy rushed into the hall.

'Papa, where've you been? You were s'posed to come and sit next to me for breakfast.'

'I am sorry, Peter. I expect I was tired from helping *der Weihnachtsmann* last night.' He gave his son a wink.

'But I told you he's not—'

'Peter.' Carl put a hand to his lips. 'Not another word. If the children want to believe in magic you must allow them to do so.' He caught Lana's eye. 'Sometimes magic does happen when you do not even know it is a possibility.'

Lana flushed. 'Why don't you let Peter take you back to the dining room and at least have some toast and tea. And then you can spend as much of the day as possible with him.'

'Can we, Papa?'

'I'd like that very much.' Carl caught Lana's eye. 'Shall we all go for a walk later?'

'I think it should just be you and Peter,' Lana said, knowing she'd said the right thing when Peter's face broke into a beam as he looked up at his father.

★   ★   ★

All through the day there never seemed to be a chance when she could see Carl alone – not even for half an hour. Because the children were on holiday they seemed to be everywhere in the building, including the library, which most of them normally hardly ever bothered about. Finally, Lana asked Maxine if it might be possible for her and Carl to talk in the chapel after the children's service in the afternoon.

Harvey, who played the mouth organ, had asked Peter if he would help him do a jigsaw puzzle, and the two children went off together, Harvey talking non-stop.

'You'd never see that when the Fierce One was in charge,' Kathleen said, laughing as she came out of Maxine's office and watched them.

'She sounded a right dragon,' Lana said with feeling.

'She was a dragon, all right,' Kathleen said. 'Beats me why she wanted to be in charge of an orphanage. I think it was for the power. She made it quite plain she couldn't stand the children. Most of them were scared of her. We all cheered when she left and June Lavender took over.'

The afternoon couldn't come quick enough for Lana. The children had decorated the chapel to look quite festive, setting sprays of artificial flowers and silvered cones, and real holly and mistletoe at the altar. Carl arrived only a minute after her.

He must have been waiting for her to appear, Lana thought, feeling a little light-headed.

'I have a gift for you.' He took from his jacket pocket a small flat box.

'Oh, you shouldn't have. I didn't get you anything.'

'I didn't expect anything.' Carl gave her a smile and handed it to her. 'Please open it.'

She took the box and lifted the lid. Something wrapped in tissue paper. She took it out of the box and laid it in her palm. It was a pearl bracelet.

'Carl, I can't take this.'

'Of course you can. I want you to have it. You are missing a bracelet.'

She looked at him, puzzled.

'You told me you gave your bracelet to Priscilla for her Christmas present. So this is in its place.'

The pearls gleamed up at her in the soft light from the stained-glass windows. 'You didn't buy this specially?'

He shook his head. 'I wish I had but there is no time to do shopping in this new life of mine. No, the bracelet belonged to my wife. I bought it for her on our wedding day. It was a set.'

'It's far too precious to give away,' she murmured, running her fingertips over it.

'Lana, I do not give this without thinking. *You* are now precious to me. The bracelet does not mean anything sitting in a metal box. If I know you wear it sometimes, then I know you are thinking of me. And now . . .' Carl pressed her hand, 'will you allow me to put it on?'

She nodded. What else could she say? It easily slipped over her slim wrist and he clicked the safety clasp.

'It's so beautiful.'

'Not nearly so beautiful as you.' His eyes were fixed on hers. '*Liebling*, you came to my door last night.'

He said it as a simple statement.

'Yes, I did,' she whispered.

'You do not know how very much I wanted to open that door. But I knew it would be wrong and later you would regret it.'

'I know.' Lana dropped her eyes.

He cupped a hand under her chin tilting her face towards him again.

'Lana, my darling, when this war is over, I want us to be married. I want you to be my wife and a mother to Peter.'

'I don't know what Peter would say about it,' she said.

'He's fond of you already.' Carl kissed her forehead. 'And he will come to love you.'

'But he'll need you to himself,' she said. 'He's missed you for half his life. He's lost everything with his mother, and then his grandmother. And not hearing anything from you for a year or more, not knowing if you were dead or alive. I can't barge in and take over like that.'

'Give him time, Lana. The war is not ending yet but it is turning in favour of the Allies. They will win, I am certain. And when it happens I want you to be by my side.'

She couldn't answer. Her mind whirled. It was all too soon. But there was one very important question she needed to ask him.

'Would you like another child one day?'

Carl's face clouded. 'It would be a miracle for us to have a baby. But this is not a nice world for children. I think we will have enough to do to give Peter the love he has missed these last years, don't you?'

Lana nodded but it wasn't the answer she was hoping for. She fingered the pearl bracelet, her heart torn.

'Kiss me, Lana.'

He lowered his head and she felt the touch of his lips.

The door clicked open.

'Papa!'

Guiltily, she drew back.

'You have forgotten to knock before coming into a room,' Carl said in a firm tone.

Peter's face fell as he entered the room. 'I wanted you to see the jigsaw Harvey and me have done.'

'Harvey and *I*,' Lana automatically corrected, holding up her hand, the bracelet slipping back a little with the movement.

'Harvey and I,' Peter repeated impatiently, glancing at Lana. Then he looked down.

Too late she tried to hide her hand.

'That's my mother's. Why are you wearing her bracelet?' The boy's face was red with accusation.

'Peter!' Carl reached out his arm, but Peter burst into tears and rushed from the room.

'Wait here, Lana. I will go to him. Explain.'

'There's no need, Carl. We both know this can't go on. Every moment is precious to him. It isn't fair for me to take you away – even if it's only a few minutes here, an hour there. Which is all it can be.'

She didn't know how she managed to keep her voice steady. Carl caught hold of her arm and pulled her up, then held her close.

'Don't say any more,' he said. 'Don't speak. I can't bear it. Just when I think I have found some happiness you want us not to see each other.' He looked down at her. 'I thought we have a future together after this evil war.'

She shook her head. 'Carl, nothing changes the fact that I'm English and you are German. You wouldn't want to live permanently in England.'

'*Nein*, of course not. I want to help rebuild my country. It's where I belong when we have purged this terrible regime.' He kissed her forehead. 'And you will be by my side.'

No!

Without warning, her temper flared. He was taking it for granted that she would give up her country without even a discussion. He wasn't interested in her feelings, her concerns.

'No, Carl, I couldn't do that. Being away from my family . . . I don't speak or understand the language, I'd be treated suspiciously by some people—'

'No. Only the stupid ones.'

'It's not just me – it's Peter.'

'And you will make him a wonderful mother.'

'No. He sees me as a threat now when he saw you kissing me, and then his mother's bracelet on my arm. There's a huge hole in his life and only you can fill it. I will always do my best by him until the war's over, but I can't promise anything more.' She looked at him. 'Carl, please say you understand.'

'I don't understand. If we love each other—'

'Don't say another word.' She touched his lips with her fingertips.

'Would this make you change your mind?'

He'd never kissed her so passionately, so urgently. Her senses reeled. Her knees trembled. She clung on. If she hadn't she'd have fallen backwards like a rag doll. And then with all the willpower she had, she pulled away and said, 'Go to him, Carl. He needs you so badly.'

Carl set his mouth in a determined line and without another word walked out of the chapel leaving Lana drained of all emotion – and alone.

CHAPTER 38

Lana never knew how she got through Christmas Day, trying to be cheerful and enthusiastic in front of the children. But she couldn't bring herself to go to the chapel for the service and sit in the very place where she'd hinted that anything between her and Carl was doomed. She knew Carl had understood the real meaning behind her words.

The worst part was when she saw Peter in the Great Hall after dinner as he was leaving to go for a walk with his father. Carl didn't even look her way but Peter did. He shot her such a look of anger and resentment it was clear she wasn't welcome to go anywhere near them. She longed to tell Peter he had his papa to himself now. But of course she couldn't. She could only stand and watch as Peter turned his back and put his hand in his papa's, just as Charlie opened the oak door to let them out of the front door.

She busied herself in the kitchen in silence, helping Bertie and Reggie to prepare the supper. In her heart she knew Maxine could probably do with her support with the children's games, but she didn't want to talk to anyone. Bertie threw some curious glances at her. Reggie simply got on with the preparations, only speaking to Bertie when he had a question or wanted to stop for a bite to eat.

The afternoon dragged into the evening. The children were worn out with games and extra food and the excitement of their toys. Somehow, Lana managed to dredge up the energy to help Dolores with their bath time and finally get them into bed. She was grateful the nurse was not a particularly talkative woman, and her practical manner was a comfort.

'Right. I think we've got them all settled,' Dolores said, as they closed the younger boys' dormitory door. 'Do you fancy a sherry in the common room, Lana? I think we're all going to meet in there for some adult Christmas cheer.'

'I have a blinding headache,' Lana said. It was true. She'd had very little to eat and drink all day, and she was beginning to feel light-headed again.

'Maybe you should go to bed early with a couple of aspirins,' Dolores said.

'I think I'll take your advice, Nurse Dolores.'

'You go on up and I'll bring the aspirins to you.'

'No, please don't worry,' Lana said. 'I'll probably fall asleep straightaway.'

'If you're sure . . .'

'I am. But thank you for being so kind.'

She had to turn away. It would provoke a lot of

questions if Dolores saw that she was on the verge of breaking down.

'Would you tell the others for me, and give my apologies?'

'Of course I will.' Dolores hesitated. 'This might not be the right thing to say, but I wish you a Happy Christmas.'

'Thanks, Dolores. I wish you the same.'

Lana slipped between the sheets, Dolores's 'Happy Christmas' sounding in her ears as she fell into an exhausted sleep.

Somewhat revived the next morning, Lana was determined not to let whatever had taken place between her and Carl turn into a quarrel. She knew he loved her and she loved him. Above all, she desperately wanted him not to leave Bingham Hall angry or upset with her.

'Can you take Carl to the station this morning, Lana?' Maxine said as she hurried by to her office after breakfast. 'Harold's not back until the day after tomorrow.'

'Yes, of course.' Lana hesitated. 'Maxine, do you think Peter should come as well to see his father off?'

Maxine frowned. 'No, I don't think he should,' she said, finally. 'It will upset him all over again. I think he should say goodbye to him from here.'

Lana nodded. At least it would give her a chance to put things right.

'He needs to catch the nine-forty, so I'd leave

here at nine. I'll tell him to be ready then. That should give you plenty of time to get to Liverpool. The roads should be quiet as it's Boxing Day.'

She was ready in the Great Hall at ten minutes to nine. Carl came down the stairs carrying his overnight bag when Peter spotted him and flung his arms around him.

'I don't want you to go, Papa. Why do you have to go?'

'I don't want to either. But I must.' His eyes fell on Lana for an instant before he turned again to his son. 'I have a lot of work to do so the war will end soon. And you,' he looked down at Peter, 'must be a good boy and do your lessons, especially your German.' He kissed the top of Peter's head. 'And you don't forget to write to your papa.'

Peter shook his head, a tear running down one of his cheeks.

The doorbell rang and for something to do Lana opened it. Her mouth fell open. Frank stood there with a wide grin on his face.

'Aren't you going to invite me in?'

With burning cheeks, Lana stood back while Frank came in, removing his cap. He put a small packet, wrapped in brown paper, into her hands.

'It's a little something for you,' he said, his eyes twinkling. 'I'm sorry I didn't make it yesterday but there was an emergency with several sheep at one of the neighbouring farms. I think they've picked up something. I was there hours. I hope you'll forgive me.'

Lana didn't need to look at Carl. She felt him stiffen even though he was several feet away. Frank had obviously not noticed him as a group of children had suddenly rushed through the hall.

'Cat got your tongue?' Frank chuckled.

'I'm sorry I can't stop, Frank,' Lana said, feeling highly awkward and embarrassed. She mustn't let Frank realise Carl was someone special. 'This is Carl Best, young Peter's father.' She turned to Carl who seemed to be watching her every move. 'Mr Best, this is Frank Drummond, our local vet – where Rupert, our lovely cat, came from.' She knew she was gabbling but she couldn't stop herself. Why am I feeling so guilty? she thought, crossly.

The two men shook hands, eyeing each other and murmuring they were pleased to meet.

She drew a breath. 'I'm taking Mr Best to the station. In fact, we have to leave right now, or he'll miss his train.'

The sooner they both left, the better she'd feel.

'I've only just dropped by to wish Lana a belated Happy Christmas,' Frank told Carl. 'But I'm passing the station on the way to friends so I'd be glad to give you a lift.'

Before Lana could answer that it was no trouble at all for her, Carl said, 'That would be most kind, Mr Drummond. Thank you.'

As though he couldn't bear to be alone with her.

Carl turned to Lana. 'It was nice to see you again, Miss Ashwin. Thank you for your kind

418

hospitality, and for continuing to look after Peter.' His voice was crisp.

She put her hand out and Carl took it in his own firm one. But instead of it feeling warm, his skin was cool. She dared to raise her eyes to his and stared into them. She was met with a carefully neutral expression and she half stumbled backwards, but he held on to her hand.

'It was a pleasure.' Her voice trembled.

Was it her imagination or did he give her hand the slightest squeeze before he dropped it and abruptly turned away?

'Papa!' Peter rushed after his father and Lana was thankful to see Carl break into a smile. 'Can I come to the station to say goodbye?'

'I'm afraid not, Peter,' Lana intervened. 'Mr Drummond would have to come all the way back with you, and I'm sure he has a busy day ahead helping the sick animals.' She shook her head at Frank who seemed to have lost his usual cheerful demeanour and was standing by, watching her closely.

Peter's face fell.

'We'd better go,' Frank said, putting his cap back on, and turning to Peter. 'I wouldn't want your father to miss his train.'

The two men left. She felt as though somehow she'd lost control of the situation.

And then it struck her. *I wouldn't want your father to miss his train.* Did Frank sense something between Carl and her? But how could he? All they'd done was shake hands in a formal manner and address each other using their surnames. How could that possibly raise any suspicion? She could only hope that Carl would be circumspect on the way to the station. She wouldn't want to hurt Frank for the world.

CHAPTER 39

January 1944

N ew Year passed and Lana hadn't heard a word from Frank. She'd written a note to thank him for the sweet little enamel brooch in the shape of a cat he'd left her on Boxing Day. The cat was exactly the colour of Rupert and she'd immediately pinned it on to her dress, to the children's delight.

Another fortnight dragged by. She had a brief note from Carl but he made no mention of their future, and for that she was glad. She responded in the same way, telling him about Peter and how good he was becoming at drawing. And he was now attending the village school twice a week for science taught by Mr Benton, the returned head-master. On these two days Peter usually walked there with Priscilla.

Priscilla told me they nearly always speak in German, Lana finished in her letter to him. *She says it's their secret. I'm so pleased they've formed a strong friendship. Two children who both felt outsiders are doing so well now at school. I'm really proud of them.*

Lana threw herself into teaching, thankful she was doing something she loved, but her heart ached whenever she thought of Carl and how he must be feeling. She wished now she hadn't told him she loved him. Not that she'd stopped loving him. But it would make things more difficult if he ever brought up the question again of any future together.

February brought the usual chill winds and cold rain, but towards the end of the month there was a snowstorm. Aware of a strange silence one morning, Lana pulled back her curtains to reveal a fairy-tale scene. It really was quite breathtaking. And then her mind flew to Frank. He was not the best driver in fair weather so what on earth would he be like when it was knee deep in snow. And if it froze tonight the roads would be slick with ice.

He'd still made no contact at all. She knew he was always overstretched, having let his young assistant go into the forces, but before, he'd always made time to keep in contact with her regularly. She had to admit she missed him. Missed his cheerful smile, his enthusiasm, his love for the animals under his care. There were bound to be more emergencies in this weather. She might have a word with Maxine. Ask if she would allow her to take Harold's car and go and see him. Make sure he was all right. Had enough food in. She should have checked before.

'Yes, of course you can,' Maxine said, her expression concerned when Lana explained the situation. 'Just arrange it with Harold.'

That afternoon, after class, she drove cautiously down the drive, the windscreen wipers working hard to brush away the snow, which had begun to fall again, quite heavily. It hadn't had time yet to freeze, she thought, and it was only a short drive to the vet's.

The road leading to the village was snow-laden and although she could feel it was slippery under the tyres, the Rover held the road well. She was making good progress with the village in sight when an oncoming car skidded. It made straight for her.

She wrenched the steering wheel to the left and the car gave an almighty bang as the front wheels went into the ditch. She barely felt her head bump into the steering wheel before everything went black.

Someone was tapping on the car window.

What . . .? Lana pulled herself up from where she'd fallen forward, holding her head. She felt confused. Where was she? And then she remembered. That car. It had been about to plough into her. To avoid it she'd had to pull right over. So why did she feel as though she was tipping forward?

Oh, God, she must have plunged into the ditch. The car must be stuck nose down.

She looked at her hand. There was blood – quite a lot of it. Her head spun. She closed her eyes. Maybe if she could sleep she'd feel better.

The tapping was louder. For goodness' sake. Whoever it was would surely break the window. Gingerly, she turned her head towards where the voice seemed to be coming from. A man with a cap, his mouth moving but she couldn't hear any words. He seemed to be shouting something and pointing. She tried to open the window to hear what he was saying but it wouldn't move. She tried the door. Nothing. Drawing in a shaky breath she tried again but it had somehow locked itself. She rattled it but it wouldn't budge.

The man outside shook his head and disappeared.

'No, don't go,' she gasped. He couldn't leave her. But he hadn't heard. She put a hand to her head again, recoiling at the sticky blood. Where was her bag? She fumbled for it on the front seat but it was empty. Maybe it had fallen on the floor. She bent down, relieved when her hands closed over the handles. She raised her throbbing head and opened her bag, pulling out a handkerchief. She held it to her forehead where the bleeding seemed to be coming from. Oh, where was that man? Please let him have gone for help. Tears of self-pity swam before her, making everything out of focus. She felt the car shake and tried to see out of the window. The man in the cap was outside, pulling on the door handle. He looked up and gave her a wave, then a shout of triumph as the door swung open.

He stuck his head in.

'Are you all right, Miss?'

'Yes, I think so.' Her voice sounded far away.

'What's that bleeding? Let me look.'

It was the last thing she wanted – to be examined by a man with dirty hands. But he reached in and took the handkerchief away.

'Oh, nasty. You might need a stitch or two in that.'

'No, I'm sure it will be fine if I can get it washed and a plaster over it.'

'Where were you going?'

'To the vet's.'

'Frank Drummond's place?'

Lana nodded, making her head throb even more madly.

'I'll get you out of the ditch, but I'm not sure you should be driving with that cut.'

'I'll be okay, honestly. It's only half a mile away.'

The man nodded. 'I'll get one of the Shire horses. Shan't be long. You stay right there.' He went off chuckling at his little joke.

Furious now with the unknown driver who must have driven off without stopping to see if she was hurt, Lana swore out loud, tears of anger spilling down her cheeks. If it wasn't for the kind man who must have seen the accident . . . She shuddered, dreading to think what might have happened if he hadn't been there.

As good as his word the man soon returned with an enormous horse and a length of rope. She glimpsed him disappearing underneath the rear of the car – to tie the rope around the back axle, she guessed. Minutes later he'd attached it to the horse's harness and was shouting instructions. The car began to heave and groan as the horse pulled. Once she felt a slight hesitation and her heart plummeted, but then the car gave an almighty judder. She felt a thump as it righted itself on the road. Oh, the relief to be on level ground.

She looked out of the window. It was getting dark and she rubbed her numb fingers, trying to bring some life to them, all the while thinking how the dear man and his even dearer horse had rescued her. She opened the door and tried to stand, but her legs gave way and she sat back on the seat again. The man in the hat popped his head in the car again.

'There you are, Miss. Saved by Clemmie – she and Winnie are the best Shire horses in the county, but Clemmie here seemed the most eager to come and help.'

'What wonderful names,' Lana said, managing a wan smile. 'I can't thank Clemmie enough – and you, of course. Are you one of the farmers?'

'Yes. Sid Smithers at your service, Miss. Lonsdale Farm, just over yon.' He jerked his head, then looked up at the darkening sky. 'And I believe you're up at Bingham Hall.' She nodded. 'It's going to freeze tonight so be sure you're not out in it. Wouldn't want you to come another cropper. I might not be nearby the next time.'

'Did you actually see what happened?'

'Oh, no, Miss. I was in the stables. It was the driver who nearly ran into you. Almost had hysterics telling me.'

'Did you know him, by any chance?'

'Yes, but it wasn't a man, it was the local midwife – Celia Daniels. Have you met her?'

Oh, not that woman.

'What the hell was she doing driving like a maniac in this weather? Couldn't she—'

The farmer interrupted her. 'She was too upset to do anything but asked if I would come and get you out of the ditch.'

'Oh,' Lana said. She gave him a weak smile. 'Yes, I have met her.' She retrieved her glasses and put them on. 'Thank you again, Mr Smithers. I'll be all right now. I'm only a couple of minutes away from the vet's so I think I'll carry on.'

'You drive safely then, love.'

'Lana! Dear God, you're hurt. Whatever's happened?' Frank's eyes were wide as he practically dragged her inside and took her by the hand, through the waiting room to a room marked Private. A dog barked somewhere.

'It's Barney,' he said. 'He heard you and wants to say hello, but I'm going to leave him in the kitchen for now. Come. Sit here.' He gently pressed her into the only armchair in the room. 'Let me go and wash my hands and I'll have a look at that wound.'

427

He was back immediately. 'It's not bleeding much now,' he said, his capable fingers probing a lump that was beginning to feel the size of a walnut. 'Just a nasty bang. Heads always bleed and look worse than they are.'

'Yes, but you're comparing me with the heads of dogs and rabbits and horses,' Lana said, trying to inject a little humour. For some reason she felt safe now she was here with Frank. He was a vet, yes, but he would know about wounds caused by accidents, whether on animals or humans.

'The farmer who rescued me said he thought I'd need a couple of stitches.'

'No, I don't think so,' Frank said. He put a white cloth in her hand. 'Hold this over it while I get some water to clean it thoroughly. Then I'll put a dressing on and we'll see how it heals. But first you're going to have a brandy.' Frank disappeared and came back with two glasses of amber-coloured liquid.

'Drink it,' he said. 'It will calm your nerves. In fact, I'm having one as well.'

'I'm not that keen on—'

'I'm ordering you to drink it. It's medicinal.'

'Well, in that case . . .' She swallowed a mouthful, then coughed, and looked up at him. 'Not used to it.'

'Give it another go,' Frank said, 'and meanwhile, can I leave you a minute while I make the tea?'

Lana nodded. All she wanted to do was lean her head on the back of the shabby armchair with its embroidered cover and close her eyes. She'd almost nodded off when Frank appeared with a tea tray.

'I've put sugar in yours, whether you take it or not.'

'I haven't taken sugar since the beginning of the war,' Lana protested.

'It's good for shock.' He handed her a cup with a couple of biscuits in the saucer and pulled up a chair opposite. 'Drink your tea, and then tell me exactly what happened while I clean your forehead.'

Lana told him how Farmer Smithers, with the help of Clemmie the Shire horse, had pulled her out of the ditch.

'Nice chap, old Smithers,' Frank said, dabbing some TCP onto the cut and ignoring Lana's wince. 'Thank God he was there. You could have frozen to death if no one had come along.' He frowned. 'What happened to the other driver? Did he stop to see if you were all right?'

'I don't know,' she said. 'I must've fainted. But Mr Smithers said she alerted him there'd been an accident, and could he help get a car out of the ditch.'

'Not another woman driver.' Frank smirked.

Did he really believe *he* was a good driver? Lana's temper flared. 'Excuse *me*, but *I* wasn't the one skidding all over the road. Celia was driving much too fast for the conditions.'

Frank's jaw fell. 'Celia? Celia Daniels?'

'I'm sure there's only one Celia,' Lana returned coolly.

'She's a bit of a menace,' Frank said, as he fixed the dressing in place, 'although she does have a good reputation as a midwife. I just wish to God I'd never taken her out those few times. She puts far more into it than I'd ever meant. Drives me nuts.'

'She thinks you're in love with her but don't realise it.'

Frank's eyebrows shot up. 'Did she tell you that?'

'Yes, in no uncertain terms.'

'Well, there's no need to be jealous of Celia.' Frank's eyes gleamed.

'I'm not sure about that,' Lana said, swallowing her irritation. 'She's an attractive woman.'

'And always right,' he said with a roguish grin. 'Imagine living with that level of perfection on a daily basis.'

'I couldn't imagine.' Her tone was cutting. She should leave now. Politely thank him and go.

But before she could move, Frank suddenly became serious. 'I'm glad you managed to get here, Lana.' He put his hand lightly on her arm. 'Where were you going before the accident?'

'I was coming to see *you*. I was actually getting quite worried not hearing from you. At first I thought you were busy, but all these weeks have gone by with nothing.' She might as well get things out in the open. She looked directly at him. 'I wondered if Carl Best had said something to you.'

He wore an expression she couldn't fathom. What did he know?

'I'm sorry I haven't been in touch,' he said finally, rubbing his eyes. 'You're right – I *have* been busy with one emergency after another, but that's not particularly unusual.' He looked up. 'What was *Herr* Best supposed to have said?'

'You realised he was German, then?'

'You couldn't disguise *that* accent.' He drank the rest of his brandy in one gulp. 'Go on, Lana. Please don't take me for an idiot.'

Lana wished she hadn't started this. But it was too late.

'I just thought he might have said something about him and me.'

'He's German, for God's sake. He didn't talk about anything except the weather and how he hoped his train wouldn't be delayed. He's obviously a refugee or a detainee. I'm surprised he hasn't been interned, so I reckon he must be working for the British to be freely roaming the countryside.' He paused and looked at her directly. 'So what were you afraid he might say?'

To Lana's fury she felt her face redden.

'You see, he didn't have to say or explain anything.' Frank looked away but went on without waiting for her reply. 'There was no need. It was crystal clear when I saw your face as you said goodbye to him.'

'What do you mean?'

'I think you know. But if you want me to spell it out, it was perfectly obvious you're in love with him.' She was silent. 'I *did* mean to ring,' he continued. 'But as the time went on, I thought it best to let you be free to go to him.'

'Did you get my note to thank you for the brooch . . . which I love?' she added lamely, pointing to the lapel on her dress.

'Yes.'

'And you didn't think to reply?'

'No. You didn't need me to complicate your life any further.'

Lana bit her lip. Frank was obviously terribly hurt. She should have gone to see him weeks ago. How could she have left it so long? He must have felt used, the way she'd gone out with him in between times. She'd felt at the time it was fine because they were just good friends. But something had changed between them and his next words took her completely by surprise.

'You see, Lana,' he said, taking hold of her hands, 'it's been very hard for me because I've fallen in love with you. And just when I gathered the courage to tell you, I saw that your heart belonged to someone else.'

'Dear Frank,' Lana gazed at him. Something stirred within her. He looked so vulnerable. 'I wouldn't hurt you knowingly for anything in the world. I always felt we were friends. We've always got on so well together, and I've loved spending time with you – going to the pictures, even changing your wheel . . .' She tried to make him smile.

'But you never regarded our time together as

anything serious,' Frank said. 'Whereas I hoped you might come to love me one day. I even asked you if you loved someone else? Do you remember? And you said you weren't sure. So I didn't give up hoping until I saw you with Herr Best at the orphanage. And at that moment you looked very sure.'

Lana shook her head, truly not knowing what to think. What if Carl had never come into her life? More and more she was beginning to think she and Carl could never be together. Peter wasn't ready to share his father. And Carl wanted to take her away from her country, her family, her job with the children that she loved without even a discussion. It wasn't that Carl was being thoughtless or didn't care – it was just how he was. The culture must be so different in Germany.

But Frank was everything in a man she'd ever wanted. His openness, his values, his love of nature – reminding her not for the first time of Dickie. And she loved how he looked after the animals in his care, treating them as precious individuals. He was well read, he had an endearing sense of humour, and they liked a lot of the same things. She always felt safe with him. And completely comfortable. Until now. Her heart squeezed with the pain she was inflicting on this dear man.

Frank went to the window and peered out.

'It's gone very dark all of a sudden,' he commented, pulling the curtains. He turned round. 'And by the way, Miss Ashwin, you're not going anywhere tonight. It's pitch-dark now, and the roads are going to freeze again.'

He always called her 'Miss Ashwin' when he was teasing her.

'I'm fine now I've had a cup of tea – and the brandy you forced on me,' Lana said, smiling, trying to keep it light. There was no way she could possibly stay here overnight. The villagers' tongues would wag right out of their mouths.

Frank shook his head. 'I didn't train at veterinary school for seven years not to know when an animal is fit to be sent home, or not – and I'm afraid the same goes for you.'

'I don't have anything with me – no toothbrush, no nothing.'

'I always keep a new toothbrush,' Frank grinned. 'Never know when one might have an unexpected guest.'

Celia? She shook the unwelcome thought away.

'Frank, I must go back. It's only a few minutes' drive and Maxine will be getting worried—'

'I'm going to telephone her right now.'

He returned within minutes. 'Your nice matron perfectly understands. She says under no circumstance are you to drive home in this weather with a cut on your head. And if you don't feel much better tomorrow she'll send for the doctor. I told her I would keep an eye on you and she said she was most grateful. So,' Frank smiled, 'it's bed for you, young lady. You're going to rest in the guest room for at least a couple of hours . . .' He looked at his watch. 'And then I'll come and see how you are. If you feel hungry – and I think you may by then – I'll make you a boiled egg with some bread and real butter. How does that sound?'

Lana had begun to shiver, but she simply said, 'You're very kind.'

'I'm not being kind,' Frank said abruptly. 'Anyone would do the same.'

CHAPTER 40

Lana removed her blouse and skirt and stockings and pulled back the covers. The room was clean, but unaired, and plainly furnished, though there were a couple of landscape paintings on two of the walls. She pulled back the sheet, dreading a cold bed, but to her relief Frank had put a hot water bottle where her back would lie. He'd drawn the curtains and left a bedside light on, together with a glass of water and two aspirins. What a thoughtful man he was.

'Any problems, call out,' were the last words she remembered hearing before her head touched the pillow and she was sound asleep.

For the first few seconds after Lana awoke she had no idea where she was. Pushing herself up too quickly, she fell back again. Her head swam. She put her hand to the dressing on her forehead. The accident. She was in Frank's house. It must be well after midnight. She reached for the glass of water and drank deeply. Her stomach felt empty and she remembered Frank had promised to make her a boiled egg. It was too late now. She'd slept through supper. Too bad, as she felt quite peckish.

There was a gentle tap at the door.

'How's my patient?' Frank stepped in. 'Hungry?'

'Not half. But it's too late for you to be cooking now.'

'It's only coming up to eight. Perfect time. I'll bring it up to you.'

'No, please let me come down. I'm much better, honestly.'

'Well, if you're sure.' He closed the door behind him.

She dressed quickly and came down the stairs.

'I'm in the kitchen,' Frank called. 'Come on in. Barney's going mad wanting to say hello.'

Barney greeted her with a few wet licks on her hand and some happy-sounding barks. He wagged his tail, then went to his basket and curled up again, as though satisfied that he'd made her acquaintance again.

Frank had set the table for two and gestured for her to sit down.

'How do you like your egg?'

'Soft, please,' she said. Frank set the egg timer. 'I'll just wash my hands from Barney's welcome.'

He moved to the side of the sink; she was conscious how near he was as she put her hands under the tap. But he didn't touch her or make any remark. She could smell the maleness of him – warm and musky. She mustn't think like that.

It must be the shock of the accident that had her senses reeling.

Frank had made more tea, and they ate and drank in companionable silence.

'Better?' Frank said, when they'd finished.

'Much.' She smiled at him, feeling almost at home.

'Was it the brandy or my perfectly cooked egg?'

'A combination,' she grinned, then became serious. 'Frank, I'm going back to Bingham Hall. Don't try to dissuade me. I'm truly better and it's not late. Not even nine o'clock.'

'I can see you've made up your mind,' Frank said, 'but will you promise to telephone as soon as you arrive?'

'I promise.' She looked at him. 'I can't thank you enough for what you've done for me. Especially after . . . after . . .'

'After I said I loved you, knowing you don't love me?' Frank finished for her. 'Don't give it another thought. I hope we'll still be friends. I want us to.'

'I'd like nothing more,' Lana said.

He fetched her coat and bag and when she was ready to go, she turned to him. 'Don't leave it so long next time.'

'I won't.' He kissed her on the cheek. 'I'll come with you to the car.'

'There's no need, honestly. You're not dressed for it. Just stay in.'

He made to follow her.

'Please, Frank. I'm perfectly all right.'

She picked her way carefully to the car, slipping every few steps, but at least it had stopped snowing. She pressed the starter button and on the second attempt the engine spluttered into life. Turning her neck to see Frank watching her from the door, she waved. He waved back.

After ten minutes of careful driving over the icy road, this time with no mishaps, she was back at Bingham Hall.

'I'm going to have a look at that forehead,' Maxine said, as soon as Lana appeared the next morning.

'Really, Maxine, I'm fine. I didn't sleep too well, but it was nothing to do with the accident.'

'Now, Lana.' Maxine's voice was firm.

'All right, Matron – if you insist,' Lana grinned, then wished she hadn't. The cut seemed to stretch, giving her a spike of pain. But it had stopped throbbing, at least.

In the sick ward Maxine gently removed the dressing and inspected the wound.

'It's weeping a little so I'll clean it again and put some antiseptic cream on it.'

After Maxine had finished she said, 'Now, I want you to watch my finger without moving your head.' She held up a forefinger and slowly moved it in front of Lana's eyes, then back again. 'Good,' Maxine said. 'I'm pretty sure you don't need to go to the hospital. But if you have *any* problems

– headache, feeling sick or dizzy – then come and see me. All being well I should be able to take the dressing off in the next day or two and let the air get to it.'

'Thanks, Maxine.'

'You need a hot drink,' Maxine said, washing her hands. 'I'm going to ask Ethel to bring us some tea to my office. I want to hear all about it.'

'Can you believe it was the ubiquitous Mrs Daniels who alerted Farmer Smithers?' Lana said.

'Oh, I can,' Maxine said. 'But the question is – did you mention this to Frank?'

'Yes, I did, because he asked if the driver had stopped to help me. When I told him it was Celia Daniels he told me he wished he'd never gone out with her as she made more of it than he'd intended. And Frank always strikes me as being absolutely honest. But I didn't bother to tell him she more or less threatened me to lay off her man.'

Maxine smiled. 'I suppose one can't blame her. He *is* a very good catch. One of the few, I think, in Bingham. No wonder she doesn't want to let him slip through her fingers.' She gave Lana a piercing glance. 'I shouldn't pry but do you feel any different towards him after yesterday?'

'Well, a man doesn't necessarily have to rescue me for me to have warm feelings towards him,' Lana laughed. 'I liked him very much before that.'

'And Carl?' Maxine paused, her turquoise eyes

fixing steadily on Lana. 'I had a feeling you were in love with *him*.'

She had to tell someone. Someone she trusted about how confused she was.

'Maxine—'

'Don't answer if you don't want to.'

'But I do,' Lana burst out. 'He told me he loved me when he came at Christmas, and I told him I loved him too. And I do. It's just that—'

'You're not sure of a future with him,' Maxine suggested gently.

'He seems to take it for granted that I'll go back to Germany with him as his wife. He wants to go back to help build it up again. I can't blame him. But Germany is not my country. I can't see myself there. I don't speak the language. I doubt I'd get a job because unemployment is bound to be awful. The people won't be comfortable about him bringing back an Englishwoman, whether we win the war or not. He thinks we'll win and I have to believe that, but there's no guarantee. Besides,' Lana glanced across at the young matron, 'I don't want to give up my life here. Bingham Hall's done so much for me . . . helping me get over Dickie. Given me a better outlook on life. You said it would.' She gave a self-conscious laugh. 'You said the children helped you as much as you did them. And I now know exactly what you meant. But there's something even more important than *my* wishes.'

Maxine raised her eyebrows. 'Oh?'

'It's Peter. I've thought long and hard about him. He needs the full attention of his father.'

'But Peter likes you,' Maxine said. 'And trusts you.'

'He tolerates me as I'm a link between him and Carl. But he'd be very resentful if Carl and I ever got married. And Carl's made it clear he doesn't want children, whereas I do.'

Lana could have bitten her tongue out, mentioning wanting children. More than once she'd wondered if the twin babies had been adopted yet – please God, together in a loving home – but hadn't voiced it as she hadn't wanted to bring up the subject of adoption. However, Maxine seemed quite calm as she leaned back in her chair and studied Lana with a narrowed gaze.

'Mmm. That's an important issue. He'd probably change his mind once you were his wife.'

'No.' Lana shook her head. 'Carl won't say what I want to hear. I know that now. I'm resigned to it.'

'Where does Frank come into all this?'

'If I hadn't met Carl I would have fallen head over heels for Frank.'

'Really?'

'Yes. This sounds awful, but yesterday Frank and I had an honest talk. He said he saw my face when I said goodbye to Carl and could tell I was in love with him. Then he said it was very difficult for him because he'd fallen in love with me himself.'

'Good gracious.' Maxine's eyes were wide. 'It must be wonderful to have two such attractive chaps madly in love with you.'

'But it's not,' Lana protested. 'I can't work out what to do.' She paused. 'Let's change the subject. There's something I *do* want to do if you agree. It's Priscilla's birthday next month. She'll be thirteen on the twenty-first. Her birthday last year must have been terrible as it was the first one since her mother and father died. I'd like to make this a special one.'

'I'll be delighted to help,' Maxine smiled as she flipped the page of her calendar. 'And we'll need to let Bertie know so she can save up coupons for the sugar and the dried fruit for the cake.'

'Apart from the three of us,' Lana said, 'can we keep it a surprise? Priscilla hates any fuss – look at how she shrugged off our attempts to make a mention in class of her helping the children to escape on the night of the fire. I wouldn't put it past her to say she doesn't want any special party. But I think she deserves it.'

'She does.' Maxine looked at Lana thoughtfully. 'Just before you go, Lana, I will say one thing . . . and it's serious. If you really, *truly* loved Carl, you'd go anywhere in the world with him . . . as I would with Crofton, if he asked me to.'

Lana gave a sharp intake of breath.

'Would you really, Maxine?' she said in a soft voice.

Planning Priscilla's surprise party helped Lana to push any possible future with Carl into the back of her mind. She knew she would have to confront it but not now. Not yet.

The following day Frank telephoned to ask her if she'd like to go to the pictures the following Saturday.

'Just as friends,' he said. 'No strings.'

For an instant she wished he hadn't said that. She wished he'd just asked her to the pictures and that was that. But she understood he was trying not to put her under any pressure.

'I'd like that,' she said, and added, 'very much.'

To Lana's relief Frank appeared perfectly friendly and natural, although he carefully avoided touching her. But once they were in the cinema, Lana couldn't help her eye straying to Frank's hand resting lightly on his thigh. Not for the first time she noticed how strong and capable it looked, and she itched to feel her hand in his. Just as a warm and friendly gesture, she told herself. What if she put her hand into his? Would he snatch his away? Or would he curl his fingers around hers? Would he think she'd fallen out of love with Carl? Biting her lip, these thoughts ran through her brain, and she kept both hands tightly together on her lap.

When he bent his head towards her she was startled. As though he knew her topsy-turvy thoughts.

'Would you mind?' he whispered.

'No, of course not,' she whispered back, thinking he was about to take her hand. She was disappointed when he merely took out his pipe.

She was aware of him taking out his leather pouch and pushing some tobacco into the bowl, then lighting it. The aroma was rich and mellow, and somehow comforting. He looked at her, but she couldn't see his expression in the dark.

'Did you enjoy the film?' he asked when they were strolling into the foyer.

'Yes,' she said, hoping he wouldn't question her too closely about this latest Humphrey Bogart film as she hadn't taken much of it in. 'But the news is what really cheered me up. It was so horrible last time when we saw all those bombs landing on Berlin, though I know it was supposed to boost our morale that we were giving as good as we got – and more. But it had the opposite effect on me.'

'The war is definitely turning our way now,' Frank said, helping her on with her coat, 'and not before time.' She was almost certain his fingers deliberately brushed her bare neck. Quickly, as though she hadn't noticed, and to save both of them any embarrassment, she edged away and wrapped her scarf around her neck. He gave her a glance but didn't comment.

'Would you like to go somewhere for a drink?'

She couldn't stay in his presence, so close to him, any longer.

'Can we give it a miss this time? I'm feeling a little tired.'

She was relieved when he gave her one of his warm smiles.

'Of course.'

He braked hard outside Bingham Hall causing the gravel to fly. She raised her eyes. Much as she was tempted to tell him it was bad for the car, she held the words back. There was no point in spoiling the mood. He switched off the engine and went round to open her door.

'Thank you so much for a lovely evening,' she said, as she swung her long legs out onto the drive.

We're the same height when I'm wearing heels, Lana realised, as they stood facing one another. He kissed her cheek.

'When's your day off?'

'It varies, but sometimes a Thursday.'

'I'd have to work in the morning, but how about if I get away around two? We could go to Sefton Park if the weather's reasonable. We seem to be having a dry spell but who knows how long that'll last? Not that Barney minds what weather it is, so long as he's out.' Frank looked at her. 'Sorry, I never asked – would you mind if we took Barney?'

'I shouldn't like it if you left him at home,' Lana smiled.

CHAPTER 41

'Prissy's birthday – it's Prissy's birthday,' the children chanted when Priscilla came slowly down the stairs on the morning of 21st March to clear blue skies.

'Your birthday and it's the first day of spring,' Lana told her. She'd been waiting at the bottom of the stairs to be the first one to say Happy Birthday, but some of the younger children had beaten her to it. 'You've done your hair differently. I like it pulled back with the ribbon.'

'I wish they wouldn't call me Prissy,' Priscilla muttered, ignoring the compliment.

'You know, when people shorten your name, it means they like you.'

Priscilla's grey eyes narrowed.

'It's the same when they tease you,' Lana added. 'People don't bother to tease if they don't like you. And if you get annoyed it will only make children do it all the more. Just smile and thank them for acknowledging your birthday.'

Priscilla didn't look convinced. It was such a shame. When she did give a rare smile she looked so lovely, Lana thought sadly. She hoped the young girl would enjoy her birthday as Bertie and Reggie and Ethel had worked hard to make this a special one. Well, there was still time.

'Now for the cake,' Bertie said that afternoon as she brought out an iced cake from the pantry. She set it on a plate covered with a doiley. 'Reggie, did you put the balloons out, like I told you?'

'Yes, Cook, I did.' Reggie's tone was mocking but Bertie was obviously used to him now, Lana thought with amusement, as the cook didn't come back with her usual snappy reply. 'But I'd better go and check everything's in place,' he added.

'The cake looks superb,' Lana commented when Reggie had disappeared. 'Incredible that you managed to ice it and produce all the candles.'

Bertie grinned. 'We have our ways, hen. Jerry isn't going to take over quite yet.'

Lana and Maxine had chipped in to buy Priscilla a songbook. Lana had spotted it in a second-hand music shop in Liverpool and seized it. Barbara had painted a portrait of Rupert, and the rest of the staff had put a little bit of cash in an envelope for her. Bingham village school had even sent her a card. The young girl's place setting looked exciting with the presents and envelopes.

The children rushed into the dining room all talking at once, not noticing at first the festive air.

'Prissy, come and sit next to us,' one of the twins shouted.

Priscilla hovered in the doorway, hesitatingly.

'No, she's going to sit with me,' Betsy called out, and plonked herself down.

Priscilla made for her usual place at the far end, but Lana stepped forward.

'I believe you're over here, next to me,' she said, taking the girl's stiffened arm, feeling her reluctance as she barely allowed herself to be led to her new place at the table.

Lana watched the young girl's face as she scanned the two wrapped gifts and envelopes containing her cards.

The children simmered down when Priscilla opened the first card, which was so large it wasn't in an envelope. Every child had signed their name in it. Some had drawn a miniature picture or written a small note. She spent a long time reading the card, and when she turned to Lana the expression in her large grey eyes seemed to carry a question.

'Are you all right, love?' Lana said.

Priscilla nodded and chewed her bottom lip. She opened the card from the school, read it and put it to one side. She picked up the last one, which had no envelope, and leaning over, Lana noticed a crayoned drawing of a striped orange cat with a message ballooning from its mouth, though the words weren't clear. Priscilla opened the card, a frown creasing her smooth forehead; then the corners of her mouth twitched mischievously before she handed it to Lana.

'May I read it?' Lana mouthed.

Priscilla shrugged, though she gave Lana a half-smile.

Lana couldn't understand a word. But a warm feeling stole round her heart. It was more than she'd hoped for. Peter had taken the trouble to make a special card for Priscilla and write it in his own language so no one else could understand it. Priscilla looked across at Peter and Lana was gratified to see a secret smile pass between the two children.

When Priscilla unwrapped the songbook her eyes shone as she began flicking through it. 'Thank you, Miss Ashwin. These are lovely songs.'

'It was from Matron as well.'

'Yes, I know. I'll thank her.'

'And Miss Graham has offered to help you practise – she says she'll accompany you on the piano.'

But it was Rupert's portrait that stole the occasion. Barbara had captured him beautifully.

'Oh, I *love* him,' Priscilla cried. 'Mrs Steen is so clever. I wish I could paint like her.' Then her face dropped. 'But I don't know where to put it.'

'I have the perfect solution, Priscilla.' Maxine had left her table and stepped over to Priscilla's seat. 'From now on you have your own bedroom on the nursery floor.'

'Oh, thank you, Matron. It will be like I was – when I . . .' Her eyes welled up with tears.

'You're almost grown up,' Maxine said. 'You should have some privacy.'

'Thank you, Matron, and for the songbook.'

Maxine patted her on the shoulder. 'Enjoy the rest of your birthday, Priscilla.'

'Excuse me, all. I need to put this cake down.' It was Bertie holding a large tray with Priscilla's cake. She set it on the table. 'You know what you have to do, hen?' Priscilla looked up at the cook. 'You have to make a wish.'

'I'll never get what I always wish for,' Priscilla mumbled under her breath.

'I'm going to light the candles anyway,' Bertie said firmly, striking a match.

'Don't cry, Prissy.' It was little Betsy. For some reason she'd taken a shine to Priscilla and Lana noticed Priscilla always treated her kindly. Betsy put her thin brown arm on the young girl's. 'Make a wish anyway, but you're not allowed to tell anyone – else it don't come true.'

'Or else it *won't* come true,' Lana corrected.

Bertie finished lighting the candles, then stood back.

'Make a wish, make a wish, Prissy!' the children bellowed.

Priscilla leaned over and blew out the candles in two goes and only Lana noticed the tears in the young girl's eyes as the children shouted, 'Hurray!'

Lana rose to her feet and clapped for the children to quieten down. All eyes turned to her. 'This is a special day we're celebrating, and not just because it's Priscilla's birthday. We've never thanked her properly for helping all the girls in their dormitory down the fire escape on the night

451

of the fire. There may have been more burns and injuries if she hadn't acted quickly and sensibly. So please give her a big clap.'

Piping voices from the girls calling out 'thank you', and some cheers from the boys, and everyone's enthusiastic clapping added to the cacophony, but Priscilla's eyes were downcast. She doesn't like this kind of attention, Lana thought. She was used to being the only child at home with her family, maybe only allowed to talk when she was spoken to. Lana almost wished she hadn't gone to such lengths. Then Priscilla suddenly looked up, her eyes flicking round the table. She rose to her feet, her chair scraping loudly on the floor. The dining room hushed, the children all turning in Priscilla's direction.

'Thank you for the lovely card from all of you. It was very kind,' she said in her clear voice, then looked across the table at her friend. '*Und danke schön, Peter, für deine Geburtstagskarte,*' she said softly.

Then she sat down, tears streaming down her cheeks.

To Lana's disappointment Frank phoned at a quarter to one on Thursday, the day they'd arranged to go to Sefton Park, to say he'd had an emergency call from one of the farms. A young ram had been attacked by a rogue dog, which had gouged a wound in its side.

'I'm hoping to save him,' he said apologetically on the telephone, 'though he's in quite a bad way.'

'Don't say another word,' Lana said. 'I don't know anything about rams but if there's anything I can do to help, please ask.'

'Maybe come over and make me a cup of tea,' Frank said, already sounding exhausted, 'and keep Barney company. Vera's gone to have lunch with her daughter and I told her not to rush back. Of course, I didn't know about the ram at the time.'

'I'll be over right away,' Lana said, pleased she might be useful, if only to provide hot drinks. He probably hadn't had anything to eat either, she thought. At least she could make him a sandwich.

Harold had taken the car to get the bumper straightened out from when it had plunged into the ditch, so Lana half ran to the surgery. She knocked and tried the door. It was open.

'Frank, it's me,' she called.

'Go down the hall,' his voice called back. 'It's the second door on the right after the waiting room.'

A strong smell of disinfectant hit her as she eased the door open and let herself in. Frank looked up, keeping his hand on the poor animal who was stretched out on the long narrow table with a rag wrapped around its nose. Its eyes were closed but it was twitching. The towel it was lying on was covered in blood, and for a moment Lana felt queasy. Then she mentally reprimanded herself and approached the table where a lamp was trained on the ram's injured side. The sight of the deep gash almost had her rushing to the lavatory, but she gripped the edge of the table and pulled her stomach in hard.

'What can I do?' Her voice shook but thankfully he seemed too busy to notice.

'Wash your hands over in the sink.' He jerked his head towards one of the corners. 'Then hold him down while I clean the wound. He won't struggle. I've doped him.'

An hour flew by as Lana handed him instruments he gestured towards, not always picking up the right ones, but his voice was steady as he corrected her, and towards the end she frequently worked out what he needed before he asked for it. Full of admiration she watched him absorbed in his work, nodding and muttering, until finally he completed the last stitch and cut the thread. He stretched up and rolled back his shoulders.

'I'd forgotten how difficult it was to perform an op on one's own,' he said, 'but you were marvellous. You'd make a great assistant.'

'I didn't have a clue what I was doing most of the time,' Lana said truthfully. 'But I'm glad if you thought I was some sort of help.' She looked at the animal who was now breathing regularly. 'Will he survive?'

Frank glanced down. 'I think he will. He's young but he's a tough beast. But it's going to take a while for him to recover. Luckily, Grayson's one of the better farmers and he'll give him the time he needs. I'll keep him here overnight and take him back tomorrow. Then I'll be sure he's no longer in danger.'

'Please let me know,' Lana said, anxiously. 'You will, won't you?'

Their eyes met. She caught her breath.

'Yes, I'll let you know,' he said.

Two days later Frank rang Bingham Hall.

'How's my new assistant?' he asked, and Lana could picture his eyes twinkling.

'I'm well, thank you, but more important – how's the patient?'

'Young Lightning? He's a bit wobbly on his pins but he'll be fine.'

'I'm so glad. You were wonderful, Frank. It was a privilege seeing you in action.'

She heard him chuckle.

'We never got to Sefton Park. Any chance over Easter?'

'Can we leave it for the following Sunday? I promised my parents I'd go and see them over the holiday.'

'Look forward to it.'

The receiver clicked. She had to smile. He didn't really waste words. The thought suddenly occurred as to what her parents would think of Frank. But she didn't have to wonder. She knew they'd both approve unreservedly. *Even Dickie? Would he approve?* a small voice questioned. *Yes, even Dickie.* That certainty made her feel perfectly content.

★   ★   ★

Lana received a postcard from Carl wishing her a Happy Easter, and hoping she was well. She couldn't grumble about the brevity of his message because she hadn't sent him anything. Every time she began a letter she became so worried that she might say the wrong thing that she'd put her pen and notepaper away, telling herself she would write it later. In the end she sent him a brief letter to tell him she and the other teachers were planning an Easter egg hunt. The children were getting excited as they'd never heard of such a thing before. She asked if they had the same tradition in Germany.

She sealed the envelope and decided to walk to the village to post it. He might just get it in time for Easter.

Strolling in Sefton Park with Frank, Lana almost forgot that the country was still at war, the Allies embroiled in heavy battles at Monte Cassino as they tried to advance on Rome. Here in the park it was so peaceful. There were a few couples enjoying the air and an old man on a bench was tucking into a sandwich, but there were no children, only a nanny briskly pushing a pram. Frank hadn't brought Barney after all, but he took on a mysterious air when she asked where he was.

'Vera, the nurse, takes him home sometimes if I'm going somewhere they don't welcome dogs.'

'But it says you can bring dogs into the park,' she said, but he didn't comment.

They were walking in step but apart. Taking a chance he might rebuff her, she slipped her hand through his arm and he looked down at her and smiled.

'You can't believe there's a war on, can you, when you hear the birds and see the flowers?' he said. 'Pity about the daffs. They're more or less over, but we've still got narcissi.' He pointed to several clumps around some of the tree trunks.

'The sun's a bit weak but it still feels as though spring is really here,' Lana said, happily falling in with his mood.

'My favourite time of the year,' Frank said. 'I love summer but it gallops away, whereas spring gives you all the colours of green and you know you have it all to come.'

'It's wonderful. And the primroses. I wish they didn't grow so low down so we could smell them.'

'Go ahead,' Frank laughed. 'They do have a perfume, but I can tell you're not a country girl if you're worried about getting your knees dirty.'

'It's my stockings I'd worry about,' Lana said seriously. Then she gave a mischievous grin. 'Maybe I'm not a country girl but I'll show you.' She crouched, feeling her skirt ride up her legs, but it was too late. She'd taken up the challenge. She put her hands on the ground and face down inhaled their scent. After some seconds Frank held out his hand to pull her to her feet.

'And?'

Lana smiled. 'It's not like any flower I know. I

can't really describe it but it's sort of innocent. Like spring itself.'

Frank looked at her intently, then chuckled.

'What are you laughing at?'

'You.' He pulled out a pale blue handkerchief and gently wiped the tip of her nose.

'Primroses act like little cups,' he said, his brown eyes merry. 'They hold the raindrops.'

She put her hand to her nose and laughed. 'Well, I'm obviously not a country girl but neither am I a sophisticated city girl.'

'You're perfect just as you are.'

The air stilled between them.

They wandered over to a vegetable plot where a gardener was bent almost double planting potatoes in one of the raised areas. He looked up when he heard them.

'Morning.' He lifted his cap and they watched as he dug another hole the depth of his trowel and popped in the sprouting potato. 'King Edwards,' he said, with a satisfying grin. 'You can't beat them.'

Frank tucked Lana's hand in his arm as they walked the circular tour, admiring the waterfalls and pools, but she had to reluctantly remove her hand when they faced the stepping stones over a stream and he gently guided her in front.

'Take it slowly,' Frank warned. 'There's algae on some of them.'

She'd almost got to the last stone when her foot skidded and she would have toppled over if Frank hadn't grabbed her waist from behind.

'Steady, Lana.' She was aware of his hands.

She couldn't look round or she would have fallen again.

This time he took her hand as they walked back to the car. When she glanced at him he gave her hand a gentle squeeze. 'For your own safety.'

She grinned at him. 'Thank you, kind sir.'

He grinned back. 'Ready for some lunch?'

'Definitely,' Lana said. 'Do you know some-where nearby? I still don't know my way round Liverpool.'

'Nor do most Liverpudlians,' Frank said, with a grim expression. 'Since the Blitz it's hard to recognise anywhere.'

'Do you think the war will be over soon, Frank?'

'Hard to tell. But it's turning our way now.'

She couldn't help her thoughts straying to Carl. Firmly, she pushed him to the back of her mind.

'How were your parents when you went to see them?' he said.

'My mother went through a serious illness but she's much better now. And happy that things have worked out for me at the orphanage. They both know how I love teaching . . . well, most of the time,' she laughed. 'It gets a bit tricky some-times.'

'I'm sure it does,' Frank said.

She enjoyed walking with him, matching her rhythm to his.

'We'll see if we can get into the Adelphi,' Frank said as they rounded the corner into Ranelagh Street.

'I never expected this,' Lana said. 'I'm not sure I'm dressed for it.'

'I've been admiring that skirt showing your gorgeous long legs ever since you bent down to smell the primroses.' He chuckled. 'So I'm sure the Adelphi will allow you in with no trouble at all. But they certainly wouldn't Barney.'

They were shown to a table in the dining room where huge cone-shaped chandeliers hung from an ornate ceiling, and crisp white tablecloths covered tables for four.

'What a beautiful room,' Lana said, removing her hat. A waiter appeared to take their jackets.

'By the way, this is my treat for being my assistant with Lightning,' Frank said.

'I didn't want anything.'

'I know. That's why I'm treating.' A waiter came over to hand them the menu. 'Order whatever you fancy,' Frank went on, 'but I'm having game pie, which I can strongly recommend.'

She wondered how often he came here and who with.

'That sounds lovely.'

'And we're having a glass of wine – to celebrate.'

'What are we celebrating?'

'Today. This reprieve from work. Us.'

'You never talk about yourself,' Lana said. 'I don't even know if you're married.'

'You can find out by talking to anyone in Bingham,' Frank said, rolling his eyes. 'Most of them love a gossip.'

'I'd prefer to hear it from you.'

They were interrupted by the waiter who took their order.

'There's not that much to tell,' Frank said when the waiter had disappeared. 'I'm forty-three. I was only fourteen when the last war started but my father used to prepare the horses to go to the front. When I was a bit older – the war was still going at the time – and found out what had happened to them I made up my mind to save animals, not send them to such terrible deaths. So immediately after the war when I was eighteen I began my training.'

'I think it's a wonderful vocation,' Lana said, lightly resting her hand on his.

'You have to be dedicated.' Frank glanced down at their hands. 'Two years more than a doctor, probably because one minute you're looking at a sick cow and the next you're trying to work out why a goldfish has lost its zest.' He grinned at her. 'But I wouldn't want to do anything else in the world.'

'You're a natural. I could see that when you were operating on Lightning. Anyway, go on. You married at one point?'

'I married far too young – before I qualified.' His face took on a bitter look. 'She thought it would be glamorous to be married to a vet, but it's the complete opposite. The worst for her was that I was on call all the time. We rarely went out. And apart from inevitable emergencies, there's overnight lambing where I'd be gone hours – still do it, of

461

course. But it has its rewards,' he went on, his mouth now relaxing into a smile, 'knowing you've saved an animal that would have surely died.'

Lana was silent, listening to his every word. The waiter came and poured them a glass of wine, then left. When Frank didn't continue, she ventured, 'And your wife?'

She hated thinking he had a wife who couldn't see what a wonderful husband she had in Frank.

'Ex,' he said quickly, as though to reassure her he was well and truly single. 'Three years into the marriage she left me. But before she did she gave me hell.' He shrugged. 'My divorce came through last year.'

'I'm so sorry.'

'Don't be. I was relieved.'

'Have you children?'

'No. Rhona wasn't keen. She was too conscious of her figure. But I'd love to have them.' He looked at her intently. 'Even now.' He paused. 'What about you?'

Lana blinked. 'I was engaged to a lovely man who was in the Merchant Navy. His ship was torpedoed in 1941. That was it.' Her eyes filled with tears. 'We both wanted children.' She swallowed hard.

'Oh, Lana, how awful. It must have been a ghastly time for you.' His eye went to Dickie's ring. 'I mean it. But now you have Herr Best.'

She wished he hadn't mentioned Carl. It was like a cloud hanging over them.

'Frank, I don't—'

'Sorry, I shouldn't have brought him up. I just can't see you trotting off to Germany after the war, that's all.'

'I have no plans to do that,' she said firmly.

He gave her a level gaze. 'I'm glad.' He picked up his glass. 'Let's toast this wonderful day. I feel happier than I've felt in ages. How about you?'

'I'm happy, too,' Lana said, surprising herself that it was true. She clinked her glass with his. 'To this wonderful day.'

'And more wonderful days to come, I hope,' Frank said, smiling at her.

CHAPTER 42

There was something in the air, everyone said. Vague rumours about a big push on the Continent. One evening, on the sixth of June, Lana and Maxine, together with Athena and Dolores, were in the common room listening to the wireless. Maxine was knitting a pullover for Peter.

'I started it a year ago,' she said, shamefacedly. 'I'm hoping to get it finished by winter but I'm still on the first sleeve.'

'He could freeze to death if it takes you that long,' Lana chuckled.

Suddenly the music stopped. As one, the four women stopped chatting. Maxine put down her knitting as a BBC announcer spoke.

'This is the BBC Home Service. Here is a special bulletin read by John Snagge. D-Day has come. Early this morning the Allies began the assault on the north-western face of Hitler's fortress. The first official news came just after half past nine when Supreme Headquarters of the Allied Expeditionary Force issued Communiqué Number One. This said, "Under the command of General

Eisenhower, Allied naval forces supported by strong air forces began landing Allied armies this morning on the northern coast of France.'"

Barbara broke the silence.

'About time,' she said.

'My goodness,' Lana gasped. 'There've been whispers but it's really happening.' She squeezed her eyes shut. More lives to be lost without doubt. How many hundreds, thousands . . .? Her practical self said that something of this kind had to bring the Germans to heel once and for all. But what if the Germans retaliated and dropped more even more bombs to crush the British into submission . . .?

She closed her eyes, breathing out a deep sigh. Please let this latest action prove successful and bring the war to an end soon.

But exactly a week later Lana was sickened and scared to read that Hitler had sent his new secret weapon over to England: flying bombs – what Hitler called his vengeance weapon. You couldn't see it, the article in the paper said. But you could hear it. And as long as you could hear it you were all right. It was when the noise stopped . . .

Lana gave an inward shiver. It seemed the new bombs – the Londoners were calling them doodlebugs – were directed once again on poor old London. Would Liverpool be next? A black depression came over her. How much longer could they keep going? But they had to. The alternative was terrifying.

The weather wasn't helping. It was much cooler than normal summers and dull nearly every day. If only the sun would come out it would lift us all, Lana thought, as she rang the bell for the end of class. The children banged their desks shut and joined in the struggle to be first out.

'One at a time,' Lana called, but her order fell on deaf ears. She sighed. History was not really her subject but she was doing her best to bring the Iron Age to life. The girls weren't interested at all, and the boys only wanted to know what weapons the men made so they could fight. It was so sad that many of these children only knew war.

She'd begun seeing Frank regularly. After that glorious day in the park they'd been to the cinema a couple more times, and even managed to get a glimpse of the damage that had been done to the Albert Dock – a shocking spectacle from what they could see of it, reminding her of how lucky she was to be at Bingham Hall away from the brunt of the bombing. But Frank didn't ever touch on anything personal between them. As far as he was concerned they were friends, and for that she was grateful. He obviously respected her feelings for Carl. But often she wished Frank might kiss her again . . . properly. It seemed ages ago since that one and only time.

She'd written a letter to Carl but her heart for some reason hadn't been in it. Neither of them ever mentioned the current state of the war, but now she was determined to steer him away from anything personal even though his last letter had sounded desperate.

> Lana, have you thought any more about our talk at Christmas? It seems a long time ago but I was serious when I asked you to be my wife. I know I am not really in a position to ask you. But if we love each other we can wait.

She'd fobbed him off. It was the only way to describe it, she knew. She'd told him they should wait until the war ended to see how they both felt and to give more time to Peter. She decided not to tell him that Peter had begun to wet the bed again – almost every night. Only that morning Lana had stopped one of the maids who was carrying a pillowcase. She'd told Lana it was Peter's soaked sheets she was taking to the laundry room. An hour later Lana had caught Jack chanting:

'Peter, Peter wets the bed,
If he don't stop he'll soon be dead.'

'And if *you* don't stop that at once, Jack,' she'd said sharply, 'you'll go straight to your room after supper.'

How cruel children could be, Lana thought, as she wrote Carl's address on the envelope. The clouds hadn't lifted but she needed some air. She'd walk to the village and get it off to him.

As she approached the post office building she took the envelope out of her handbag ready to buy a stamp and walked up the steps. There was only one person in front of her in the shop. He had a familiar set to his shoulders and she smiled to herself.

She tapped him on the shoulder and Frank turned round, his face breaking into a grin. Giving her a peck on the cheek he said, 'Here, give me that.'

Before she realised what he was doing he'd taken the envelope out of her hand.

'Frank, I—'

'I think I can treat you to a stamp, Lana.'

She felt sick.

'Two letter stamps, please,' he said. The woman behind the counter pushed them through the grille.

Lana's heart beat hard. Frank licked the stamp for his letter, then turned her envelope over. For a split second his hand seemed to freeze in mid-air. Then slowly he turned to her and handed her back her envelope and the stamp.

'You'd better take care of this,' he said. 'I wouldn't want to sully your love letter.'

Abruptly, he turned and stalked out.

She gulped, trying to dislodge the lump that had formed in the back of her throat. Automatically, she stuck the stamp on, then looked down at the envelope, almost not knowing what to do with it.

'I'll put it in the postbag,' the woman behind the counter said. 'It'll go out at four o'clock.

Somehow Lana thanked her and stumbled out. She could just make out his figure in the distance, but she couldn't have run after him if she'd wanted to. Her leg muscles felt like they had seized up.

'Frank,' she called. But he didn't turn round.

Resolutely, Lana started walking back to Bingham Hall, her steps slow and dejected. She dragged her feet the last hundred yards, her head down, not noticing the lush green of the avenue of lime trees, angry with Frank for assuming she'd written Carl a love letter. If only he'd given her the chance to tell him it was almost the opposite.

But how would she have explained? She was so confused about her feelings for Carl. She'd thought she loved him. Was it only infatuation? No. It went far deeper than that. Raw passion? Her face flamed with the idea. Was loving someone forbidden? A German who'd worn a Nazi uniform was certainly the last person in the world she would ever have thought she'd fall in love with.

And Frank. Where did *he* fit into her confused world?

CHAPTER 43

Whilst she could understand his initial reaction, Lana couldn't forgive Frank for not allowing her to explain why she was writing to Carl. She'd thought they were good friends, but he obviously didn't value it as *she* did. Only this morning she'd bumped into him as he was making for the village café with Celia's hand tucked into his arm. For a few seconds she was consumed with fury. Hadn't he told her Celia 'drove him nuts' with her possessiveness? He'd insisted there was nothing between them, yet there he was, about to have a cosy chat with her in the Cosy Corner café. At the very least, he was encouraging the woman.

Lana felt as though a dark cloud had settled on her. Frank needed a very special woman who genuinely loved him and his work in almost equal measure, not some glamour puss with a loud voice who seemed intent on winning him more as a trophy.

Lana was determined not to let him see her by keeping her head down, but at the last second she couldn't resist looking up, only to see he'd steered

470

Celia in front of him through the entrance but had turned back to gaze at her. She could have sworn that he wanted to speak to her, but Celia dragged him inside. Lana hurried on, anger spurting up into her throat again at the weakness of men, as she walked onwards to the library to change her book. She was saddened to think Frank was so stubborn he had brought their friendship to such an abrupt end.

Aren't you being what you're accusing Frank of? a little voice inside asked her. *You're just as stubborn. You could easily go and see him – explain – and all would be back to normal.*

Why should she have to persuade him? He should know her better by now and trust her. But she couldn't blame Peter entirely for the reason she was keeping in contact with Carl. She gave a deep sigh, and rubbed her forehead. Why was life so complicated?

'You know it's Peter's birthday on the 10th of next month,' Maxine said as Lana was having a cup of coffee one morning in the matron's office.

'Let's hope the weather picks up for him,' Lana said, immediately thinking of Carl. Would he come down to see his son?

'They say this could turn out to be the dullest July since records began,' Maxine said with a grimace. 'We've virtually had no summer. It *has* to improve in the next fortnight for his birthday. I was thinking of a picnic for all the children if it's fine.'

'I think that's a good idea,' Lana said. 'We should start preparations soon.'

'I was wondering whether Carl might be able to get over,' Maxine said, watching Lana closely.

'I'm sure he'd be pleased to be invited,' Lana said, but her insides were in the usual state of turmoil whenever his name was mentioned.

The following week Lana received a letter from him.

My dear Lana,

After all these months I am allowed to see my son again for his birthday. They have given me freedom to choose for Peter to come to Bletchley or for me to come to Bingham Hall.

Mrs Taylor has invited me again, so I would like to accept. I will come early on the morning of the 10th to be there in good time for Peter's birthday picnic and will return on the following morning.

I will be very happy to see you both again.

Until then,

Carl

Lana chewed her lower lip. Despite what she'd said, he seemed to think of them as a family already.

She slept badly the night before Peter's birthday. Trying to get back to sleep for a further hour or two by mentally going over the arrangements for the picnic didn't work. Carl's image – his handsome features – kept pushing to the front of her mind. In the end she gave up.

After breakfast Maxine asked Harold to fetch Carl from the railway station. When Lana saw Harold drive off late that morning she felt almost relieved she didn't have to meet Carl on her own.

'Papa's coming for my birthday today,' Peter announced to anyone within earshot.

Lana saw Priscilla's mouth tighten but she was pleased the young girl didn't make any comment. She knew Priscilla was always a little jealous that Peter had a parent and she didn't. But at least it hadn't spoilt their friendship, and Priscilla's German, according to Peter was, in his words, 'not bad'. Praise indeed. She smiled to herself. Both children used the language between them as a secret communication, much to some of the other children's annoyance. Lana gave Priscilla a wink, and to her surprise Priscilla sent one back.

Judging by the noise level, the picnic was a huge success but Lana's head had begun to throb with the children's screams and shouts of laughter. After they'd eaten and begun to play games, she decided there were enough adults around and that no one would miss her, except possibly Carl. Perhaps they would have some time together this evening. She took an aspirin and lay on her bed. The headache was due, no doubt, to a scant two hours' sleep last night. She drifted off, but when she awoke an hour later she felt worse.

She'd go to the kitchen and make herself a cup of tea.

'You look white, Miss,' Reggie said when she stepped into the kitchen.

'A headache, that's all,' Lana said.

'Och, you're getting too many of them, hen,' Bertie said. 'Something's worrying you.' She swung round. 'Reggie, put that kettle on.'

It was rather nice to be fussed over. She could just spot Rupert through the open doorway in the scullery curled up in his basket, but when he heard her he got up languidly and stretched out, then strolled over to her for a stroke. He then proceeded to give himself a good scratch.

'He's been scratching quite a bit lately,' Bertie said.

'It'll be fleas.' Reggie curled his lip. 'It's disgusting.'

'No more disgusting than when you had head lice, Reggie,' Bertie flashed back.

Reggie's face turned red. He'd taken to the kitchen, Lana thought, but he'd never wholeheartedly taken to Rupert.

As she sipped her tea and finished one of Bertie's fairy cakes from the picnic, Lana felt decidedly better.

'Thanks, Reggie,' she said, getting up and rinsing her cup at the sink. She'd go and see how the children were getting on.

But she didn't make it outside. On her way to the front door Carl came towards her in the Great

Hall and held out his hands. He took hers, and Lana was thankful there were no prying eyes with everyone in the garden.

'I was worried about you.' His extraordinary blue eyes looked down at her intently.

'I'm sorry I wasn't here when you arrived,' she said, feeling a little shaky. It must be the aspirin. 'I had another headache and felt I needed a rest. I didn't have a lot of sleep last night.'

'I'm worried about you with so many headaches.' Carl watched her. 'If you are feeling better this evening can we go somewhere to talk?'

'Maybe this evening in the library,' she said.

'You two probably need some time together,' Maxine said after supper.

'Yes, we need to talk,' Lana said. 'I was wondering if we could use the library.'

'Why don't you go there after the children are in bed? You'll have some peace then.'

'Thank you, Maxine. You're such a good friend.'

'I hope so.' She laughed at Lana's serious expression. 'Don't look so worried. Everything will turn out for the best.'

'I'd like to believe that,' Lana said with feeling. But she was a long way from thinking it was really possible.

'I love the smell of books in a library,' Carl said, as he followed her into the baronial space. 'This one has a wonderful aroma.' He went over to one of the shelves and lifted out a bound copy, holding it to his nose. 'Mmm. *Introduction to Greek Mythology*.' He looked up and smiled. 'I would welcome the opportunity to read this.'

'You may borrow it while you're here,' Lana said as they crossed the floor to the round-table room. She felt nervous as she drew a chair out for him and sat down herself. Where should she start?

'It's wonderful to see you again, *mein Liebling*. Your letters—'

'Carl,' she broke in, 'I have something I must tell you.'

'You look so serious.' Carl took her hand in his and covered it with his other. 'But of course it is very serious what we have to say to one another.' He smiled at her encouragingly.

'I told you at Christmas I can't live in Germany.'

'I have been hoping – *praying* you will change your mind.' His eyes flickered with uncertainty. 'You know I cannot live in England after the war ends.'

'Yes, I know that.'

'Then how can we—'

'Carl, there's no easy way to say this. I've thought and thought. But I realise I can't marry you.'

'But we love each other.'

She looked at him directly.

'You think you love me. I truly thought I loved you. But if I did, I would follow you to the ends of the earth – but I know I can't. Our love was impossible right from the start.'

Carl's eyes shone unnaturally. He looked at her with intense longing.

'Lana, if you come with me to Germany after all this is over, I promise I will make you happy.'

'I know you would do your utmost, Carl.' She squeezed her eyes to stop the tears that threatened. 'But I wouldn't be being true to myself.'

'Oh, darling, are you certain you can't love me enough?'

She nodded miserably. 'I am, Carl. And I want you to take this back.' She held out the pearl bracelet but he shook his head.

'Please keep it. It's my gift to you. I don't want it back. I want to imagine you wearing it.'

'But suppose you meet someone else?'

He shook his head more vehemently this time.

'No, I'll never change my mind. Please, Lana, do as I say. I want you to think of me when you wear it.'

She looked down at the bracelet, its soft glow.

'All right, but I won't wear it here because I don't want to upset Peter again.'

He nodded, then looked away, silent for a minute. 'Oh, Lana.' He turned back to her, his eyes glistening. 'You would have made me so happy if you said you would be my wife. But I will try to respect your decision.'

'You must.' She gulped. She had to say it. 'And one day, after this awful war, you will meet another woman. A good German woman who will understand all you have gone through and love you all the more for it. For your bravery, your integrity, your loyalty – and your devotion to your son.'

'So many good things, it is a wonder you can resist me.' Carl tried to joke but his last words caught in his throat.

'I didn't want to hurt you,' Lana said, her throat tight. 'I'd lost Dickie – you'd lost your wife. If our countries hadn't been at war we would never have met. We were just two people who met in the wrong place at the wrong time and thought love could overcome everything. I realise now it can't. But there's one very important thing you've done for me, Carl. I was full of hatred when Dickie was killed. So bitter. I blamed every German for his death. I hated every single one. You've shown me there are good Germans – good people in every country, along with the evil ones. I won't make that mistake again. You don't know how much that's helped me with Dickie.' She traced the outline of his face with her fingertips. 'And I'll never forget you, Carl.'

He pulled her up and held her close, kissing her hair.

'And I will never, *never* forget *you, mein Liebling*.'

CHAPTER 44

A fortnight later on the 25th August the announcement came over the wireless that Paris was liberated – the Germans had surrendered.

'Oh, thank God,' Lana said out loud when she heard the news. Everyone she spoke to in the village was saying this was a sign that the war was coming to an end. She hoped it was true, but she doubted it. Even though there was a welcome lull in the bombing, nobody celebrated – the news was still terrible in the Far East.

'You look as though you could do with a holiday, Lana,' Maxine said when they were in the common room that evening.

'I thought she looked a bit peaky lately.' Kathleen blew out her cheeks. 'We probably all need one. But first things first. Hands up anyone for cocoa?'

'Me, Miss,' Lana, Maxine and Athena chorused.

'So that's everyone,' Kathleen said, getting up.

'I'll come and help you.' Athena closed her book.

When they'd disappeared, Maxine said quietly, 'I don't want to pry but we haven't had much opportunity—'

'I told him I couldn't marry him,' Lana pre-empted her.

Maxine waited a few moments, then looked Lana straight in the eyes.

'I think you were right,' she said. 'It would have been a very complicated relationship. How did he take it?'

'As I hoped. The perfect gentleman. Very sad but resigned.'

Maxine sighed. 'And Frank?'

'I don't want to talk about him,' Lana said, in a sharper tone than she'd meant. She tried to smile. 'Sorry, Maxine. Don't take any notice of me. It's just that I feel so on edge. But I'd like to spend some time with my parents. They're getting older and—'

'No need for any further explanations,' Maxine said. 'Take the time off until we start the autumn term, and if you need longer—'

'Maxine, you know I've been very happy here at Bingham Hall, don't you?'

Maxine nodded. 'I'm not sure I want to know what's coming.'

'We have to talk about it. You know history and geography were never my subjects. I just stood in when Judith Wright took off without any notice. My passion is teaching English, but you have Athena for that.'

'Don't forget, you're my substitute driver.'

'Not now,' Lana said. 'Harold's made a complete recovery from his operation. I want to go back to

Yorkshire, then decide what to do. I've been teaching for ten years and I'm ready for a change.' She hesitated. 'What I'm saying is that I'm giving you my notice.'

Priscilla turned from the common room door, which one of the teachers had left slightly ajar, not believing what she'd just heard. Her favourite teacher, Miss Ashwin, whom she trusted and loved above all the others, had just given in her notice and was going back to Yorkshire. She couldn't let her go. She just couldn't. But what could she do to persuade her to stay?

It was almost time for her to get ready for bed so there was no chance to do anything until tomorrow. She had to work out a plan. And she needed someone to help her. Someone who would be upset to see her go. It was no good asking Matron. Priscilla knew Matron would do her best to persuade Miss Ashwin to stay on, but she had the feeling Miss Ashwin was prepared for that and wasn't going to allow her to change her mind. No, it had to be someone different. Someone unexpected. Someone who not only liked Miss Ashwin but who Miss Ashwin liked back.

Early next morning Priscilla got up and washed and dressed, then trotted downstairs to say hello to Rupert and to give him his breakfast. She loved this time alone with him, stroking him and talking in a silly cat voice.

Someone poked his head in the scullery doorway.

'Reggie. What do you want?'

'Nothing.' Reggie was gruff as usual. He lit a cigarette and blew the smoke over one shoulder, just missing Rupert who was waiting for her to put his bowl down.

'Don't know why you're so fond of that fleabag,' he said.

'Don't call him that – it's horrible.'

'Well, he is. Always scratching himself. He's definitely got fleas.'

It was as though a light had shone onto her problem, showing her the next step.

'I suppose he must have,' Priscilla said contritely. 'I'll get him some flea stuff. That'll sort him out.'

She would walk over to the vet's. See the nice Mr Drummond. She'd always thought he was soppy about Miss Ashwin, so there was a good chance he'd be just as upset as *she* was.

Priscilla was greeted by the nurse when she'd first run crying to them about the injured cat.

'How nice to see you, love. Come in, won't you?'

Two minutes later the nurse called her in to see Mr Drummond.

'You haven't come across any more wounded cats, I hope.' Mr Drummond looked at her, his eyes twinkling with laughter.

He was exactly the sort of man she would have picked for Miss Ashwin. Just like the doctor hero in the latest book one of the maids had lent her. Well, maybe Mr Drummond was older but then, so was Miss Ashwin.

'No, I haven't, and I hope I never have to again,' she told him seriously.

'And Rupert?'

'He's got fleas.'

'Ah, he needs some special powder.' He smiled broadly at her, then disappeared. He was back a few moments later with a small tin.

'Sprinkle this around his ears and on the back of his neck where he can't reach it. Don't let him lick it off if you can help it. And don't let it get into his eyes. You should see an improvement in a few days. Repeat after a month. Do you think you can do it? Miss Ashwin will help you, I'm sure.'

Priscilla burst into sobs.

'Come, come, child, fleas are not the end of the world. Rupert will be fit as a fiddle in a couple of days' time.'

'I'm – I'm not c-crying about Rupert.'

'What is it then? Sit down and tell me. I'm sure it's nothing that can't be resolved.'

'It's not about me,' Priscilla said, looking upwards into his nice craggy face. 'It's Miss Ashwin.'

She saw Mr Drummond give a start of surprise. 'Miss Ashwin?' he said. 'Is she ill?'

'She's been very sad lately,' Priscilla said, sniffing. 'And she's going away.'

'Well, we all need a holiday, Priscilla,' Mr Drummond said, sounding to Priscilla like he badly needed one himself. 'I expect Miss Ashwin does, as much as anyone.'

'You don't understand, Mr Drummond. She's leaving Bingham Hall. She's going back to Yorkshire . . . back home . . . for good. And I'll never see her again.'

Frank Drummond tapped his unlit pipe on the table. 'How do you know she's going away for good?'

'I heard Matron and Miss Ashwin talking. And that's what Miss Ashwin said . . . that she was giving in her notice.'

She was gratified to see him give a start.

'What was Matron's response?'

'I don't know because I had to leave.'

'Hmm.' Frank Drummond lit his pipe, taking a while to get it going. He glanced at her, and she saw a glint in his eye. 'I don't think I'll allow you to de-flea Rupert after all, Priscilla. I'd better go there myself to sort him out. What about this afternoon? Do you think you could have Rupert ready for me?'

'Yes.' Priscilla wiped her eyes with the back of her hand. 'Thank you very much, Mr Drummond.'

As Priscilla stepped out of the clinic her lips curved into a smile. Until now she'd thought she'd be a teacher like Miss Ashwin when she left school – but her meeting with nice Mr Drummond had changed her mind. She was going to be an actress!

CHAPTER 45

The front bell rang immediately after dinner-time. Lana heard a man's voice quietly ask to speak to Matron as she was carrying out a stack of plates for the kitchen.

'Frank!'

He'd come to apologise for not listening to her explanation. Her heart gave a little leap that now all would be well between them. She hated the thought of going back to Yorkshire without being friends with Frank again. In fact, the idea made her feel quite panic-stricken.

'Hello, Lana.' He'd lost his usual warm smile. 'A little bird told me Rupert has got fleas so I've brought some powder that should see them off.'

He hadn't come to see her, after all.

'I haven't seen him all morning,' she said shortly. 'He's usually wherever Priscilla is.'

'Here's the girl herself,' Frank said, looking over Lana's shoulder. 'Hello, young Miss. Where's that famous cat of yours? I've come to show you how to de-flea him.'

'He's in the scullery waiting for me to bring him some titbits from the dining room.' Priscilla threw him a look, which didn't seem entirely innocent to Lana. 'How do you know he's got fleas?'

'All cats have them at some time or another. Does he scratch himself a lot?'

Priscilla nodded.

'Can you hold him for me?'

'I promised to help Mrs Steen tidy the art studio straight after dinner,' Priscilla said. 'Miss Ashwin, could you do it? Rupert trusts you.'

Lana gave Priscilla a quick glance. Something wasn't right but she couldn't put her finger on it. Almost as though they were reading from a script. It must be her imagination.

'Yes, I'll hold him,' she said, turning to Frank. 'Just follow me.'

She led him to the kitchen where Bertie was taking a pie from the oven.

'Bertie, Fra – Mr Drummond is going to de-flea Rupert in the scullery. Is it all right if we come through?'

'Yes, but I'd prefer you to do it outside. I don't really want all that stuff wafting into the kitchen.'

Frank nodded. 'As it's not windy we can take him outside. We just need a table to stand him on.'

'There's an old iron table outside with some pots on it,' Bertie said. 'Just set them aside.'

Lana picked Rupert up and put him over her shoulder. His purr was loud in her ear. Outside, she stood him on the table but Rupert immediately struggled. She pressed him down as firmly as she could without hurting him, but he was too powerful for her. He squirmed his head and she could feel the muscles tighten in his neck. Without warning he sprang from under her hands and shot off like a ginger streak.

'They always know something's up,' Frank said. 'And they're not going to hang around to find out what it is.' He looked at her properly for the first time. 'We can't try again today, but I'm sure you and Priscilla can do it between you when I'm not around. He'll probably behave himself for her.'

Lana nodded. Paradoxically she wished he would go, now he'd made it clear he hadn't come to see her. But it was her chance to tell him that she was leaving.

'Frank, I want you to be the first to know I've given in my notice.'

He raised his eyebrows. 'Oh? Why's that?'

'I need a change.'

'You've not been here long enough to need a change, I wouldn't have thought.'

'No, I mean a change from teaching. I've done it for ten years. It's time to do something different – my heart isn't in it the way it ought to be. I feel I'm letting the children down.'

'I doubt that,' Frank said. He paused. 'Do you fancy a walk?'

'I don't know. I don't know anything any more.'

He threw her a sharp look. 'Come on. Let's walk down the drive.'

'All right.'

She was silent as they walked. She should be

feeling relieved that she'd told him she was going, but there was a knot in her stomach.

As they walked out of sight of the house Frank unexpectedly took her hand. Tears pricked the back of her eyes and she told herself off for becoming a sentimental fool. He didn't mean anything by it. She tried to edge her hand gently away, but he gripped it tighter.

'Lana, we must talk. Why don't we go back to the clinic. It's half-day so there won't be anyone around.'

'All right.' It seemed she was only capable of saying those two words.

She fell into step with him as she used to. It felt natural, comfortable. But she mustn't read things that didn't exist. He didn't speak either, though it wasn't awkward. Instead, she was even more conscious of her hand in his – their skin touching. She felt she could walk with him forever, so long as he held her hand. Her face warmed but she blamed it on the sun. For once her mind quietened as they kept perfectly in step. She felt she was walking her troubles away. As she gave him a surreptitious glance he caught her.

'What is it, Lana?'

'N-nothing.'

A dog barked as they opened the door, and Barney rushed to greet his master.

'I've brought Lana to see you,' he said, patting his head. Barney gave an obligatory wag of his tail and licked her hand.

'Come and sit in the kitchen while I make us some tea,' Frank said, taking off his jacket. But it was when he undid his tie and threw it over the back of the chair, and undid the top button of his shirt, that something hit her so hard she thought she'd been winded.

Frank. Dear God, all this time it was Frank who she loved. Who she would go anywhere with so long as she was with him.

And she could never tell him. He would laugh in her face. Remind her she was in love with Carl. Make her feel she was two-timing her German friend. He'd never believe her in a million years.

'Frank.' She tried to hide the desperation in her voice. 'I think I'll say no to the tea.'

He came and stood close to her. 'Why is that?'

'Because . . . because . . .' She turned away, tears spilling down her face.

'Lana.' He took her arms and turned her so she faced him again.

And then he kissed her. At first it was gentle. And then she heard his sharp intake of breath. His kiss deepened, and she hungrily kissed him back. She never wanted him to stop.

'Lana,' he groaned, as he drew away. 'What are you doing to me? You're in love with—'

Lana's breathing was coming in short jerky sounds. 'I've told him I can't marry him.'

Frank's eyes sparked as he pressed his hands on her arms.

'What are you saying?'

'I'm saying I don't – didn't love him enough to go to Germany with him when the war is over. Maxine said something to me that I couldn't grasp at the time, but she was so right. She said, "If you *really* loved Carl you'd go to the ends of the earth with him."

'But I was making all the excuses possible to Carl why I would never live in Germany,' she went on rapidly, trying to explain. 'I couldn't speak the language. The people would regard me as the enemy whether the Allies won the war or not. And if we lost, it would be even more unthinkable to live in Germany. And there was Peter. He needs his father. He's been without him for four years and has no one else, poor little chap. So we said goodbye on Peter's birthday a fortnight ago.'

'Why didn't you tell me at the time?'

'What was the point? You didn't let me explain that time at the post office why I was still writing to Carl. It was mainly because I've always told him how Peter's doing. He worries himself sick about his son, and I can understand why.'

'I see.' Frank's tone was neutral.

She looked at him, still feeling the imprint of his mouth.

'Then I saw you arm in arm with Celia Daniels the other week going into the café. I thought you must have made it up with her.' Lana gulped. 'I didn't want to come between you.'

'What are you talking about?' He gripped her arms. 'She's doing a fund-raising event in her garden for the war – we're on the same committee, that's all. I've told you before – there's nothing between Celia and me. Never was – never could be. So there's no need to be jealous – though I must say I'm rather glad if you are.'

'I wasn't jealous,' Lana protested, then saw his raised eyebrow. A flicker of anger bubbled. 'I've never thought she was right for you. But you never rang or anything.'

Frank buried his face in her hair.

'I'm sorry. Sorry for acting like a lovesick schoolboy. I was so jealous of him. So sure you loved him. I thought the best thing would be to let you go.'

'What made you change your mind?'

Frank smiled.

'Go on, tell me.'

'It was Priscilla. She was terribly upset because she overheard you saying to Maxine that you were giving in your notice. She thinks the world of you.'

'She came to tell you that?'

'Yes, using the flea excuse.'

'Little monkey.'

Frank kissed her forehead. 'You have to hand it to her. She's obviously very fond of you and it looks like she was trying to bring us together. Even saying she had to help one of the teachers so you'd have to hold Rupert.' He chuckled. 'You remember when I told you I'd fallen in love with you?' She nodded. 'I've never stopped. Not for one minute. And when you helped me with the young ram – you didn't have a clue what you were doing—' He broke off and grinned at her. 'But you were determined to help me pull Lightning through.' He kissed the tip of her nose. 'I loved you even more then.' He squinted at her. 'And of course I realised how jolly useful you are when it comes to changing wheels.'

'Now you're mocking me.' Lana pretended to clip his ear.

'Oh, my darling.' He hugged her to his chest again, then released her and dropped on one knee. 'I love you so much. Would it be enough of a change for you to do me the honour of becoming the wife of a middle-aged vet?'

'Who would that be?' she said, fighting to keep her face straight. 'I don't know anyone that old.'

He lifted her hand to his lips and kissed it. 'I'm giving you five seconds to answer.'

'I suppose I'd better before Celia Daniels or anyone else beats me.' She couldn't stop her beam of happiness.

'They're all queuing up,' Frank chuckled as he scrambled to his feet. 'But I'm grateful you've not kept me waiting the full five seconds – this stone floor was killing me!'

CHAPTER 46

Lana's feet were light as she floated back to Bingham Hall in the early evening in time for supper. Frank had wanted her to stay longer but she needed some quiet moments on her own to take in all that had happened. It seemed impossible that they'd both acted so foolishly and nearly lost one another. If it hadn't been for Priscilla . . . Lana smiled to herself. Who would have thought Priscilla was so insightful? The young girl had changed remarkably from when Lana had first set eyes on her at the school. Although Priscilla would never truly settle at Bingham Hall, she was beginning to make a difference to some of the other children's lives – particularly little Betsy, and Peter. And she'd added so much to Lana's own life and happiness.

'That was a long walk,' Maxine said laughing, as she met Lana in the Great Hall. 'But I can tell by your face it's all good. Supper's going to be half an hour late today – I think Reggie had a bit of a disaster – so we can have a cup of tea and you can tell Auntie Maxine all about it. I can't wait to hear.' She paused. 'And then I'll tell you *my* news – or rather Priscilla's.'

'Priscilla's?'

'Yes. But yours first.'

Maxine jumped up from her chair in the office and hugged Lana.

'I'm thrilled for you. Frank is a darling and absolutely perfect. So that means you'll stay on.'

'For a while, anyway. But I wanted to ask you if I could just fill in when you need me – for holidays and sickness – even for *you* when you have a holiday, if you'd like me to—'

'I did that for June and it worked well, so yes, I'd be happy with that.' She looked at Lana and grinned. 'I might even be able to take a few days off to get married.'

Lana's eyes flew wide. 'Oh, Maxine, there I am going on about Frank and me and all the time—'

Maxine chuckled. 'Don't worry. The wedding will happen one day. Crofton's away at sea at the moment, so it won't be just yet.' She sat down again and Lana followed suit. 'What will you do the rest of the time?'

'Join the WVS,' Lana said without hesitating. 'I can drive. Help with their canteen on wheels – anything really. And in between times, marry Frank. And something else.' She caught Maxine's eye, hoping their friendship could withstand her next confidence. 'He'd love to be a father. So if it happens, that should be enough to keep me out of mischief.'

To Lana's great relief Maxine beamed. 'That's wonderful he hopes to have a family, and I'm sure it will happen.' The young matron paused. 'Is it going to be a fancy wedding?'

'No, the very opposite. We both want a quiet one. And it'll be in Yorkshire so my parents can come. Mum has a nervous problem, so it's hard for her to travel anywhere. But I hope you'll come – with Priscilla, of course. If it wasn't for her . . .'

'If you plan to wait until the war's over, Priscilla may well not be here.'

'What do you mean?'

'This came in this afternoon's post.'

Maxine held up a big brown envelope with large spidery writing. It was addressed to 'The Matron'. Lana glanced at the postmark and frowned. Chicago? That was America.

'Shall I read you the letter?'

'Do.'

Maxine cleared her throat. 'The date is 4th July 1944.' She looked up. 'Independence Day, written in brackets.' She bent her head and began:

'Dear Matron – I apologise for not knowing your name.

I am writing first to you and will go on to explain why. I come from Liverpool but fifteen years ago I went to a jazz club when I was out with my friends one evening. There

495

I met a jazz musician called Donny. To cut a long story short, we fell in love and he wanted me to go back with him to his hometown in Chicago. My parents were shocked enough at that, especially when I told them he was ten years older than me. They said they would stop any wedding – I was only eighteen, so I had three more years to go – but when one of the neighbours told them he was black they completely disowned me. They forced me to leave home. Their parting words were that they would never speak my name again. As far as they were concerned I was dead. But worse than anything was to say goodbye to my baby sister, Priscilla.'

Maxine looked up briefly as Lana gasped, then continued.

'She wasn't even three and we adored each other. I was practically a mother to her because Mum was never motherly and quite frankly neglected us every weekend to be with her smart friends. She knew I'd always look after my baby sister and see that no harm came to her. I hugged her tightly and I remember Priscilla looking at me. I told her she had the most beautiful grey eyes I have ever seen. The colour of a greyhound's coat, I told her. In my heart I thought I would probably never see her again. Of course she didn't realise I was saying goodbye forever. I kissed her and picked up my suitcase and

496

never turned round. I couldn't bear to see her little face at the window waving to me as she always did when I left for work every morning.

'Anyway, Donny and I went to Gretna Green and got married and soon after we sailed to America. We live outside Chicago and have three children – two girls and a boy. Every time I had a baby I'd write to my parents, enclosing a photograph of their latest grandchild but they ignored me. Eventually, after years of silence I gave up. But I never stopped thinking about my sister and worrying about what had happened to her.

'Then about three months ago the American Red Cross wrote and said my parents had been killed in the blackout. It had taken all that time for them to track me down. But there was no mention of Priscilla and I feared the worst. I wrote back thanking them and said would they ask about my sister in the British branch. And last week I had the most wonderful news from them that she had been taken to Bingham Hall, which was only about ten miles from where we lived. I hadn't realised it was now an orphanage as it was a grand country house when I knew it. The war has changed everything, I guess.

'I'm enclosing a letter to Priscilla telling her that when the war is over Donny and I want her to come and live with us as a member of

497

our family. The children can't wait to meet their aunt. I've put a couple of photographs in her letter. Tell her I can't wait to see my darling little sister again, though she must be getting quite a young lady by now.

'Thank you for your patience in reading this long letter. I wish I could be there when you tell her about me and she reads my letter to her.

Sincerely,
Prudence Byrd'

Maxine gazed at her as though on a second reading she still hadn't taken it in.

Lana pressed her palms to her cheeks. 'I can't believe it.' She felt her eyes prick with anger at Priscilla's parents.

'Nor could I at first,' Maxine said soberly.

'It was so cruel, the way they treated their daughter,' Lana burst out. 'And poor Priscilla will have to know that. She'll be devastated – she almost worshipped them.'

'I know,' Maxine said. 'But thank heavens she now has a sister who wants to take care of her. In the end it's really the most wonderful news.' She looked across at Lana and smiled. 'Let's call her in.'

Priscilla sat in matron's office, her mouth open. Maxine hadn't read out the letter but simply described what had happened to Prudence when

Priscilla was a little girl, deliberately leaving out the part where Prudence had said her parents had forced her to leave home, and as far as they were concerned she was dead.

Priscilla couldn't stop shaking her head. 'I can't believe it,' she said. 'I have a sister who I never even knew existed.'

'Do you remember once when I told you what beautiful grey eyes you have?' Lana said.

Priscilla nodded slowly.

'And do you remember when I asked if anyone had ever told you that before, and you hesitated? Then you said a lady once told you the same thing and hugged you, but you couldn't remember who she was. Not surprising when you weren't quite three. But that was your sister. So you *had* known her all along. She sounds so kind and loving. And she'll take great delight, I'm sure, in filling in all the gaps, and she'll want to know all about you, too.'

'But why didn't she come and see me before she went to America?'

'She probably thought it would be too upsetting for you after all those years,' Lana said. 'And too upsetting for her to leave you for the second time.' She caught Maxine's eye. 'I'm sure she can answer all those questions when you see her.'

Priscilla burst into sobs. 'Mummy and Daddy should have told me I had a sister. They never mentioned her – not *once*.' She looked up, the tears streaming down her face. 'I'll *never* forgive them.'

Lana put her arms round her. 'It's all right, love. Cry as much as you want.' She shook her head as she glanced at Maxine. 'Try not to be too hard on them. They loved you and wanted the best for you.' She stroked Priscilla's back until the tears stopped. 'Here, blow your nose.' Lana put a handkerchief in the young girl's hands. 'Do you want to read your sister's letter in private in your room, or do you want to stay with us? Oh, and she says she's put a couple of photographs in with her letter to you.'

'I'd like to look at the photographs here.'

Lana handed her a letter opener. Priscilla sliced the envelope and unfolded a sheet of paper that was wrapped around two photographs. She stared hard at the first one, finally turning it over. With wide eyes she handed it to Lana.

A toddler with straight blonde hair, grinning at the camera.

'It's you, Priscilla, at the age when Prudence left home.' Lana offered the photograph to Maxine. 'You look adorable. That's how your sister remembers you. She's going to have a shock when she sees how grown up you are.'

Priscilla gave a tearful smile and looked at the second photograph for much longer, then again gave it to Lana.

A happy family. A fair-haired, exceptionally pretty woman, with a little girl of about six on her lap, her other arm round an older girl, and a smiling, dark-skinned man with a mass of black curls, his hand on the shoulder of a young lad, the image of his father.

Lana handed the photograph to Maxine who gazed at it and smiled. 'Your birthday wish has come true, Priscilla,' she said, looking up. 'When the war's over – not long now, everyone thinks – you'll be reunited with your sister and meet her family.'

'But I didn't know then I *had* a sister.' Priscilla gave a disbelieving shake of her head.

'It was your dream to leave Bingham Hall and have somewhere to call home,' Maxine said. 'Miss Ashwin and I could tell that by your face when you blew out your candles. But dreams can sometimes turn out differently from how we imagine. Sometimes they're even better . . . like this one.'

Priscilla lowered her eyes to the floor. It was a lot for the young girl to absorb, Lana knew, but after Priscilla had been silent for over a minute, Lana began to worry.

'What's the matter, love?' Lana asked, putting her arm round the thin shoulders.

'America's a long way away, isn't it?' Priscilla said in a muffled voice, her head still bent down.

'It is, but it's a marvellous country. Nearly new compared with England. It'll take time to get used to everything . . . but you'll have your own sister to help you and show you round. I think you're going to love it.'

'Yes, I'll have Prudence, won't I?' Priscilla said, raising her head, her eyes red and swollen. 'But what about Peter? He's my best friend.' Tears ran silently down her cheeks.

'You can write to Peter,' Lana said. 'In German,' she added, 'so you don't forget all he's taught you. And when he's older, maybe he can come and visit you.'

'Do you really think so?' Priscilla's face had visibly brightened.

'Yes, I'm sure,' Lana answered.

'How long will it take to get there?'

'About a week,' Lana said, thinking of Dickie. His ship had often taken much longer to arrive in America when the captain had to zigzag over the Atlantic to escape the U-boats. And then do the same trip coming back to England with vital supplies. The kinds of missions that kept the country from starving. She swallowed hard and drew a long breath. 'You'll be sailing on an ocean liner,' she smiled encouragingly. 'It'll be a wonderful adventure. You'll be the envy of all the children.'

Priscilla's eyes widened. 'An ocean liner,' she repeated. 'Can you believe it, Miss Ashwin?' She gave Lana a shaky smile in return but it quickly faded. 'I wouldn't want to leave Rupert. Can he come with me?'

'No, love. He'd hate the journey. And he wouldn't be allowed to go anyway. He's best to stay here where he knows for the time being.' She paused. 'Would you allow *me* to take care of him?'

Priscilla nodded. 'Yes, Miss Ashwin, I'd rather know he was with you than anyone else.' She looked at Maxine in dismay. 'I didn't mean to sound rude, Matron, but Miss Ashwin—'

'I'm well aware that Miss Ashwin is Rupert's second favourite person,' Maxine said, chuckling.

'But when I marry our nice vet,' Lana intervened, 'we'll adopt him as our own cat . . . that is, if Matron agrees.'

'You're going to marry Mr Drummond?' Priscilla's eyes nearly popped from her head. 'Oh, you *will* have the wedding before I go away, won't you? Can I be your bridesmaid?'

'So many questions,' Lana smiled. 'And yes to all of them, seeing as you played such a big part in bringing us together.'

Priscilla giggled. 'I did, didn't I?'

'You certainly did, love, but please keep this a secret for the time being. It's only going to be a quiet wedding in Yorkshire – where my mother and father live.'

As soon as she uttered the last words Lana wished she hadn't. But giving a surreptitious look at Priscilla allayed her fears. The young girl was glowing with happiness.

Lana handed her back the photographs, which Priscilla tucked into the envelope.

'May I be excused, please, Matron?' she said, calmer now as she rose to her feet. 'I'd like to go and read my letter from my sister.' She hesitated, then glanced at Lana. 'But first I'm going to find Peter. I want to tell him before any of the others.'

She shot out of the door, pulling it firmly closed behind her.

'I was really anxious about her at one point,' Maxine said. 'Those two have become firm friends and it's natural she doesn't want to leave him. But she's a changed girl now from when she first came to us – no doubt about it.'

'The friendship's been good for both of them,' Lana said with feeling. 'She'll have time to get used to the idea of going away – though please God don't let this war go on much longer. But I'm positive they'll always keep in touch through letters.'

'And maybe Carl will take Peter to see her one day,' Maxine said quietly, her eyes on Lana.

Hearing Carl's name, Lana's chest tightened. She momentarily closed her eyes. She'd never intended to hurt him. He was a good man and one day he'd find happiness again – she was sure of it.

'Talking of letters,' Maxine broke into her sombre thoughts as she picked up an envelope, 'this came for you a little while ago. Hand delivery.'

Frowning, Lana opened the envelope and took out a small sheet of paper and read it aloud.

'Dear Lana,
    Just a note to hope you've settled in at Bingham Hall, and to tell you something that will make you laugh. I bloody miss you – even Priscilla! And not just missing a spic-and-span

504

cottage. I'm trying hard to keep it tidy! Come over for tea sometime when you have a spare hour after work and see for yourself. I promise not to snap your head off.

Maybe we could go to the theatre or something.

Janice'

'Well, well.' Maxine grinned. 'Wonders will never cease.'

'Strange how you can get the wrong idea of someone,' Lana said, smiling now. 'That goes for her *and* me. But poor Janice has had a rough time. Sounds like she's finally decided to live a little.' She put her hands on each side of her face. 'It's making my head spin, all this excitement. Tomorrow's going to feel a bit flat. Maybe we should do something to celebrate.'

'Let's see.' Maxine put her elbow on the desk and tapped her fingers on her cheek. 'Priscilla's dearest wish has unbelievably come true, and you've finally realised you're head over heels in love with your lovely vet, so I suppose they're two good enough reasons. And now, of course, we've got Janice turning over a new leaf.' She sprang from behind her desk to give Lana a warm hug.

'You know something, Lana? In spite of this damned war, we're going to throw a party, and even include Janice now she's eaten humble pie—' Maxine's eyes glittered with mischief. 'Anyway, as I was saying, it'll be a party to remember . . .

one for the children to tell *their* children about.' She grinned. 'What do you think?'

As Maxine was speaking, Rupert strolled in, trilling his usual greeting. He leapt onto the other visitor's chair, sat upright and stretched his jaw in a lion's yawn, succeeded by a full-throated meow.

Lana fondled the top of his ginger-and-white-striped head. 'We didn't ask you for *your* two pennyworth, Rupert,' she admonished, 'but I believe we can take that as a meow of approval.'

The two women dissolved into laughter as Rupert nonchalantly blinked, then settled down for his usual five-hour catnap.